OFF
BOOK ONE
PLANET

USA TODAY BESTSELLING AUTHOR
AILEEN ERIN

INK MONSTER  LOS ANGELES, CA

ALSO

The

The

Th

O

First Published by Ink Monster, LLC in 2019
Ink Monster, LLC
4470 W Sunset Blvd
Suite 145
Los Angeles, CA 90027
www.inkmonster.net

ISBN 9781943858217

For Isabella and Jeremy.
You inspire me every day.
I couldn't do this without you.
Love you both more than words.

managed to wrap an arm around me even with the constraining pads, and I nudged him softly. "Don't be afraid to rip into this guy."

"Hey," Roan's light green eyes filled with laughter, and he tugged on my long braid. "Don't listen to Maité. I have plans tonight. Don't want to mess up my face."

"That's why you're going to put on the mask I gave you," I said.

"You didn't tell me Yvette was in this class," Roan murmured in my ear. "Been trying to get a date with her sister for years. Think she'll put in a good word for me?"

"Roan." The word was a warning, but he looked at me with wide, innocent eyes. I elbowed him in the stomach—this time harder—and he let out an *oof*.

Roan wasn't the least bit intimidating. At three inches shorter than me and a little too energetic to be anything but adorable, he was more like a speedy teddy bear than anything else. He could keep up with me and made me laugh constantly. Which is why he'd been my best friend for nearly a decade, but his timing needed work.

"If anything happens to them because you were goofing off when—"

"Come on, Maité. I'll do my job here. But that doesn't mean we can't make this fun."

"This is too important to mess up," I whispered. The truth sat like a ball of molten lava in my stomach. Life was dangerous out there for all kids. They had to be able to defend themselves. "All right. Who wants to go—*Motherfuckingshit*." A sharp burn ran through my finger, and I couldn't stop the curse from flying out as I shook my hand.

A couple of shocked gasps came from my students.

"Sorry. I..." I glanced at Roan, not sure how to fix this.

Roan looped his arm with mine. "One second. Gotta talk strategy with my girl before we start." Roan dragged me toward the makeshift locker room.

"We'll be right back," I said, looking over my shoulder at the class. "Try doing bunkai number eight to stay warm. Yvette? You help lead."

Yvette nodded, her chin lifting up as she stepped forward to take charge. "You got it."

That gave us a second, and by the look on Roan's face, I was about to get an earful.

"Jesus. You're going to get us killed," Roan whispered as soon as we were through the curtain. At least he wasn't mad enough to start yelling. If anyone—even one of my students—found out I was a halfer, we'd both be as good as dead. "The implant still bothering you?"

"Bothering is too nice of a word." I bit down on the tip of my finger for a second, feeling the microscopic chip beneath my skin. "It feels like a hot poker is stabbing my finger. The alerts from my contact lens were bad, but I turned them off. It's been two weeks since it was implanted, and I'm still feeling the frequency shifts."

Roan's eyes widened. "How often?" His voice was threaded with worry.

"It feels like every other minute, but maybe more like every ten. I thought shutting down my email would help, but... I hate it." I spat out the words. It was the truth. I hated every damned second that this piece of shit tech sat under my skin. "I have to get it removed or I'll end up cutting it out or—"

"No. You can't." His tone made it clear he wasn't kidding around. "Not after everything we went through to get it in the first place. The fake ID. The sketchy doctor. And I could get in so much trouble if they find out I was the one who took your blood sample. No fucking way, Maité." He stepped closer to me, and I could almost feel the heat of Roan's anger. "We've talked about this. You gotta start blending in better. Most people have their neural lace implanted straight onto their brain by now, and—"

"But I'm half *alien*."

"Don't say that word." His tone was outraged, but for no good reason.

"It's not a dirty word. It's what I am. I'm half Aunare. And the alien side of me is stronger than the Earther side. My kind can't have implanted tech. I'm too sensitive for it. This will kill me—or worse—drive me insane. There's no way I'd survive lacing my brain, so don't even start with that again."

A neural lace hardwired all of a person's apps, calls, games, and everything else they wanted straight into their cerebral cortex for maximum convenience. Earthers loved it, but if a simple finger implant and AR contact lens nearly drove me crazy with jolts of fire-hot pain, that kind of tech would kill me for sure.

"So what now?" Roan took a step back from me, shaking his head. "You get your dinky-assed implant taken out and then go back to using a wrist unit? And then what's going to happen to you?"

"It worked before." My words were mumbled. I knew I couldn't go back to that. I'd stick out, and I already looked too Aunare as it was.

"It worked because we were kids. We all had wrist units back then. But in a few months, you're going to be twenty. You can maybe pass for sixteen—*maybe*—but not once someone talks to you. You act and sound much older than you are. And I get it. But by sixteen most people already have the neural lace. You *need* this implant or you're going to get caught. And we *both* know what happens then."

He was right. I knew it, but I still wanted the implant gone. It'd been a couple of weeks, and the burning pain was getting worse. Maybe if I—

"No way. Stop it." Roan cut off my thoughts. "I know that look. You're about to argue with me, but you're just stubborn, and you're *wrong*. You're just going to have to suck it up. SpaceTech will kill you if they find you. Your family and your friends. Anyone who spent any significant time with you. Which means *me*. You have to get your shit together and stop cussing every time that thing gets an alert. If they find out who you are, there will be *war*."

I rubbed the bridge of my nose, trying to find my Zen. "I know. I know. I'll figure something out and—"

Someone tapped on my shoulder, and I spun. One of my newest students—Hillary—let out a gasp at my too quick movement.

Shit. Shit. Just fucking shit.

Aunare weren't like Earthers. They were an elegant race built for speed and fighting. It's why I taught the class. Fighting for me was like breathing. But I couldn't show these kids who I was. What I was. I couldn't move that fast or they'd know.

When I taught my classes, it was painfully hard not to give in. Not to let my body move like it could. And in that one second, I'd given myself away.

Hillary's eyes were wide as she stared up at me. She'd had a close call a couple weeks ago and ended up in my class a little battered and bruised, but I saw the will to fight burning inside her. I wanted to make sure that next time, she'd fight and win.

"Are you—? Was that—?" She was too afraid to ask what I was.

Roan was right. I hadn't lived this long to be stupid now, but the implant was distracting me. It was making me too on edge, and I couldn't afford to forget my Earther facade for even a second.

"Sorry. You startled me." I'd found that if you explained a movement away as being scared or excited or some other extreme emotion, most Earthers dismissed it. They didn't want to find an Aunare living on this planet, especially if it's someone they'd been spending significant time with. Hillary had been here every night for three weeks. She didn't want me to be Aunare.

"Oh. Sorry," she said, and her shoulders relaxed. "I didn't mean to startle you."

"Everything okay?" I asked.

"We only have twenty minutes left in class." She swallowed. "I need the practice." Her words were barely audible.

"Of course. I'm so sorry I got distracted. Apparently, I'm having a day." I shoved through the curtain. "Okay, everyone. I promise to stay focused on your training for the rest of class." My finger burned again, and I bit my tongue. I swallowed the coppery tang of blood in my mouth along with another curse that was begging to slip out.

This might not get any easier for me, but these kids? I could help them. Volunteering here three hours a day, six days a week took its toll on me. Especially since I also had my shifts at the diner. But if teaching them to survive was the only thing I did before SpaceTech caught me, then that was something I could be proud of.

"We're going to work off of the bunkai we were just practicing while sparring with Roan. Each movement in the bunkai is something that can be used to fend off an attacker. Roan is covered in padding, so don't be afraid to let loose," I said as I settled back into teaching.

Everything was going to be fine. I could do this. I could stay hidden, teach my classes, and save my money. One day, I'd be light-years away from here and safe. Until then, I'd dream about making my escape from this godforsaken planet.

CHAPTER TWO

I SAT at my desk in the dark and watched the news on the vidscreens. The students had all left hours ago, and Roan was now changing in the back. He'd stayed to spar with me, sans padding, after my classes. It was nice of him, especially since he knew I was going to kick his butt.

It'd been a good workout, but I was still on edge from my slip-up with Hillary. If I wanted to relax, then I needed to let my body really move. But I couldn't do that, even with Roan. He could barely keep up with me at half-speed.

Now that everyone was gone, all I wanted to do was go home and hide. It was getting harder and harder to hold myself back. One of these days I was going to do something I couldn't talk my way out of, and that one slip-up was going to be the death of me and everyone I loved.

I scanned the screens for any sign of trouble outside. I could always tell my mom I was sleeping here if there was a riot or the police were out searching for their latest target. She wouldn't love it, but spending the night in this shithole of a warehouse was better than risking my life to get home.

Supposedly, it hadn't always been this dangerous. Way before I was born, SpaceTech—the biggest corporate conglomerate—took over all of Earth's governments. I didn't know the specifics, but I hoped whoever thought that was a good idea was rotting in hell. It'd turned into an unmitigated disaster for everyone on Earth. As long as it didn't hurt SpaceTech's bottom line, they didn't care what happened to us. They didn't care that we lived in a world with too much violent crime, corruption, and poverty.

SpaceTech was good at one thing—expanding to grow a stronger power base. Their colonization and trade routes spread across the galaxy and they'd found dozens of other species to exploit along the way. In all their greed to find more profits and expand colonization across the galaxy, SpaceTech finally met a race that was stronger, smarter, and had better tech than them.

From all the stories, it had been nice between Earthers and the Aunare for nearly a decade, but a few weeks before my seventh birthday, SpaceTech assassinated all high-level Aunare officials living on Earth and then started hunting everyone else on any of their colonies with ties to the alien race. In less than two weeks, most Aunare or part-Aunare people living on a SpaceTech-controlled planet were murdered. Except the few of us that got away.

That was why I forced myself to watch the news multiple times a day. I couldn't get caught. Especially since my mother and I were the only two high-level Aunare targets that managed to run before SpaceTech could murder us. There was a hefty reward for anyone who had information on our whereabouts. And if someone actually turned us in, their whole family would be set for life and then some.

If things could get worse, I wasn't sure how.

The news tonight was normal. One image caught my eye. A massive SpaceTech warship was landing on Terra 10—one of the colony planets on the edge of SpaceTech's official empire. A report of increased Aunare activity in the area sparked SpaceTech's IAF—Interplanetary Armed Forces—to arrive in force, quickly securing the area.

If they said the Aunare were dangerous, and they needed more forces in the area, then it had to be true. Right?

Except it probably wasn't true. I'd bet my day's wages from the diner that the Aunare weren't even close to that colony. SpaceTech wanted the humans to feel the alien threat all the time and used it to justify all the crap they did.

Another image caught my eye. The Albuquerque spaceport. Large ships—some commercial, but most were SpaceTech issued— lined up, waiting to land as far as the eye could see. The ticker underneath said that there was going to be a gala for the ground-breaking of the spaceport's expansion.

I shook my head at the screen. That meant that there were going to be SpaceTech officers showing up for it. I needed to be extra careful until they cleared out.

Slowly, all six channels—including my off-the-grid ones— changed to cover a new story happening on Earth. I flicked the button, linking all the vidscreens to show one large image: a half-Aunare guy, maybe a couple years younger than me, being dragged into an execution arena in Ohio.

Damn it. I looked away for a second but then made myself watch.

He was bleeding and dirty. Whoever had found him had beaten the crap out of him. SpaceTech liked to make a big spectacle of murdering any person with Aunare blood or ties left on Earth. There was a sizable reward for whoever turned in the enemy, and they got the added bonus of the best seat to watch the execution.

I whimpered and squeezed my eyes shut, but that didn't stop the sound coming from the screens. The guy pleaded for his life, and the crowd yelled, calling him names that should never be uttered. Not ever.

It wouldn't be long before a pack of rabid dogs would be let loose in there. When this kid started fighting for his life, he'd move with his inhuman speed. And, if he was from a strong Aunare bloodline, his skin would give off a golden glow like it was lit from within and tattoos would appear along his skin.

Once it was over, SpaceTech would come on the screen and tell Earthers here and across all the colonies how the Aunare were the problem. The Aunare were the reason Earthers' lives sucked ass. The Aunare were why there was so much crime and poverty.

What a crock of shit.

"Hey," Roan said as he gripped my shoulder. He'd changed into a pair of black pants and a bright blue button-down shirt, sleeves rolled up to his elbows, and a shiny pair of kicks I hadn't seen before. He looked a little more dressed up than usual. "I've been calling your name."

I shook my head and pointed to the screen.

"I saw the alert and hurried. How many times do I have to tell you not to put yourself through this?" Roan shut down the screens with a flick of his finger. "You okay?"

I nearly laughed at the absurdity of his question. "Is any of this okay? That kid will be dead soon and for what?"

"I know, but—"

"But nothing," I snapped. "There's nothing we can do about it. It's done. That kid did nothing wrong except exist, and that's how it is for all halfers. I have to hide or that's happening to me. And if SpaceTech ever finds me, I'll be wishing for the end that poor bastard is about to get right now. I haven't even heard from my father since I was six, but that won't matter to them when they make an example of me. Or worse. Use me to start the war they've wanted to fight for the last thirteen years." The air was rushing in and out of my lungs in quick gasps, and I knew I had to calm down before I really lost it. Roan wasn't the one I was upset with. This wasn't his fault. I shouldn't be yelling at him.

I wiped a hand down my face, giving myself a second to get it together. The mad started to fade, and bone-deep exhaustion took its place.

A searing pain ran through my finger, and that was it. I was done. My eyes burned, and I struggled to keep the tears from falling. "I'm sorry I snapped at you. It's been a long day. I worked a twelve-hour shift at the diner before coming here to teach, and I need to get home and—" My voice broke and I cleared my throat, trying to cover it up.

He reached a hand down, and I took it, letting him pull me out of the chair. "I'll walk with you," he said.

I took in his outfit again and remembered. "It's gamer night at Starlite, right? That's where you're heading?"

"It is."

"Then go. Have fun and forget about me and my problems."

"Come on, Maité. Don't be like that. I'm not letting you walk home alone. Not tonight. Not when you're upset."

"I can take care of myself, and you have plans. Just because a halfer fifteen hundred miles away is being brutally ripped apart by savage, diseased dogs doesn't mean I will be. At least hopefully not tonight." I tried to laugh, but Roan just stared at me.

"I know you're capable of handling everything on your own, but we both know it's better if I go with you. No one will bug you if we're together."

He was right. A girl walking alone at night attracted too much attention. I didn't want to mess up his evening, but if he was offering, I couldn't afford to refuse him. "You're right. I hate it, but you're right. Will you please walk with me?" I asked as I zipped up my hoodie, put my backpack on, and tightened the straps.

"That's why I offered." He pulled me toward the door. "Come on. Let's get you home. I know how you like that beauty rest."

I gave him a small smile. "Sleep is very important. Critical even."

Roan opened the door, holding it for me. "I'm aware." He might have heard it from me a time or two.

"Well, as long as you know."

I set the lock for the warehouse and then quickly undid my braid. I bent my head down, letting my long hair fall to shield my face as we stepped into the crowded streets. Patrol bots zoomed overhead, scanning everyone. I'd yet to be picked up by facial rec, and I was doing everything I could to make sure it stayed that way. I tried to wear neutral colors that didn't attract any attention.

Since I hadn't even broken a sweat tonight, I kept on my black active leggings and tank top. I pulled my hood up over my head.

Someone bumped into my shoulder as they pushed through the crush of people, and Roan tugged me closer to his side.

A ship flew low over the mishmash of buildings in Albuquerque's warehouse district. The engines were so loud I had to cover my ears. I watched it disappear from view but kept looking up for a second. Smog and light pollution hid any inkling of the night overhead, but I still tried to make out the stars. Hoping to see something to wish on. Hoping that something would change. But hoping never did me any good.

A Tykson revved its engine down the street. The single-person, hovering motorcycle was on the wish list of every eighteen-year-old I knew, except me. I was saving every little bit I had to buy my own ship so that I could safely get off this planet. It was my only chance at not getting caught. Another solid five years, and I might be close to having enough.

The blast of air under the Tykson spat dirt along my leg as it zoomed past. "Asshole. SpaceTech isn't even attempting to clean up the city anymore."

Roan ignored me because I could go on forever once I started on the company. "Haden stopped by during your intermediate class."

I winced. I'd seen my ex stop by, but thankfully, I hadn't talked to him. "What'd he want?"

We separated for a second to let someone pass between us. The side streets were way too crowded tonight. It was making me antsy.

"Jorge has a new recruit for you to train."

"What's the recruit's story?"

Jorge was the head of the ABQ Crew. He'd been the one that found my mom and me nine years ago when we first got to New Mexico. He set us up with a safe place to live and papers so we could finally stop running. I owed him everything.

In return, I trained his recruits for free so they could help patrol the streets. Someone had to make Albuquerque safe, and Space-Tech wasn't doing shit. This city owed a lot to the Crew, even if SpaceTech viewed them as a vigilante gang.

"Guy a year older than us wants in. He's got some medical training, so he'll be an asset, but he has to learn how to handle himself in case shit ever goes bad."

Anyone with medical training was welcome in the Crew. "I can do that. He'll have to start in my beginner class, just like everyone else. No bitching about being in with kids."

"That's fine. He's already agreed and won't be complaining. He'll be there tomorrow."

"Frosty." Teaching was the only thing I actually liked doing on Earth. It made me feel like I was making a difference.

"And…"

Oh boy. Roan never hesitated to say anything unless he was about to piss me off. "What?"

"Haden wanted to talk to me about something more personal," Roan said as he pulled me back to his side again.

That didn't sound right. "More *personal*? With *you*? You're not even friends with him."

"He, uh… He wanted my opinion on how to get back together with you." Roan blocked his face as if I'd hit him.

I rolled my eyes dramatically, and Roan stood straight again.

Haden was a bad decision that wasn't going away. "No. He *thinks* he wants to get back together with me."

Roan laughed. "How is him *thinking* he wants to be with you different than him actually *wanting* to be with you?"

"Because as soon as we're together, he'll start whining again. I'm not opening up. I'm not letting him in. Blah. Blah. Blah. He's got this picture of what we'd be like in his mind, but when it's not actually like that, all he does is complain. I couldn't ever be myself around him." And that had been the downfall of our relationship.

"Honestly, I'm starting to think I'm not built to be with anyone," I said. "Haden was sweet, caring, has a good business. In his spare time, he cooks for the homeless with the Crew. In theory, he's pretty perfect. Maybe even too perfect. But I don't know. That night when… I just wasn't feeling it. He touched my tattoo, and I ran. And then he kept calling and calling and *calling*. The more he called, the more I wanted him to leave me the hell alone. He doesn't deserve that. He should have a girl who actually wants to answer his calls."

"You're so touchy about your tattoo. Vanessa did a good job on it."

"I know it's weird, but I don't want anyone to see it, let alone touch it. It's personal."

Roan was quiet for a second, but I knew he didn't understand. I wasn't even sure I understood what my hang-up was.

"Well, you're the girl Haden wants," Roan said finally. "And that he showed up to talk to me? That takes balls."

"I guess, but don't you think it's a sign that you're my best friend and you're not friends with him?"

"No. He's in the Crew, just like us. Which means he's already been vetted. And I'm not in the relationship. That's just you and him. He really wants to try to see what's between you two, and you say he's perfect, so maybe it's worth another shot?"

Enough with this already. "Don't make me feel bad about it. I didn't feel a connection with Haden, and I tried. That's it. It's over."

"But did you try? Did you open up to him?" Roan raised his voice over the sounds of the people around us as we moved through a crowded intersection. "Did you tell him about your dad?"

"Are you crazy? No. Of course I didn't tell him about my dad." The only people who knew exactly who and what I was were my mother, Roan, and Jorge. Telling Haden was too big of a risk. One I couldn't afford to take.

"Maybe you should've."

I shrugged off his suggestion. "I just didn't get that feeling. That click. And I knew I couldn't tell him the truth."

"But you told me barely five minutes after we met, and I've never said anything."

I glanced at Roan for a second as we waited for the next crosswalk to light up. There were too many people around to really talk openly, but I knew what he meant.

Roan could've turned me in and become one of the richest people on Earth. The bounty on halfers was big enough to set a person up for life, but the bounty on me and my mom? It was astronomical. But Roan hadn't turned me in. I'd be shocked if he told me he'd even considered it.

Roan stared at me pointedly, giving me his best *see, it's okay to open up* expression. But he was wrong. For me, opening up meant death.

"You're different. I trust you." I wasn't sure what was different about him, but it was a gut feeling. I'd learned the hard way to trust my gut, and it said that hanging out with Haden was okay—he was damned pretty to look at—but nothing more.

"You could always just date me," he said way too loud, and I laughed. He gave me one of his big, infectious grins.

The light changed, and we started making our way closer to the intersection. Some girl pushed me into Roan as she wove past us. "Aww! Give him a chance. He's cute!"

I gagged. "Nope. Not happening." The idea of being with Roan wasn't appealing at all. I didn't have a sibling by blood, but Roan was more than my friend. He was my brother. He felt the same way, but we hung out so much everyone liked to think we were a couple. It'd turned into an inside joke with us.

Roan cupped his hands around his mouth. "Thanks for the support." He climbed up the light pole to stand above the swarm of people moving across the intersection in all directions. "Maybe you could meet me one night? I chill at Starlite every Thursday. It's frosty," he shouted.

The girl laughed and waved as she disappeared from sight.

Roan looked down at me. "I might have scored a date!"

His grin was infectious. "Dude. You're living in dreamville. She didn't even turn when she waved at you."

"No way. I'm so in with her. Trust me."

I laughed a real, gut-deep laugh for the first time in weeks.

He gasped, pretending to be hurt. "If I didn't know you as well as I do, I'd be offended right now."

"That's why I love you. Now will you get down from there before we get into trouble." I waved at him to hurry up. He was attracting way too much attention.

"Don't worry so much." He hopped down. "I love you, too. I just wish you could be happy."

"I'm as happy as I can be given my circumstances." That had to be good enough.

He dragged me across the intersection as the light changed to yellow.

I jerked my hand from his. Roan knew I didn't like to break any laws—even jaywalking—but it was already too late. We were the only people in the intersection now, and that was bad. I hurried across, dragging Roan behind me.

"Chill out. It's still yellow," he said as it turned to red.

Shit.

"Freeze!" A booming voice came from behind us. "IDs. Now."

We froze as ordered. The cop's words echoed in my ears, and I closed my eyes. My ID would never pass an official inspection, but running now would be worse.

This so wasn't happening. It was a bad dream. A nightmare.

I opened my eyes to find a SpaceTech police officer standing in front of us in his navy and gray uniform. He didn't have any medals over his right pocket, so I knew he was a newbie, but that was almost worse. Newbies liked to find ways to prove themselves.

The traffic and commotion around us had slowed a little as lookie-loos all stared, wanting to see what the officer was going to do to us.

"What's the problem, officer?" I asked in what I hoped would be a calm voice, but it came out way too high-pitched.

Roan grabbed my hand, and I wove my fingers with his.

"After your buddy here illegally climbed that light pole—which as you know is official SpaceTech property—you crossed the intersection on a yellow."

"I'm sorry, officer. We didn't notice it had turned yellow until we were already in the intersection. It won't happen again," I said a little too quickly.

The cop's eyes narrowed as he spotted something behind me. "Halt! Right now!" He lunged past me.

Across the street, some kid took off running. People started yelling as the kid pushed into the crowd, holding a bag in his arms. The cop dashed across the street, a speeder missing him by a fraction of an inch.

Roan dragged me to the curb so that traffic could move again, but I could barely move. I stood there frozen as people walked around us on their merry way. Meanwhile, my world had been seconds away from ending.

I tried to calm down, but all I could hear was my heartbeat thundering in my ears as if it was urging me to run, run, run, yet my feet stayed firmly in place.

"Maité?"

I swallowed, but I couldn't speak. Not yet. I wasn't even sure how to process the fear that still coursed through my veins. I felt Roan's arms wrap around me and I crumpled against him, my forehead resting on his sternum.

"Inhale."

Roan was quiet for a second, and a moment later, the sound of a pod stopping to hover in front of us made me jerk away from him.

I blinked a few times at the bright yellow, double-capacity pod. I almost didn't believe it was there. "You called a cab?" They traveled on tracks above the human-driven vehicles and had a sharp fee as a result.

"I think we've had enough excitement for one night. My treat."

As we sat down in the cab, that smelled way too much of body odor and cheap booze, I wondered how long I could actually keep hiding. My heart-shaped face made me look all too much like a female Aunare. I wasn't as tall as their women—they were six feet at a minimum, and I was five feet, seven inches. But if the shape of my face didn't give me away, the size of my eyes might. They were a little too big. Thankfully, I had my mother's light brown eye color instead of the brighter shades of Aunare blues and greens. Still, if anyone looked too closely, they'd know I was a halfer.

Roan took out a small case from his pocket. He carefully opened the lid, pulled out the fingernail-size device inside, and flipped it on. Now we could safely talk. The tiny piece of tech would disrupt all video and sound recording that SpaceTech mandated for every public transportation vehicle by adding static to both feeds so that our faces were now blurred and anything we said would come out as unintelligible hissing.

"Are you okay?" Roan said, breaking the silence.

My breath shook as I released the air I'd been holding in. "That was too close."

Roan pulled me into his chest, squeezing me tight. "It was my fault. I shouldn't have rushed through the light. And I really shouldn't have climbed the light pole. My flirting almost got us killed, and I'm so fucking sorry. I just… That was so iced. Seriously, Maité. SpaceTech Police Force *never* does that. They never stop people on the street. They have bigger problems and they—"

"I know." That wasn't the point. That wasn't why I was freaking out. "How much longer do you think I can keep hiding? Really. I mean, let's be honest here. It's only a matter of time before I do something wrong or someone notices. I can't change what I am. I'm terrified that—"

Roan pulled away and grabbed my face. "You won't get caught."

"You don't know that."

There was every chance that sooner or later, someone would

catch me. Every couple of months SpaceTech would remind the world who my mother and I were. My mother had altered her appearance some, and the aging they'd done on my toddler picture wasn't totally accurate. It's the only reason no one had turned us in yet. Someday someone would look at me, and they wouldn't see Maité Martinez.

They'd see Amihanna di Aetes. Daughter of Rysden di Aetes, the head of the Aunare military and second to the Aunare King.

And when that happened, there would be no more running from my fate.

CHAPTER THREE

I'D NEVER BEEN HAPPIER to be home as I was that night. Roan had paid the exorbitant cab fare and then left on foot for Starlite as soon as I'd entered the apartment building. He'd asked me to join him, but the close call with the cop was almost more than I could handle. All I wanted to do was hide in my darkened room for the next day or ten. But as I approached the front door of our apartment, voices seeped into the cement-lined hallway.

For a second, I dismissed them, but Mom's voice rose above a deeper one, and I stopped walking.

We rarely had anyone over at all and *never* at this hour. Something was going on, and it couldn't be good.

I tiptoed the rest of the way, pressing my ear to the door.

"I tried to contact you. I really did." Mom's voice was muffled, but I could make out her words. "But how could I know if he'd come for Maité after all these years?"

It felt like something slithered around my chest and tightened. Someone had come for me. But who?

Between the next three heartbeats, a few scenarios ran through my mind.

One. The cop from earlier had sent another officer to bring me in, but STPF didn't move fast, especially for an idiotic ticket.

Two. SpaceTech had found us. Two of Earth's Most Wanted. But if that were true, then there would be fighting and screaming and the sounds of my mother begging for them to leave me alone.

Then the third idea came, and I took a big breath.

There was only one other possibility. They were here. The Aunare were here. I'd stopped dreaming years ago that my father or the Aunare would show up to rescue us. I wasn't sure what this meant except that my life was about to change in a huge way.

The fluttering in my stomach started small and crescendoed into thousands of flying butterflies. I wasn't sure if it was excitement or nerves, but specifics didn't matter.

Better face this now.

I slid my backpack off my shoulders and unlocked the door.

I expected to see an Aunare person sitting in my living room, but I was wrong. The man sitting in the metal folding chair I'd painstakingly painted my favorite rich blue-green shouldn't be here. He shouldn't be relaxing, his feet on our crates-and-plywood coffee table like he was chatting with an old friend. Not just because it was late and he was a stranger. But because he was SpaceTech.

I stepped inside the apartment, closing the door softly behind me. My mother was sitting on the worn-in couch, leaning toward the man, and the look in her eyes said she was hopeful. Excited. Happy. But he was *SpaceTech*. His blond hair cut painfully close to his head and his rod-straight posture as he sat up, dropping his feet from the plywood, and watched me were a dead giveaway. SpaceTech guys all had the same look. Like it was beaten into them when they joined the corrupt company. But there was something different about him.

He wasn't wearing the navy-and-silver dress uniform of an officer or even a navy-and-gray one of a low-level SpaceTech grunt —instead just a plain white T-shirt and jeans with a little rip in one knee—but I knew what he was. Except he wasn't arresting me.

And he wasn't disgusted, hateful, violent like other humans when faced with a halfer.

"It's you," he said, and if I wasn't mistaken, there was more than a touch of awe in his voice.

His gaze traveled over every inch of me as if he were making sure I was here, real, and unharmed. He might as well have been touching me for all the weight it carried. And the worst thing—as he grinned, something in me softened.

This was so iced. I couldn't actually be attracted to a SpaceTech officer. Sure he wasn't much older than me—maybe a year or two at most—but he was *SpaceTech*. They were the worst.

His light blue eyes sparkled as he slowly stood. "You're here."

"Yeah." I let the bag slip from my fingers, thudding onto the floor. I needed my hands free in case I had to fight. "But you really don't have to cry about it."

"Maité," Mom said, but I couldn't tear my eyes away from the guy in our living room.

That might have been out of line, but he was making me uncomfortable. Who was he? What was his story? And why was he happy to see us?

"Maité." Mom's voice was firmer. Her eyes were glassy, her hands clasped at her chest, and her face screamed that every hope and dream that she'd had for the last twelve years were coming true. We were saved.

But I wasn't that naïve. "Where's my father?"

Mom and the stranger shared a long look, and I understood completely. "He sent some SpaceTech double agent douche instead of coming himself? Classy."

The stranger's laugh, a deep rolling sound, lit a flame deep inside me. One I instantly wanted to snuff out. How could I be attracted to a SpaceTech officer? It was absurd.

I shoved that feeling down, and a new one came bubbling to the surface. Anger that my father wasn't here.

I knew I was being unreasonable. Of course he couldn't come

here himself. He was an important Aunare. He was the enemy on this planet. If he was caught, it'd be bad for everyone.

But that didn't stop me from being hurt that my father hadn't come. And when the disappointment finally hit me, it was too much. Everything that happened today piled up to one big emotional shitshow. The implant in my finger driving me crazy. When I'd moved too fast in front of Hillary. Nearly getting caught by the cops. And now this guy was here?

My breath started coming in bigger and heavier gasps. My emotions boiled over, and my skin started to glow.

It wasn't like a full-Aunare glow—the one that showed power and lit up Aunare skin with tattoos showing their paths in life. My skin hadn't ever done that. I wasn't sure why, but it was probably better that it hadn't. This minor glow was alien enough that I resented it. It was a giveaway I couldn't conceal or control. I didn't always hate what I was, but right then, right there, I did. I never liked to show myself in front of anyone but Roan, my mother, and Jorge. This guy might not be turning us in, but he was still a stranger.

"What's going on here?" I needed some answers.

"This is Declan. He's a friend."

"He's SpaceTech." I spit the word out with bitterness even though I knew that this particular officer wasn't a threat. I knew that he was somehow connected to the Aunare and maybe even my father in some way. But it still didn't make any sense to me. SpaceTech officers weren't to be trusted. Full stop.

"I am SpaceTech," he said. "But I'm also a friend."

"That's an oxymoron if I ever heard one." I took a breath, trying to calm down. To stop the glow. To find some kind of normal to hang on to while my world was upended. "Do we need to run? Are they coming?"

"No." My mom stepped toward me, and I stepped back, holding out a hand to stop her from coming any closer.

I wasn't sure what the glow was about. It didn't happen often, but when it did, it scared me. There hadn't exactly been any

Aunare I could ask about what it meant. I didn't trust what Space-Tech said completely, but apparently, Aunare were dangerous when glowing.

"I know I need to find out what's happening here, but I need a second to calm down. Clearly." I headed down the hall to my room.

"You don't have to hide what you are from Declan. I promise," Mom said, but she didn't come after me.

I closed my door to shut out the sound of their whispers. Air. I needed air. Even if it was lung-coating, polluted, smoggy air.

I tucked my hands in my sleeves, pulled the hood low over my face, and went out the window. I sat on the fire escape and gave myself a second to breathe. Tonight had gone from messed up to completely bizarre. The Aunare had sent a SpaceTech guy to get us. I'd never seen that coming, not in a million years. As far as I could tell, the Aunare hated SpaceTech as much as SpaceTech hated them. Although the Aunare had a much better reason for their animosity.

I threaded my legs through the rungs in the railing and leaned my forehead against the cool metal. From fifteen stories up, the people on the street looked like tiny toys. Cars and pods rushed this way and that. People wove through each other on their way home or to a party or a late shift at work. I was sure some of the Crew were down there patrolling. I was restless enough to join them, but I had to deal with this guy—Declan—and whatever it was that he wanted.

Everything came at a price. Even the Crew had strings. I just had to figure out what strings Declan came with.

Slowly, the glow faded from my skin, and I started to feel a little less anxious. I sat there, watching the movement and lights from the city below me, and for a few minutes, I could just be. But then my bedroom door opened and softly shut, signaling the end of my solitude. Someone walked through my room, climbed out my window, and settled down beside me with his back against the railing

I glanced over. Declan. "My mom sent you to calm me down? Probably smart. Of her. Not you." I rested my head on the railing again. "She knows better than to come after me. You should've definitely bowed out."

"Nah. I'm not one to back down from a challenge, and I figured this was a chance to start the catching-up portion of our conversation."

"Catching-up?" I studied his face again, and I definitely didn't recognize him. "To catch-up implies we have a history, and I've never seen you before."

The sounds from the street below were softer from up here. We were far above even the pod lines. The wind whipped around the buildings, and the bots were tiny black dots buzzing around as they tracked movement on the streets.

"We do have a history. But your mom told me about what happened, so it's okay that you don't remember me." He grinned. The way he was looking at me like I was a long-lost friend, was actually nice. I just wasn't sure why he seemed to feel like that about me. If I knew him, it was before Albuquerque. At least nine years since we'd had any sort of friendship, and I'd been a child.

Maybe I was reading him wrong. I didn't think so, but maybe. "You're happy to see me?"

"Yes." His answer was so instantaneous and vehement that I knew he was telling the truth.

This wasn't what I pictured happening when a SpaceTech officer found me, but apparently, Declan was a different kind of SpaceTech officer.

But why? Who was he? What was his story? I had questions, and I wondered if he was going to answer any of them. I assumed not, but it wouldn't hurt to ask. "Why're you happy to see me? You're SpaceTech. It doesn't make sense." If the Aunare had some allies in SpaceTech, why wait until now to use them?

"I'm not just SpaceTech, so it makes perfect sense." Declan grinned bigger if that was even possible. "I'm immensely happy and relieved and thankful because you're alive and healthy and

God—" The grin faded as he looked away, and I missed it. "I imagined all kinds of things over the years. All the things that could've happened to you... I don't have to worry anymore. That's a really good feeling."

"Sorry." Some strange guy spent thirteen years worried about me? It was kind of weird.

"Don't be. Rysden—your dad—"

I huffed. "I know who he is." I might not have seen him since I was six, but I knew his name well enough.

"Of course you do. Stupid. Sorry. I'm just nervous. I finally found you, and it's like a weight that I've been carrying for thirteen years has finally eased. This nightmare is almost over, and fuck if I'm not excited right now and making a total ass of myself."

The click happened. Right then. Just like it had with Roan years ago. Call it intuition or a gut feeling, but he was being truthful. I didn't think he could fake that rambling admission.

"You might be handsome—"

"That's nice to hear." The megawatt smile was back.

"But I honestly don't think I know you. I don't remember anyone named Declan from my past."

"You're wrong." He shrugged. "Or wrongish. I lived next door to you a long time ago."

"How long ago? We've been in Albuquerque for nine years."

Before then we never stayed in one place long enough to make friends. Some people made an impression along the way, but most of those early years we spent running from one place to the next were a blur. It didn't help that I'd been so young, too.

"It's been four thousand, seven hundred, and thirty-two days since I last saw you."

An exact count in days? That wasn't what I expected. I did some quick math in my head. "Before Liberation Week? You knew me from back then?"

"Exactly."

"And you're old enough to remember me?" He didn't look that much older than me. A few years maybe.

"Calling me handsome *and* young? Careful. You're going to do all kinds of things to my ego." He tilted his head as he watched me as if trying to get a read on me.

I just stared at him for a minute. My gut said to trust him, but I still wasn't sure what to make of him. He thought he knew me, but he didn't really. I was barely a person at six.

"I was ten when you were born," he said, finally. "That makes me thirty now. And you're turning twenty in a couple months."

He was right about my birthday, but he could've learned that from Space Tech records.

"So, yeah, I remember you, but I don't take it personally that you don't remember me. You were just a kid when everything went to shit. Plus, your mom helped those memories fade."

"Right."

My mother had my memory wiped when we first started running. I was having a hard time not speaking in Aunare, and she said I kept talking about things that would get us caught. So she took me to a doctor to help me forget that part of my life.

I wasn't sure how to feel right then. It was weird that someone besides Mom, Roan, and Jorge knew who I was, especially when I didn't really know him.

I stared out at the skyline, not wanting to hold his gaze anymore, but I could feel his eyes on me. Watching me. Waiting for me to ask another question.

I had to get up the nerve to talk about the one thing I didn't want to talk about. After a minute of quiet, I finally asked him. "My father sent you?"

"Among others. There are a lot of people looking for you."

So it wasn't just my father. I shoved down the disappointment and asked another scary question. "SpaceTech? But you're not going to turn us in."

"Exactly," he said. "SpaceTech is looking for you, but there's not a chance in hell I'd ever turn you in."

I gripped the railing a little tighter to keep from running. It was one thing to assume SpaceTech was still after me and another thing to have confirmation.

"But that's not who I meant," he continued.

"Who? Besides my father and SpaceTech, who would care?"

"It's a long story, and I'm not sure now is the time."

No. That wasn't how this was going to go. "If there's someone after me, then I should know about it. Now."

"He's not after you. Not like you mean. He's not a danger to you." His cheeks turned the slightest bit rosy. Good. He should be embarrassed by all his rambling, especially if he wasn't going to spill.

"Now I'm really confused."

"I shouldn't have said anything."

"I guess not." Because now I wanted to know, and that he wouldn't tell me was annoying. But there was one question that was possibly more important.

"I noticed your room is a painted deep blue-green, same as that chair."

That was an odd thing to bring up. "Yeah. It's my favorite color."

He gave me a funny look, one I didn't know how to interpret. "It doesn't remind you of anything? Anybody?"

"No. I just like it. Makes me feel calm." I shrugged. "So where is he?"

"Your father?"

Oh my God. Was he trying to annoy me? If he wasn't going to tell me who this other person was that was looking for me, then he needed to drop it. "Yes. My father."

"On Sel'Ani." The Aunare home planet. "It was too dangerous for him to come back to Earth, but we've been looking for you for a while. We weren't sure if you lived through the initial attack at your house, but Lorne said—"

"Lorne?" I cut him off. "That's the other guy looking for me?"

"Not the point. Sorry. I'm rambling and saying things I shouldn't. It's not like me... Shit." He looked up at the sky and let out a long breath. "I'm really messing this up royally, but it's so surreal. I've been searching for you for *thirteen years*."

The smile he gave me felt a little awkward because he was obviously genuinely so happy. But since I didn't know him, I didn't share his excitement. At first, it felt nice to cause his excitement, but now it was making me uncomfortable.

"Here you are. Just like that."

"Yeah. Here I am. But how'd you find me? Why now?"

Jorge had paid to fix my files when we got to ABQ, but the patch-up was a piss-poor job. When we were twelve, Roan checked the files and added more schooling information, some medical charts, and he even put in some shopping history to make it look like we'd been in Albuquerque my whole life. As far as my records went, I was Maité Martinez, born and raised here. I'd been Maité so long that my real name didn't feel like me anymore. I wasn't even sure I'd answer to it if someone used it.

"Well, it took me a long time. Clearly. Mostly because my brother is an asshole and never liked your family. He figured I knew your escape route, and he was right. Your father told Lorne and me what to do if something happened, but nothing went as planned. It took me a week to shake my brother, and that week was enough for you to slip away. I almost caught you at a train station in Austin, but after that, your mom ditched the plan, and I couldn't find you. Until now."

Our four years of running were all a blur now. We'd been moving so fast, not really sleeping and homeless for chunks of it. I didn't even remember being in Austin. "And? Why now? I must've messed up somehow, but when?"

"Ah. Your implant." He tapped my finger. "They had to run your blood—"

"They didn't run my blood!" No. I'd been careful. I started to get up, but he held my leg for a second, stopping me. That pause gave me enough time to think.

"They couldn't run it," I said, more calmly this time, "because they didn't have it. Roan was with me. He—"

"They didn't run it, but techs had to report the vial missing. There are a lot of strict rules about implants and handling of blood. Even with third-rate doctors."

"You're messing with me. Right?" This was bad.

"Unfortunately not. No one thinks that SpaceTech would keep track of this kind of stuff, but… If you'd replaced it with a different sample, you'd have been better off. And since your blood was handled by such a seriously shitty doctor…" His voice was getting louder, and I could see the anger growing in him. "That dirty office? That man… He barely qualifies as a physician. He could've maimed you, and—"

"I know. Okay. I *know*," I said quietly. "But it's not like I had much of a choice. I have to blend. And don't you judge me." I stood up, unable to stay sitting next to him. "You don't know me. You haven't been through what we have. Don't you dare judge me."

He held up his hands. "You're right. I'm sorry. But honestly, no one would've run the blood if you'd have left it. The way that office is set up, they weren't actually testing it. Only keeping track that it was accounted for. But since it went missing, it was marked as someone trying to hide something and…"

Ice-coated shitballs. I hadn't even thought of that. I was so screwed. I leaned back against the railing, sliding down to the floor of the balcony. I hugged my knees to my chest, silently cursing myself for making such a massive mistake, but how was I supposed to know they wouldn't actually test the blood?

Declan slowly stood up. "The record of the missing vial went into the system with your picture. Anyone in the system with your stats goes into my search folder. I'd know your face anywhere." If I wasn't mistaken, he was almost wistful with his words.

If he knew my face, then that meant that others would, too. We were going to have to run. If not right now, soon. "But SpaceTech doesn't know where I am?"

"No. Not yet. But if I found you, it's safe to say that someone else will, too. It's time for us to get you out of here."

"And my mom." I wasn't going anywhere without her.

He nodded. "And your mom."

I couldn't believe that this was finally happening. After the scare I'd had tonight, I'd thought I was inches away from being caught. And I was kind of right. Except this particular officer was probably the only one that wouldn't turn me in.

I didn't even know how to feel. What would it be like to see my father again? Would he even like who I was now?

What was it going to be like not to be afraid anymore? "So what now? Do I pack or…?"

"Take whatever you want with you, but honestly, if you came as you are now, that'd be fine, too. Your dad is just ready to have you back."

That last statement was so emotionally loaded. I didn't even know how to separate the swirling mix that was brewing deep inside. My skin started to glow, and I groaned.

Declan reached down to run a fingertip along my cheek, and I shied away from it. "It can't hurt me, and you shouldn't have to hide it."

That it wouldn't hurt him was something, but the rest… "I hate it. I can mostly hide, but this…" I squeezed my eyes shut. "I can't always control it."

"You can *always* control it if you—"

Knocking came from inside the apartment. Three loud thumps followed by even more then some garbled commands.

My skin grew brighter to glow like the moon.

Only one type of person would knock like that.

CHAPTER FOUR

I JUMPED up and shoved Declan into the railing. "You!"

"No. I had nothing to do with this." He held up his hands. "I swear. But please, let me handle it."

I was pushing past Declan before I could think, to dive back through the window into my bedroom.

Declan grabbed my arm, and I gasped. I'd moved fast, yet he'd managed to catch me?

"Calm down," he said. "We have to think."

"My mother is in there." I wrenched my arm away and sprinted through the apartment. This time I was too fast for him to catch, but I froze when I hit the living room. Mom was sitting on the couch wringing her fingers, but she hadn't answered the door.

For the second time in under an hour, I was confused. The only people in the building that IAF would be here for were us. I was pretty sure of it.

Mom shook her head slowly and pointed up at the ceiling.

The pounding came again.

Thump. Thump. Thump. "Interplanetary Armed Forces. Open up or we'll be forced to break down the door." It wasn't until I heard the voice that I realized it was still too soft. IAF—Interplanetary

Armed Forces—was here, but not at our apartment. They were upstairs.

Telly and Frank lived up there. They weren't Aunare. They were just an older couple with too many cats.

Footsteps sounded overhead. The officers yelled. My palms started sweating.

IAF couldn't do this. Not to them. Telly was sweet, and Frank wouldn't hurt anyone.

The sound of something shattering and a thud had me moving across the room.

"No, Maité," Mom said. Her knuckles were white as she twisted her hands. "It's too late for them. You have to leave it be."

"I can't. This is wrong. I have to go help them." Another thud had me racing for the front door, and then all of a sudden, I was on my back. I tried to move, but Declan's legs were pinning mine, and one of his thick arms was across my shoulders, firmly pressing me into the floor. "What the hell are you doing?" This guy was about to be on my shitlist. I didn't care if he was here to help me. Not anymore.

His smile was gone. "If I let you up, are you going out there?"

What was his problem? "Of course I'm going out there. They need help."

"Then I can't move."

I ground my teeth as I tried to rein in my temper, but he was pissing me off. Didn't he get that Telly and Frank were nice, innocent people? Whatever was going on in their apartment, I was sure they didn't deserve it. "Get off me or I'm screaming."

He slammed a hand over my mouth. "No. I didn't come this far and work this hard to find you to have you throw it all away for whoever the hell is up there. They're expendable. You're not."

Expendable? How could he say that about anyone?

A thump was followed by Telly's cry, and I struggled to get out from under Declan. He pressed down on his arm across my collarbones. I shoved at his arm, but it was like moving a boulder, and he had all the leverage. For now. All I needed was an in, and I could flip him. I'd move too fast for him to stop me.

He removed his hand from my mouth. "I know you want to help them, but you have to think. What will happen if you go up there?" He paused. "We both know that they'd start asking you questions. They'd ask to scan you. Anything legit would drive a halfer with the weakest Aunare blood to distraction, and you're from the second strongest Aunare line."

He was right. I knew it, but that didn't change what was happening above my apartment.

"We both know that useless piece of crap in your finger doesn't count to IAF. Like you said—it's to blend. That's it. You'd be scanned, and that would be a huge red flag. You'd be thrown into a cell for interfering, which would give them enough cause to run a full scan on you. Not that they need cause."

I knew where he was going with this, but I hated it.

"You'd be outed as a halfer, and if they find out exactly who you are... It's not just your neighbors' lives on the line here. IAF takes you in, it's war. *Millions* will die. The only reason the Aunare haven't made a move against us yet is because, until tonight, *no one* knew where you were. Not SpaceTech. Not your father. But now your father knows... This is dangerous. So fucking dangerous."

My lip trembled as I heard Telly pleading with the IAF upstairs, and then something heavy hit a wall.

"You can't save them. Not now. But you can maybe save everyone else," Declan said.

He was right. God, I hated it, but he was right. The glow started to fade to nothing as I gave in.

A chunk of the ceiling rained down on us, and I gave up fighting, relaxing into the carpeting under me. My heart felt like it was shattering for them, and I squeezed my eyes shut. Hot, silent tears poured down my face.

This was so iced. I was from a strong Aunare line—a line of generations of fighters—and still, I couldn't do a damned thing for my neighbors. "I'm letting them die so I can stay hidden. How can I look myself in the mirror after this?" He'd pinned me pretty well, but if I'd fought him harder... If I'd actually used my Aunare strength and speed...

He settled down beside me, staring up at the ceiling like I was. "Over the years I've done a lot of things I'm not proud of. I've blurred the lines so that I could stay in the good graces of Space-Tech. So that maybe I could change things. So that one day I could find you and your mom alive. Hell, for a lot of reasons I guess. But there were times I could've stood up and saved someone but didn't. I've always tried to look at the bigger picture. The times when I didn't stand up against something that I knew was wrong? I'll have to live with them."

I stared at his profile as he talked. He was pretty, even his bad company haircut couldn't hide his perfect nose, square jaw, and light blue eyes. A little scar on his right cheek only gave him a bit of character.

He caught me staring and smiled, but it wasn't as happy as it was earlier. His eyes didn't crinkle in the corners. "I'm telling you only because I don't want you to feel guilty about not saving your neighbors. When you look in the mirror, you'll hold your chin high because I was the one to stop you. This was my bad. You can put this on my shoulders."

No. I couldn't let him take the guilt for my inaction. "Why make me feel better when you were just trying to do what's best for me? Why do you care so much about me? I still don't get it." There was a scream from upstairs, and my hand found his.

He squeezed my fingers tightly. "You know that saying about not being able to pick your relatives but picking your family?"

"Sure," I said, focusing on him and his words as the noise upstairs descended into deathly quiet.

"Well, I picked my family because the one I was born into is deplorable. But I got away. I spent a lot of time on Sel'Ani as kind of an exchange student and—"

What? "I didn't know there were programs like that."

"It was kind of a one student thing. I don't think it went quite how they were hoping." He turned away from me and was quiet for a second. Lost in his memories.

I wanted to ask so many questions, but I bit my lip to stop them from pouring out.

"Anyhow," he said after a moment. "I got to know your dad and his family pretty well. And Lorne and his family. And you and your mom. You all took me in, overlooking everything about where I came from and who my family is. I think it's safe to say that your father helped me survive a shit childhood and shaped me into the man I am today. Even if I have some things in my past I'm not proud of doing, I still can be proud of who I am. I can never repay him for that. So helping you now, it's a given. You're family."

"With that kind of loyalty... You make my dad sound like an amazing person."

"He is."

"I wouldn't know. I don't remember him at all. All I know is what I see on the news. He's as much a stranger to me as you are." A few years ago, this would've bothered me more, but I'd found my own family. I had Mom, Roan, the ABQ Crew, and my students. I'd come to a place where I was okay. I was surviving.

Sure I was scared. Every damned day. But I had a plan. I'd been taking flying lessons on any kind of craft I could find on the odd chance that I'd find something I could afford to buy one day. It was slow, and I'd had a few setbacks, but I was going to get there.

But everything was changing again, and it felt like I was caught in some weird alt reality. Now I was here, talking about my father?

"To hear you say that you don't know him would break your father's heart."

"He's right, *mija*." I nearly jumped at the sound of Mom's voice.

I let go of Declan's hand and sat up to see her, still sitting on the couch. Tears glistened on her cheeks.

"He hasn't tried to find us," I said. "If he really cared, we would've been out of here a long time ago."

"That's not true," Declan said. "I'll let him explain for himself, but not knowing where you were and if you were okay—it wasn't just me going through that torture. You're his only child. He loves you more than air, and not being here right now is killing him."

I didn't know what to say to that. It felt so surreal to be sitting here talking to a stranger—who wasn't exactly a stranger—about my father—who was also a stranger... To be thinking about actually leaving this planet soon?

"What's the plan, Declan? When do we leave?" Mom asked.

"That part is trickier than I anticipated."

Shit. Now that he said we were leaving, I wanted to go. Now. Waiting was going to kill me. Possibly literally. "What's tricky about it? Besides the obvious harboring fugitives part."

"My brother is here," he said as he stood up.

Mom hissed.

He reached down and pulled me up off the floor. "Exactly." He let go of my hand, and I felt cold without it.

I rubbed my palm off on my pants to stop myself from reaching out to him again and moved to sit next to Mom on the couch. "Why does your brother being here make this trickier?" I felt like I was missing something.

Declan moved to the door, leaning against it as if to stop anyone from coming in. "My brother hates the Aunare. He's made his career outing halfers, and it all started with you and your family. It's a lot to get into right now, but let's just say he blames you specifically for everything that's gone wrong in his life. Catching you is everything to him. He thinks it will bring him closer to our father. Closer to finally getting back at me for every wrong he thinks I've done him. Closer to starting the war both he and my father want."

"Jesus. What did I do to piss him off so badly? I was a kid."

"Nothing." He crossed his arms as he stared fiercely down at me. "You didn't do anything, and you've got enough to worry about without worrying about a past that you can't change. What matters right now is that we have to be very careful with what our next move is." He let out a long sigh.

If he felt nervous about this whole thing, I wasn't sure how I was supposed to feel about it.

"You got that implant over two weeks ago, and I've known exactly where you were since then, but I couldn't come. Not until I had a good reason. I used the groundbreaking of the spaceport's expansion as my excuse to get here, and my brother was off on VegaFive. He shouldn't have come for something like this, and yet he landed an hour after me. I got to your apartment about five minutes before you did. And not long after that, IAF takes in your upstairs neighbor?"

I always knew that things were crazy dangerous for me, but it felt more real in that moment than ever before. To know that IAF had been that close to picking me up was terrifying.

"My brother knows I'm in this building, but it'll take him a few days before he realizes that he sent IAF to the wrong apartment. Or maybe he'll never realize his mistake. I don't know if we'll be that lucky, but either way, I know now exactly how closely I'm being watched. And that this building is also being watched."

I didn't like that. Not at all. "We should leave. Right now."

"No. I can't risk moving you. You're the pawn my brother needs to draw the Aunare into a war."

It wasn't safe to stay, and it wasn't safe to leave. I wasn't sure what that left us with. "So what are we going to do? We can't just wait for him to find us. We have to leave."

"That's exactly what he wants. You run now, and he'll know. AI will be searching for anything out of the ordinary on their surveillance cameras. Any coming and going that's not routine will stand out, and you can't afford to stand out. Especially not now. The spaceport gala is in three days, and this city is going to be a madhouse with over five thousand SpaceTech officials already arriving from all over the galaxy. After that, everyone will leave, including my brother. I'll make sure of that. Once he's gone, it'll be much easier to sneak you out of here. He'll be in cryo for his trip back to VegaFive, and the STPF here is lazy. They'll have been working nonstop for days, and won't care anymore. They'll be ready for a break. Without him on their asses, they'll drop their search."

"So four days?" Mom asked.

"Hopefully four. Five max. I'll be keeping an eye on both of you, but I won't make contact. Not unless I have to. I just can't mess this up. There's too much at risk."

Mom put her arm around my shoulders. "We'll wait a little longer. A few days won't matter to us."

"Thank you for being understanding. Keep doing your normal routine until I come back. Go to work. See friends. Whatever it is you normally do, do that. Don't deviate too much, because AI will be looking for irregularities in traffic." He moved away from the door, stepping closer to me. "I wish things were different but... Just be ready. Because when I come back, it'll be time for us to run." He took another step closer. "I won't leave you a second longer than I have to."

"Okay." After everything Declan had told me, I trusted him. Maybe more than I should. So, when he said we'd leave as soon as we could, I believed him. "We'll be here."

"Good." He closed his eyes for a second as he let out a long breath. "Good." He walked to the door but stopped before opening it. He glanced at me over his shoulder. "It really is good to see you again, Amihanna."

The sound of my birth name made my chest tighten. I wasn't her. Not anymore. "My name's Maité."

"Right. Maité." He gave a stiff nod and stepped outside.

When the door shut, I gave my mom a squeeze before she could start asking me if I was okay or what I thought of Declan or any of the other million questions I could see running across her face.

"I need time to process. We'll talk in the morning?"

"Okay. But if you change your mind, come get me. I'm not sure I'll be sleeping anyway."

"Okay." I slipped out of the room, heading back to my bedroom. If I thought I needed a minute before... Overwhelmed didn't begin to describe how I felt now.

I crawled up on my bed until I was pressed into the corner. It felt nice, having the walls at my back. It made me feel like nothing was going to sneak up behind me. I hugged my knees into my chest and took a breath.

A few days and this nightmare would be over. I might be heading into a totally different life. I didn't know what that would mean, but at least it would be a change. That was a start. It was more than I'd had to look forward to in a long time.

CHAPTER FIVE

IT'D BEEN three days since I found Declan waiting in my apartment. Since then, the city had been swarming with SpaceTech's goons. I know that he said it was only going to be a few thousand of them, but it felt like everywhere I turned there was another uniformed officer. Everything in me said I should lay low and hide, but I kept hearing Declan's voice in my head telling me to do my normal routine. The AI would be looking for changes in the routines of locals. So that's what I'd been doing, but it wasn't easy. Especially this afternoon.

There'd been a table of ten SpaceTech officers in the diner. I'd been terrified every second of showing what I was. Of one of them recognizing me. Of something happening to mess up my chance of getting away. When I took them the check at the end of the meal, I wasn't thinking about anything other than getting them gone as quickly as possible.

As I left the table, one of them knocked over a bottle of ketchup, and I caught it. I *caught* it. My reflexes had been too good to be human.

Stupid. So stupid. So *unbelievably* stupid.

Who cared if it made a mess? None of them caught on, but it'd been close enough that I'd moved slowly through the rest of my shift, even if it pained me to do so. I wasn't messing up again.

After thirteen years, I was on the verge of actually having some freedom. All of the waiting for someone to find us was done. All of the hiding and pretending and lying was almost over. Almost over. But not yet. I wasn't quite there yet. This last little bit of waiting and pretending felt more intense than what I'd felt the last thirteen years combined. The stress of staying hidden was eating me up inside, devouring me.

Mom had been trying to keep me calm during my shift, but she was too busy cooking in the diner's kitchen to handle my freak-out. We'd been slammed. As soon as my shift was over, I waved goodbye to her and sprinted straight to the warehouse gym. When my last student was gone, and all my classes were done, I decided to take a second for myself. Instead of rushing home, I'd set up some equipment to work out. It was just me and my thoughts, but once I started thinking, my skin started glowing. I'd been moving nonstop since then.

Sweat coated me, but the workout hadn't been enough to stop the glow. At this point, I wasn't sure it'd ever be enough.

I'd turned on some music an hour ago because the silence was too much, but no matter what I did, I couldn't dampen the glow. It was almost as if working out was making it worse, but I didn't know how that was possible. Usually working out calmed me down and the glow would slowly start to fade until I'd snuffed it out entirely.

A whistle cut through the warehouse, and I stopped moving. Roan.

I spun to see him walking through the door, slamming it behind him. His shirt looked wrinkled, and his thick, tightly curled hair was sticking out even poofier than normal. He waved a dark finger through the air, and the music instantly turned off. "Have you been here since your last class?"

"Yeah." My words sounded hollow as I tried to catch my breath. "Just trying to get in a good workout."

"It's three in the morning. I'd say you should be done, but looking at you tells me otherwise."

"Is it really that late?" I'd only planned to stay until my mind and nerves settled, but that hadn't happened yet. I wasn't paying attention to the time.

"Liz is losing her mind."

My mom. Damn it. I'd forgotten to call my mother, and it was totally understandable that she was upset. Especially since I'd turned off all my message and call notifications. "I'll call her."

"Good. She woke me up, convinced that you were out with me, but except for your classes here, I haven't seen you in days. You're shutting me out, and now you're here all night, looking super-Aunare, and all that's telling me that something's going down. What happened?"

"Nothing happened." Lie. "I'm fine." Another lie.

He stared me down.

Roan had a point. The glowing skin was a dead giveaway. It usually only happened in times of extreme stress, and even then I could get it to go away pretty quickly. But not tonight. Tonight was a whole new level of Aunare that I wasn't prepared to deal with.

I walked to my bag and grabbed a water. I wasn't sure I should tell him what had been going on, but he was right. I'd been avoiding him for days, and that didn't sit right with me. I wasn't sure how to tell Roan I was about to leave. I'd probably never see him again. Saying goodbye might kill me.

I wanted him to come with me. Leaving him here didn't seem like a good option. If anyone found out that he was my best friend and that he knew exactly who I was, then he'd be in danger. But asking him to leave his family and friends and home? That was a huge price to pay for my friendship.

If I asked him to come, then where should I draw the line? Should I ask Declan if we can take Roan's family, too? Jorge? The whole Crew?

I should've kept to myself all these years, but I wouldn't have survived without Jorge. Without the Crew. And for sure, not without Roan.

"Is it the SpaceTech douches?" Roan broke the silence. "I know it must've been hard the last few days, but the news says most are gone this morning. In, like, a few hours."

"It hasn't been easy, but no. I... Something's happened." How could I tell him I was leaving? It seemed impossibly hard.

I lay down on the floor, staring up at the ceiling. Now that I wasn't moving my body ached. I'd pushed myself too hard.

Roan stood over me. "Just say it. We haven't had any secrets between us ever, and I don't think we should start now."

He was right. Again. "A man came to my house a few nights ago." I spit out the words as quickly as I could. "*I'mleaving-intwodays*."

"Leaving? What the hell are you talking about?" Roan sat down hard next to me. "What man? Where are you going?"

"He's SpaceTech, but an ally of my father's. He found me because of the implant—"

Roan's dark skin paled, making his green eyes look brighter. "But we were—"

"I know. We were careful, but the missing blood was flagged." I closed my eyes. "I'm scared of leaving you behind. If anyone finds out—"

"You're skipping a few steps. Are you sure you can trust this person?"

"I think so." I took a breath. That wasn't true. "Yes. I absolutely trust him."

"Seriously? You're sure."

I opened my eyes. I knew Roan well enough to see the concern on his face. That tilt of his chin and wrinkling between the eyes said it all. "Yes. I'm leaving for Sel'Ani tomorrow or the day after."

Roan was quiet for a long while, staring off into the distance before he finally let out a breath. "I knew this would happen eventually, but I'm not ready. How're you doing?"

I held up my hands. The golden shimmer from them wasn't

super bright like I'd seen from full-blooded Aunare, but it wasn't nothing either. "I've been working out for the past five hours, and it's not getting any better."

Roan touched my hand carefully with his fingertip. "You're glowing brighter than I've ever seen."

I itched to pull my hand away, but Declan said it was safe. At least now I knew I couldn't hurt anyone when I was glowing, but I felt even more clueless about what it meant and how to make it stop. "It's never lasted this long before."

"Shit, Maité." He ran his fingers through his hair, making it even poofier. "How are you going to get home like that?"

"Exactly. I might have to sleep here." I shrugged. It sucked, but as far as I could figure, it was my best option. "I'll keep moving until I drop, and then maybe I'll be able to sleep. But I forgot to tell Mom. I'm sorry she woke you."

"Don't worry about that. I can try sparring with—"

The lock beeped as it disengaged. The only person besides me and Roan who had the code were my mother and Jorge.

I popped up from the floor when I saw it was neither of them. "What are you doing here? How do you know the code?"

Declan grinned. "I have my ways." He was wearing a pair of loose black active pants and a dark gray shirt. He was a little sweaty with a touch of red in his cheeks, but he didn't look out of breath. I wondered if he'd been out for a run.

Roan moved to stand between us. "Who the hell are you?"

It was nice that he wanted to protect me, but I could do that just fine on my own.

"This is the guy I was just telling you about." I stepped around Roan. "Do we need to leave now?" I asked Declan.

"No. I'm just checking on you." He gave a nod to Roan. "Hi, I'm Declan. A very good friend of her family."

"You turn her in, and I'll kill you." I'd never heard Roan's voice so deep and dark. He meant every word.

Roan was the best.

"You don't have to worry about me. I promise," Declan said to

Roan before turning his attention to me. "You okay? You've been here for a long time, and I got worried."

Roan laughed. "You don't need to worry about Maité. She can more than take care of herself."

"Just because she can take care of herself doesn't mean that she should have to."

Roan's smile disappeared. "You think you know her better than I do?"

They stepped closer together, and I could feel the fight brewing under my skin.

No. This wasn't the time or the place. I put myself between them again. "Roan, this is Declan. He's an old family friend." I turned to Declan. "This is my best friend, Roan. Please be nice to him. He's family to me."

"Who is this guy? He looks familiar."

"I get that sometimes. I'm SpaceTech and have been for a long time, but I work to help ease the tension between Human and Aunare."

Roan crossed his arms. "Ease tension? Is that a joke? After what we did to the Aunare—what we're still doing to them—it's a wonder they don't slaughter us all. Must be a fun job."

Declan let out a long sigh. "It's not easy, that's for sure. We're in the middle of a very deadly chess game, and Amihan—"

I cleared my throat. Roan knew my name, but I didn't like hearing it. The name gave me hope, and even with Declan right there, I wasn't sure I could believe that he was going to whisk me away and everything was going to be fine and dandy in a day.

"*Maité* is the mother of all pawns," Declan said.

"I don't know if I like the comparison. I don't want to be some piece that could be moved around and played." That turned me into an object, and I was a person.

"I wouldn't either if I were you, but it doesn't change the truth." He gave me a solid once-over that had me squirming. "You're glowing."

"I'm aware." It wasn't something anyone could miss.

"Why?"

My cheeks heated. I didn't like to show weakness, but this was one I couldn't hide. "I don't know. I can't get it to stop."

His eyes widened. "What do you mean?"

"What do you mean what do I mean?"

"Okay. Why won't it stop?" He said the words slowly.

Was the man being annoying on purpose? "How the hell should I know? I'm a little stressed at the moment and—"

"I'm an idiot." He wiped a hand down his face, and when he looked back at me, his mouth dropped open slightly. He finally understood. "You were never taught how to control it. You don't even know what it means, do you?"

"No. It's not like there are any Aunare around that I can ask, and I can't trust any information that SpaceTech puts out."

"You can't hide when you look like that." He was stating the obvious, but at least he was getting it.

"Exactly. I can't leave here. I'm stuck. Usually working out helps, but apparently not tonight."

"What do you do when your skin starts glowing out there?" He motioned toward the door.

He wasn't wrong to be surprised. It was kind of a miracle I'd survived this long.

No part of surviving had been easy for me. "I learned to cover all my body parts whenever I'm in public, so it's just my hands and face I have to worry about. If I start glowing, I shove my hoodie over my head, use my hair as a shield, keep my head down, and stick my hands in my pockets. All while moving as fast as possible to a safe place." I stared off at nothing.

This whole conversation made me feel too exposed. I didn't like that my skin was giving away my feelings, and I didn't like talking about my feelings to a stranger. Even one that I trusted. The glow gave too much of it away, and talking about my survival methods just seemed odd to me.

"It used to happen only once in a blue moon, but it's been getting worse the last year or so. But I'm on edge. I'm going to keep working out, and it'll stop." Declan tilted his head as I said that, and my heart sank. He said he'd be keeping an eye on me, which meant that he knew I'd been here, working out, for over five hours. "It has to stop, right? Eventually?"

"No. It actually doesn't. The glow has to do with energies. I can help some, but I'm not Aunare. I don't really understand it all." He pointed to the desk. "I'm going to make a call. You need to talk to someone who can explain it to you better than me. Just need a second, and I'll get it connected."

He went to the desk and placed three small devices on it. I wasn't sure if he wanted privacy for the call or if he just needed the desk for the devices, but I was going with the latter.

I walked toward him. "What are those?"

"I need to make an untraceable, off-the-grid call. This will help me do that."

"Is it safe?"

He gave me a fierce look. "I would *never* do anything that would put you in danger." His voice was firm but had a tinge of hurt in it. He was mad that I would even question that, but what he didn't get was that I always had to make sure.

I let out a breath. "Okay."

"But, as I said, you need more help than I can give. You need to talk to another Aunare." He powered them up and started tapping his fingers in the air. "Hey."

"Is there a problem?" A rich voice came through the line. He sounded worried, but the voice—the timbre and texture of it—sent shivers through my body, and I'd pay my hard-earned money to listen to the man talk all day.

I'd thought that Declan's voice was nice, but this one was out of this world.

I almost laughed at that thought. Whoever he was, he was out of this world. Literally.

"No problem. At least not how you mean," Declan said.

"What does that mean? Did you find her? Is she okay? What's—"

"She's here with me now. She's fine. I'm—"

"You're in the air then? When do you—"

"No."

"What do you mean?" The voice deepened to a low rumble before he switched to Aunare. I gasped as Declan did, too.

I'd only heard it in old videos, but it was a beautiful language. Full of lovely hushing sibilant sounds that soothed my soul. I didn't understand the words, but they felt familiar.

Mom said my first language was a mix of Aunare and English. They decided before I was born that she would speak to me in English and my father would speak to me in Aunare. But once Liberation Week happened, it was too dangerous to say even a single Aunare word. Ever. The brain wipe the doctor had done got rid of every Aunare word I knew.

Now the language seemed familiar but forgotten. Like if I could just clear away the fog, then I could understand what they were saying, but as it was, I didn't understand a single word.

"Is that my dad?" I asked. The voice sounded familiar, but I didn't know how. Maybe it was the memory wipe.

Declan and the other man stopped talking.

"Amihanna." That one word felt like a caress that slithered its way into my heart and grasped it. The timbre of it surrounded me, and all of a sudden, I was filled with heat and drowning in want.

My throat was dry as I blinked my eyes, trying to figure out why the light was suddenly so bright, but then I realized it was me. One word to me from the Aunare man and I was wrecked.

If I'd thought my skin was glowing before, I was wrong. Now it was so bright I could've lit up the entire city.

This was so messed up.

CHAPTER SIX

THE ROOM WAS SILENT, and I knew I wasn't the only one holding my breath. I'd never seen my skin glow so impossibly bright before. There weren't any tattoos on it like the ones I'd seen in pictures of the Aunare, but the glow was just as bright. I didn't even know this was possible.

I dropped my chin to my chest as I realized that there might be nothing I could do to make my skin stop glowing. This was it. I was going to have to move into the warehouse. Become a hermit. Because I wasn't going to be able to leave until the glow was gone, and I was having zero luck stopping it before the Aunare man did whatever he did to turn it on full-force.

"Whatever you just did, stop it," Declan said.

Me? "I didn't *do* anything." I was trying to stop it, not make it worse.

"I know." Declan blew out a long breath. "Lorne did something."

Lorne? That was the guy who was looking for me. If I wasn't so exhausted, I would've tried to find out more about him, but right now, all I cared about was making the glow stop.

"I didn't do anything, Declan," Lorne said. "I literally spoke her name, and that made her skin glow more?"

"This can't be happening." My voice sounded whiny, even to me. "I'm so screwed. I can't hide like this. What am I going to do?"

Roan shrugged at me, and I knew he felt my helplessness. I could see my glow against him as if I were a bright light shining on him.

"I worked out for hours to make the glow fade a little, and now... I'm serious. I'm open to suggestions. I've tried everything and I'm so tired and I can't—" I was trying not to panic, but my breath was heaving in and out, and I was so tired. So unbelievably tired. I just wanted to go home, but that wasn't happening.

"Saying your name shouldn't have done anything," Lorne said. "I need to see you."

"No," Declan said.

"Declan. I'm not asking." His tone was all demand. "I need to see her. Turn. On. The video. Feed."

"No." He massaged the bridge of his nose, and I wondered if he was as freaked out as I was. "Jason's here. I think he suspects —" Declan stopped, as if speaking it aloud would make it true. "Trust me. I can't risk using a stronger signal. He knows what to look for, but voice should be fine. The signal isn't as complex."

Lorne muttered something in Aunare. "When does Jason leave?" The name "Jason" was soaked in hatred. I couldn't imagine hating anyone that much, but I was sure he had a good reason.

"Nine a.m."

"And you'll leave after him? Come straight here?"

The way he was asking the questions—more demand than anything else—I wondered who this guy was and why he cared so much about getting me back to wherever he was.

"Yes. Tomorrow evening." Declan looked at me. "Everyone will have cleared out. It should be safe by then."

I closed my eyes for a second, thankful that this was actually happening. I really hoped it'd be safe tomorrow. I needed to get out of here before I got caught. Especially since the whole glowing thing was getting worse.

"Good." Lorne heaved a heavy sigh. "Good."

"Wait. Jason?" Roan said. "Who is Jason?"

"Jason Murtagh is—" Lorne started, but Roan cut him off.

"I knew you looked familiar. You're Declan Murtagh, Space-Tech CEO's black sheep son. Jason is the golden boy, primed to take over for your dad whenever he retires. And Lorne ni Taure? Heir to the Aunare throne?"

Declan froze and then looked to me. If I wasn't mistaken, there was guilt in his eyes. He'd withheld his last name, and I hadn't asked. I assumed he was just someone who worked for SpaceTech, but I knew those names as well as I knew my own.

I didn't know what to say. I hadn't realized who Declan was. I trusted him with my life, but he was almost as high up in the SpaceTech food chain as he could get. Maybe I shouldn't have trusted him, but then again, if that really was Lorne ni Taure on the line, then I wasn't the only one trusting a Murtagh.

Declan stood there, waiting for me to either kick him out of the room or reaffirm my friendship with him. I knew if I asked him to leave, he would. But I didn't want him to leave.

In that moment, I realized that the fact he was a Murtagh didn't really change anything. Not to me.

Declan must've seen a change in me because he looked away briefly to Roan as if to ask *Can I trust him not to turn us in?*

"You can trust Roan. I swear. He's known exactly who I am for nearly a decade, and he's never said a word about it to anyone." Something didn't add up. "Why are you helping me if you're a Murtagh?"

"It's a long story." His voice sounded as tired as I felt.

"You're full of those," I said. "One day you'll tell me what exactly what's going on."

Declan huffed and gave me a half-smile. "One day. Maybe."

"Who else is in the room, Declan?" Lorne asked. His voice had a sing-song quality to it, and I found myself inching closer to the desk. I wanted to hear more of it.

"Me, Maité—the name Amihanna's used for the last ten years—and her friend, Roan," Declan said.

"Is he just a friend?"

"I think so?" Declan looked at me for confirmation.

I wasn't going to answer—it was a bullshit question that didn't require a response—but Roan thought otherwise.

"Am I her boyfriend?" Roan laughed. He was enjoying this a little too much. "If you're interested in her at all, you just made a massive critical error. Trust me. The last guy that pulled possessive needy shit on her—"

"Last guy?" Lorne started talking very quickly in Aunare.

"Just ask her," Roan said. "You got a question, ask. Maité's straightforward. No games."

I wanted to slow clap my best friend. This was why we'd stayed so close over the years. He got me, just like I got him. "And stop talking in a different language about me. If you have a problem, just say it."

"It's not that he has a problem exactly," Declan said.

"I wouldn't say that." Lorne's voice had a predatory rumble to it that made my insides hum in response.

Whoever this guy was, I wasn't sure I ever wanted to meet him. The way he made me feel from just the sound of his voice was too much.

"Forget him," Declan said to me.

Lorne muttered something softly in Aunare, and I wanted to reach through the stupid device and wring his neck. What was he saying? "Switching to a language I don't know to talk about me when I'm *right here* is insanely rude."

Declan rubbed a hand over his mouth. He cleared his throat as if to stop a laugh, and when he moved his hand, the smile was still there. "We have a problem if you have a boyfriend, because once we leave, who you were here on Earth will most likely come out.

Anyone who knew about you might be in trouble. So is there someone we should be worried about?"

Okay. So there was a valid reason for the question, but the verdict was still out on Lorne, and I wanted to know what Declan thought was so funny. "I was just talking to Roan about that before you got here. I have to say, I'm really worried about a lot of people. Especially Roan and his family."

"We'll protect him and his family, and your mother already told me about Jorge. We'll see if we can get them to a safe place with new identities before the news hits. Probably to one of the colonies, but if not, we'll move them to an Aunare planet."

"Seriously?" Roan said, and I couldn't tell if he was excited or pissed or both.

"Yes. I was going to find you tomorrow. Jorge, too." Declan was quiet for a second, and I could almost see him thinking through what he was going to say.

"Is there anyone else that would be brought in for questioning because you and your mom went missing? Anyone that you spent more than a few hours with, one-on-one?"

"Not really. They wouldn't drag in the whole Crew, would they? Or the people from my classes?"

"No," Declan said. "They'll question them, but you were in hiding. They won't hold them accountable."

"What's the Crew?" Lorne asked.

"One thing at a time, Lorne," Declan said. "Anyone you've been dating?"

I swallowed down the knot forming in the back of my throat. How many people's lives was I going to mess up just by being around them? Haden didn't deserve to be ripped from his life here on Earth. I didn't love him. I never did. He'd been nice and convenient, and I'd been so unbelievably lonely. I'd just wanted to be normal for a little bit, and he gave that to me. At least for a while.

The idea that Haden could get into trouble didn't sit right with me. I never should've started something with him, no matter how many times he asked me out. "I was dating a guy, but he doesn't know anything about me. He—"

Roan snorted. "Haden couldn't crack her, no matter how hard he tried. Poor heartsick guy showed up a couple nights ago trying to figure out how to get—"

"Seriously!" My cheeks grew hot, and I wanted to punch my best friend. "Shut up. What happened between Haden and me isn't anyone's business," I said. "And since he doesn't know who I am, he should be fine."

"No. Keep going, Roan. I was enjoying—" Lorne started, but Declan cut him off.

"Let me handle this." Declan took a breath. "Okay, but this Haden spent one-on-one time with you that can be tracked. Is that right?"

I shrugged, trying to come off as casual, but I felt like I was being interrogated and I didn't like it. I knew he was just trying to figure out who was in danger, but it still felt weird. "I guess that's accurate."

"Okay. I'll check Haden out. Anyone else?"

"Nah. She didn't spend much time with anyone. Maité keeps it all locked up tight—" I shoved Roan, but he just laughed and happily kept on spilling about me. "Only people who know anything about her are Jorge and me. She's always stressed though, so I've been trying to get her to hook up with someone. A little one-nighter might help her relax and get rid of that glowing problem."

My mouth dropped open, and for a second, I was too pissed to say anything. But that passed quickly. "*Ohmygod.* Shut the fuck up, Roan, or I'm going to murder you."

"And you never offered?" Declan asked, ignoring me. His eyebrows raised in curiosity.

Roan and I shared a look. This happened a lot. "Gross. No," Roan said.

I agreed with him too much to be insulted by his disgust.

"Oh. He doesn't like girls," Lorne said.

"I like girls, but Maité is just... No. That's not happening. Ever. *Gross*."

"Did you have to say gross twice?" I was going to be offended in about two seconds.

Roan rolled his eyes. "I didn't mean it that way. You're hot. Lorne, I know you can't see her now, but..." Roan let out a slow whistle.

"This just keeps getting worse." I sat down on the floor. If everyone was going to ignore me, I might as well get comfortable.

Roan shot me a wink. "And she can kick some fucking ass. She's totally frosty when she gets going, but no. She's like a sister to me. Thinking of her like that? It just ain't right. I don't see that ever changing."

"Back at you." I sighed. "Look. I get that whoever I might have come into contact with could be in danger, but I don't understand why we need to get into my whole dating history. It's really a nonevent. Suffice it to say that I'm just not wired that way. I'm a fighter, and that's that."

"Bullshit, Maité."

Oh man. Roan was about to slip into the same argument we've been having for the last few years.

"Everyone's wired that way. You just haven't met the right one yet. You can't move like you can and—"

"That's *enough*!" I said. "I've had a really long, really hard day." I narrowed my eyes at Declan. "A group of your cronies were at the diner, and I swear one of them knew who I was and I've been panicking ever since. I'm done with this. All of this. I mean what the hell am I going to do? I can't leave the warehouse like this. I look like the goddamned North Star. Nothing I'm doing is stopping this glow, and to be honest, I'm exhausted. I've been hiding for so long, I just don't want to do it anymore. I want it to just end. For everything to be over. I'm *done*. I can't take one more day..."

I flopped on my back before I got too emotional and squeezed my eyes shut. But it was true. I was so close to getting away, but it still felt like a distant hope. Like it wasn't real. And the fact that I couldn't even get a handle on my skin after hours and hours… I was wrung out.

"Amihanna?" Lorne's voice felt like a hook in my soul. The way he said my name made my skin hum.

"Please. Stop." I didn't mean for it to come out as snappy as it did, but I couldn't help it. "You make it worse every time you talk to me."

"I can't fix a lot of things, but if you want, I can stop the glow."

"You can?" I wanted his help. I wanted it more than anything because I was so tired and the glow wasn't going away. But Lorne wasn't even in this solar system. How could he possibly help?

"Yes. If you'll let me," Lorne said. "How much do you remember about me?"

I glanced at Declan. He was sitting at my desk again, watching me carefully. I'd been through this last night with him. I don't remember Declan. And I really didn't remember anyone named Lorne. "Will you still help me even if I don't remember you at all?"

"Yes."

I was desperate, but I couldn't lie. "I don't know anything about you except what I've seen on the news. I'm not even sure I know what you look like. I don't know how you and I and Declan are connected. I know my father is basically best buddies with your dad—that together they rule the Aunare—but other than that, I don't understand why you'd even care enough about me to help me."

Lorne's long sigh felt like a stab in the chest. "Declan. Please. How could she forget?"

"Her mother had parts of her memory wiped."

Lorne started quietly muttering in Aunare. I glanced at Declan, and he motioned to hold on.

"It's not as bad as it sounds. Wipe is too strong of a word. Liz had them dulled enough that Ami wouldn't remember you or me or her father or much about the Aunare. When they were on the run, Ami was really scared—with good reason—and kept asking for you and crying and asking to go home to Sel'Ani and speaking in Aunare. It sounds like it was a really terrifying few months. They were almost caught a couple of times. Liz had to make sure Ami didn't say something that would get them killed. She was desperate. Liz said it got easier in some ways after the wipe."

"Can it be undone?" His words were clipped, and I wondered what he was thinking. What he was feeling. Who he was to me.

"Liz told me that Ami should learn Aunare quickly once she's exposed to it. Once she feels safe, she might start to remember some of her memories, but again, her age at the time of the wipe is a factor. Some of those memories would've faded anyway because she was only six the last time she saw any of us. The wipe gave them an extra push. Although some part of her might think of us as familiar, she said to think of this as a fresh start with her."

"I just...I thought she'd remember me. Us." His voice wavered.

I felt terrible that I'd hurt him. I didn't like that there were things that I was forced to forget. It felt too much like a betrayal, even if I understood why my mother had done it. Getting a little kid to keep quiet must've been an impossible task.

"I know," Declan said. "Me, too. But I think that's why she's reacting to your voice. The memories are really buried in her subconscious, but they must still be there."

"That had to be a very skilled wipe. Removing a language and memories of people, but leaving who and what she was."

"Yes. Liz used all of their money for it."

A loud gasp came through the line. "How did they survive without the money we left for them?"

I didn't know much about the wipe, but this was a question I could answer. "We worked. Wherever we went, we found odd jobs. Cleaned houses. Mom did hair for a while. Babysat for neighbors. Did handy work. I read a book on plumbing and..." I let out a breath as I remembered all the times I'd been scared. The times when we didn't have enough money for food. The times when we huddled together with only a blanket to keep us warm as we slept on the cold pavement.

"None of it was easy, but we made it work." I didn't know

what all Mom had told Declan, but I didn't feel like spilling my guts about the last thirteen years. And I certainly wasn't going to argue about the choices my mother made to ensure our survival. "Can you help me with my skin? I want to go home. I need sleep. My shift starts in five hours, and I haven't been to bed yet. I just need to get through the next day."

"Your shift?"

"For the last five years, I've been waitressing at a diner during the day. My mom is a cook there, too. She got me the job once I was old enough. In the evening, I teach martial arts to people—mostly teenagers. I don't make money on the classes though. But I'm going on twenty hours of no sleep after a double shift, teaching, and my workout—"

"You've been working out since ten, and it's now past three in the goddamned morning. That's more than a workout, Maité," Roan said.

"I had to do *something*. Once you left, the glow…" I took a breath. "Lorne. Can you help me? If not, I'm just going to crash here and see if sleep will help."

"I can help." He was quiet for a second, and I wondered what was running through his mind. "If you've been working out for hours on end, you might have thrown your energies too far in the wrong direction. We're very sensitive to frequencies and energy shifts—especially emotional ones. Lie down and relax. I'm going to try and align them. This way is a little slower, but it's all I can do from here."

I lay back and closed my eyes, waiting for something to happen. After a minute, he started playing some instruments that sounded like soft bells. Sometimes the notes from the bells seemed to draw out endlessly. One note melded into the next, and then a bell would toll. I'd never heard anything like it before, but the vibrations of the instruments—whatever they were—made my hands and feet tingle.

And then he started singing with them. I didn't understand the words, but the tingling worked its way toward my heart until I felt something in me loosen. Align. Unlock. It left me with a feeling that everything was going to be okay. I wasn't so on edge anymore, and that was a huge relief.

I didn't want it to end, but when the last note finally faded into nothing, I stayed quiet on the floor. I knew Declan and Roan were still there, but with my eyes closed, I could pretend that it was just me and Lorne and his impossibly seductive voice and the instruments he was playing. It was beautiful.

"What was that?" My mouth was dry, and I knew I had a water tube somewhere in the warehouse, but I didn't want to get up. "How did you make me feel so…relaxed?"

"It's an ancient Aunare healing tune, and I used crystal bowls to enhance the effect. It's the first one we learn as children. Balance in all things."

He took a long, slow breath, and when he spoke again, he sounded sad. "I can appreciate what your mother did, and I understand that she's managed to keep you safe this long, but I'm glad Declan finally found you. You are out of balance. Out of practice. And without any training, you're in a very dangerous position."

"Dangerous position?" I wasn't sure what he meant by that.

"If what Declan says is true, you don't know what it means to be Aunare, let alone what it means to be from the di Aetes lineage."

He was right. "No. I don't know what any of that means."

"It's okay. You'll learn. But you should know that this is just a bandage. Tomorrow, when you wake up, you could feel more on edge than ever. And that's okay, too. Just remember, you'll be safe soon." He was quiet for a second.

Lorne seemed to think things through before he spoke, while I tended to just vomit out words. I wondered if all Aunare were this careful with what they said or if that was just Lorne. "Declan?"

"Yeah." Declan's voice popped the little, peaceful bubble I'd been in, surrounded by Lorne's voice.

I blinked my eyes open, and for the first time in hours, my skin didn't have any glow to it at all.

Roan and Declan were standing together against the wall. They looked like they'd been talking, but I'd been so focused on Lorne's voice that I hadn't heard them at all.

"Teach her the Aunare breath. It could help," Lorne said.

His crystal blue gaze found mine, and he gave me a nod. "I will."

"Is there any other reason why your energies would be so out of tune? Hearing my voice shouldn't have done that."

Something about energies out of whack made me think of something. "I have an implant."

"Remove it, Declan." His response was quick and vicious. "She can't survive with that in her. Especially someone with her lineage."

"Sure. I can remove—"

"No. He can't remove it. I *need* it," I said. "I hate the stupid chip. It puts me on edge and hurts all the time and is generally driving me insane, but if someone notices that I don't have one, I'm dead. They're used for everything, and I can't blend without it. It's only one more day."

"No. No. I hate this. I want you to leave *now*. Get off the planet. Who cares if Jason finds out? Use the Aunare boost on your ship. If I hurry, I can meet you just outside the Naustlic System and take you the rest of the way. They won't be able to keep up with my ship."

"You come inside SpaceTech territory, it'll be an act of war. Too many innocent people would die." Declan took a breath. "And I can't get through the checkpoints as they are now even if I wanted to leave. The boost won't help with that. Once Jason is gone, they'll lighten. They won't think twice about me, but I won't risk her getting caught. Not now. After talking to Liz… I just can't risk it."

I wanted to know what he was talking about, but I didn't think he'd answer me now. "I agree with Declan. I've been doing this for thirteen years. A few more hours isn't going to kill me."

Lorne was quiet for so long that I wondered if the signal had been severed.

"Fine," Lorne finally said. "Teach her. I want to stay on the line, but it's hard for me to not be there and…"

"I understand. I'll take care of it, brother."

"Thank you. Amihanna?" Lorne said.

The way he said my name sent shivers through my body. I couldn't control or stop them, and it was driving me crazy.

Why did hearing my true name from him make me feel like I was falling from the top of a skyscraper with no parachute?

"Yes?" My voice was weak, but there.

"Soon."

The single word—part promise, part threat—had my heart beating way too fast.

My mind was instantly empty of everything except echoes of that one word.

Soon.

Soon.

Soon.

It felt like someone ran their fingertip up my spine, and I shuddered and then let out a startled laugh.

What the hell was that?

Roan was staring at me as if he didn't know me. *What was that?* He mouthed to me.

I shook my head. Some guy had just rocked my world via galactic teleconference. I wasn't sure there was anything I could say about it.

Declan quickly hung up and packed up the device, and I was left feeling like part of me was gone.

What the hell?

Declan slid it into his pocket and then glanced at me. "You ready?"

"For?" I honestly couldn't remember.

"The Aunare breath. It should help you. It's something to use before the glow gets this bad."

I had a second to be disappointed. To wish that Lorne was still on the line. He should've been the one to do it, but the more I thought about the way Lorne made me feel, the more relieved I was that he was thousands of light-years away. It was too much. Way too much.

I forced all my questions about Lorne out of my mind. The only thing that mattered right now was learning how to control the glow of my skin. Because if the next day went even a little how the last few days had gone, I needed that knowledge.

"I'm as ready as I can be for someone who hasn't stopped moving in almost twenty-four hours." My shift had started at eight a.m. yesterday, and we were now pushing six a.m.

For the next hour, Declan taught me the calming breathing patterns of the Aunare. Little by little, it started to make sense and feel familiar to me.

"I think you've got it now. You ready to go home?" Declan asked, finally.

"Yeah." I was too tired to see straight. I had to get to my bed before I crashed.

"Come on. I'll drop both of you off."

Roan was curled up on the floor with the pillow and blanket I kept stashed in the makeshift locker room. I was going to have to wake him up, and he would have questions for me. Questions I didn't want to answer.

"Is it safe to leave with you?" I asked.

"I think so, but I'll keep an extra close eye just in case. Okay?"

I nodded. "Thank you."

"You don't have to thank me."

But I did. I was thankful for Declan. I hadn't known him for long, but he felt familiar. I wondered what I was forgetting. What did my mom have wiped?

And Lorne?

Lorne.

Just thinking his name after hearing his voice had me on edge, and I felt like there were so many things that Declan was keeping from me. So many things about Lorne. About the Aunare. About why he was here helping me when he should want me dead, just like his father and brother did.

One more day, I told myself. One more day of pretending and hiding and lying. One more day, and then I'd be far away from here and have all the answers I wanted. I just hoped that I made it through the day without anything else going wrong.

CHAPTER SEVEN

I'D ONLY MANAGED to get a couple hours of sleep before Mom woke me up for my shift at the diner. She was too afraid of someone noticing my absence to let me skip it, even though I begged. Two hours into my shift, I regretted listening to her. Lorne wasn't kidding about waking up and being more on edge than ever. The stupid implant wasn't just making my finger burn constantly anymore. It was starting to malfunction, which meant I was messing up every entry. As I jammed in the order via the kitchen's tablet, I wished I'd let Declan cut it out. The thing was a pain in my ass and now slowing me down while I worked. It was useless. I was seconds away from grabbing a knife and getting rid of it myself.

The more the day wore on, the more I realized staying polite to my customers was going to be an impossible feat. The one currently sitting at my counter was looking at me and licking his lips like I was a juicy steak he wanted to take a bite of. I wasn't sure I had it in me to be civil to him, let alone polite.

The man gestured to the line of display bottles behind the counter. "I'll take an Orange Fizz."

Figured he'd want such an expensive drink. The way he was

looking at me like he could own me if he wanted, made me think he must have money.

"Plus, eggs scrambled with extra cheese. Extra bacon. Extra butter on my toast." His gaze traveled over my body as he spoke, making my skin feel extra greasy.

I showed him my teeth, hoping he'd mistake my expression for a smile. "Anything else?" My tone was a little too sharp, but he didn't notice. His gaze stayed fixed on my chest.

"Not right now, sweetheart. But maybe later."

I bit back a retort and turned around carefully. Spinning too fast would make my short skirt rise, and no way would I let him see even a glimpse up my skirt. I reached into the metal fridge, bending at the knees to find the Orange Fizz.

It took me entirely too much time and effort to find the last bottle hiding under a mountain of other sodas and ice cream. When I turned back to the jerk, his head was tilted to the side.

Pervert.

I knew it. I had him pinned from the second he walked in the door. He was at least a decade and a half older than me—maybe more—and he was trying to see up my skirt? Disgusting.

I grabbed my multitool from the counter, popped the cap off the bottle, and barely stopped myself from slamming it down in front of him. Losing my cool wouldn't be smart. Especially not when I was so close to escaping this hellhole. But, thankfully, Declan had been right. Not a single officer in uniform had entered the diner today. This perv's haircut had me wondering for a second if he was one in plain clothes, but he was too tubby around the middle to be SpaceTech. They had fitness requirements because of all the space travel that was required of them.

I dropped the multitool in the sink under the counter, placed a glass of ice next to the bottle, just in case, and showed him my teeth again. "Anything else?" Even with my clipped tone, the idiot mistook that as an invitation, wrapping his fat hand around my arm before I thought to pull away.

My finger burned again, and the urge to unleash every emotion

I was holding inside grew so strong my hands shook. It was taking everything in me not to kick his ass, grab my go-bag from my locker, and leave the diner.

But that's not what Declan said to do, and I wasn't about to blow my chance at getting away from here by losing my temper with some random customer.

I clenched my fists. *Don't do it. Don't do it. Don't be stupid now, Maité.*

I let out a breath for the count of six, and then let the air slowly back into my lungs for a count of three, using the Aunare breathing technique just like Declan had taught me.

Tonight, I'd be gone. I could do anything for a few more hours. I'd been through so much worse.

But still, as his thumb moved up my arm, I couldn't think of one worse second in my life.

"You been in Albuquerque long?" The sound of the perv's slightly nasal voice irritated me.

"All my life." The lie I'd uttered so many times before slid smoothly off my tongue. I had to get away from him without causing a scene, but how?

"You ever been off planet?" he asked.

An idea came to me. This would end in bloodshed, but not his.

The perv's eyes stayed glued to my breasts as I slowly reached for the multitool again. "No," I said.

"This close to the oldest spaceport on Earth and you've never gone anywhere? You've never been off planet? Not even once?"

"No, sir." My heart hammered. Why was he asking me this? What did he care?

"You ever meet any Aunare?"

"No, sir," I answered him as calmly as I could. My voice didn't waver, but it was a little higher than normal. I had to fix that. "I was only a little kid when Liberation Night happened. I don't remember them at all." My voice sounded more natural. I knew he wasn't asking because he suspected anything. He didn't know anything about me. The perv was just being a jerk.

"You sure? Pretty girl like you would attract them. You almost look like one, but then you can't be a halfer. Right? I saw you using a chip earlier."

Shit. I should've worn my hair down.

I took another practiced breath, hoping to prevent my skin from glowing. He didn't know anything. Not yet. But I couldn't give him any reason to ask more questions, and I had to get out of there. Now. "The Aunare were exiled from Earth when I was barely more than a baby, so there's no way that I could know any." I flicked the corkscrew open under the bar with my thumb and twisted it around in my hand. It was awkward, but I managed to slice my palm.

"Ouch!" I said with a heavy dose of whine and jerked my arm free from his grasp. "Damn it." I held out my bleeding palm. "Excuse me. Gotta clean this up." I tucked my palm against my chest and spun toward the kitchen a little too fast.

My skirt flew up. Air brushed the back of my legs.

I tugged it down but it was too late, and his chuckle made me feel dirty. I moved a little faster to get away from him before I did something I'd regret, but the sound of his laughter followed me into the diner's kitchen.

What a perv.

The diner's uniform wouldn't bother me so much if it wasn't so revealing. The dress was supposed to look like the diner's original 1950's uniform, but the manager updated them two years ago. It was now made of a stretchy fabric. The top clung to me like a second skin. The bottom was still flared, but it'd lost three inches. For most of the customers the waitresses were invisible, but every once in a while someone would come in here and think the missing three inches meant that we were open for other kinds of business.

The noise of the kitchen covered up his laughter as the door swung shut behind me. A round bot zoomed past, nearly nailing me in the face with its bowl of chopped onions. "Watch it!"

Mom caved a couple weeks ago and let the boss buy a bot to

help her with prep work. I wasn't used to it flying around here yet. It made the diner more efficient during rush hours, but neither of us liked it.

Mom was alone in the kitchen, busy in front of the large griddle top. Bacon strips sizzled as she placed them on the hot surface. Her thick black hair was pulled back in a ponytail as she cooked. It was just us here today, thankfully. From the way she was working—a little slower than her usual frenzy—I knew I wasn't the only one tired and on edge.

I spotted a towel and grabbed it.

"Order up, table five," Mom said as she looked over her shoulder at me. She spotted me wrapping my hand in the towel, and her eyes went wide. "What happened?"

"It's nothing, but there's a guy at the counter. I needed a distraction to get away from him and—"

"Maité. Don't you dare pick a fight with anyone. Please. I know you're on edge, but…" She wiped her hands on what used to be a white apron and looked at the screen to check the orders. "It won't be long now. Just stay focused. Do your job."

Was she serious with this? "I *am* doing my job. I just—"

"I don't want to hear it." Mom's voice was more than snippy. "The sun was almost up when you came home. You had me so worried. Anything could've happened, and you didn't call or message or answer any of my million messages."

"You're right. I wasn't paying attention, I was…" I'd been so focused on trying to stop the glow that I'd filtered everything else out. It was a shitty thing to do, especially now. "I'm sorry. I've been on edge, but that's exactly why I was out late. I was at the warehouse, burning off some energy." I had to keep my emotions in check, and working out helped. She knew that. "I don't know why we're even talking about this right now."

"We're too close to leaving for you to mess up," Mom whispered, even though there was no one around. There wasn't any surveillance at all in the kitchen, and the bot was so basic, it barely counted as a bot at all.

Mom didn't even look at me as she flipped over some hash browns. Her cheeks were red, and the circles under her eyes were darker than I'd ever seen them. I knew that was probably at least a little my fault.

"I don't need to be worrying about where you are or wondering if you're running around with the Crew playing savior to people who would hate you if they knew who you really are." Her movements were sharp and choppy as she added cheese to an omelet. "Especially when you're supposed to be at home, where I can keep an eye on you."

Was she really saying that I was going to be the one to mess it up? I knew she was tired—we both were—but I didn't deserve that. "Mom. Seriously?"

When the silence stretched on, I glanced out the back window. Soon we'd be far away from here, but Mom was kind of right. I had to be nice to our customers until then.

"I'll *continue* to be polite. Even if he's a giant skeeve. And—just so you know—I haven't been going out with the Crew. If you were worried, all you had to do was ask. You didn't have to snap at me."

Mom finally stopped moving and closed her eyes. "I'm sorry. I'm just…scared."

"I am, too. Every damned day. But we can't let that fear take over our lives."

Mom's eyes grew watery. "How did you get so smart?"

I shrugged. "Maybe I learned from my mother."

Mom rolled her eyes at me dramatically. "Sucking up now?" She reached down into a cabinet, pulled out a first-aid kit, and crossed the kitchen. "Let me see it."

"Don't worry. It's fine. Not much worse than a paper cut." The angle of the corkscrew had been too weird to do any major damage.

"We can't let it get infected. We can't risk going to the doctor. Not ever again."

I winced. I hated when she brought up that nightmare. "Fine." I held out my hand. She doused it with disinfectant, and then covered the cut in a clear liquid bandage.

"There." She brushed a kiss against my forehead before getting back to work.

I silently loaded three omelets and a basket of biscuits from the warmer to my tray and shoved through the swinging door. Today would be over eventually, and soon, I'd be light-years away from here. Until then, I'd hang in.

Mr. Creeptastic waved me over as I served the food to another table, but I pretended not to notice. I had at least five minutes until his food was ready, and I planned to respectfully ignore him until then.

I strode through the kitchen, waved at Mom, and went out the back door. I'd already taken everyone's orders so everything would be fine for a few, but I needed a break. I really, *really* needed a break.

I leaned against the brick building and stared out at the mostly abandoned train cars. There was a family living in one, but none of them were in use anymore. At least I didn't have it that bad. Not anymore. And even if the last few days had been exceptionally stressful, things were going to get a whole lot better.

I tried to let that thought relax me, but then I started thinking about what life would be like on Sel'Ani and my mind started spinning. So, I quickly gave up on relaxing, pulled up my messages. I had one unread from Roan.

How're you doing today?

I typed a quick reply. *Better. Just want today to be over.*

I'd only been working at the historic Route 66 diner for five years, but it'd been around for centuries. Working here, with the vidscreens decorating the walls, showing how Albuquerque used to be before the Spaceport made me miss a past I never knew. Life seemed simpler then. Not to mention easier. I used to watch screens and think maybe it could get better—easier—here, but it never did. Now I just wanted today to be done, so that we could leave.

My finger burned, and a floating bubble appeared in my vision. I swiped to the left, and Roan's face popped up. With one tap, I accepted the call.

"Hey." Roan's voice came through the tiny device I kept clipped to my ear. "How are you hanging in?"

"I'm fine." I lied and then felt instantly terrible about it. "It's been a long day, and it's only just started."

"You look like you're doing okay though." He kept it vague because we never knew if someone was listening in, but the worry in his voice was thick.

"Order up," Mom said through the door.

She didn't have to say which order it was. I shouldn't let the perv wait, but going back out there… "Listen, I'm working. I can't really talk now."

"Roger that," Roan said. "But I want to see you before that thing tonight."

"Pick me up after my shift." I checked my watch. Only eightish more hours to go. "I want to see you, too. Okay?"

"I'll be there."

"Good." I ended the transmission and pushed away from the wall.

"Go take the man his food. *Por favor*," Mom said as soon as I stepped into the kitchen. "The quicker he's fed, the quicker he's gone. And be polite."

I wanted to say something snappy back to her but stopped myself. "Will do." I grabbed the plate from the warmer and shouldered my way through the door.

Be polite. I could totally be polite. I'd been doing this for years now, and he wasn't my first handsy customer.

I needed to check on my other tables, so I went around to the customer side of the counter and set the plate piled high with his breakfast—extra everything—in front of the perv. "Do you need anything else?" I gave him a smile.

If only Mom could see how freaking polite I was being.

Without the counter between us, he grabbed my arm again before I could pull away.

I had a moment to think about how I shouldn't have gone to his side of the counter before my body tensed. I waited to see what he'd do, but each second seemed to last an eternity.

I couldn't mess this up. Not now.

"Why don't you sit right next to me, sugar? Keep me company while I eat." He pulled me toward the seat next to him.

I could be polite for maybe two more seconds but not longer. I had to get out of this. Quickly.

"I'm working." I motioned to a full table across the room. They'd finished their omelets, and one of them looked like they were about to snap their fingers at me. "I have to go see what they need."

I stepped back and tried to wrench my arm free, but his fingers dug in painfully.

No. This was bad. This was very bad.

"Please let me go. You're hurting me." I said the words a little louder. People were noticing, and maybe if they noticed more, he'd back down.

But from one second to the next, something changed in him.

I'd told him he was hurting me and now he was grinning.

It wasn't the crooked leer from before. It was the smile of a person who was finally getting what they wanted.

He liked that he was hurting me, but there was something else to it. Maybe it was that I was cornered. I was powerless. A guy like him must love that.

My mouth felt like it was filled with cotton balls as I tried to figure out what to do next. If I fought back, I'd be screwed. He had money or he wouldn't be ordering what he ordered. Which meant he'd call the police.

I had to get free before I lost my shit, but there was no corkscrew to save me this time. "Please release my arm, sir."

His fingernails felt like fat daggers digging into my arm.

"Don't be that way. I'm sure we can both have a good time."

He jerked my arm, and I fell against him, my chest pressed against his and I didn't have a second to think before he squeezed my butt under my skirt.

All thoughts fled my mind except that I wanted him gone. Now.

His fingers slid under my panties, and I couldn't breathe. It was like all the air had been sucked from the room, and I just wanted him to let go. He had to let go. And I knew in that instant I'd do whatever it took to get him off me.

I tried to shake free, but he was still gripping my arm painfully tight, and I was pinned between his body and the counter.

I couldn't get away without hurting him, and I shouldn't hurt him. Because he'd call the po—

His hand slipped deeper into my underwear, his finger trying to press inside me, and I snapped.

Everything that I'd felt for the last few days—for the last few years—boiled up. I couldn't stand having this slimeball touching me. Not there. He didn't get to do that. He didn't get to violate me like that without getting his ass handed to him.

I moved fast—Aunare fast. In between one racing heartbeat and the next, I slammed my fist into his face.

Blood splattered onto me as his nose crunched and for the first time in a while, I smiled and meant it.

He screamed a pile of curses and released my ass to hold his face with one hand. The asshole wouldn't release his grip on my arm. That had to change. Now.

His short nails ripped into my skin as I tried to free myself again, but I couldn't get him to loosen his grip. Not without hurting him again.

"Let go." It was the last warning I was going to give.

"You bitch—"

I spun, twisting my arm as I did, and he went with me. His shoulder gave a sickening pop as it dislocated.

There was a fraction of a second where I felt proud of standing up for myself—proud that I took this fucking pervert down because he *deserved* it. Who knew what he'd done before to someone else. What he was capable of doing to someone who didn't know how to fight back. How many women he'd pawed and gotten away with it because he thought he was owed.

But then his screams brought me crashing back to Earth.

I froze as I took in the blood covering his face and the way his arm dangled from his shoulder.

Oh shit. Oh *shit*. What had I done?

Even with him lying there, I could still feel where his fingers had been in my underwear. I felt dirty as I stepped away from him, straightening my skirt and pulling it down as far as the material would stretch. But no matter how dirty I felt, I knew I'd fucked up beyond all repair.

This was the worst moment of my life. With one action—one time that I stood up for myself—I'd given SpaceTech everything they'd always wanted.

I'd be arrested. They'd figure out who and what I was. And then, there would be war.

What now? What the hell was I supposed to do now?

"What's going on out here?" Mom's voice cut through my panic. She was stepping out from the kitchen, her eyes wide.

I glanced around the diner. Everyone was staring. Oh shit. Oh *shit*. This was really bad.

CHAPTER EIGHT

"THIS BITCH HIT ME. She's under arrest."

I took a stumbling step away from the perv. Under arrest?

Wait. *He* was arresting me? Was he actually a SpaceTech officer?

"Oh my God? What have you done?" Mom asked as she came to stand between me and the perv. I couldn't stop staring at the blood dripping down his face, plopping onto the checkered tiled floor.

"Have you gone *loco*?" Mom's face was pale as she handed the officer a clean towel for his face. "Put pressure on your nose. It should help with the bleeding."

Oh shit. The blood. There was so much of it. All over his face. All over his ruined clothes. It was too much blood.

Oh shit. It was all over my hands and face and dress.

Oh *shit*. What had I done?

I'd never get away with this. I'd just iced myself.

As Mom stood up, she whispered to me, *"Run."*

She was right. I had to leave before the STPF arrived. The man was gesturing with his fingers, and I would bet my life that he was calling the police. Or calling backup if he was STPF.

I started to back away from them, but I hesitated.

"What about you?" I whispered.

Mom stepped forward, grabbed another towel from behind the counter, effectively blocking my view of the officer. "I'll be fine as long as you're fine. *Run. Now.* Before it's too late."

I pressed my forehead against hers for a second and then spun.

I ran through the kitchen, dodging the stupid bot. When I got to the back door, I didn't stop. The sun blinded me, but I kept running. My feet hammered the pavement. People on the street stared at me, but I didn't care. I moved as fast as I could without giving away what I was to everyone I passed.

I wove around buildings and traffic, not stopping until I was miles away. My breath came in gasps as I slowed to a stop. My legs were burning from the effort. I was still bone tired from last night, and I needed a second.

What do I do now? Where should I go? Where can I hide?

I collapsed on a transit stop's bench. I needed to get off the street. There were cameras everywhere. The quicker I got off the grid the better. Using the city's system was a no-go. Too much surveillance and too easy for SpaceTech to stop the bus or trail or pod and hold me until they got there. But I couldn't hide if I was on foot either. Running was too slow. The cameras would easily track me, but I didn't have transport.

Wait. I didn't, but Roan did. He got a beat-up Tykson with a few hundred thousand miles last year. He didn't use it much, but as far as I knew, it was still running. I quickly dialed him.

Roan's semitranslucent image popped up in front of my face. "What's up?"

"I need help."

A little crease formed between his eyes. "Is that blood on your face?"

I swallowed, but I didn't need to say anything else.

"Send me your location. I'll be there in five." His image cut off, but I glimpsed his helmet in his hand.

At least one thing was going right today.

Time seemed to move painfully slow as I waited for him. Two

of my knuckles were split open and bleeding. I sucked on them to stop the sting. Perv's face was harder than it looked.

I couldn't stop my knees from bouncing together as I waited for Roan. I was so screwed. I'd broken some rich guy's nose and dislocated his shoulder. This was so bad. I ran my hands over my face, smearing blood—

Oh God. That wasn't just my blood I'd sucked off my knuckles.

I stumbled to the nearest alley and threw up.

Once I was done heaving my guts out, I moved behind a dumpster, I could still see the street to watch for Roan, but I was less visible.

I wiped my face on my uniform top as cars, pods, and hover-cycles raced by, the whir of the wind mixed with the high-pitched hum of the machines. I watched, not really seeing cars, and tried to figure out what to do. But my mind came up with nothing. Any way I spun the scenarios, I came up with the same ending.

My life was over because of some groping asshole.

As I went over the scene again in my head, I could feel the heat of his hand against my butt. I gagged again but swallowed it down. I needed a shower. I wanted to crawl out of my skin. To be anyone else but me.

I let out a breath when the familiar silver Tykson stopped at the curb. Just the sight of my best friend made me feel like maybe I could get through this. Maybe I could figure something out.

The battery stuttered as he powered down. That wasn't good. He was going to get stranded one day, and I hoped I was around to laugh at him when he did. But today his cycle needed to work.

"Let's get you out of here." His voice was muffled through the padded helmet.

"Thanks." I stepped up to the cycle, and he handed me his passenger helmet. As soon as I had it on, all the surrounding sound was wiped out.

"What happened? How much trouble are you in?" Roan's voice echoed through the helmet's connected speakers. Not only could we talk to each other while riding, but we also didn't have to worry about being overheard.

"Customer wanted to get friendly, and I broke his nose." I didn't want to tell Roan what'd happened. I hadn't even processed it yet, but if he knew, he might be tempted to go back to the diner. He couldn't do that. I was in enough trouble for both of us.

"You had to do that today? Of all days?"

I ground my teeth at his accusation. "It's not like I was trying to get into a fight!"

"Are you okay?" His voice was a little calmer.

"No. Not even close to okay." I wrapped my arms around Roan's waist. "Get me away from here."

He pressed the START button, and the battery powered up. My stomach dropped for a second as we jerked a foot off the ground and zoomed into the slow flow of late morning traffic.

The city rushed by for a few precious minutes until we hit a red light. The electronic billboards downtown had mostly burned out, but one at this intersection still shone. A soda ad, with brightly animated cartoons flickering over its screen. The accompanying jingle was more earworm than song, but I couldn't help but watch. Which was exactly the point.

The music changed, and the image shifted to a recruiting ad for SpaceTech IAF. A familiar face came up, and my body went cold.

The light turned green, but I needed to see this. I needed to watch.

"Pull over." I punched Roan's shoulder. "Now. Now!"

"Okay. I heard you."

I started to tumble off the cycle as it jerked to a stop, but Roan reached around to hold me steady.

"What's going on?"

"Shh!" I pointed at the billboard hanging at least ten stories above us.

Perv's face stared down at me. It was an old ad from ten years ago. I must've seen it a hundred times without really watching it, but before today, I didn't really have a reason to pay attention to it.

There was exactly zero chance that I was going to be recruited, and generally, I ignored anything SpaceTech. But now I was noticing. Now I was paying attention.

He looked about twenty pounds lighter, and they'd done something to his eyes, made them softer—less pervy—but that was him. "SpaceTech is working hard to build profitable planets throughout the universe." His voice echoed among the scrapers. "But we need strong citizens if we want to reach our goal."

The image switched to young men and women in navy-and-gray SpaceTech uniforms as they patrolled through neighborhoods on one of the colonies. The houses were all the same, with perfectly manicured lawns and spotless streets. The place might seem nice to some people, but to me it seemed totally sterile and utterly void of any personality.

"Creating a safe place for families free from Aunare is a big part of the mission."

The screen flashed to Sergeant Pervo handing a ball to a little girl while her parents watched. "Five years on Tellus protecting families like these can earn you a slice of the good life on VegaFive."

Perv's face filled the screen again. "I'm Jason Murtagh, President of Security for SpaceTech, and I say join up. Make a difference. Earn your place among the stars."

The billboard went black for a second before becoming an ad for a burger joint.

I suddenly felt cold. "Ice-coated shitballs. That was him. I just broke Jason Murtagh's face. I *decimated* the guy next in line to own and run SpaceTech."

"You didn't." Roan shook my shoulders. "Please tell me you didn't beat up Jason Murtagh right before his brother was going to get you away from this fucking planet!"

The helmet suddenly felt as if it was two sizes too small. I ripped it off before the damned thing suffocated me. "I did. I smashed his face in and dislocated his shoulder. Maybe more. I don't know. I ran. I just—I ran."

Roan flipped up the visor on his helmet. "God, Maité. What the hell are we going to do?"

I was going to throw up again, but I had nothing left. "I didn't do it on purpose." My hand shook as I wiped off the cold sweat beading on my forehead.

"Not on purpose? How the fuck do you beat the shit out of someone by accident? This is serious. You could die. *I* could die! Fuck, Maité. What—"

"I know!" It was as if he'd parked his Tykson on my chest. My breath was shallow, and I couldn't get enough air in as the panic slowly strangled me.

"He's a Murtagh, Maité. A Murtagh!" Roan was pissed and with good reason.

I couldn't believe this was happening. This was a nightmare. It had to be a nightmare.

"I don't even know if Declan can help you now. Do you have a way to call him?"

"No." Gray dots peppered my vision.

"He said he was keeping an eye on things. So he'll fix this. Right?"

"I don't know." I wasn't sure anyone could fix this. My hands shook so badly, it took me three tries to slide my helmet back on.

I'd known fear my whole life, but I'd never known fear like I felt in that second. Every part of me screamed to run as far and as fast as I could. But I had to think it through first. I couldn't mess this up any worse than I already had.

"I need a plan. I'm going to have to figure out how to hide my trail and run." Except I couldn't figure out anything through my panic.

And then I remembered something. "Damn it. I had a go-bag in the diner. I had money. Laundered, clean money. I had tech. I had clean clothes. And I didn't even think to take it with me." Fear was making me dumb. I climbed back on the Tykson, and Roan followed. "We need to go. I have to get out of sight of the cameras.

And I'm going to need to go get my backup bag at the abandoned depot. Head there first."

"I can't fucking believe this…" Roan muttered as he sped into traffic again, cutting off another Tykson. Horns blared and tires screeched behind us, but that didn't slow him down. He knew what was at stake.

I leaned my helmet-clad head against his back. I'd seriously stepped in it this time. I had a sickening feeling I'd be seeing Jason Murtagh again soon. I just hoped that didn't mean I was sentencing everyone else to die, too.

CHAPTER NINE

AS ROAN DROVE us through the city, I tried to suppress the panic that strangled my chest, but it wasn't working. The fears running through my mind were too loud to shut down. How I was going to be arrested. Then executed. Or maybe they'd find out who I was, and the real fun would start. But I was worried the most about Mom.

I'd left her. I'd *left her* there at the diner to deal with my mess, and I wasn't convinced she could handle it. What if she was arrested? What if they found out who she was? What if they killed her?

The only thing keeping me from running back to the diner was the fact that she wasn't Aunare. If SpaceTech took her, she'd be held and questioned, but even if they did a scan, nothing would come up. They might not love her files, something might seem off, but she would always be human, and being human meant that she wouldn't get killed just for breathing.

Plus, Declan was watching. He'd know what happened, and he'd help her. He *had* to help her.

But even knowing all of that, leaving her to deal with STPF

didn't sit right with me. Not even a little bit. That didn't mean I could go back. Not if I wanted to live.

The good news was that I didn't have a tracker. Declan was right to assume that my implanted chip was basic. The shady doctor thought it was weird that I didn't want all the bells and whistles—we actually paid *more* than normal for him to implant something lower tech—but that was the only way I could handle having the chip. GPS devices gave off way too many signals.

Roan was the only person I knew besides Mom and me who didn't have a tracker. He was even more against implants than I was, but only because he wanted to give SpaceTech as little insight into his life as possible. Roan's chip was nearly as basic as mine. But even though we were without trackers, that didn't mean SpaceTech wouldn't find us.

I couldn't stop running. Not for a while. Cameras could be repositioned. Satellites could be moved. And then they'd know exactly where I was.

I needed a plan. I needed to think. I needed to get my shit together. If I made one wrong move, I'd be screwed.

For everyone's sake, I had to get away. One step at a time.

"How long until we get to the abandoned depot?" I said through the com in our helmets.

"Ten minutes," he said after a second.

"Can you make it any faster?"

"I'm doing my best." His voice was still snippy, and I knew he was still mad at me. He slid the bike into fourth and started weaving through side streets.

If there was one thing I could always count on, it was Roan. I wasn't sure how I'd ever pay him back for this, but I'd find a way.

The abandoned train depot was just outside of town. I'd hidden my bag in one of the trains because no one ever went there. During Liberation Week sixteen years ago, the city turned into a murdering mob slaughtering the Aunare, and the humans needed a place to put the bodies. They'd left thousands to rot at the depot. It'd been officially decommissioned nearly seventy-five years before then and was turned into a train museum. But after Liberation Week, the depot was a much different place.

I was pretty sure that the humans felt at least a little bad about what they'd done because as far as I could tell, no one came within eight kilometers of the depot. The surrounding neighborhoods sat empty and abandoned. Locals liked to say that it was haunted.

Since no one came close to it, there was no monitoring at the depot. Running electricity to the cameras alone was considered a waste of SpaceTech resources. Which meant it was a dead zone in a lot of ways. It was the perfect place to hide until I figured out my exit strategy.

The bag I'd stashed there had money, clothes, and essentials to get Mom and me moving. Except I was going to have to run without her. That hit me like a laser burning through my chest, and it took everything in me not to turn around to go find her. I had to believe that Declan would go ahead with his plan. That he'd leave today and take her to Sel'Ani. She didn't deserve to be punished for my screw-up.

Buildings flew by, making streaks of color along my vision. I replayed the last hour in my head as we entered the dead zone. There was no way in hell I'd get away with what I'd done. The more I thought about it, the more I realized that running might be pointless. I couldn't believe that I'd survived homelessness, poverty, and hunger, only to be taken down by one powerful SpaceTech pervert.

They knew exactly what I looked like now. It wasn't some aged pic from when I was a baby anymore. They might not know who or what I was exactly, but they'd be able to find me so much easier. STPF could back up the recording from the city surveillance system until they saw me leaving the diner, and then follow me from there. Satellites would support the cams in blackout spots. Probes would track our various possible routes. Eventually, they would see everything. The depot didn't have surveillance, but they'd see where we fell off the map and be looking to see when we reappeared around the dead zone. It wouldn't take a genius to figure out where I'd gone.

My only hope was that if SpaceTech could find me, so could Declan. If I managed to stay out of SpaceTech's grasp long enough for Declan to get to me first, I still might have a chance of getting out of this alive.

Roan finally turned the Tykson down the deserted road to the depot. Dirt and rocks had scattered over the pavement. The airstream from the bike kicked up a layer of dust and sand, coating my legs in it. I tightened my arms as we jolted over rocks and headed toward the gates. They used to be electrified, but since no one came out here, SpaceTech didn't bother. Tall lights rose above the tracks, but they were turned off. Even if the sun wasn't high in the sky, the lights here never turned on.

As we got closer, I noticed a break in the fence big enough for the Tykson, and I pointed to it. "That way."

Roan went off the road and entered the depot. Bones and half-decayed clothes littered the ground. I winced at the crunch of Aunare bones breaking under the Tykson. Roan weaved through a few trains before jerking to a stop. I swung off and shoved my helmet at him.

No sounds. No people. No surveillance. Just us.

"Fuck!" I screamed until my lungs were empty. I picked up a rock and chucked it as hard as I could. It *thunked* against one of the train cars, but it wasn't enough to curb my panic.

It wasn't nearly enough.

I kicked the nearest train. Pain ricocheted up my leg. I was still wearing my work shoes—soft-toed pieces of crap. I limped away from the train, cleared a spot free of stray bones, and sat down in the middle of it to rub my toes through my shoe.

"You done?" Roan asked.

I grunted. "I don't know." I flopped onto my back. "I really messed up this time." Tears threatened to fall, but I blinked them away. I couldn't crumble. Not yet.

He rubbed a hand down his face. "I know we've been over this, but I still say I could sign up for mining runs on Abaddon. With the bonus I get from finishing all five runs, I could buy your—"

"Not happening." My outrage at the idiocy of what he was saying burned through my panic. "Mining lucole is a death sentence and I—"

"It's the best shot we have! You hide while I clear the five mining runs to Apollyon, get the money, and go to Tellus 5. I'd have more than enough cash to get some legit files made for you then. You get off this rock. Meet me there. Once we're away from here, we can find a way to reach Declan without his brother knowing, and you can finally be safe."

He was nuts if he really believed that was an actual possibility. "You make it sound easy when *none* of it is. Let's just put aside the idea that I'd be able to successfully hide long enough for you to sign up for duty and actually clear all five runs because, with all the surveillance that SpaceTech has, that's going to be impossible. It would take you at least a couple months to get to Abaddon, train, and finish all five runs. I can't hide from them for months. Days, maybe. Weeks, probably not. And months? You're delusional."

"It won't—"

"Yes. It *will* take you that long. Say you sign up tomorrow and leave the same day, which isn't happening, but for the sake of argument, let's just think of the best case scenario. Once you take off, you'll be in cryo for at least a couple weeks to get to Abaddon. I'm sure once you get there you'll have to do some sort of training. Add a week for that. And then you'll complete all five runs to Apollyon."

I got up and started pacing. White bits on the ground cracked under my feet. With every noise, my chest grew tighter. This place was a reminder of how many had failed to outrun Space-Tech. I wasn't sure how I could possibly fare any better than them.

"Are you okay?"

I spun to Roan. Was he crazy? Of course, I wasn't okay.

He held up his hands. "Don't get pissed at me. You've been quiet for like the last couple minutes, pacing around here."

"I'm just thinking. This place. This situation. SpaceTech. And now you're thinking about signing up for mining runs? It's all so iced. All of it. But you can't do this. Not for me. Not ever. It's way too dangerous. You'll die trying to mine fuel for SpaceTech—the most evil company in the known universe. Is that really how you want to end your life?"

"No. I'm not sure what's going to happen, but I can't abandon you. So don't even ask."

"I won't, but…" I let out a breath. But I couldn't abandon him either. I kept pacing, trying to sort out my thoughts.

I wasn't sure what Declan had in store for Roan and his family, but it had to be better than lucole mining. I understood Roan's reasoning, but it was foolish and pointless.

But there were too many steps. We needed more money than I had stashed in my go-bag to get us off planet. I'd never be able to get a job since SpaceTech knew my face. The only way Roan could make enough money was…no. I couldn't really be thinking about letting him sign up. It was so wrong.

Abaddon was the worst planet in the known galaxy. It was named after the Angel of Death for a reason. Its surface was covered in active volcanoes, spewing ash and sulfur into the air. Without a suit, a human would boil to death in seconds. The fact that SpaceTech had a base there at all was insane, but Abaddon's moon, Apollyon, was the only place that lucole existed. The moon would've been a safer place to put the base but refining lucole required an intense amount of heat, which was why SpaceTech had gone to the trouble of building a base on the lava planet. The crystal was refined on the base, and then shipped all over the galaxy. It powered their rockets, ships, cities, you name it, but mining lucole couldn't be easy.

Why else would they give a monstrous sum of money, plus housing *and* land on Tellus 5, to anyone who could get five full loads of lucole in the five trips to Apollyon and back? We couldn't be that desperate or foolish yet.

"Listen to me." Roan's voice snapped me from my thoughts. "If you stay here in the dead zone and hide out in one of the cars with the bones, then you have a shot. They won't search them. No human wants to step foot in here. We can make a dummy from the bones here, put it on my bike, and I'll draw them away from you. When it's safe, I'll ditch the dummy and the bike, sign up for mining runs, and I'll have Jorge drop off supplies to you here. It won't be fun, and maybe you're right. It might take me a few weeks, but I've been doing the sim runs and—"

I knew where he was going with this, and I was ending it. "I don't care how good your sim runs have gotten, you'll die on Abaddon." I didn't leave any room for negotiation in my tone.

"I'm good. I can do it. I don't want to owe *any* Murtagh, even Declan."

I stopped pacing to sit in front of him. I gave him a long look, hopefully conveying how full of bullshit he was.

"We've both been taking extra flight lessons," he said. "You're better than me. I swear you could do it in your sleep. And if you can, then that means I have a real shot, too. I'm telling you, it's not impossible. The only reason people keep dying during the runs is because they're a bunch of morons."

"You're making my point for me. Anyone who signs up for runs to Apollyon is a moron. And if you do it? You're just as fucking stupid as they are." I huffed a laugh that had no humor in it. The guy was living in a land of delusion if he really believed that he could pull off all five mining runs. "This is stupid. I can't believe we're arguing about this. We need to find a way to get in touch with Declan. He's the key."

"Okay." He used the same tone I'd use to pacify Mom.

Arguing with him when he was like this would do no good, so I dropped it. For now. We had bigger problems to deal with first.

"What's the plan? How do we find him?" he asked after a second.

"I don't know. I can't figure out a way to contact him. I should've asked for a secure number or messenger or something. A guy like that has to have one. He called Lorne for chrissakes." Why didn't I think about getting his number? "I guess the plan is to stay away from SpaceTech long enough for him to find us. He said he'd be watching, but what if he somehow missed what happened? How will he find me?" It was hard for me to think past what'd happened. What Murtagh said to me—asking me if I knew any Aunare and that they'd like a girl who looked like me—made me think he knew exactly who I was.

"What? What are you thinking right now?"

I looked up at Roan. "Jason Murtagh was asking the strangest questions. And when I wouldn't answer them, it's like he wanted me to act out. He was grinning when he grabbed my arm hard enough to hurt and wouldn't let go." I looked away from Roan. "He thought it was funny when he stuck his hand in my underwear," I said quietly.

"Jesus, Maité." His words were harsh in the quiet of the depot. He grabbed my chin, forcing me to look at him. "He stuck his hand in your fucking underwear?"

The revulsion was back, and I stepped away from Roan. "That's why I broke his face."

"You should've done more." I'd never heard Roan's voice be that cold before. "He should be dead."

That look in his eyes was trouble, especially now. "Don't do anything. Don't be stupid. Not like me, because I think I've been played." I wasn't sure if I should laugh or cry but damn it. The more I thought about it, the worse this whole situation got. "I think Jason was moving me—*his pawn*—to the place he wanted. But what does he want? What's his goal? Why bait me like that? If he knew who I was, why not just turn me in and start the war SpaceTech has been itching for? I don't get it. It doesn't make any sense."

"We have to find a way to contact Declan without his brother finding out."

I sighed. "I don't know how. I mean, we could look up some of his public accounts, but those will all be monitored. That would give our location straight to SpaceTech. But Declan said he was watching. I'm hoping that means that he's taking care of Mom, and if I can stay away from SpaceTech long enough, maybe he can catch up to me. It's been a while since I've been on the run, but I'm sure I'll remember what to do. Maybe he'll get to me before Murtagh finds me again."

That was a couple more maybes than I wanted.

I got up and started walking around the train cars.

"Where are you going?"

"I'm getting my go-bag. That's the whole reason we came here." I'd made a little star mark on the side of a blue car. Three rows in. Five cars down from the entrance.

I paused when I spotted it. "Here. It's here." I tried to open the door, but it was rusted shut. "Help me with this."

"You're going inside? It's full of bones."

I looked back at him. "Yes. As you said, no humans would look in there."

He muttered something but came to help. A few good tugs and the door moved just enough for me to squeeze through the opening.

I climbed over the piles of bones, moving to the back corner. The bag was about a foot under there. In retrospect, I probably didn't have to do such a good job of hiding it, but at the time, I wanted to make sure no one ever found it.

As I dug through the bones, I tried to tell myself that it didn't matter. That they were just bones. That bones didn't care that I was shoving them around, but these had been people. Aunare with full lives that had been ended too soon. I could almost hear the ghosts of them screaming for revenge, but there was nothing I could do. Not right now.

I found my bag and dusted it off. Roan was pacing outside the train car as I squeezed back through the opening and jumped down.

"What now?"

"My mom and I had a plan if someone found us. We'd come here. Grab the bag. We marked a path through the dead zone. There's another bag there with enough supplies for me to hike to Santa Fe. We have a contact there, and—"

"You're leaving me."

I hated the hurt in his voice. "It's for the best. I probably shouldn't have called you. I'm going to get you into trouble for sure." This sucked. "Maybe I should—" My finger started burning. I bit down on the chip when the burning didn't let up. "Christ. It's not stopping."

"I'm not getting any alerts."

I stood up slowly, looking around the sky. A little tingle rippled along my skin.

Energy.

That frequency. I knew it. SpaceTech's own special com channel.

It grew stronger until I saw the lights.

No. No. Not yet. It was too soon. I should have had hours. A half-day at least. I hadn't even had time to breathe, let alone figure out a plan.

My heart pounded as I waited, praying with everything I had that I was wrong. That they were just passing by. That it was just a random coincidence. That it was Declan instead of Jason.

But then I heard it. The soft, high-pitched whine that was getting louder by the second.

"They're here." The words were strangled, but I managed to get them out.

"What?" Roan said as he searched the sky, but he didn't feel the energies like I did. He wasn't Aunare. He couldn't feel them approaching.

I pointed. "There." The dragonfly-size scout drones zoomed overhead.

"Shit." Roan swatted at one as it lowered to scan his face. The tiny bot sped back, but they could take a hit and keep going. "Let's go."

"It's too late." My skin grew cold as I stood motionless watching the black dot in the sky grow bigger as it flew toward us. It had to be a SpaceTech jet.

There wasn't anything I could do anymore. It was over.

The jet came toward us, hovering above the trains.

I never even had a shot at running. Not if they were this quick. "How the hell did they find us so fast? We don't have trackers..." It didn't make sense.

"I do." Roan's voice was barely more than a whisper, but the way it cut through all the noise in my head, he might as well have shouted it.

I spun to him. "What! When did you get a tracker?"

"I started at the plant yesterday." He pulled up his long shirt-sleeve. A tiny incision marked his wrist. "They made me switch out my chip. It was required in case of an accident. They said they had to be able to find me."

"And you didn't think it was worth mentioning?!" How did I not realize... I should've felt the tracker frequency, but I'd grown so used to sensing them in everyone around me, that I ignored the tiny hum. I didn't even know he was getting a new job.

This was so iced. I told myself it didn't matter—that they would've caught me anyway—but I didn't know that for sure.

I pulled at my hair. "Fucking shit, Roan!" The scream tore through my throat. "How could you not have told me?"

"I forgot! I was a little distracted by the whole beating the shit out of Jason Murtagh thing. And you've been MIA lately. I didn't get a chance to tell you about it. It didn't seem important in light of what I learned last night," he said over the growing noise. "You have to get out of here. You have to run. Take my Tykson." He shoved his helmet at me, but I stepped back.

I'd never lose them. Not now. Not with a ship already in sight. "You go. It's me they want." I shoved my bag at him. "Run. There's a path. Two cars down, take a left. Then fifty-seven steps. Then straight to the trees. You'll see an "A" marked into a tree. Follow the letters. When you get to Santa Fe, find out what happened to my mom. If Declan isn't taking care of her, use the money in the next bag." He was staring at me, not moving. "What are you waiting for? Run!"

"I can't leave you."

I gave him a shove so hard that he fell to the ground. "Go! Get out of here! Now!"

He stood and paced for a second as the ship closed in, then strode back to me.

What the hell was he doing? Was my best friend really this stupid?

I was going to die as soon as they realized what I was, but that didn't mean that he had to join me, too.

"Go. Or we'll *both* be worm food." Tears flowed down my face, but I didn't care. Not anymore.

He threw his helmet on the ground with a curse and wrapped his arms around me. "Damn it. You can't cry. You have to show them how tough you are. Don't give them anything. Maybe they won't scan you. Don't you ever give up hope."

I wanted to tell him not to be a moron—they'd definitely scan me—but I clung to that idiotic hope. I wiped my face and tried my best to shove all the fear away. It wasn't going to help me get through this. I had to be strong. I'd done nothing wrong, no matter what that perv said.

Dust filled the air as the ship stopped overhead. I covered my eyes and lifted my jumpsuit collar to protect my nose and mouth.

Roan had waited too long. Why hadn't he run?

A zipping sound filled the air. I squinted. Six figures rappelled down cables while the jet hovered above us.

"On the ground. Now!"

I shivered as my blood turned to ice. My knees hit the earth hard, and with that impact, I felt like I was floating outside of my body. Like this was happening to someone else. Except it wasn't. It was happening to me.

Two of the soldiers grabbed Roan, and my heart pounded painfully in my chest.

"Leave her alone. She didn't do anything wrong." Roan's voice sliced me.

"Stop struggling or you're going to lockup with her," one of them yelled over the noise.

"I'll be okay," I lied, but that didn't stop Roan's tirade.

I closed my eyes as hard hands groped me, searching for weapons. My heavy, panting breath sounded like it belonged to someone else as they twisted my arms behind me, locking them in cuffs.

Roan was still yelling, but it was drowned out by all the other noise. The ship. The STPF. The drones. The sound of my heart hammering in my ears.

Strong hands spun me around. The biggest block of a guy I'd ever seen towered over me, dressed in a navy-and-gray camo uniform. His mouth opened and closed a few times. "You're just a kid," he said as he shook his head.

What was he expecting?

He hesitated. For a second I thought he'd do the right thing and let me go. Then the moment was over.

I'd been an idiot for thinking that, even for a second.

He gently wrapped the cable around my waist before looping it through his gear and securing it. "Target acquired. We're a go," he said, and my feet lifted from the ground.

Roan was left alone among the derelict railroad cars, watching me. He yelled something that I couldn't make out, and then snapped on his helmet and sped off. I watched as he disappeared from sight. He was the last bit of home I'd see. Maybe ever.

The soldier held me as we were sucked into the ship.

Roan was right. I had to hold it together. I couldn't show any weakness. Even if all I wanted to do was curl up in a ball and cry until they came to kill me.

CHAPTER TEN

THE JET HOVERED JUST above the roof of STPF's headquarters in downtown Albuquerque. My vision was a blur as they shoved me out of the jet and hustled me inside. I didn't notice anything except the gray concrete floor and the way my breath was whistling as it left my lungs. I slipped into counting my breaths, like Declan had taught me, to keep from glowing. So far, it was working, but I wasn't sure what I'd do if it stopped. I still felt like I was floating through this nightmare. I was living it but also removed from it. Distanced. I wanted to poke at that feeling to make it go away, but I was sure if I did that, then this would feel too real, and then the glowing would start.

It didn't take long for the STPF to get me booked into the system. My chip held up enough to give them access to my forged file, which didn't immediately set off any alarms. The vidscreens on the walls streamed the streets outside. The faces were scanned as people walked by, and their records pulled up beside each face.

I watched those screens the whole time I was inside. I couldn't look at the files they were making about me. I didn't answer their questions. They didn't really care what I would say. They had everything they needed on me. They'd proven that when they played video from the diner. I was still in the same uniform. Jason Murtagh's blood was still on my face. I was guilty, and everyone knew it.

I'd been holding my breath, but once I was given wipes for my hands and face and ordered to strip down and change into the orange jumpsuit, I knew I was over the first big hurdle. They'd taken my contact lens and deactivated my chip but left it in my finger. It wasn't sending out painful signals anymore and could be turned back on easily, but at least it'd done its job. From what the officer could tell, I was a normal, everyday, troublemaking Earther.

When were they going to scan me?

Maybe I was wrong about everything. Maybe Murtagh didn't know shit about me, and he was just a pervy asshole after all. Maybe it was just bad luck that he'd come to my diner. Maybe they didn't automatically scan people to see if they were Aunare like I thought.

I never wanted to be more wrong in my life as I sat in the booking room and prayed that I'd somehow avoided them finding out the truth about me.

Officer Perez—the female guard they assigned to my booking —had been surprisingly respectful. After a while, she told me to get up and follow her. She led me through a few locked doors, to the cell block.

I tried to step back, but Officer Perez pushed me forward. I didn't want to go into a cell. I didn't know what was going to happen next, but it was only going to get worse from here. I knew it.

I forced myself to keep moving, slowly marching my way into the cell, and Officer Perez slid the door closed. Metal slid along metal. I jumped as the lock engaged, clanking and beeping as the alarms activated, and suddenly everything felt a little too real. I was back in my body, and I wished with everything I had that I could go back to that floating feeling.

"Stay away from the bars. They become electrified if you get too close. They won't kill you, but it'll sting like a bitch."

"Okay." I swallowed the knot of dread. I wished I'd researched more about the whole process of being sent to jail. At least I'd know more about what to expect. Not knowing when I was going to get scanned was driving me crazy.

Breathe. I had to remember to breathe.

Officer Perez started to turn away. I was safe. I was stuck in a cage that could shock me, but no one had scanned me. If I was being treated like a normal human, then I had a shot at getting through this alive. I took a breath, thankful that maybe Roan's job on my file had been thorough enough that SpaceTech didn't require a scan.

But Officer Perez stopped.

"Shit. I almost forgot." She tapped in her code, unlocking the cell. "Scanner's down. Your file checks out, but it's procedure."

Any hope I had left went down the toilet. "The scanner's down?" My voice sounded hollow.

"Yeah. Broke a few hours ago. It's never broken before, so I'm not used to doing it this way. It's throwing me off my game. All out of order." She pulled a little rectangular device out of her pocket. "Just need a little blood for the lab. Arm, please."

My heart hammered in my chest as I held out my arm. My pulse was going so fast, so hard, it almost looked like it was jumping from my skin.

I tried to breathe but I couldn't. Not if I was supposed to hold still. I wasn't sure how the glow was staying away, and I knew I had to get control soon.

Officer Perez looked at me. "You okay?"

I didn't trust my voice, so I gave her a tight-lipped nod.

The officer took the gray, one-inch by two-inch box and pressed it against the inside of my elbow. A few lights told her where to place it, dinging when she'd aligned it with my vein. "All righty. This might sting for a second."

I hissed as the needle pierced my skin. That one sting was it. Would it tell her the results instantly? I wasn't sure if they'd figure out that I was Amihanna from that one test, but they'd know I was Aunare.

"Okay. That's everything. Just settle in. It'll take a bit to process the blood. With the scanner down, the lab's backed up. You won't see me until dinner unless there's a problem with your blood."

Unless some miracle happened, she would be back much sooner than dinner.

"Okay." It came out a hoarse whisper, but it was all I could manage.

The sound of the locks engaging barely registered this time. I watched the officer until she was gone from view. The tiny box with my blood locked inside was my death sentence. I wanted to shout through the bars that this wasn't right. That I didn't deserve to be here. For her to come back and let me out. Instead, I stayed frozen, unable to do anything but watch as she left. A high-pitched whine slipped from me, and I stifled it as I tried to find a shred of hope to cling to.

I don't know how long I stayed there, staring down the hallway before I finally made myself move. It smelled like something had died in the cell, but I forced myself to step farther away from the bars and find a space clean enough to sit on.

Everything in Albuquerque was dirty. With the winds and the sand, there wasn't any way for a place to stay clean for long, but this cell was beyond foul. Black and brown smeared the gray cement walls. Some of it must've been old blood, but I didn't want to know what the rest was. The metal toilet in the corner was splattered with shit. I choked back the bile rising in my throat.

Two metal pallets stuck out from the walls. I perched on the edge of the lower one, making sure not to examine it too closely, and pulled my knees to my chest.

This was so iced. The worst thing that could ever happen had happened, and there was nothing I could do but wait for everything to end. There was a tiny drop of relief in that. No more hiding. I wouldn't have to be scared anymore because I'd be dead.

The absurdity of that thought made me want to laugh and

scream and cry all at once. A whimper escaped before I could stop it. I slapped a hand over my mouth to muffle the sound. Air whistled in and out through my nose as I held my hand tight against my face.

I was a fighter. I'd trained my body for years. I could think of something. But what?

My mind was broken, and I couldn't come up with anything that could help me out of there.

I sat there until I couldn't sit still anymore. Nervous energy forced me to move. I got up and started pacing. Ten steps forward and turn. Ten steps back and turn. Ten steps, turn. I went back and forth, moving just slower than a jog. It didn't clear my head the way I wanted, but at least I was moving. At least I was doing something.

A clang sounded at the end of the hall, and I stopped moving. There were other cells in the block, but my mind kept picturing Officer Perez coming back with that gray box. Maybe she'd been wrong about the lab being backed up.

I held my breath, counting six, before I let it out, counting to three. Then inhaled quickly for a count of three again and let it out for a count of six. I stayed as quiet as possible, listening to the footsteps echoing and counting my breaths the way Declan had shown me.

When I finally gathered the courage to look down the hall, it wasn't Officer Perez like I'd thought. A wall of a woman dressed in orange was coming toward me. I assumed there was an officer behind her, but if there was, I couldn't see them.

The locks disengaged on my cell without anyone entering a code, and the door slid open. The woman stepped into the cell like she was the freaking queen of the prison. She topped six feet easily and was thick with muscle. Her hair was buzzed into a mohawk, and she had body mods in her forehead, giving her horns. The woman probably wanted to terrify people on sight. I'd bet she achieved it for most, but I was too busy being scared of my little vial of blood getting processed to be afraid of anything else.

The doors closed and I heard footsteps walking away, but the woman blocked my view of the officer that dropped her off. It wasn't until she moved in closer that I noticed the sleeves of her jumpsuit were torn, exposing red geometric tattoos.

She was a Roja. The criminal gang that the Crew fought against all the time.

Why couldn't I just wait alone for my fate to catch up with me? Why did I have to share my space—maybe even my last moments alive—with a fucking Roja?

"You're in my spot," she said.

Fantastic. She wanted a fight, but I wanted to avoid one. I was already in enough trouble for one day.

"Sorry," I said as I shifted out of her way.

Her feet were heavy on the cement, but she wasn't moving to the bunk to sit down. She was coming toward me on the other side of the cell, cracking her knuckles.

Yup. This was going to be a fight, no matter what I did.

The Rojos were all about shows of strength, not precision attacks. Chances were the she-beast would be no different. She was easily twice my weight. That counted against me. But it was probably safe to say that I had considerably more training. Even if I didn't use my Aunare skills, I could probably finish this quickly and easily, but I didn't want it to start.

"You're still in my spot." She sneered, revealing her teeth. Fake silver canines stuck out from her mouth. I'd bet money on them being razor sharp.

My muscles tensed. She was trying to intimidate me, but that didn't mean I had to fight. And yet, the Aunare in me—with all the stress and fear that I was bottling up—begged me to let loose on this woman.

But that was wrong. It wouldn't solve anything for me. In fact, fighting her could only get me into more trouble. I forced my muscles to relax.

This made the Roja laugh, revealing her mouth again. I took a long look at the fangs in her mouth. They were definitely sharp.

Why someone would want something like that in their mouth was beyond me, but the she-beast and her teeth weren't going to take me down. Not with how my day was going.

"Why don't you tell me what's not your spot, and I'll go there?" I tried to sound placating, but it came off condescending.

Way to go, Maité.

"It's all my spot."

Perfect. If she wanted a fight, I wasn't sure how I could avoid it in such a confined space. I shook out my arms, getting ready for the inevitable.

She stepped toward me again.

I took one step back before what she was doing hit me.

She was trying to put me in the corner, and that was bad during a fight. Especially with the she-beast. One hit and I'd be pinned. I'd be forced to use my speed and strength, which I couldn't do. I didn't see any cameras in the cell, but I'd have to be an idiot to assume that they weren't there. Getting me on video moving fast would be bad. Not as bad as the vial of blood in the lab, but still something to avoid.

I clenched my fists and watched her shoulders. As soon as she moved, I easily slid between her and the wall without using my Aunare speed. Now she was the one in the corner.

Before she could turn, I kicked the back of her knee. My foot found the sweet spot, slightly off center. Her knee snapped as tendons ripped, and it buckled under her. She hit the floor. Hard.

Well, that was easier than I'd—

"Bitch!" She snagged my foot.

I wasn't fast enough to kick free before my shoulder smashed into the floor.

Damn it.

Her fist hit my stomach, and all my air was gone.

Gasping, I twisted on the floor and kicked her wrist, breaking her hold. I crab-walked back a few steps, before regaining my feet.

She faltered, trying to get up, but she wouldn't be able to. Not with the way her knee was bent, sticking out to the side.

I slammed my foot into her face, and she slumped to the ground, less than an inch from the electric bars.

My hands were shaking from the adrenalin rush as I sat on the edge of the cot, but after a second of staring at the Roja's prone body, I realized I'd made a mistake. I should've let her win.

Fighting in a cell looked bad. If I lost, maybe I would've gotten some pity points. Fighting and winning? That was so shortsighted. On the off chance that I somehow didn't get found out as a halfer and made it to an actual trial, I'd have another mark for the judge to hold against me.

I bent to check her pulse. It was strong. At least I hadn't killed her.

I leaned back on my heels. Ice it to hell. I should've taken the beating.

Footsteps echoed again, and I glanced up to see Officer Perez sprinting down the narrow hallway. "You were supposed to be alone in there. Shit. I'm going to have to move you to solitary because of this." Her shoulders slouched as she waved her finger through the air. She gave clipped instructions and then ended her call.

"You okay in there?" she said when she was done.

No. I wasn't remotely okay, but she was talking physically. Pretending to be hurt was an option, but that wouldn't get me anywhere. I rubbed the ache in my stomach. The she-beast had hit me hard, and I was going to have a giant bruise. Other than that, my shoulder ached a bit from where I hit the floor, but that was nothing major. I was way better off than the Roja, who was still unconscious on the floor.

"I'm all good."

"She's twice your size. You some sort of ninja expert or something?"

I huffed a laugh. If she only knew… "Or something."

Officer Perez entered the cell and inspected the Roja before she pushed the round, black button on her com again. "Medic needed in cell six." She scanned me head to toe. "Well, you seem fine to me, but I have to ask. You need any nanos?"

"No." A hurt shoulder was way better than the feeling of little bugs under my skin, pinching and poking me where I should never feel anything pinched or poked. Nanos and I didn't mix. I'd learned that the hard way.

Officer Perez stood and stared me down with her hands on her hips. "You going to cause me any more trouble?"

I hoped not. I didn't want to make my situation any worse than it already was. "No, ma'am. I'm sorry about this." I thought about telling her that it wasn't my fault, but I was pretty sure she wouldn't care.

"Good. I don't feel like cuffing you." She waved me out. "This way."

I almost smiled. Almost. Maybe she realized I wasn't a bad girl. I was just in a totally crappy situation.

We went into another corridor. The noises of people yelling to be released, arguing with their cellmates, and more than a few people muttering to themselves filled the hallway. "Why is this one so packed and mine was empty?"

"You were in temporary holding. That's why there were only three cells there. After your blood processed, you would've been moved to one of the cells here, but now you're going to solitary."

We took a few more turns and the noise of the prisoners faded. I chewed on my lip as we walked.

If Jason Murtagh knew who I was, why wouldn't he turn me in?

We stopped at a solid door. This one had only a tiny barred window and a covered slot in it.

Officer Perez opened the door. "It's only for a little while. I hear your trial's getting fast-tracked."

That was something. At least I wouldn't have to wait long before I found out what my fate would be, but she still hadn't said anything about the lab test. The question begged to come out, but that would be dumb. A human wouldn't ask about the results.

They'd just assume it was fine. So I bit my tongue and stepped into my new cell.

It was the size of a tiny closet. Only one metal pallet stuck out from the wall. This mattress was marginally more inviting than the last one. In the corner was the same type of metal toilet, although noticeably cleaner. My jumpsuit was a little dirty now from the fight, but I didn't care. It seemed like a superficial worry. I didn't care how dirty I was, I just wanted to get out of here alive.

"I'll be back to bring you some food in a couple hours."

Food? It must've been a long time since I'd eaten, but I wasn't hungry. Not even a little bit. I nodded at Officer Perez as she closed the door and slid the bolts in place. A second later, it gave three deep beeps, and I knew I was stuck.

Time ticked by and I stayed paralyzed on the pallet. Perez came with dinner, but I didn't even bother getting up. Whatever was on the tray stank like moldy greens, and I had bigger issues than hunger.

Had the test results come back yet? I couldn't ask, but she said she should have them by dinner.

As I sat there, I tried to grasp at any hope I could come up with. That something happened to my blood to make it not come up as Aunare. That Declan could help me even given the fact that I was now in SpaceTech custody. That Roan had gotten away and was with my mom somewhere safe. That Murtagh had no clue who I was. That somehow I'd get out of here a free woman. But the more I thought about it, the worse it seemed.

If I was right and putting me in prison was Jason moving a pawn in this dangerous game between the Aunare and Earthers, then what was his next move? Tell my father? Use me as bait?

Declan said that my father wanted to come, but it was too dangerous for a high-ranking official to come to Earth. It would be seen as an act of war. So, if luring my father here was Jason's goal, then what?

He wanted war.

Even if it was too late to save me, part of me knew my father would come for me, and he wouldn't come alone. He would bring all of the Aunare army. He had more than enough reason to destroy Earth after everything that SpaceTech had done to the Aunare people.

SpaceTech would be stupid to bait my father. The Aunare army was the most feared in the known universe because of their advanced tech.

There had to be something I was missing. SpaceTech wouldn't draw my father here unless they had some way to defeat the Aunare.

Had I walked into Murtagh's hand? Did he attack me just so I'd fight back and he'd have reason to arrest me? I hated that, but I wanted to live. So I'd fight. Whatever Murtagh threw at me, I'd keep fighting for as long as I could. I was stubborn enough to never give up.

Eventually, I lay down on the cot, trying to get some rest. I had to be ready for whatever came next, but sleep seemed impossible. Every time it came close, my body would jerk me awake, ready for a fight.

The only thing that I knew was morning would come, and life was most certainly going to get a whole lot worse.

CHAPTER ELEVEN

BY THE TIME someone keyed the lock outside my cell, my eyes burned, and I was exhausted. Emotionally. Physically. Mentally. In every way, I was done. A part of me was dying in the jail cell, and maybe that was for the best. I was doomed anyway. They'd come with breakfast a couple hours ago, but I'd ignored it. I wasn't hungry.

The door swung open, slamming against the wall with a bang. "On your feet."

I stood and stretched out my muscles. I wasn't sure what was happening now, but I was in no rush to get wherever we were going.

A woman with blonde hair pulled back in a severe bun stared at me with her arms akimbo and feet slightly apart. Her badge said Officer Hill.

Her squinty scowl and tight lips told me she was either a fan of Murtagh or not a fan of me, the prisoner. Whichever it was, we weren't going to be friends.

Officer Hill didn't speak to me as she cuffed my hands and led me through the hallways. I wondered where we were going but didn't need to know badly enough to engage in any sort of conversation. If my test results had finally come in, then I'd find out soon enough. Delaying that as long as possible was my best way to stay sane.

But with each step we took, my nerves wound tighter. I pressed my fists into my stomach, hoping to ease the ache there—nerves, not hunger—but there was nothing I could do except put one foot in front of the next.

She paused at a door labeled IR 5. Interrogation room. She knocked twice before opening it.

A man I'd never seen before sat in a metal chair on one side of a small metal table. He wasn't in a suit, but he managed to look fancy enough in his crisply pressed button-up. His long hair was tied back in a low ponytail. Fine lines spread out from the corners of his eyes, but he wasn't smiling.

I was about to ask Officer Hill who this was, but then I noticed Declan standing in the corner.

My knees started to fold at the sight of him, but Officer Hill uncuffed me, then shoved me toward an empty metal chair. "Sit there and wait."

I didn't quite register her barked order before she left the room. The relief I felt seeing Declan… For a split second, I thought everything might be okay. His job was to find me and protect me. He could fix everything. But then I saw my reflection in the mirrored wall behind them. The bright orange of my jumpsuit hurt my eyes.

Declan couldn't fix this. Not even if I wanted him to more than anything in the world. I was about to say something but the way Declan held himself—his spine rod-straight in his navy and silver officer's dress uniform—made me pause.

The four cameras hanging in the corners of the room buzzed as they repositioned themselves to focus on me. They could've been so small that they'd have been virtually unnoticeable by the naked eye, but SpaceTech liked their presence to be known—and felt.

I looked back to Declan. He was a double agent, which meant

he had to pretend he didn't know or care about me in any way if he didn't want to blow his cover. Declan's uniform and posture made a whole hell of a lot more sense. This wasn't going to be fun.

A dark-skinned brick of a Native American with a tribal-patterned tattoo across his face strode into the room, slamming the door behind him. His head was perfectly shaved, and from the look of him, he was older than Declan—mid-forties maybe.

"Sit down, Miss Martinez," Declan said. His tone was brisk and cold and nothing at all like the warm tone with a smile that I was used to.

I swallowed down the dread. Declan had been my last hope. He was the one miracle that I thought was going to come through for me, but I wasn't so sure that was possible anymore.

I lowered myself into the chair—sitting as straight as Declan now was—and looked from the guy in the button-up across from me to Declan to the tattooed man and back again.

"Shall we begin?" the tattooed man asked.

The guy in the button-up cleared his throat. "We can. I'm Jim Waterson, your lawyer," he said to me. "You've gotten yourself into a lot of trouble."

I glanced down at my orange jumpsuit. "Yeah. I figured that much out already."

I blew out a long breath. That'd come out testier than I wanted, but I didn't like being backed into a corner, and that's exactly what I felt like now. Declan and the new stranger shared a look that said they were about to deal me a shitty hand, and I honestly wasn't sure how much worse it could get at this point.

"Court-appointed?" I asked Jim. Because if he was, then I was going to have to be extra careful with what I said around him.

"No. Jorge sent me."

A little part of me relaxed. That was good. At least that meant that two out of the other three people in the room were friendly. The tattooed guy was staring at me as if he'd take pleasure in gutting me, frying me up, and having me for breakfast.

I kept my gaze on him. He was the wildcard.

"I'm IAF Specialist Ahiga. I'm here to find out more about the attack."

If this was a fair room, I'd wonder what attack he meant—mine or Jason Murtagh's? But I was the one in jail.

"Did you know who you were attacking?" The tattooed man's voice held no emotion.

"No. I was only aware of his hand inside my underwear."

If I hadn't seen the tiny tic in Declan's jaw, I would've thought he was angry at me. But he looked down and away, and I knew it wasn't me he was angry with. In that moment, I was pretty sure that he hated his brother just as much as I did.

"All right. There are some inconsistencies in your files, and they've set off some questions. Your blood was processed, and that checks out. But we need answers."

I fought to keep any shock off my face at the news that my blood checked out. I wasn't sure how much I could say or what he wanted me to say. I was sure that this was all for show, but beyond that, I was clueless. Staying silent seemed like the safest option.

Ahiga leaned forward and grabbed my wrist, hard. He slapped on a thin film, and my skin burned as it powered up. A little line appeared, flat and even, but when I moved, it jumped.

"That's a lie detector. You answer my questions. Yes or no. Answer them honestly." Ahiga's low, rumbling orders were said with a cold calmness that had my heart racing.

The thin strip of tape lit up and started beeping in sync with my heart. Too fast. It was going too fast. A tiny readout of my beats per minute, along with my body temperature, appeared on the tape.

"That's right. You're getting the severity of this now."

My gaze jumped to Declan. He stayed quiet but did a slow, long inhale, prompting me to do the same. Just like he'd taught me in the warehouse.

I counted my breaths. Six in. Three out. Three in. Six out. Four in. Eight out. And just like that, I was calm. I could do this.

"You live in Albuquerque?"

Eight in. Four out. Six in. "Yes." My heart rate stayed steady. It wasn't a lie.

If he was annoyed at how slowly I answered, he didn't show it at all. "Have you always lived here?"

Three out. Three in. Six out. "Yes." A lie, but the beeping stayed the same, so I kept the measured breathing going.

"Your father is deceased?"

Four in. Eight out. Eight in. "Yes." Lie.

"You're a member of the gang who calls themselves the ABQ Crew?"

I kept my even breathing going, though this one wasn't a lie. "Yes."

"Have you ever done anything illegal as part of the ABQ Crew?"

"No." Also, not a lie.

I assumed there was no change in the readout of the detector, but I kept my gaze locked with Declan. I wasn't sure what the cameras would make of that, but he was breathing with me. Keeping me calm. If he hadn't been in the room, I hoped that I would be this calm, but that was probably a bigger stretch than I wanted to admit. If I was honest with myself, I would've been freaking out without him here. I couldn't look away.

I don't know if he knew what I was thinking, but he gave me a small smile and a nod. As if telling me that I was welcome. That he had my back. That I wasn't alone in this.

"Have you ever knowingly fought against SpaceTech's authority, rule, or laws?

"No." True.

"Do you support the rulings of SpaceTech, its officers, leaders, judges, and laws?"

"Yes." Lie.

"Have you now or ever come into any contact with any of SpaceTech's enemies, including but not limited to the Aunare?"

"No." Lie.

"Are you absolutely certain?"

I swallowed. Eight in. Four out. Six in. Three out. "Yes." Bigtime lie.

"So this was just a random coincidence? That you attacked Jason Murtagh? Son of the CEO of SpaceTech?"

"Yes." At least as far as I knew when I was in that diner.

"And why did you attack him so violently?"

"That's not a yes or no question."

Ahiga slapped his hand on the table. "Don't be a smart ass with me. Answer the question."

I shivered at the coldness in his voice. "Because his hand was in my underwear."

"And I'm to believe it wasn't wanted?"

"Yes." True. So fucking true...

"You moved fast. Fought hard. Your blood test showed no Aunare blood, but the video shows otherwise."

Also not a yes or no question. Eight in. Four out. Six in. Three out. Three in. "Jorge has been training me with his Crew since I was a little kid. I teach martial arts classes after my shifts at the diner. I wouldn't be a very good instructor if I couldn't hold my own when being attacked." I leaned toward Ahiga. "Because make no mistake—your beloved Murtagh sexually assaulted me and deserves to be the one in orange. I'm not sorry for breaking his fa—"

Jim slapped his hand on the table. "That's enough. Don't answer any more questions, Ms. Martinez. You've asked her all the ones on my list, Specialist Ahiga. If you want to do any more interrogating, you're going to have to do so at a later time. I now need the room to talk to my client. I will assume that you will adhere to protocol and shut down surveillance of this room."

Ahiga twisted in his chair to look at Declan. "Do you have any other questions for her?"

"No. I believe you've covered everything my family wanted."

"Good." Ahiga's gaze narrowed as he looked at me, but he

turned to the lawyer. "I will shut down audio, but video will remain. Regardless of her answers, she attacked one of the most senior officers in SpaceTech. She is under strict 24-7 surveillance. You have ten minutes." Ahiga strode to the door, opened it, and waited for Declan to exit the room.

Declan didn't say anything to me. He'd barely said a word, but even if he hadn't spoken up for me, he'd been there. He'd helped calm me. Helped keep me breathing so that I could answer the questions.

He stopped beside me and reached for my wrist. "I'll take care of this." He quickly ripped off the piece of mechanical tape, and I hissed. An angry red welt rose on my skin. He gently ran his thumb over it.

He wasn't saying anything, and I hadn't known him long, but I knew the caress was the only apology he could give me. He was going to take care of this. I hoped that meant what I thought it did. That he was going to somehow get me out of here. But if he could've gotten me out, wouldn't he have done it already?

My heart hammered at the apology on his face as he dropped my hand and exited the tiny room in a few quick strides, slamming the door behind him.

I stared at the door for a second, wondering what I was going to do. What was happening? How I could get out of this mess I was in?

"All right. Let's get started." Jim's voice startled me. I'd almost forgotten he was here.

I glanced at him but felt completely lost. I didn't know what to say.

He looked quickly to the cameras and then back to me. "They might've turned off the audio, but I wouldn't doubt that they're reading our lips, so the whole not listening to us thing is out the window."

I pressed my fist against my stomach, trying to calm my nerves bubbling and brewing inside me. "I figured as much."

"So I'm not going to say much other than that you're screwed."

I almost laughed. "Tell me something I don't know."

"I wish I could, but..." He pointed to the cameras again. "Here's where a lot of trust is going to come into play."

"I don't trust a lot of people." And I hadn't gotten that click with this guy. I didn't know him, and I wasn't sure I could put my life in his hands.

"I can understand that, but those you do trust sent me. I'm very good at my job, but there's not much I'm going to be able to do to help you."

"Shit." The word was more of a hushed whisper as I closed my eyes. I knew it. I knew he couldn't help me, but hearing him say it out loud made it so much worse. "So what now?"

"I can only tell you what I know." He leaned across the table. "Murtagh played you. He's an asshole, but from what I can ascertain, he's never laid a hand on anyone like that. He wanted you to act out. He wanted you in jail. The problem is, I don't know what his plan is. All I know is that he has it in the works to move you tomorrow, after your court date. You'll not be found a traitor. You'll not be sent to the execution arena. But other than that, I'll have to come up with a plan to help you once we find out what game he's playing."

"You know? About me?" I couldn't say more. Not with the cameras rolling.

"Yes. I know everything about your life, Ms. Martinez. Rest assured that I am on your side, regardless of who is footing the bill."

I tried to stay calm, but it was getting harder by the second. I felt my skin starting to grow warm, but I couldn't let it glow. I went back to counting my breaths. "Tomorrow I'll go to court then? Isn't that fast?"

"Yes. He's got a game going, and I don't know what it is. Neither do the people who care about you." He meant Declan. "We're trying to avoid something very bad, but we don't want to lose you either. No matter how this goes, know that there are a number of people watching out for you."

If they didn't know what was happening, they didn't have a real plan. They couldn't. Having no plan, let alone three or four backups? That went against every instinct I had. "Ice it all to hell." I had one big question. "My mom?"

"All your known associates have been moved to safe locations. Do you have any other questions that I can answer at this time?" He glanced at the cameras again.

No. I hadn't forgotten, but I needed to know my mom and Roan were okay. And, yes, I had so many more questions, but I wasn't sure what I could ask. I didn't want to put anyone in danger. I didn't want to fuck this up any more than I already had.

So I shook my head. "No. I don't have any more questions at this time."

Jim started talking about paperwork and proceedings that would happen tomorrow, but I didn't hear a word of it. All I knew was that for some messed up reason, Jason wasn't going to out me as Aunare. But everything else? That was up in the air.

I rubbed the welt on my wrist. What the hell was going to happen next?

The door opened.

"Time's up," Officer Hill said. "Move it."

I gave a nod to Jim and followed Officer Hill back to my cell.

I sat there for the rest of the day, my whole body numb. I couldn't breathe. I couldn't think. I had no idea what was going to happen, but at least I wasn't going to have to wait long. Tomorrow was going to come soon enough.

My stomach was killing me by the time Officer Perez brought me dinner. She stepped inside instead of sliding the tray through the slot in the door. "You gotta eat this time, kid." A nasty stink filled my tiny cell. I was on the company dime until the trial. Which meant the "food" wasn't really food. It was genetically modified and grown in a lab by SpaceTech. The nutrition levels were there, but it was cheap to make and smelled like warmed-up ass. I was sure the taste would be worse.

"How positively delightful."

Officer Perez laughed. "You know you made the news?"

Now that caught me by surprise. "No shit?" Why would Jason ever release that footage if he wasn't planning on sending me to the execution arena?

"Yup." She relaxed her stance. "The footage from the diner went viral for a minute before the authorities could pull it down, but you can't unsee something. You know?"

"Yeah." I couldn't unfeel his hand groping me either. And knowing it went viral? That meant that Jason hadn't leaked it. I wondered if Declan had. But why would he do that? It didn't make any sense.

"According to the story, you've got Jim Waterson as your lawyer."

I didn't know anything about lawyers, but I was sure Officer Perez would have information. "What do you know about him?"

"He's the best. If anyone can help you, it's Mr. Waterson."

I took the plate from her. "The thing is, I'm not sure anyone can help me."

"What he did…" She touched my shoulder. "I'm rooting for you."

"Thanks."

She left, sliding the locks home as I stared down at the plate of food. "Dinner" consisted of green mush and a slice of crumbly bread. I poked the unknown substance, and it jiggled. It seemed to have a life of its own, and for a second I actually thought it might roll itself off the plate. Nasty. I grabbed the bread and shoved the plate back out through the slot in the door. I wiped the gunk off my finger, and it left a clashing stripe of green against my orange pants. I nearly inhaled the bread even though it was stale.

I pulled up my jumpsuit collar a little bit, so that my hair wouldn't touch the mattress, and lay down. Not much for me to do but wait.

I wondered what Mom was doing now. Where she was. If Declan was going to get her to my father. It was what she wanted, and I hoped she'd go. She missed him, even if she didn't talk about him anymore. She'd never even dated anyone else, although I knew Jorge had a thing for her. There was no reason for her to stay here, even if I was rotting away in jail. She didn't need to be here for that.

Hopefully, Roan and his family would be better off wherever Declan had stashed them.

Declan. I wasn't sure whether to be thankful for him or pissed off. He'd popped into my life a few days ago and given me hope. If he hadn't found me, maybe I wouldn't be in this mess. I couldn't think like that though. I had to focus on getting through this, whatever this was.

And still, I was left with this gnawing feeling that I'd failed everyone. My mom. Roan. Declan. My father. The Aunare. Two civilizations of people that might go to war. It wasn't my fault, but it didn't matter. I should've found a way to get Jason Murtagh off of me without smashing his face in. He was touching me and deserved it, but I should have found another way. I should never have let my anger take hold. I'd been so close to getting away from all of this, and now...

Sweat chilled my skin, and I leaned my head against the cold concrete wall. If I'd just had enough control to stop my fist, I'd be at home. In my own bed. Eating my own food. Maybe even escaping with Declan, along with everyone I loved. I could've been safe.

I'd wanted a change. I'd wanted off planet. But not like this.

A sob slipped free, and I rolled over, shoving my face into the dirty mattress as I cried my frustration, helplessness, hopelessness away. I knew I wasn't perfect. I definitely wasn't an angel, but I didn't deserve to be here in this cell waiting for some asshole to determine how I was going to live out the remainder of my life. And I definitely didn't want to be used to start an intergalactic war.

This much pressure shouldn't ever be on one person. I didn't ask for this. I didn't want it. All I wanted was to be left alone. To be safe. To be given every other right that every other Earther had.

My heart shattered as I cried and quietly prayed for something —anything—to save me. To find me and take me far away from here. To give me a life where I wouldn't have to hide or be afraid anymore.

But no one came. No one ever came.

CHAPTER TWELVE

THE LOCKS on the door beeped as they disarmed. I wasn't sure how long I'd cried, but I knew I hadn't slept. If someone was here, that meant it was time to go to court. Which meant life was about to get a whole lot worse.

"Off your ass," Officer Hill said. "Let's move."

Spots filled my vision as I rose. Maybe I should've tried to eat that stuff last night, but the pain in my stomach was more than hunger. It was exhaustion and fear and a whole load of anger.

Officer Hill shoved my wrists back into the cuffs and gave me a push. I somehow managed to follow her down the hallway, but my feet were dragging. I didn't know what was going to happen, and I was in no hurry to get there.

I made the mistake of catching my own reflection in a window. I barely recognized myself. My hair looked like something had nested in it. Dark circles lined my eyes. The orange jumpsuit made my skin look embalmed.

I guessed twelvish hours of tossing and turning and pacing in a tiny room would do that to a girl. I'd be making a killer first impression on the judge. Not that it mattered. This was probably all for show since Jason was moving all of his pieces on the chess-board right now.

"Keep moving." She reached back and pushed me ahead of her, not hard, but I was so tired that I stumbled. This woman was a real delight. "Hurry up."

I imagined at least six different ways to take her down, but it wasn't her that I was angry at, even if she was an asshole. The worst part was being stuck. There wasn't a damned thing I could do to help myself as I followed her through hallways and into a system of underground tunnels. I just had to keep moving.

Our footsteps echoed against the cement walls. The wet, cold air made the tunnel feel coffinlike, which seemed fitting. It felt like death in here. I wasn't sure what I was going to find at the end of the tunnel. Jim said that I wouldn't be executed, but I wasn't sure if I should believe him. Death could very well be on the horizon.

We took one last turn and then climbed dimly lit stairs. The lights flickered, seeming to warn me of the danger to come. But nothing was going to stop what was about to happen. I was a pawn in this messed-up game. I was going to find a way to change that, but I just wasn't sure how yet. My skin started to tingle, and I needed to calm myself down. There was no place to run and hide here, so I went back to the breathing that Declan had taught me.

Six in. Three out. Three in. Six out. Four in. Eight out. Eight in. Four out. Six in.

I counted as I walked. Each footstep a beat of breath. I was going to survive this. I had no other choice. I didn't know much about my father or the Aunare, but I knew the di Aetes line never gave up. That was something my mom had whispered to me over and over, especially on nights that had been particularly hard and scary. It had gotten me through then, and it would get me through today.

Finally, we reached a door. Officer Hill placed her hand on the sensor. It beeped twice, and then the click of the lock sounded. My chest tightened as the door opened, revealing the courtroom. It was small. Four rows of benches sat behind two desks. One for the prosecution. One for the defense—for me.

Officer Hill was in front of me again and moved behind me, releasing me from my cuffs, and motioned to the chair. "Sit there." She gave me one last stare down before turning and leaving the same way we'd come.

Declan sat behind the prosecution desk in his navy and silver SpaceTech IAF dress uniform. He watched me as I walked toward him. Studying me.

I didn't squirm and met his gaze straight on. I wanted to use his presence to give me confidence, but seeing him in his uniform and sitting behind the prosecution desk made me nervous. I would've felt much better if he was on the other side of the court-room, but I knew it was all about appearance for him. If he'd had a choice, he'd be wearing something else and sitting behind me.

I sat next to Jim, who was typing away, his fingers furiously flicking through the air in front of him.

I studied the desk to keep my panic down. The wax coating on the wood was thick and sticky. Years of doodles had been scratched into its surface. The ceiling of the courtroom was painted midnight blue with golden stars. I spotted constellations and wondered why they'd gone to so much trouble. It seemed too pretty for a room like this.

A man with slicked-back hair walked into the courtroom. He'd gone way overboard on product, turning his hair into a glossy helmet. The fabric of his suit shimmered as he moved and I knew it had to be expensive.

I didn't trust shiny men. The shinier their medals, their suits, their shoes, the dirtier they were inside. I guessed that's what was throwing me off about Declan's uniform. Too many shiny medals.

Loud knocking from the front of the room startled me. I tried to calm myself, but it was impossible. Only concentrating on my breathing was keeping the glow at bay.

A court officer stepped through the doorway beside the raised judge's dais. "All rise." A ripple of motion moved through the courtroom as everyone followed his order. When I moved too slowly, my shirt collar was yanked up from behind.

"Up you go," Jim said.

No witty retort came to me. All my energy was focused on not throwing up.

"The Thirteenth Court, Judge Parson, presiding," the court officer said as the judge entered the room.

The judge's black robes billowed behind him, a nod to times that had long since left Earth. Some traditions kept the people passive. This was one of them. The illusion that there was a justice system. That people were innocent until proven guilty, but that wasn't true. Not anymore. Anyone who was arrested was guilty. SpaceTech had decided that long before anyone ever stepped foot inside the courtroom.

The judge sat, his chair groaning under his extreme girth. The company's silver logo was backlit with a blue light behind him—the angular font "ST" for SpaceTech. It hung over the judge as a reminder in case anyone ever forgot who was really in charge.

The judge looked down at us from his high-up chair, making me feel mouse-size. He popped a hard candy into his mouth before tapping his gavel. "Case number 34532, SpaceTech versus Maité Martinez is called to order." The candy rattled in his mouth as he spoke, garbling his words.

Everyone sat down, and I followed, thankful that I hadn't fainted yet.

"Your Honor, the State charges that Ms. Martinez attacked Jason Murtagh, Head of Security for SpaceTech Corporation, breaking his nose and causing both extreme physical and mental trauma."

Yup. I definitely beat the crap out of Jason. Not that anyone would know now. He'd probably shot up with nanos before he left the diner that night. He'd have been back to normal in a few hours or less.

The judge's hand waved through the air, and I wondered if he was scanning my file through his lace. "The penalty requested is one year of service on Abaddon."

I gripped the wooden chair, nails digging grooves into the wax layer.

Abaddon? That wasn't a prison sentence. Murtagh was sending me off to do work detail? Why?

SpaceTech needed their powerful lucole mined and refined to keep their space fleet operational, and that took a whole base of people working on Abbadon to keep production up. It wasn't just people working with the lucole, but also a large support staff— doctors, cooks, janitors. But who would want to scrub toilets on a volcano planet that could blow up any second when you could do it safely on Earth? So, SpaceTech filled the base with prisoners and called it a work camp.

Convicts usually served out a shorter term on Abaddon than they would on Earth, but some of the jobs were beyond dangerous. A lot of them didn't survive their term, no matter how short it was.

"Defense, how do you plead?" the judge asked.

"Not guilty, Your Honor. Mr. Murtagh placed his hands on Ms. Martinez's person and inside her underwear, which—as Your Honor knows—is sexual assault by Mr. Murtagh."

I went cold at my lawyer's words. Yes, it was sexual assault, but was it wise to point fingers at Jason right now?

"She was protecting herself from the unwanted advances of Mr. Murtagh, the initiating party. Her actions should, therefore, be ruled as self-defense. We have witnesses—"

The shiny lawyer stood up. "Your Honor, these witnesses' backgrounds are not—"

Mr. Waterson shot out of his chair. "Objection!"

The lawyers started arguing back and forth—each turning red in the face—but I had my eyes on the judge. He wasn't listening to either of them. He was too busy rifling through a bag of candy, searching for the right flavor.

This was a full-on farce. My anger was ramping up, and I was doing my best to keep it from showing on my skin, but it was hard

—a real struggle—as I watched the judge ignore everything being said. Every argument went unheard.

The judge pulled out a neon green one.

Green apple? That was the worst. This man was the *worst*.

After he carefully unwrapped the candy and popped it into his mouth, the judge banged his gavel three times. With each slam, I jerked in my seat. The sound was too final. My heart started hammering in my chest as I waited to hear what was going to come next. I spared a quick glance at Declan, but he was leaning forward, staring hard at the judge. His white-knuckled grip on the arms of his chair showed me that he was just as anxious as I was.

"I've heard enough. I find in favor of the prosecution. Guilty as charged."

My breath came in quick pants.

"The Court finds the Prosecution's request as to sentencing appropriate. One year at the work camp at Base STC-498, also known as the Abaddon Station."

The room spun, and I put my head between my knees. No. No. Fucking no. This had to be a mistake.

I lifted up just a bit and glanced over to Declan, begging him to do something, but he gave me a small shake of his head.

I was so screwed. If there was one thing worse than signing up for those suicidal lucole mining runs on Abaddon, it was being sent to work off a prison sentence there.

Going to Abaddon was always the worst option. How was I going to get out of this?

Jim placed his hand on my shoulder, and I twisted to look at him. "I don't understand. Why does he want me there?" I whispered.

"I don't know why exactly. This wasn't where we thought you were headed…"

"What?" That made this so much worse. If Declan didn't even think this was a possibility, then I was truly screwed. He was supposed to know his brother, but apparently I wasn't the only one in the dark here. It made me wonder if Declan's cover was already blown.

"I have to talk to your friends. We need to get a plan ready before..." He must've seen something through his neural lace because he froze and his skin grew pale.

"Before what?"

Declan got up, shoving his chair away and stormed over to us. He grabbed the collar of my jumpsuit and twisted it, lifting me from my chair.

"What the hell?!" I yelled, trying to shove him away. What the hell kind of game was he playing?

"You listen here, you little bitch. You fucked with the wrong fucking family." He screamed the words in my face, spit flying. He gave me a sharp shake, and then lifted me off the ground by my jumpsuit. My feet weren't even grazing the ground as he leaned into my ear. "You stay alive." His words were so quiet, I could just barely hear him. "I don't care what it fucking takes. You do what you have to do, but you make sure you stay alive."

I started to cry. "How?"

He gave me another shake. "Give me three weeks. Four max. I'll have you out of there. I promise, but you have to stay alive for me." He pressed a soft kiss against my neck. "I'm so, so sorry. You're going to have to make this look good."

I was about to ask what he was talking about, but I didn't have to. He threw me down, and I crashed into the chair hard enough that it wobbled. Declan looked at me like I was the lowest scum in the universe and then slapped me across the face.

I didn't have to fake it. My face felt hot, and I could feel the shape of his hand like a brand against my skin. I'd been hit harder before, but not like that. Not when I was barely hanging on. Tears streamed down my face. I'd never felt more alone than I did in that moment.

I knew that he only did it because he was being watched. My neck was still warm from the soft kiss. But the look he gave me was worse than the slap, even if it was just as fake.

I watched Declan as he disappeared from the courtroom. The doors swung shut behind him, and he never looked back.

The judge started banging his gavel again.

"The court is remanding Ms. Martinez into the custody of SpaceTech Officer Ahiga for immediate departure to Abaddon." The judge slammed the gavel a final time.

Of course. The asshole who interrogated me. That just made my day.

I watched him approach me with a small med-gun in his hand. He grabbed my arm before I could move and placed the med-gun against my arm. A tiny chip floated in saline solution inside the chamber.

A tracker. "Shit." I glared at Jim. "I—" I couldn't have a tracker. It'd drive me crazy before the week was up. I tried to free my arm, but Ahiga's fingers dug in.

"Hold still or it'll hurt worse," Ahiga said. "Don't make another scene."

I closed my eyes and swallowed down the cry of panic that was threatening to break free. My former life was gone. As crappy as it was, it'd been mine. Fighting with the Crew. Teaching. Even the shitty job at the diner. It might not have been much, but it was mine.

"Son of a spacebat!" Pain radiated, numbing my arm. "What? No count to three?"

He grinned, showing his full set of perfectly straight white teeth. "Easier when it's a surprise."

I waited for the tracker's onslaught to my system but oddly felt only the tiniest of blips. It wasn't nearly as bad as the implant in my finger had been, which made no sense. It had to have been modified for Aunare. I didn't even know that was possible.

I stared at the doors Declan had disappeared through. Was the tracker his doing?

Ahiga yanked me to my feet before I could think too hard. "Let's move."

This was actually happening. I couldn't believe this was actually happening. I was going to be alone up there. Completely under SpaceTech's control. In that moment, loneliness and dread threatened to swallow me whole. Only Ahiga physically dragging me down the hallway kept me upright.

When we got outside, a black SpaceTech-issued armored hover vehicle sat at the curb. Ahiga shut off the alarm with a swipe of his finger and opened the back passenger-side door. "Get in," he said.

The last twenty-four hours of my life had been surreal, but this just seemed off. I was walking out into the daylight wearing a shitty orange prisoner jumpsuit, and no one was stopping me. No officers were watching. It was just Ahiga and me standing beside a car. "Don't I need to be, like, processed or something? Or hand-cuffed? Or—"

"Do you want to be handcuffed?"

"No!" I sighed. "I just… Is this how this normally happens? I thought it'd be more—"

"Traumatic?" Ahiga grunted. "No. This isn't how it's done, but Declan personally requested you be remanded into my custody. That means I decide how I handle you. It'd be best if you never, ever questioned me again." His words held a whole hell of a lot more than a hint of threat. "Get in the car."

The words had a bit of a snap to them, making me think I was pushing his patience level, but he mentioned Declan putting me in his custody. *Declan's* move, not Jason's. Did that mean that he was an ally? I wasn't sure. Maybe the interrogation was clouding my judgment. Maybe Ahiga was a good actor. He'd have to be to play both sides.

I climbed into the car and took a deep breath to steady myself. Three out. Three in. Six out. Four in.

He passed me a packet of wipes and a protein bar as soon as he got in the driver's seat. "You're getting my ride dirty." He pushed the power button, and we lifted three feet in the air.

My back slammed into the seat as he weaved the AHV through traffic.

I stared out the window as the Albuquerque sights blurred by.

It'd been my home for a long time. Not anymore. If I had anything to say about it, this would be the last time I'd be on Earth. Hopefully, Abaddon would be a short stop on the way to somewhere better, and this wasn't the beginning of the end, but I knew better than most that hoping for something wasn't going to make it happen.

CHAPTER THIRTEEN

AHIGA WAS all business once we got to the SpacePort. He dropped me off at a cryo processing center, where I was given clean clothes and taken to a bathroom to shower. I got the feeling that it was mostly to get ready for the cryo chamber, but it also seemed like the nurse who was logging me thought I was diseased. She walked behind me, disinfecting everything I touched. Her muttering as she cleaned up would've normally bugged me, but not today. No. Today had already gotten as bad as it could get.

Abaddon. I was getting sent to *Abaddon*.

As I stepped under the hot spray of the shower, my body felt like it belonged to someone else. I wished that I could be anyone else or that this was a dream that I could wake up from. But I could only be Maité Martinez right now, and this was my life.

I wanted to believe that everything would be okay, that I was going to somehow survive on my own, but my nerves kept bubbling up inside of me and I couldn't let them take over. I needed to be able to think straight if I was going to honor Declan's demand that I stay alive until he could find a way to get me to Sel'Ani.

I scrubbed myself down with soap, trying to wash the fear and prison stink down the drain. When I'd scrubbed so much that my skin turned red, I started on my hair.

Declan had said a lot of things in the courtroom, but he'd also kissed my neck and slapped me. Both were massively distracting. My face was still sore from the slap, and the spot on my neck was so hot it was like I'd been branded. I knew the slap had all been for show—he had a cover to maintain—but the *kiss*?

What the hell was that kiss about?

I pressed my hand to my neck. The feel of Declan's lips against my neck had me wondering so many things, but none of them were important. Not when I had to focus on surviving.

Declan said he needed four weeks. In the grand scheme of things, that wasn't very long, but I didn't know what Abaddon was going to be like. The only way to survive was by shoving that kiss out of my mind and focusing on little wins. I switched the shower off and wrapped myself in a towel.

For now, I'd count the shower as my first win. It might not be a big deal, but it was a start. The water had been perfectly hot and steamy. It didn't stink of the chemicals they used to scrub all the pollution out of the water. I had soap, shampoo, *and* conditioner. The fake floral scent wasn't my favorite, but anything was better than what I'd smelled like before my shower.

It wasn't much, but it was a start to thinking positive. I was going to do this. I was going to survive. Jason Murtagh was going to regret messing with me by the time this was all said and done.

The pajamas the nurse gave me were softer than silk compared to the scratchy orange prison jumpsuit. I almost didn't mind the Space-Tech logo above my left breast. Almost. The pants were loose, but not too baggy. I pulled the drawstring and double-knotted it. The tank top was fitted, but thankfully not as thin as the pants. Otherwise, it might have been indecent. They'd given me a pair of slip-on running shoes that had papery soles with the lightest touch of rubber coating. I wasn't sure they'd hold up for anything but walking to the cryo chamber, but all in all it was way better than I was expecting for a convict.

When I exited the changing area, Ahiga was sitting in one of the cushy white chairs sprinkled throughout the mostly empty room. He was wearing a pair of navy sweatpants and a gray tank top with a SpaceTech logo on the left chest. It showed every inch of his arms. He had muscles piled on muscles. Not that I was particularly surprised. The man was massive.

I wasn't sure what to think of Ahiga. I was leaning toward him being an ally, but he was big and scary and looked like even the fires of hell wouldn't thaw the ice in his heart. The tribal tattoo that covered the right side of his face might have scared off most people, but I was in the Crew. Everyone in the Crew had tattoos, even me. Mine was a tiny little thing, just on the inside of my hip bone, but it counted.

One of Ahiga's giant hands nearly concealed the glass he was drinking from. He placed it down next to him absently. His gaze was fixed on the vidscreens across the room from him, and I could see his jaw ticcing.

The news was showing footage of one of the colonies. Ships were taking off from a massive spaceport. The reporter was yammering about IAF being ordered to a system I'd never heard of.

I glanced back at Ahiga, and his jaw was still tight. I wasn't sure what he was upset about. It looked like business as usual to me, but there was a lot I didn't know. My resistance sites had a hard time confirming their stories, and I was never sure who or what to believe.

I took another step into the room to find a place to sit, and that was enough to catch Ahiga's attention. He waved me over, and I went to stand next to him.

"Why are we the only ones here?" I figured that there would be more people waiting, but it felt like a ghost town. A way too clean ghost town.

"With the gala and everything that was going on, most ships left a few days ago. It'll be a week or so before travel resumes to normal. This flight was specifically booked to be the only one leaving from this cryo processing terminal."

"Okay, but where are the people going on this flight? It can't be just us." That would be a crazy waste of fuel and definitely not something that SpaceTech would ever consider doing.

"It's only us and the ship's crew. We're catching a ride on a supply run."

"Supply run?" I don't know why I didn't think of that, but I just assumed that every flight out had passengers.

"Not a lot of people choose to go to Abaddon," he said as if reading my mind. "And everything has to be shipped to the base, so this one's probably loaded down with food and meds and whatever else they need up on the base right now. Takes two weeks in cryo to get there, so they have to send a lot in one go. Someone else was supposed to join us—a sign-up for mining runs—but he bailed at the last minute."

"That happen a lot?" I didn't even realize you could back out after signing up.

He shrugged. "It happens. Especially after a few people bite it in a row."

The news didn't really talk about how many people made it or didn't. The ads SpaceTech ran were all about the benefits *if* you finished all five runs. I'd figured if someone did that, then it'd be newsworthy, but maybe I was wrong. "How many miners actually complete their mining runs?" Since he was being so forthcoming, I figured I'd ask him questions until he stopped answering.

"Not many. Come on." He shoved himself out of his chair. "We have a bit of a walk ahead of us, and the entrance to the ship will be a little... Well, it's not for civilians."

That was incredibly vague, and I wanted to ask more questions —not just about the entrance to the ship, but about the mining runs and the base in general—but Ahiga strode away, effectively ending our conversation.

I guessed I'd asked one too many questions.

After taking some turns, we entered an elevator. Ahiga hit the button to go up to the fourth floor, but it was the longest elevator ride ever. I could feel the upward motion, but there were minutes between floors.

The elevator dinged as we finally reached the fourth floor. My toes were almost brushing the door as I waited for them to open.

"Claustrophobic?" Ahiga asked.

"No." I let out a breath, trying to ease my anxiety. "I didn't think so, but..." Maybe I was.

The idea of being stuck in here made me want to climb the walls, but I'd only just gotten out of solitary confinement. Apparently, even my short stay in jail made a big impression on me. I hadn't enjoyed being locked up. Not even a little bit.

The doors finally opened, and I barely stifled a gasp. No wonder it took forever to get up here. We'd been indoors until then —with no windows—but now I could finally see the hangar. We were at least one hundred and fifty meters from the ground— easily fifty stories.

There were three ships inside the hangar, noses pointing to the sky. A symphony of beeps and clangs and whirring of drills filled the massive space as crews of mechanics rushed below the one farthest from us. The workers looked like little ants swarming around the bottom in a chaotic frenzy. The fact that they hustled me quickly through the court proceedings to this catwalk made me think that all of the craziness below was to rush me off planet. But not everything was about me. That could be their everyday kind of frenzy, and I could be totally wrong about which ship we were heading to.

"What's the holdup? You afraid of heights, too?" I'd stopped just outside of the elevator, blocking Ahiga from exiting.

"No." I knew that one for a fact.

Mom said my father, whenever he had time, liked to free climb up the tallest scraper in DC to watch the sunset. He'd apparently sit up there, dangling his feet off the edge like it was no big deal, waiting for the moon to rise and the stars to shine. After I was born, he'd strap me to his chest and take me with him. But I didn't know if that meant *all* Aunare were this way, or if that was just how my father and I were.

"But I'm not in a rush to get to Abaddon." I moved to the side so Ahiga could get around me.

Ahiga grunted, telling me with that one sound that he wasn't looking forward to it either. "We gotta walk across a few of these catwalks to get to the ship." He pointed at the ship I'd been staring at. The catwalks zigzagged between the ships, creating walkways at different levels across the hangar. There were lower levels of catwalks where workers were accessing panels on the ships, middle levels with more workers, and then the one with just me and Ahiga nearest the ceiling.

I started down the catwalk and winced at the feel of the sharp metal against my papery shoes. The grating was probably meant to grip shoes, but the things I had on were less than slippers.

There was nothing to do but keep going. I took another step, and something caught my eye down below. A truck was loading containers with a hazardous logo on them into a ship. I turned to ask Ahiga, but he was still standing at the entrance to the catwalk looking down at the ground. Little beads of sweat pearled on his forehead. His mouth was moving, but it was way too loud in the hangar to hear what he was saying from ten feet away.

I quickly strode back to him. "Ahiga?"

"Fucking ships. Goddamned catwalks." His gaze stayed frozen on the workers down below us as he mumbled. He wasn't talking loud enough to be talking to me, but I could make out his words well enough.

To be fair, we really were high up, but the catwalk was pretty steady and had railings. If one of them gave way, sure, we'd be a mushy pancake when we hit the ground, but I doubted that would happen. The walkway didn't even sway as I walked on it. Still, this probably wasn't the most pleasant way to board a ship, especially for someone with a fear of falling.

A bead of sweat trickled down the side of Ahiga's face, and he swiped it away with a shaking hand. "I've done this before. Just... need a second."

He was SpaceTech IAF. I was sure that he was fully able to do this himself, and it would've been easy to let him sweat it out, especially after the interrogation and how he put that chip in me without any warning... But I hated to see someone suffer when I could do something about it.

The guy was pathetic. "Come on." I grabbed his hand and gave it a little tug. "We'll get there faster this way." I took a step back, onto the catwalk, but he jerked me to a stop. "Just look at me."

"You're walking backward." His words were a little garbled.

The fact that he was scared for me told me that helping him was the right choice. "I'll be fine. Just start walking." I gave him a sharper tug, and he stumbled forward one step. And then another. And another.

Slowly but surely, we made it across the first of ten catwalks.

The more we walked, the more I studied him. Who was this guy? Could I really trust him? I wasn't getting that gut feeling, but he said that Declan assigned him personally to me. Which meant I *should* trust him.

I went back over the interrogation. I'd felt threatened and cornered, but Ahiga hadn't been mean. He hadn't asked anything out of the ordinary, and now that I really thought about it—as I held the man's shaking, sweaty hand in mine, half-pulling him across the catwalk—I realized he hadn't really interrogated me. There'd been no questioning my answers. No persuasions. He never rushed me, even when took a long time answering because of my breathing exercises. He'd been endlessly patient with me. In the moment, it'd been intense, but it'd actually been pretty mild.

Questions popped into my head, and I glanced around the hangar. There were cameras all around—some hovering in the air and others mounted to the walls and ceilings. I couldn't be sure what they were looking at or how much they could hear, but I figured there was so much going on here and it was so incredibly loud that the chances of SpaceTech doing more than keeping a cursory eye on us were probably pretty low.

I squeezed Ahiga's hand tightly, and the fear cleared a little from his eyes. "Are they listening?"

"No. Not with so much noise echoing against the metal walls. In theory, they could read our lips, but not with how close we're standing. Not here." He motioned to the small, black glass window across the hanger from us. "I've been in the control room. Camera angles are working to our advantage."

I loosened my grip on his hand. "So can I ask you something?"

"Yes. We're good until we get closer to the next ship, but keep your head down."

I glanced back. We had two more catwalks before we reached the middle ship. And then a few more before we reached ours. "You said Declan requested you to have custody of me."

"Yes."

"And why would he do that?" Declan had to have a good reason.

"Because, like Declan, I'm on your side. I don't want a war. Getting you home in one piece. Getting you to convince your father that we're not all evil shitbags. That's our one shot."

I was the one shot? That was absurd. No one could have that much sway. Especially not me. "You're placing a lot on my shoulders that shouldn't be there."

"No. I know who you are. You, Declan, and Lorne. The three of you together—you're the ones that could change this. It might seem like a lot, but that's what you were born into. I can't change who you are, but I can help you as much as I'm able while we wait for Declan."

I took a few more steps backward, pulling Ahiga with me. If he really thought I could stop this war, then he was an idiot. I didn't know my father well enough to convince him of anything. Maybe Declan and Lorne would have better luck, but they didn't need me for that.

I pushed that aside for now. "But you can't really help me on Abaddon, can you? Not if you're going to keep your cover."

"I'm *Elite* IAF, which means I'm highly qualified to keep you safe. You might not see me or hear from me, but I'll be watching. You'll have to do your job—whatever it is there—but I'm your backup. And I'll keep being your backup for as long as I'm needed. You're our best hope, and I'm taking that seriously."

"Best hope?" That was so iced.

I'd lived in fear for most of my life because of what it would mean if SpaceTech ever found me. I knew what the implications were, but I'd never heard someone else voice it quite like that. That I was the linchpin that could upend the galaxy? That the death of billions could be on my shoulders? That I could be blamed if there was a war?

The pressure that I would be responsible for so many people had never loomed over me in such a way as it did in that moment. Pressure so tangible that my ears started ringing and the air turned too thick for me to breathe.

"Your skin."

He was right. The glow was still minimal, but it was there.

I sucked in air and counted to six. Three counts out. Three in. Six out. I started walking again, pulling Ahiga with me. He watched me with wide eyes, and I shook my head. I couldn't talk about it and not panic.

Four in. Eight out. Eight in. Four out. Six in. Three out.

When I had it under control, I stopped counting.

"You okay?"

"I must look pretty bad since everyone keeps asking me that." But no. I wasn't okay. I wasn't sure I'd ever be okay.

Even in the best-case scenario—where I somehow got to Sel'Ani—I wasn't sure they'd appreciate a halfer any more than the Earthers did. With good reason. The Earthers had slaughtered tens of thousands of Aunare. Yet somehow I was supposed to bridge the two species?

No. I definitely wasn't okay.

CHAPTER FOURTEEN

IT MUST'VE TAKEN us nearly thirty minutes to inch our way to the other side of the hangar when I could've done it in less than ten. By the time we reached the end of the catwalks, my throat was dry, and I longed for a home I'd never see again.

"I'm hoping you've got it from here?"

Ahiga grunted. "Come on."

I finally turned around to face forward and was shocked to see how massive the ship was. When we first came inside the hangar, I'd thought our ship on the far side was the same size as the other two we passed—maybe a bit bigger—but it was easily three times the size. It loomed overhead, impossibly large, like a monster coming to swallow me whole. I stepped inside on shaky legs. Turning back wasn't an option, especially with a tracker in me.

"The 78X4 is the biggest in SpaceTech's fleet," Ahiga said without looking back at me.

I struggled to keep up with him as he started through the ship. I wouldn't have known it on the catwalks, but Ahiga could move faster than I'd thought for someone his size. "78X4?"

"I didn't make it up." Ahiga shrugged. "They'll be dropping off supplies for the base, and picking up lucole. To move that crap around you need a heavy-duty ship. Every speck of it weighs way more than it should."

"Right." I kind of liked that the crystal that fueled all of Space-Tech was a pain in the ass to manage.

The ship wasn't as bustling or fancy as I'd pictured. I assumed that there'd be comp panels on the walls or more doors. Maybe more people. Just more of everything. But from what I could tell, it was all empty hallways, not unlike what we'd walked through to get to the ships. No windows. Everything was shades of gray—the floors, ceiling, and walls.

As we walked deeper into the ship, I felt like it was closing in around me. My palms were sweating even though the air conditioning was blasting hard enough to chill my skin. A row of dim lights lit the floor and ceiling where they met the walls, but that was the only light. The only sound was our echoing footsteps. I couldn't hear anything from outside. It was like an enormous gray coffin.

I wondered if that was what SpaceTech had wanted. It would've been easy enough to brighten up the ship a little, but having only been inside it for a few moments, I felt a certain doom. Like anyone in here was heading to their death. But that could've easily been me projecting my feelings about where I was going.

I wasn't sure what would be in store for me on Abaddon, and I didn't really know if I could keep my promise to Declan to survive. That didn't mean I wasn't going to try, but fear was making each step I took into the ship harder.

Finally, after an endless zigzagging hallway, we came to a door that whooshed open as we approached. The air inside the room brushed against my face, sending chills across my skin.

Ahiga stepped forward, waving me to do the same, and I followed him on shaky legs.

The small room was filled with cryo chambers. Each chamber was about the size of a twin bed, laid out in circles, five each, like the petals on a blooming nightshade bud. In the center of each flower was a circular console with images hovering above the head of each chamber. At the moment, they read "not in use," but that would change for at least two of them.

I counted fifteen chambers and wondered if a flight crew would be here after launch or if they'd remain empty. Not that it mattered. But I had to keep my mind focused on something or else the fear of the cryo sleep and Abaddon and whatever nightmare I was going to face next would be too much for me to control. If I wasn't careful, I was going to start glowing brighter than the sun, and I couldn't afford for anything else to go wrong. Not now.

A nurse came in behind us, her white medic uniform pristine, not a single hair out of place. "Please lie down," she said, motioning to the nearest chamber.

My hands shook as I climbed onto the bed. It would be my first time to be put into stasis. Human medical procedures and I didn't exactly have a fantastic history. The one time I had nanos hadn't been pretty.

I hoped that Declan had worked his magic on this, too. He'd covered everything so far. If he hadn't, then I'd pray that whatever they did to put a human in stasis would work for an Aunare.

I glanced over at Ahiga, who was getting into the chamber next to me. While my head was turned, the nurse pressed an injection gun to my arm. Pain radiated all the way down my bicep to my fingertips. "You could've warned me." Fear and pain made my words sharp.

"No time. We leave precisely at oh-nine-twenty-five." A little less than an hour.

A tingling sensation started running up my arm, replacing the pain. I wanted to ask if that was normal, but if it wasn't then the nurse might ask questions that I didn't want to answer. It was too late anyway. Whatever she'd injected me with was already doing its thing. I'd have to find a way to get through it.

I was still rubbing my arm when she came back with a patch.

She slapped it onto my forehead, and before I could ask what it was, she started punching buttons on the side of my chamber.

The tingling was getting worse, painfully spreading out to all my limbs, and I had to ask. "Is it supposed to tingle so much?"

The nurse scrunched up her face, giving me a look like she thought I'd lost my mind.

My heart kicked up a notch. "Forget I asked," I said quickly. Apparently, it was an Aunare side effect. That was bad. Especially since I would be trapped in here for two weeks if something went wrong.

The glass top started coming toward me from the foot of the bed. I slammed my head back on the pillow, narrowly avoiding getting hit in the face with the lid of the chamber. My panting breath was fogging up the glass three inches from my face. The patch on my forehead was starting to burn, and I itched to take it off, but I couldn't move my hands. A sharp poke hit my arm, and I glanced down to see an IV extended from the wall of the chamber, feeding liquids into my arm.

"Relax. You'll be on Abaddon before you know it." The nurse's voice was muffled by the glass. She gave me a stiff nod and then walked off.

The nurse was crazy. I couldn't relax. I whimpered as I tried to move but couldn't. As the tingles spread across my body, I became paralyzed.

I knew that I was supposed to be falling asleep, but I wasn't. I was frozen. Being awake and frozen and trapped in a tiny pod was a nightmare that I wanted out of. Now.

"Just relax," Ahiga said from the next chamber over. "The meds in your patch will hit in thirty seconds. When you wake up, we'll be on Abaddon."

When I tried to answer him—to ask if this was normal, even if I was already pretty sure it wasn't—my lips wouldn't move, and my tongue was tingling worse than the rest of my body. I only managed to make a garbled noise. I started the breathing technique again, but it wasn't working. My skin began to glow, and I lay there terrified that the nurse would come running back. That the ship's crew would come in and see. That someone would find out what I was.

I waited and waited and waited, but nothing happened. No one came back.

I'd read about cryo sleep. The theory was that the mind went into some state of perma-tranquility, like sleep but without dreaming. Everything slowed down, including aging, to help combat the effects of warping space faster than light speed. Except that everything I was feeling wasn't like what I'd read.

It was supposed to be a peaceful transition to sleep, but I wasn't falling asleep. My body was, but my mind could feel my lungs and heart slowing and panic set in.

I was frozen, and there was nothing that my medicated body could do about it.

It took longer than Ahiga said, but eventually, the patch kicked in. Except that didn't work right either. Instead of being peacefully unconscious, my mind started drifting through a trancelike state. I was completely aware of the fact that I was dreaming, and no matter what happened, I wouldn't wake up until the drugs paralyzing my body wore off. Not until Abaddon.

Like that old story I'd read about Alice and her rabbit hole, I disappeared into a dream world. Time melted away, and my mind drifted to my hopes and my nightmares.

I was thrown back into jail. Beaten in alleyways. Shoved out of jets. Thrown into execution arenas. Pain ripped through my body as I died in my dreams, screaming for release from this hell, and then my mind would shift, and the images would change to Mom being captured. Of Roan being murdered by a group of Rojos. I burned to death as Abaddon's air turned to fire in my lungs, my blood boiling as I begged for death to save me.

I dreamed of the colonies falling into destruction. Of war between humans and Aunare. Of worlds being destroyed by lucole bombs. And of being powerless to stop any of it.

Of my father hating me. Denying any help. I'd drop to my

knees, begging him to save the humans, but he would back away from me. Telling me that I was too human to be anything but garbage to him. His abandonment drove a dagger through my heart, shattering it again and again as the nightmare replayed.

Of Declan and his soft kiss. His aching slap. Him dragging me into an execution arena while I pleaded with him that he was supposed to help me. That he'd promised everything would be okay. But his face would morph into his brother's, and I'd feel his slimy hands reaching into my underwear again and again.

And when I was at my worst—sobbing in my sleep, begging for it to end—the sound of Lorne's voice would come to coax me from my full-blown panic.

And everything would change.

Lorne was the air I needed to breathe.

The soft sound of waves sliding onto shore would soothe my tormented soul. The sun warmed me, and in a flash I'd be on a beach. An Aunare boy walking toward me. I couldn't see his face, but I knew it was Lorne. At least I hoped it was Lorne. I felt the sand fall between my fingertips as I built a sandcastle. He'd laugh beside me, telling me that it was lopsided, and I'd tell him to shut up or I was going to make him eat it.

His laugh was a balm on my panicked soul.

Those were the dreams I didn't want to end.

I would climb rocks with Lorne. Practice weapon training. On a soft carpet he would read me a story about adventures across the galaxy. There I felt safe and peaceful, living in a home I couldn't remember—the one my mother had wiped from my brain. I'd get the feeling of everything being okay. That life wouldn't always be so hard.

And then Declan would come, dragging me from the beach back into the execution arena, and any reprieve that I got from the nightmares would fade into nothingness.

One dream flowed into the next without pause over and over again.

I couldn't do anything but listen to the sounds of my own muffled screaming echoing in the cryo chamber.

If anyone was there to hear me, no one ever came to help.

No one shook me awake.

I was trapped in the hell of my own mind for two weeks.

CHAPTER FIFTEEN

I WAS aware enough to feel the shift in the ship's vibrations when it started to slow. I knew we were close but wasn't sure how much longer it'd be. Each second I stayed in the cryo chamber felt like a year. I tried to stay awake and not slip back into my waking nightmares, but holding on made my heart hammer and my skin glow like lit gold. I couldn't take much more of this. I needed out of my coffin before I went completely insane.

I started counting. Before I got to one hundred the patch grew hot, and the tingling began to spread again.

When I'd first gotten into the cryo chamber, I'd hated the tingling, but after feeling nothing for so long, I welcomed it.

Thank God. At least this part was nearly over.

The first thing I could move was my lips. "I'm okay. I'm okay. I'm okay." I said it over and over. I wasn't sure if anyone could hear me or if this would somehow reveal me as Aunare, but in that moment, all I could think about was getting the hell out of the chamber.

By the time the glass slid open, I was in control enough to fling my body out. I hit the floor with a painful thump and tried to sit up but couldn't. I lay spread eagle on the floor and stared up at the ceiling. My limbs weren't totally working yet, but at least I was awake. The very real pain of my body hitting the ground told me that well enough, and that meant this particular nightmare was over.

The relief I felt was so strong that it took me a second to register that I was now out of the chamber and my skin was still glowing. That had to stop before anyone else came into the room. I took slow, measured breaths, trying to calm down. I couldn't hear anyone else moving around, but that didn't mean someone wouldn't show up any second.

"Hit the ground too hard." Ahiga's speech was groggy and slurred. "Should'a stayed in the chamber."

I wasn't sure where the nurse was, but it was probably for the best that she hadn't seen my cryo chamber exit. "I needed out of there."

"If you were claustrophobic, you could've told the nurse." His speech was already sounding better. "She'd have added a bit of relaxant to the wake-up cycle."

No amount of relaxant was going to fix what was wrong with me. "I'm not claustrophobic." At least I hadn't been, but after solitary and my reaction in the elevator and now two weeks in that chamber, maybe I was.

"Then why'd you jump out?"

I couldn't answer that without giving myself away, so I stayed perfectly silent. I licked my lips. They were dry and cracked, and I would kill for a glass of ice-cold water.

I brushed my sweaty hair off my forehead, and my arms shook with the effort. The tingling was fading, but it left weakness in its wake. I wasn't sure my legs would hold me, and that was worse than the tingling. I didn't like feeling weak. Especially not here in a SpaceTech ship. Especially not now on Abaddon. The glow was gone, but I was far from being okay.

But there was nothing I could do while I waited for the drugs to process out of my body.

"How you hanging in?" Ahiga asked.

"I'm hanging." Barely.

The urge to run beat against my mind, but I wasn't certain I had enough energy to get up off the ground, let alone run. I didn't want to be here or feel this way or have these chemicals in my body. My skin started glowing again, and I squeezed my eyes closed, taking another measured breath. Inhaling until my lungs burned and letting it out painfully slow.

Declan had mentioned that thinking of happy places and times helped when doing the breathing exercises. So I did my best and I pictured myself on a warm, sunny beach. The one I'd dreamed of, with perfectly white sand and crystal-clear water. I could almost hear the water lapping against the shore. I could smell the salt in the air.

I took another breath and happily sank into my imagination.

"Amihanna." Lorne's voice rolled through me.

My eyes flew open as I gasped and looked around. It'd sounded like Lorne was here in this room, but he wasn't.

And *damn it*. My skin was glowing brighter, and I had to make it stop.

The stupid drugs really must not be out of my system yet if I was still dreaming about him.

"Maité?" Ahiga asked.

I swallowed hard. So much for visualizing a happy place. "Did you hear anything?"

"Besides you breathing weird? No."

Which meant I'd hallucinated. Fantastic. "Sorry."

The cold, hard floor was nice against my sweaty skin. There was more than enough space for me to lie comfortably between the cryo chambers, and I was going to stay there until I got my shit together.

I focused on the wins. I made it to Abaddon in one piece and with my sanity mostly intact. I was still breathing, and that meant that I was surviving. One day at a time.

I stared up at the gray ceiling as I focused again on the breathing that Declan had taught me. After a few minutes, my skin was back to normal, and I was pretty sure I could sit up, but I couldn't walk. That didn't matter though. Without Ahiga, I didn't have any idea where to go. So I'd wait. At least I was out of the chamber.

The nurse strode in and scoffed when she saw me lying on the floor. "If you'd told me you were claustrophobic, I would've added a relaxant to your wake-up."

Ahiga let out a low laugh. "That's what I said."

"I'm not…" I started to say, but the nurse was already walking out again.

It took an hour for me to gain full use of my body, but Ahiga had been good to go ten minutes after coming out of stasis. He watched me very carefully while he waited for me to be able to move, bit by bit. When I finally stood up, his sigh was audible.

"I'm a survivor." And a di Aetes never gives up.

"I wouldn't expect anything less."

Ahiga didn't ask me any questions, but he knew something had gone wrong with my stasis. The guarded way he was watching me told me that clearly enough. There was nothing he could do about it now, but I was never, ever going to try deep space travel the human way again.

My first few steps felt like I was walking on feet made of jelly-filled plastic bags. I started to stumble, but Ahiga grabbed me before I face-planted.

"Thanks."

"No problem." He hooked his arm under my shoulders and helped me stay upright as we walked through the ship. At first, we moved slower than when I'd guided Ahiga across the catwalks, but after a few minutes, my feet started to get more feeling in them. Every step was a little stronger than the one before it. When we got to the exit, he was barely holding my weight anymore.

Ahiga leaned close to my ear. "You going to be okay from here out? Better if you show a strong front. They'll be watching."

I knew all about faking it. I could suck up any signs of weakness until I got to a spot where I could rest. I wasn't sure what was going to be on the other side of that door, but I had to be ready for anything. I stepped away from him. "How long will I be like this?"

"For anyone else, I'd say they'd be fine in an hour, but I'm not sure how long it'll last for you. The drugs should process out of your system in twenty-four hours. If you're not better by then, we'll figure something out."

I gave him a small nod, hoping he was right. That this overall dead weight feeling in my body would fade and that I'd feel more like myself soon. Because I wasn't sure I could take it much longer.

He entered a code in the panel beside the door, and it slowly opened. Heat rolled into me, and I stumbled back a step. One second in it and my tank top was already sticking to me. I pulled it away from my skin and shot a look at Ahiga.

"We're on a volcano planet. Better get used to the heat quick," Ahiga said.

For some idiotic reason, I'd been expecting to see the surface of Abaddon when I stepped out of the ship. Which made no sense. But I was kind of disappointed that I didn't even get a glimpse of it. The entire ship was swallowed up by the windowless hangar. It could easily hold downtown Albuquerque inside of it, skyscrapers and all.

This was going to be my new home, and it was important that I took note of everything I could. I was in a whole new place, and surviving meant observing everything I could about my surroundings. So I kept my eyes open as I stepped out of the ship and onto the catwalk.

Even one foot out of the ship and it was suffocatingly hot. "Is the AC running?"

Ahiga grunted, pointing to rows on rows of square blocks along the walls of the hold. "Those units are going all the time, but they just let our ship in. It'll take a couple hours for the hot air to circulate out and bring the temp back down. And by then, another ship will be here. So mostly it stays this way. It's only 107 right now."

That was a pretty specific temperature. "How do you know?"

He pointed to a vidscreen by the large bay doors. It said the temp in bright red numbers.

"Right." I took another step before reaching back for Ahiga and pulling him onto the catwalk with me. An alarm went off, and I froze. "What's that? Did I do something wrong?"

Ahiga muttered a few curses and then looked down. "Nah. See those guys there? In the heat suits?"

From up here, everyone looked tiny, but I saw a group of guys standing by one of the doors. They were covered head to toe in black suits—giant boots covered their feet, helmets on their heads, and what had to be oxygen on their backs. "Yeah."

"They're about to open the doors. The fans and cooling will combat it, but they're not miracle workers. Dangerous as fuck to go out there. The ground can be a lot even for the suits. It's volatile. No one usually goes outside, unless everything's about to go to hell and—"

Cooling systems started blasting the doors, sending a cloud of steam around the men waiting for them to open.

"What do you think's going on?"

"Dunno. Could be a problem on the surface or some repairs to the outside or they could just be doing some extreme training."

I watched as the guys disappeared and the alarm stopped.

"You ready?" Ahiga asked.

No. Not even a little bit. "I guess. Where are we headed?"

"Straight across."

"Perfect." As I walked forward, still holding Ahiga's hand, I glanced down at the people below. A group ran a weaving path through all the workers. "Why would they choose this place to work out? There have got to be cooler places to exercise on the base."

"This is a base. We train military personnel here, and—" Ahiga jerked to a stop.

When I glanced back, he was staring straight up at the ceiling. The look of pure misery on his face made me laugh. "You looked down again, didn't you?"

"Your fault." The cold look he gave me was enough to frighten the toughest of guys, but it wasn't working on me. Not when I was holding his hand to walk him across the catwalk like a little kid.

"Sorry," I said, but the laugh felt earned. I needed it.

As we reached the end of the catwalk, Ahiga let go of my hand and moved in front of me. "This way." A couple of turns later and we were in front of a stairwell.

"Are you using a chip to navigate in here?" I could buy him knowing his way around the ship. I assumed most cargo ships were laid out the same way, but this base was supposed to be different than most due to the mining and the fact that it was built on fiery hot, molten lava.

If Ahiga was annoyed by my constant stream of questions, he didn't act it. "Nah. I was here a couple years ago to work with an IAF group. Spent the longest ninety days of my life running drills and taking the guys out on the surface for twenty-minute training sessions. Swore I'd never come back."

"Should I apologize?" It wasn't my fault, but this situation was shitty for more than just me.

"Things change." He shrugged. "Don't worry about it. This isn't as bad as some other places I've been. Like NR3. That planet and its constant quakes..." His eyebrows rose, disappearing into the tattoos on his forehead. "Trust me. I'll take the heat to that place any day."

I wasn't sure which colony he was talking about, but SpaceTech kept so much information confidential that I wasn't surprised I hadn't heard of it.

As we went down flight after flight of stairs, the fitted tank top felt like it was melting onto my back. I wiped a drop of sweat from my brow with my hand. "Jesus. You'd think they'd have an elevator in this place."

"They don't like any extra machinery in this part of the base that they'd have to keep cool."

"Don't they have a way to keep it cool? I mean, it's not like fuel is a concern here, right? With all the access to lucole?" Not even SpaceTech could be this cheap.

"You'd think, but that's not the case. SpaceTech rations every ounce of it."

Well, I was clearly mistaken. SpaceTech was exactly that cheap.

Ahiga waved for me to keep moving. "We're going to miss mealtime."

"Sorry." I had a lot of questions, but if Ahiga was hungry, they could wait.

The only people we passed as we walked through the base had STIAF—SpaceTech Interplanetary Armed Forces—in big gray letters printed across their navy tees.

"What's with all the IAF?" I knew it was a base, but it was mostly for mining. Not for training. At least that's what I thought. "It's not like anyone could steal from this base. It's in the center of SpaceTech territory. And no one can make a run for it, even if they got control of one of the mining ships." The mining ships were meant for short-range at best.

And—as far as I knew—the Aunare didn't have any interest in the lucole. They had much cleaner, more efficient fuel sources. Fuel that they'd shared with some of the other species out there, but not with the Earthers. I was sure they had their reasons though. Why give an evil corporation more power?

"Better safe than sorry is one of the Murtaghs' favorite sayings. Without the lucole SpaceTech stores on the base, they would be outgunned against the Aunare. With war coming... Gotta be prepared. He's increased IAF presence on the base and in ships around the whole system."

"Right." He had a point. If I were my father, Abaddon would the first place I'd destroy. Dismantling the source of SpaceTech's fuel and weapons was a no-brainer. Still, it was in the middle of SpaceTech's territory. It'd be hard to get here without causing a war. But if my father knew I was here, he couldn't attack the base with any long-range weapons.

Maybe that was Jason's plan? Having me here definitely

secured the base. At least until my dad decided to come get me himself and blow it up on his way out the door.

The more I thought about it, the more questions and theories I had. I couldn't rule anything out yet.

The only thing I knew was that Jason had a plan. That war was coming. And that somehow—some way—I was going to have to survive here long enough to find a way to stop it.

CHAPTER SIXTEEN

AHIGA LED me through the base. I'd seen a few doors—each marked with letters and numbers—but no windows. Each hallway led to more hallways. And as far as I could tell, the only way outside was through the cargo bay. I was going to dub SpaceTech's design style as coffin-chic if this kept up.

Eventually, we stopped in front of a door. Ahiga tapped in a code, and it swung open. The room beyond was split into two sections by a counter. The space in front of the counter was empty. Beyond it a floor-to-ceiling shelving unit packed with gear—clothes, weapons, and other odds and ends— covered the walls. A small robot floated in front of them, ready to zoom to work on command.

All the clothes on the shelves were navy, which was much more my color than the diner uniform's teal or the noxious orange prisoner gear, and I'd be getting something other than the pajamas I'd been wearing for the last two weeks while traveling. Both were good news. Wins.

A man stepped away from the counter, giving me a once over. His brown hair was shaved close to his head, and his eyes were a clear-glass blue. After a long second, he turned to Ahiga, and I was glad his attention was off of me. The way he took in each part of me made me think he might've noticed what I was.

"Hey, man. Long time no see." They exchanged a head nod, handshake thing. "Who're you bringing to visit me?"

"We're gonna need full worker gear for her, Matthew." Ahiga's chin jutted in my direction.

"What'd you do to land work detail?" He crossed his arms as he gave me another stare.

"None of your business," I said because it was exactly that. I didn't want word getting around about how I punched the son of SpaceTech's CEO, especially when I didn't know what the base was going to be like.

Matthew's fingers moved quickly through the air in a series of gestures before he focused on me again. "I don't have much women's gear on hand. I'll give you what I have and the smallest size of everything else."

That didn't sound promising. "What is he talking about? No women's gear?"

"When I was here last, I was busy with the training, but I didn't see many women," Ahiga said. "That still the case?"

Matthew waved his hand back and forth. "Eh. It's still mostly men here. We have a couple females on detail in the kitchens. One woman medic. A couple here and there throughout the base." He swiped his finger through the air. "You've been slated to the red zone. I need to grab you a suit, too, but I don't keep those in here. I'll get it to Tyler before morning. He's the guy you're going to be working with."

"Okay." I assumed I wasn't going to need it before then anyway. I was doing much better, but I still wasn't up to my normal strength. I needed that twenty-four hours before I started working.

The bot stopped collecting stuff from the cubbies.

"This is it."

Matthew patted the mound of navy material the bot had collected—one pair of pants, two shorts, one shirt, three tanks, three socks, a pair of flimsy running shoes, one bra, a few pairs of underwear, and one bag labeled toiletries. A duffle sat next to it. I moved before Matthew could. I didn't want him touching my underwear. The way he was looking at me—assessing my every move—made me uncomfortable enough as it was.

I shoved everything in and pulled the drawstring, ready to get gone as soon as I could.

"One last thing. Wrist unit. This one's totally archaic, but it comes loaded with info on the base, unstable areas to avoid, your work schedule, and you might get updates from your supervisor. If I had a spare contact lens, I'd give it to you, but I don't. This'll have to do." He said it like it was a challenge.

If he thought I was going to argue with him, he was wrong. "I'm sure it's fine."

I never would've traded in my old wrist unit for the implant and contact lens if I'd had a choice. Maybe I could even get the base medic to remove the implant. I didn't love the fact that the stupid thing was still lodged inside my finger even if it was inactive.

"I've linked the unit to your SpaceTech tracker, which has an *odd* signal, but I got it to sync."

"Thanks." I hadn't even felt the chip since Ahiga injected it into my arm. I couldn't feel any signals from it. I wondered if it was some sort of Aunare tracker, but from what I knew, they didn't implant any tech at all.

"Mm-hmm. You make it the year, you can go get yourself a new contact lens, or even get a full lace." Matthew smiled at me, but his words didn't ring true at all. The way he kept talking about my implant—or lack thereof—made me wonder what he knew about me.

There was an awkward silence as I looked back at Ahiga. He gave me a tiny, almost imperceptible shake of his head.

He didn't know what Matt's deal was either. I grabbed the wrist unit and fumbled with the clasp.

"Come on," Ahiga said. "I'll show you to your bunk."

I hefted the duffle onto my shoulder and followed Ahiga through the doors without a backward glance. I wanted to ask Ahiga what Matthew's deal was, but I couldn't. Not with cameras watching our every move.

The duffle was much heavier than it looked, but maybe that was just because I was still working through all the cryo drugs. I still felt like my feet were dragging, and I promised myself I'd take a nap as soon as I found my bed.

We continued through a series of endless gunmetal gray hallways and stairwells, all with polished concrete floors. Besides the gray, the only other color I'd seen so far was the white letters and numbers on different doors. No bright colors. No vegetation. Nothing that could fool anyone into thinking that they were anywhere other than a SpaceTech work facility.

The only thing that changed depending on our location was the temperature. The stairwells were unbearably hot. Then we'd enter a level of the base, and it'd cool down a bit. I'd heard that it smelled like sulfur out there, but from inside, thankfully, I couldn't smell it.

We went up three flights of stairs, my feet clanging on the metal steps. At the top, Ahiga placed his hand on a scanner, then started pushing buttons. "The map on your wrist unit will help you figure out what they mean, but WQ361 is the women's quarters. It says here you'll share the space with seven other women, although there's room for more should the need arise." He paused his motions. "All right. Hand here."

When I didn't move fast enough, he grabbed my right hand and pressed it to the scanner. The energy passed through me, making my teeth ache. There was a series of beeps, and then it was quiet.

"Okay," he said as he dropped my wrist. "You're good to go. You'll only have access to the areas that you're approved for. Restrooms. The mess. Women's quarters and their adjoining baths. And Cargo Bay One. That's where you'll need to report in the morning."

Ahiga placed his palm on the door again. A screen lit up, saying that it was alerting anyone inside that someone was coming in, and gave a thirty-second countdown.

I gave him a questioning look.

"I'm a man opening the women's quarters. I have the rank to go into almost any room on this base, but it gives those inside a warning if they need to cover up." After a minute, there was a series of clicks and beeps before the lock clanked. He swung the door open. "Welcome to your new home."

The room was bigger than I expected. Ten bunk beds ran along opposite walls, all of them gray metal with gray sheets and blankets. A few had clothes and personal items strewn over them, giving the room its only hint of life. Thin mattresses were rolled up on the others, resting against the heads of the beds.

At the end of the room was a doorway, but no actual door. Beyond it was a row of sinks with a mirrored wall above them. I figured the bathroom had to be somewhere past that—hopefully showers, too. I needed one desperately. The smell coming off of me wouldn't help me make any friends.

The room wasn't much, but it was clean and open, which meant it was already light-years better than prison.

Aside from the things in the room, it was empty. "Where's everyone?"

"It's dinner time. They'll be in the mess, but I bet you're not hungry?"

I shook my head. Maybe it was the heat or the stress of trying to absorb everything about the base as quickly as I could, but I had zero appetite.

"It usually takes a day or two after cryo before you're back to a normal eating schedule. The chambers keep you well stocked with cals to get you through the trip. They always overdo it a bit, and with your reaction to—"

"Can they hear us?" I asked, cutting him off before he gave away any of my secrets.

"Against company policy to record in areas where there are

bathrooms and changing areas." He motioned to the other room. "Entrances to the quarters are watched, but once you're inside, you're okay."

Well, at least SpaceTech wasn't totally pervy. Now that I was alone with him, I had one big question. "What is it that I'm supposed to be doing exactly?" Matthew had said I was red-zoned, but what did that mean?

Ahiga wouldn't look at my face, and that was starting to freak me out. "What?" It didn't matter what job I had, I'd get through it. I had no other choice.

He rubbed his stubbly cheek. "You're going to be on the tarmac and roadways outside."

"Doing what?" I didn't know anything about directing airships, but I was pretty sure that was done from a control room inside the base. For everything else, there should be bots.

"Icing them down, apparently."

I laughed. Was that a joke? "I'm sorry, I thought you said I'd be icing down the tarmac and roadways?"

"Affirmative."

It made zero sense. "Don't you have bots for that? And hovering vehicles? Do you even *need* roadways? And what good does icing them down do anyway, when the whole freaking planet is lava? If they wanted a more stable place to put a base, they shouldn't have built here." I was out of breath by the time I finally stopped my rant, but I honestly couldn't come up with a more stupid job if I tried.

"Yes, there are bots for icing. Yes, the vehicles hover. And, no, we don't actually need this job to be done. The ships are much faster on smooth roadways, which can mean the difference of getting out of someplace quickly, but they can get around just fine on any surface."

I had to be missing something. "So why was I assigned this if it isn't even necessary?" I was fine cleaning toilets or scrubbing pots in the kitchen or any other menial task, but risking my life out on the surface for something that didn't even matter? That wasn't even *needed*?

The glow started small at first but quickly turned into light-show Maité.

"Shit." Ahiga went to the door and messed with the control panel, hopefully locking it, but I didn't care.

I sat down on the edge of the closest empty bunk. "I can't believe this." I shouldn't have been so surprised and pissed off, but I was. I'd honestly thought Jason was going to have me cleaning toilets with a toothbrush, but to risk my life—

"According to the report on file, all the bots have been called in for maintenance." His face was getting a red tinge to it as he answered, but his words remained calm. "Indefinitely."

I wanted to scream with frustration. "Is Jason trying to kill me in the quickest, stupidest way he can?"

"Very possibly." Ahiga's jaw ticced.

None of this made any sense to me. "Why ship me here just to kill me? He could've done that on Earth."

"I don't know, but I'm sure he has a reason, and whatever it is, we're not going to like it."

"I don't think I like any reason for me dying." This was more than iced. For one blessed moment when I stepped off the ship, I'd actually thought that maybe he'd stashed me here so that my father wouldn't blow up their primary fuel source. But I'd been so unbelievably wrong and stupid for thinking that.

When my father found out about what I was doing, he'd lose his mind. I had no doubt that it wouldn't be long before someone purposefully leaked it to him. Jason might even be goading my father into starting the war. "How quickly can you get me shifted to another work detail?"

"I'm already working on it. My first request to the CO was immediately denied. I'm going to go talk to him now. I've messaged Declan, but it might be a bit before he hears. I got an automessage that he's in cryo right now."

This was all kinds of messed up. I was going to be working on the surface of hell. Fine. But Declan needed me to survive for a month, maybe more, and I wasn't sure that was possible with that job. Even in a cooling suit. I wasn't sure I could survive a week out there.

"Did Declan say when he'd be out of cryo?"

"No. He didn't say when he went into cryo, when he'd get out, or where he was headed, and before you ask, no. We didn't get a chance to regroup once we got your sentence. After you were arrested, Roan leaked the footage of the diner and—"

"Roan did that? I thought Declan had." When Officer Perez mentioned that the footage went viral, I hadn't understood how or why, but I assumed it was something Declan or maybe even Jason had done.

"Roan thought it might help you. He did it before running with your mom, his mom and sister, and Jorge. Declan caught up to them while you were in jail. He planned to get them somewhere safe and then head to wherever you were sent, but he didn't leave word via our normal lines. I don't know why the hell—" Ahiga squatted down in front of me and reached for my hand. I gave it to him.

I'd helped him before, and now he was here for me. At least I had one friend here. That was something to be thankful for. I focused on that and tried to calm the glowing with my breaths.

He continued. "This work detail assignment is coming from Jason, and since I was denied the transfer so quickly, I have to think that the base's CO is in the know. I don't think I'm going to have any luck changing it."

"So what then? I'm screwed until Declan gets me out of here somehow? So weeks? Maybe a month?" I didn't think it'd be possible to sweat more than I already was, but I was wrong. "I'm going to die." My heart was pounding out of my chest, and if I'd had any food in my stomach, I would've thrown up. "Jason's going to send me out there to burn to death." I'd dreamed about that during cryo. It had been awful, but I knew that when it actually happened, it was going to be way worse. The walls were closing in on me, and it wasn't just the heat that was making me dizzy.

Ahiga grabbed my shoulders and gave them a good shake. "You're not going to die. You'll have the suit. I'll go back to Matthew and check it myself."

"What's Matthew's deal? Does he have anything to do—?"

"Matthew doesn't have any say over the work detail assignments. Something was definitely wrong with him today, but you don't have to worry about him. He monitors all the supplies on base, and because he does that, he knows everyone that comes and goes through here. He used to be Elite IAF, but he got hurt a while back and scored this cushy job."

"Does he know what I am?"

"He doesn't know anything, and even if he guesses, it doesn't matter. You'll never run into him again. The good news—and it might be the *only* good news here—is that you really shouldn't ever see any SpaceTech officers. They're watching, but they only pop in if someone isn't doing their job."

"So the Tyler that I'm working with isn't an officer?"

"No. He's a convict."

At least I wouldn't have to deal with any officers. I was trying desperately to see the bright side of this, but every time I thought about the job I was supposed to do here, the more I wanted to run. Except there was no place to run to. There was no escaping the base. I was hundreds of light-years from the nearest colony. The only thing on this planet was the base.

I was stuck. I might not be in a cell anymore, but I may as well have been.

"You gotta stop freaking out on me. You're going to be okay. If something starts going bad out there, you come in. Simple as that."

I snorted. There was no way Jason would've assigned this job for me if it was going to be that easy, but there was no easy way out of this, no matter how much I wanted it.

"I'm going to figure something out," Ahiga said. "We just got here. Give me time to work on the CO."

What a load of shit this was. Just being on Abaddon was dangerous, but I never—not in my wildest dreams—thought my job here was going to be this asinine.

"Here's what you're going to do." Ahiga stood up. "You take a shower. You had a hard trip here, so just try to calm down, and then you go to sleep. But don't skip breakfast in the morning, okay? Your body is going to need all the calories it can get tomorrow, and drink as much water as you can stand so you stay hydrated out there. Water will also help you flush out the rest of the cryo drugs."

"Thanks for the tip." That came out shittier and snappier than I wanted, and I winced. "Sorry."

"Don't apologize. That'll just piss me off. Pick a bunk and get settled. The glow is lessening, but it needs to get gone before your bunkmates get back."

I took a breath in for a count of six. "I'll work on it."

"Good. And check your wrist unit for where to go in the a.m. Don't be late. I'll find you when I have news." Ahiga didn't wait for me to say anything before spinning on his heel. The door slammed behind him.

I wanted to run after Ahiga and ask where he was staying, but it didn't matter. He was an officer here. If they separated the workers from the officers, then it might be a while before I saw him again. He was here to help me, but I couldn't lean on him too hard or else his cover would be blown.

I strode down the line of bunks. I didn't really care which one I had. There were plenty available, so I threw my bag down on a lower one and sat.

The detail I'd been assigned was total bullshit. Maybe the suits would be enough to keep me alive out there, but Jason had clearly gone out of his way to put me on tarmac detail. Something told me my chances of survival weren't great.

So I had to think of something. I stood and started pacing up and down the aisle between the bunks. Now that I was here, the insane idea of going on mining runs sounded less and less crazy. Roan said he thought he could do it, and if he could, then…

I wondered if I could switch.

Mining should be dangerous enough if Ahiga pitched it the right way to the CO. Maybe not as flashy a death as burning on the surface of Abaddon, but blowing up on its moon had to be a draw for Jason.

It was a crazy plan and had a lot of ifs, but it was a start.

Was I really considering this?

No. Not yet. But maybe one day I'd be desperate enough to try.

The glow faded completely, and I slowed my pacing. There was nothing I could do now except follow Ahiga's advice—shower and sleep.

Tomorrow, I'd figure out if I really was desperate enough to beg for mining duty. If there was one thing I knew, I would *not* be doing a stupid robot's job for long. My stubbornness wouldn't allow it.

CHAPTER SEVENTEEN

I WOKE WITH A START. My head slammed into the bunk above me as I fought to get out from under the sheets. Even the paper thin cotton was enough to make me feel trapped.

It took me a few long seconds to realize where I was. I got up, looking up and down the row of bunks, but everyone was already gone.

I went back and sat heavily on my bunk. I hadn't even stirred while my bunkmates were getting ready, and I wasn't sure when it'd gotten so uncomfortably stuffy in the room. It felt like the AC had gone off sometime in the night, and I wasn't sure how I managed to sleep through that. I didn't think I'd been dreaming, but with how I woke up—with my heart racing and a panicked scream threatening to break free—I must've been dreaming something terrible.

I glanced down at my wrist unit and realized I had an hour and a half before my first day started. Not wanting to be late for work, I quickly headed to the showers.

The bathroom had a row of open shower stalls, and I gritted my teeth as I walked toward them. The water flow in my old apartment's shower had been weak on a good day. It took five minutes just to get my hair wet, and the water had been lukewarm. From the shower I'd taken last night, I thought I might hate the showers here more. At least at the apartment, I'd had privacy. I didn't like being naked in front of anyone. No one was here right now, but I wouldn't always be that lucky.

I almost skipped a shower, but I'd sweated so much in my sleep, I could feel a layer of stickiness along my skin. That was no way to start the day.

Picking the closest showerhead, I turned on the knob. No matter how hot I turned it, the water stayed cold. I would've thought that with how hot it was here that the water would also be hot, but no.

I quickly shed the shorts and tank I'd used as pajamas. Holding my breath, I stepped under the icy stream. I yelped as goosebumps broke out across my skin and moved as quickly as I could. It was a shock at first, but then, when I got over the initial jolt, it was a refreshing break from the thick heat in the room. Still, I didn't linger for long in there. Not like I had in the spaceport shower.

When I finished, I slapped my hair into a messy bun and threw on another pair of shorts. At least I thought they were shorts. They were skintight and made of the same water-wicking material as a lot of the other stuff. The tank top was fitted, but soft. Going out in so little clothing wasn't my usual MO, but it was too hot to even think about pants.

I had a little over an hour before I had to show up for work. That left me just enough time to follow Ahiga's advice to have a good breakfast. My appetite was still nonexistent, but if Ahiga said food would help me survive, I'd eat as much as I could shove down my throat.

My hands shook as I checked my hair. Going out on the surface seemed pretty terrible, but I'd gotten through plenty of sticky situations. I wanted to believe that I could do this, but the nerves were still there.

I checked the screen on my wrist unit. There was an emergency info app, a calendar—which had my shifts—and a few other things that I'd check out later. But no access to any browsers. Aside from an alerts app from SpaceTech, there was no messaging on the unit that I could find. A map icon was also nonexistent, but there was a little SpaceTech icon labeled "SPB-14278."

A basic menu bar popped up, and I realized Matthew was right. This wrist unit was pretty archaic. It looked like something programmed decades ago. One more click and the map popped open. The blinking blue dot on the screen showed my position. A little search told me that there were two mess halls—main and an officers' club. The main mess was a few buildings away. I quickly navigated, checking the map every few steps as I wound through dimly lit hallways until I finally reached a door with a barely visible metal plaque labeling it "Mess Hall."

I scanned my hand on the unit next to the door. This time it didn't make my teeth hurt, but the buzz along my body was uncomfortable. The door unlocked, and I stepped into the noisy room.

A couple hundred guys sat eating at long tables with benches. As I walked through the center aisle between them, the men stopped eating to stare. The movement rippled from front to back. My fingers itched to tug down the shorts, but I didn't want to give off the impression that I was uncomfortable, even if I was. They might mistake my lack of comfort for fear, and that could quickly escalate into one of them trying something with me, which wouldn't go well for them. But my skin crawled as I fought the urge to turn around.

Ahiga said food. So I was getting food.

I scanned the faces staring at me. No women in sight. Not as far as I could tell. For a second I wondered if I was in the right place. Maybe I'd mixed up which mess hall I was supposed to be in. Or maybe I missed a women-only mess, but I quickly ruled that out. There were only two, and from what Matthew and Ahiga said, there weren't many women here. Having a separate mess hall wouldn't be a good use of resources.

A whistle cut through the air, and I realized that maybe the other women weren't in this room for a reason. Maybe I was the dummy for coming here to eat. But where were the other women?

I tilted my chin up, not wanting to show any nerves, and walked evenly paced steps as I made my way to the counter at the back of the room. A lady with a hair net grunted at me. Finally. Another woman.

"Good morning," I said in what I hoped was a friendly tone.

The answering stare down made it clear she didn't want to be friends with me.

Fine. I grabbed a tray from the stack and shoved it under the protective glass. Some sort of neon yellow egg substitute hit the metal with a wet plop. I struggled to keep the disgust off my face. Choking down this slop was going to be a chore. A serving of potatoes, a hunk of bread, and some gray-looking sausage quickly followed. I thanked her and went to find a place to sit.

A man with long, stringy hair who stunk like he hadn't showered in weeks had a large empty space beside him. He seemed like he was paying zero attention to the room, so I figured it was a safe place to sit, even if he did stink. But as I moved to the empty part of the bench, the man slid over, stopping me before I could throw my leg over the bench.

Okay, not welcome at that table. The guy seemed to like his meal in peace. I understood that well enough.

The third time it happened, I started to get annoyed. The guy looked and smelled normal, so I wasn't sure why I was getting the cold shoulder. I didn't have to be soul mates with whoever I sat next to, but I needed a place to sit so I could attempt to eat this crap before my shift started. I didn't have time for their juvenile behavior.

"You can sit by me," someone said behind me. The slime in his voice made me cringe.

I chose to ignore the offer, not even looking back at him.

Worst case scenario, I could always take my tray to my bunk.

"Maité!"

I stumbled at the sound of my name. It didn't sound like Ahiga or Matthew, and I assumed they'd be in the Officers' Mess. Who else here knew me?

I spun, scanning the faces and trying to find the source.

"Over here!"

My mouth dropped open. "Holy shit," I muttered under my breath.

John Santiago was a short guy, but thick and made up for his height by lifting some insanely heavy weights. His head was shaved, but he didn't have as many tattoos as some of the other ABQ Crew guys. None of them showed in the standard SpaceTech tank and pants that he was wearing, but the matador fighting a bull on his chest was memorable. The over-the-top expression on the matador's face used to crack me up when we sparred. I wasn't sure why he'd gotten that particular tattoo exactly, but the guy loved to laugh and to make everyone around him laugh. So I figured that had a lot to do with it.

He was smiling big, showing me a mouthful of pearly whites, and I felt my shoulders loosen. "¡*Tanto tiempo!*" he said, bumping my forearm with his.

It was good to see a friendly face. "No kidding. It's been what…three years?"

"Yo! Move down!" he yelled at the guy sitting next to him.

There was some grumbling, but a few guys slid down the bench, opening a seat next to Santiago. I'd been trying to ignore everyone else—I'd had enough hostile looks—but as I put my tray on the table and sat down, I saw Ahiga sitting across from me.

"What are you doing here? I thought officers didn't mix with workers." It came off a bit ruder than I wanted, but I didn't want to come across as friendly anyway. Not when SpaceTech was watching.

"You know her?" Ahiga asked, ignoring my question.

"Yep." Santiago's tray was empty. Guess someone liked the food. "She's the Crew's best fighter. Man, you should see her spar. It's, like, crazy. She's fast and sharp and dude, you just never see the girl comin'. When she was a kid, Jorge would test out his top guys against her. She always won. It's like she knew what they were going to do before they did it. She just took them the fuck down." He slammed his hands on the table, rattling our trays.

The guy was talking too much, but in that moment, it was so nice to see an old friend that I didn't care.

"We'd time it and set up bets and shit." Santiago laughed. "My money was always on Maité though. I ain't stupid. She beat my ass five times—"

"Seven." He wished it was five times, but he was wrong.

"No way, *chica*. It was five. It's not something I could forget."

"Apparently, you did. It was seven." I grinned at him, but my smile quickly faded when I realized the guys within hearing distance had quieted to listen to us.

Damn it. I didn't want any more attention than I already had.

I avoided their gazes by staring at my food. They'd forget about me in a second. They had to.

I quickly glanced up, and any hope I had to remain anonymous here deflated to nothing. I'd been so happy to see Santiago that I'd forgotten to keep my mouth shut. I'd totally abandoned my plan to keep my head down until Declan got here. Everyone in the Crew loved him, and apparently the same was true here.

I stabbed a hunk of potato and forced down the grainy bite, trying to ignore their stares. How the cook managed to ruin potatoes was beyond me.

"You're not saying different, so that means you really think you beat me seven times. The first time got me by surprise. Wouldn't forget that shit." Santiago started counting on his fingers. "Two. Three. Oh yeah. Three was a bitch. You kicked me so fucking hard in the leg I limped for weeks. Couldn't afford the nanos and I wouldn't let myself admit a child hurt me that badly. Hit my pride hard." He huffed. "But I got over that the fourth time. Then five. So what am I forgetting?"

I shrugged. No way was I answering that, especially since he hadn't elaborated on a couple of them.

"Wait. Wait. I got it. That time when you did that bounce-off-the-wall kick thing makes six." He slammed a hand on the table, and the water in my glass sloshed over the rim. "Oh shit. How did I forget the time you flipped me so hard I flew across the room? TKO." He smirked at me. "That's embarrassing. Seven. She beat my ass seven times, and she was just a kid. How old were you then? Fifteen? Sixteen?"

"Twelve. I was thirteen when Jorge switched me to teaching."

"Sounds like you're a girl full of surprises," Ahiga said.

"You already met Ahiga?" Santiago asked.

I glanced up and froze, waiting for Ahiga to say something. I'd already given away that I knew him by my reaction when I sat down. But Ahiga didn't say anything.

This was getting awkward. "We were on the same ship here. It was only us in the cryo room. So not really. Just to say hi, I guess. How'd you end up here, Santiago?" I asked, hoping to change the subject off to something—anything—other than me.

"Eh. You know I got caught takin' down that Rojo a while back. Been here ever since. I was going to get ten on Earth, but it's only four here. Almost done."

"Seriously?" If he'd lasted nearly four years, it gave me hope that maybe I could last out my one year. Or at least until Declan came. Maybe it wouldn't be so bad? Sure, my job was the pits, but maybe life in general on the base wasn't as terrible as SpaceTech made it out to be.

"Yeah."

"I didn't think people lasted that long here."

Santiago leaned back in his chair and gave me one of his easy smiles. "It's not as bad as people make it sound. I'm a mechanic for the mining ships. It's what I did before, so it ain't all bad. Man. That's the crazy part of it. Those assholes who sign up for runs." He shook his head. "Those mofos drop like flies. Anyone with half a brain would stay away. Hell, anyone with a few working brain cells should know better."

The men nearby nodded their agreement.

I wanted to scream and shout and curse the fact that everything

I came up with turned out to be a dead end. "Ah. Well. That's interesting." Once again, the little bit of a plan I'd thought up disappeared. I'd been hoping to somehow transfer to the mining runs. On Earth, Roan said that he thought we could make it, but I'd told him then that it was suicidal. Apparently, I was right the first time.

Damn it. I hated being right all the time. Just this one time I wanted Roan to be right. I needed him to be right.

Santiago leaned into me. "So...uh...since we're both gonna be working on base together, you gonna show me your tattoo?" He waggled his eyebrows.

I snorted before I could stop it. "No." My cheeks burned. Why did he have to say it like that in front of all these guys? I already felt like too many people were paying attention to me, and now they were probably mentally undressing me.

"Her tattoo?" Ahiga said, looking at me. "Most people who have them don't mind showing their art."

"Yeah. Maybe people who have them on their face don't mind it, but not me. Mine's personal."

I didn't know why I felt that way about my tattoo, but when I'd been trying to pick what to get, I could only come up with one thing that I was okay with forever marking my skin. And when the artist was done, it felt like I'd made a part of my soul visible. Suddenly, I was vulnerable in a way I didn't like.

I'd made Vanessa—the tattoo artist—promise never to tell anyone what it was. I'd even taken the sketches of it and burned them.

Thankfully, the tattoo was hidden on the inside of my left hipbone and small—about two inches by one inch. The only people besides me and Vanessa who had seen it since was Roan—because he'd been with me when I got it—and Haden.

I regretted that Haden had ever seen it, and the one time he'd ever touched it... I could still see the shock in his eyes as I slapped his hand away from me. We'd been hot and heavy one second, and then he caressed that spot, and I suddenly felt dirty. I'd grabbed my clothes, barely bothering to dress before I was out the door.

I didn't answer his calls after that night. It's why I don't date. After that night, I knew I was too much of a mess to handle a relationship. It wasn't worth the time.

I stared down at my plate. I'd barely managed a few spoonfuls of this lab-grown junk.

Someone kicked me under the table, and I glanced up.

"You watching your figure?" Ahiga asked.

"Girl doesn't need to watch shit. She fine," someone yelled from down the table.

I stared so hard at Ahiga that I was pretty sure he knew I was murdering him in my mind.

"Eat," he said, clearly not bothered by my stare.

Fine. I knew I had to eat, but it wasn't my fault that the drugs had mutilated my appetite. I mushed the soupy eggs around with my fork. I was going to have to try them, but I wasn't looking forward to it. I forked a small bite on the bread, hoping that would make it edible, but gagged. "This is *disgusting*." It was so awful it was making my eyes water.

"You'll get used to it." Santiago chuckled as I made a yucky face at him. "I've spent too much time with the guys placing bets on what Maité's tattoo is."

Was he still talking about my freaking tattoo? "Shut it."

"Not unless you show me."

"No." And if he kept bringing it up, I was going to kick his ass for the eighth time.

"One of my girls gave it to her—it's an initiation thing, so I know it's there—but Maité won't let no one see. Vanessa won't spill where it is but said no one would ever guess what it was. ABQ Crew members have to have one of an animal, but everyone gets to pick theirs. Some think maybe she chickened out and Vanessa's just covering Maité's ass." He slapped his hand on the table. "Guys have been trying to get at her just so they can see the tat, but no one gets through to Maité. Except for Roan. He—"

"Shut up!" I loved Santiago, but he was killing me. The guy was spilling way too much information. No one could know a weak spot, especially about Roan. "I like my privacy. Remember that or I'll be forced to remind you."

I had to survive, and the best way to do that was to keep my head down. Being a woman on a male-dominated planet was already going to make that difficult enough. And if the guys thought I was a challenge, the target on my back would only get bigger. I'd already made it bad enough when I corrected him earlier. This needed to be shut down. Fast.

"No way. I'm not going for number eight. I'm older now. I break, dude." Santiago held up his hands in surrender. "Sorry, *chica*," he said, more quietly. "I forget that about you. About you liking privacy."

"Doesn't everyone?" I wanted to be pissed at him, but Santiago was clueless. That was always his problem. His positive, fun-loving nature made up for it.

"Nah. I don't need privacy." He rubbed his head. "I'm an open book."

Ahiga laughed. "That's because your book is mostly empty."

I nearly spurted potatoes on the table. By the time I stopped laughing, my sides ached, and tears were running down my face. It wasn't even that funny, but everything had been so horrible that my mind needed the cathartic release. "Oh God. I needed that. You don't know how much. Thanks."

"My pleasure," Ahiga said. "You need to eat up. Your duty starts in twenty, and you're going to need a little extra time to get into your suit."

"Suit?" Santiago asked.

Ahiga explained, keeping his cover. "Looked her up while you were spilling all her personal information. Got more information for myself. Must've pissed off someone up top, because she's got ice-down duty."

Santiago's smile melted. "No. She can't. That's total bullshit. We have bots for that shit."

"Not anymore. They're in repairs."

"That's bullshit." The joking, smiling John Santiago was gone. His face paled. "Can't you change it?"

Ahiga gripped his fork so hard, it bent. He threw it on the table. "Not up to me, kid. I'm only here for training. Just like last time."

"But it's *bullshit*. No one should have to do that. It's not even a job here. If the bots are broken, I could fix them. Fucking Space-Tech. They're the *worst*. They think that—" Santiago continued ranting at Ahiga, and I took that as my cue.

"Don't get upset on my account. I feel you on the SpaceTech front. They're pure evil, and I hate we're both here working for them. But you haven't heard why I got sent here yet, and you can be damned sure I'll spill about my tattoo before I tell you why I was arrested. Not going to happen. Ever. So don't ask." I stabbed the last bite of potato and choked it down with water.

"They're using this as punishment, and until someone stops SpaceTech, until someone isn't afraid to stand against them, they won't care about honor or what's right or anything except their bottom line. The only problem they'd have if we all died here is that their productivity would go down while they shipped more convicts up to replace us."

My wrist unit started vibrating, and I tapped the screen. "Looks like it's time for me to take off," I said. "Good to see you, Santiago." I took the sausage and bread in one hand and my tray in the other.

"Sure thing, *chica*. You're always welcome with me. I'll look out for you. Survivors Together."

"Survivors Together," I said back to him as I blushed, feeling a bit touched to have a friend so far from home. "Thanks. I appreciate that."

I dropped off my tray on the way out and headed to the cargo bay, forcing myself to eat the food as I went. The sausage was even grosser than I'd expected. It was slimy and chewy and chunky—which made eating it a chore—but seeing Santiago had been kind of awesome.

If I was looking for bright spots here, at least I had Santiago and Ahiga. Two people I could count on. I tried to keep that in mind as I walked down the deserted, hot hallways to my work duty. I wasn't sure what was going to happen out there on the surface, but my plan hadn't changed. I was going to survive until someone got me off this hell planet. End of story.

CHAPTER EIGHTEEN

I FOLLOWED the map on my wrist unit and ended up at Cargo Bay One. From what the map said, there were seven cargo bays on the base. My heart was pounding, and sweat dripped down my temples, and I wanted to believe that it was from walking through so many sweltering hallways, but I wasn't sure I could lie to myself well enough to make it believable.

This was it. I was about to endure the hell that Jason dreamed up, but I was going to do it with my head held high. I glanced at the camera hanging in the hallway. He probably wasn't watching, but I was sure someone was. I wouldn't let them see me squirm. I wouldn't give them that pleasure.

Before I could think any more about it, I slapped my hand on the door's scanner—ignoring the energy ripping through my system—and the door opened.

Stepping into the cargo bay was like entering a yawning cavern with stacks of containers climbing their way to the ceiling. I couldn't tell exactly how tall the room was because of all the piles. They seemed to tower impossibly high, and I couldn't help but hunch down a little.

It didn't seem safe for them to be placed like that, but if it wasn't then SpaceTech wouldn't allow it, especially if anything valuable was in the containers.

I forced my shoulders back and my chin high, and looked up at the stacks. The squat, round tubs towered easily twenty floors above me, ending in a black abyss overhead. Bots zoomed in and out between them at various heights, scanning barcodes on the sides and moving containers through the air to different spots. I wasn't sure what was happening exactly with the bots or the containers, but I was here and on time, and there was no one in sight.

Getting in trouble for being late wasn't on my agenda. Not on my first day. "Hello?" I called out. "Anyone here?"

One of the bots zoomed down to hover in front of my face. Four spindly arms—two on each side—stuck out from a chrome, basketball-like body. A red light blinked at me as the camera honed in.

"Name." The disembodied voice came from the bot.

"Maité Martinez." My skin started to warm, and I took a long, deep breath to stop the glow before it took root.

What the hell was that? Why had saying my name set off my emotions so much that the glow started? It didn't make sense. It'd been mine for a long time, but something in me had changed. It felt like a lie, one I didn't want to tell anymore.

"One moment, please. The appropriate parties are being contacted." The bot stayed hovering a foot in front of my face, watching me.

I wanted to hit it. Smash it into the ground. I knew the bot wasn't doing anything wrong exactly, and it wasn't judging me. The bots didn't have the programming to care about that kind of thing. But the way it stared at me, with the flashing red eye and the camera inside it recording my every movement, put me on edge.

"Hey there," a voice called behind me.

A man the size of a giant came through the doors. He had to be over six feet, five inches tall with arms thicker than my head. With how fit everyone was here, I wondered if there was a gym on the base. There probably wasn't much else to do here other than work out. And if there was, I would bet that this guy lived there.

"I was running late," he said.

He wore a tank top and biker shorts a little longer than mine. I was sure my eyeballs were popping out of my head as I looked down his body—and what I could make out under his shorts—and quickly looked back at his face. His outfit seemed even more revealing than mine, and he didn't seem to care.

I wished I could feel as confident as he did.

Sweat coated the giant man's body, making it look like he'd just stepped out of the shower. He reached out a hand, and I took it. He held my hand in a loose, gentle grip. From the size of him, I knew he could've crushed my hand, but he'd chosen to be gentle. That told me that he was kind and probably not one of SpaceTech's lackeys. Which made me think that this might not be so bad.

"I'm Maité Martinez." I stepped back, dropping his hand. "I'm not sure if I'm in exactly the right spot, but this is where the map said."

"Tyler Higgins. You're right where you need to be, honey." He winked, his blue eyes sparkling. "You're prettier than a doll."

"Uh…" I wasn't sure what to say back to that. So far he'd been nice and seemed pretty sweet—which I wasn't expecting, especially from someone his size. But was he hitting on me?

"Matthew dropped off your suit. I put it in a locker for you. You're going to want to take those clothes off though."

All my muscles tensed. I'd been wrong about Tyler. "Excuse me?" Who the hell did he think he was?

He held up his hands. "I ain't gettin' fresh. Even if I *am* open to it."

"What's your—"

"Just let me finish." His arms looked even thicker as he crossed them and stared down at me.

I should've felt more intimidated, but something about him didn't seem creepy, despite what he'd said. "You don't want to be wearing anything under your suit because it's hotter than a witch's tit in church out there, even with the cooling system. Can't expect it to work a miracle against the heat of the surface. You're going to want that cold AC on your bare skin. Best if you strip before you put it on. You can store your clothes in the locker. No one's going to mess with them, and don't you worry. I'll be doing the same."

I opened and closed my mouth but couldn't find the words. Tyler might have a point about the cold AC on your skin, but did he really think that I would undress in front of him? And the bots?

"You think I'm a perv." He laughed. "No. I won't be watching. You can find a place around one of these stacks if it makes you more comfortable, but I'm tellin' you. You're gonna regret your clothes 'bout five seconds after you step onto the surface."

I glanced down at my shorts and tank. They were moisture-wicking, thin, and skintight. I figured on or off wouldn't make much of a difference. But since I was new here, I was open to suggestions. "Maybe I'll—" A bot flew in behind me as another came closer from the side. I stepped to the right, and they moved with me. I moved the other way, and they moved again.

There wasn't an inch of privacy in this cargo bay. Jason wasn't going to allow that. Not when there was a free show to be had.

I looked directly at the bot in front of me and scratched my nose with my middle finger. "You know what, I'm from the desert. I'll be fine."

"Your funeral. This way." He motioned for me to follow him. "I'm going out there with you for part of today. Show you where stuff's at. We'll come back to refuel and cool off. Then it's gonna be on you. My duty is in here. I usually only go out to the surface in an emergency or when one of the bots needs tending, but you're replacing them now. Beats me why they've done this to you, but it ain't none of my business. I'm doing my time here just like the rest of the assholes." He laughed, but I wasn't sure what part of that was meant to be funny.

I tried for a grin, but it was pathetic at best, and I gave up.

"Don't be nervous. Most folks here ain't ever been out there.

The suit will hold you. Just find me when you clock in every day. Find me on your way out. This job ain't hard, just brutal as all hell."

I snorted.

"What?"

"Just you called it hell."

He gave me an earnest look. "It is. I'm tellin' you. Ain't fun out there."

"But the planet is literally called hell."

"It sure is."

I gave him some side eye. I still couldn't tell if he knew that Abaddon literally meant Hell or not.

A bay door at least six stories tall and half as wide took up almost the entire wall. From there I could see the top of the cargo bay, maybe fifteen or so stories up. To the side of the bay door was a much smaller one—about the size of an ordinary elevator. It was hotter on this side of the bay, but it wasn't oppressive. Either I was getting used to the heat or the walls weren't just metal like they seemed. They must've had some sort of insulation system.

A little keypad and two red and green buttons took up the tiny space between the smaller and bigger door, but they didn't seem very high tech. Both red buttons were flashing.

"Why are they flashing?" I pointed to it. "What does it mean?"

He glanced at it. "Ah. Simple's better. When people are panicked, they ain't gonna remember a code. Red button closes the door. Green opens it. Flashing means that's what it's stuck on—closed. We don't like to leave the green button pressed for longer than it takes to open the small door to the cooling chamber. Bots'll come as soon as it's open. They keep a watch on things and make sure a certain temp's maintained in here, but it doesn't matter much. Those lucole crystals can handle anything. Well, most anything. But it'll take a week for the room to cool if the big door opens for longer than a few seconds, which makes it unpleasant for me." He shrugged. "Beyond the smaller door is a cooling chamber. We'll go through it when we exit."

I turned around, staring back at the expanse of the room. The bots were back there, some watching us, but most keeping an eye on the room in general. I tilted my head to see a bit farther down the line of containers but could only see a few rows. Still, I just walked through the bay from one end to the other. This place was massive. I couldn't believe...

"I'm sorry, but you said lucole?" There had to be hundreds of thousands of the round three-foot tall bins. "You can't mean *all* of these are filled with lucole."

"They sure are."

That couldn't be true. Even with all of SpaceTech's greed for more, they didn't need that much fuel. "But some of them are food or supplies or replacement parts for bots, right?"

"No, ma'am." His eyebrows drew down. "Only lucole. That's what we do here." He considered me for a moment. "This is the main hold for the mining facility. Bay Four has some medical supplies, a good amount of food, various other necessary things, plus a bit of lucole. We usually ship out fuel to the colonies little bits at a time on Tuesdays and Thursdays. But about three weeks ago, they shut down processing and started clearing out the bays. Lotta ships coming and going these days. Bay Five was finally emptied last week, and half of Bay Six has gone, too, but Bays Two, Three, and Seven are the same as this."

I knew that it was a mining facility, but knowing it and seeing how much they were actually stockpiling were two different things. "But why do they need so much?" And why did they stop processing it? Why were they shipping so much out? I wanted to ask but didn't want to start piling on too many questions at once.

"SpaceTech guys keep saying war's coming, so we're stocking up. We gotta be prepared for it or those Aunare will kick our butts. Their tech is more advanced, but we'll make up for it in firepower. So, even if it is a bit difficult, this work we do here, it's important. Could be all that stands between survival of the human race and its total annihilation."

Stocking up? This wasn't just stocking up. This was hoarding weapons for a massive assault. You only needed a lump the size of my palm to power a ship the size of a small city for a month of solid use. Including weeks of cryo travel. I didn't even think SpaceTech had enough ships and cities and planets to use this much fuel in several lifetimes. Especially if there were three other cargo bays with at least as much stored in them. Which meant that most of the lucole had to be for weapons.

Firepower. A whole fuckload of firepower. Enough to decimate the Aunare and their allies.

Suddenly, the containers towering overhead felt a lot more ominous.

I'd been wrong. I'd been worried about the coming war. That the Aunare would come and slaughter all the Earthers. That the shape of the galaxy would change. But with this much lucole, SpaceTech could own the universe.

It wasn't the humans that were in danger of annihilation. It was the Aunare.

Did the Aunare know that SpaceTech was preparing for this kind of assault? Because if not, someone should probably tell them. Someone should stop them. It couldn't be a coincidence that they'd stopped processing and started shipping out lucole after I was captured.

I didn't have access to the outside, but Ahiga did. If he could get in touch with Declan—

Ice it all to hell. Declan was in cryo sleep.

I had to do something, but I didn't know what. Aside from blowing up the whole base, myself included.

CHAPTER NINETEEN

"AVERT YOUR EYES IF YOU LIKE," Tyler said.

I blinked my eyes as I tried to focus on what was in front of me. Tyler was shoving his tight shorts down his hips.

I slapped a hand over my eyes.

I'd been so preoccupied with the door and the containers that filled the cargo bay that I didn't even notice the lockers standing to the side of the doors. I hadn't even noticed Tyler grabbing his suit.

"Sorry." Tyler's bare ass was definitely not something I expected to see on the job.

"Don't need to worry. I ain't shy."

"That's okay," I said, my voice a little too high. "Should I put on my suit, too?"

"Only if you want to live more than thirty seconds out there. Locker five. Go ahead and grab it."

Right. I kept my hand blocking my view of Tyler as I walked to the locker. I peeked through my fingers to find number five. The suit fell on top of me as soon as I opened the door, and I let it drop to the ground. I turned my back to Tyler to give him privacy. "How hot is it exactly?" Knowing wouldn't help me, but I liked to be prepared.

"Eh. Depends on where you are and how hot the lava is. Some places, only like 260 to 315 degrees. Others, you're looking at three times that or more."

"Degrees? You're talking Fahrenheit?"

"Shit, no. Celsius."

Holy mother. That had to be like 500 or 600 in Fahrenheit.

I glanced down at my feet. The suit seemed good and all, but more protection between me and the lava sounded better. The shoes were just canvas with a thin foam and rubber sole, but better than nothing. "Can I leave my shoes on?"

"I didn't leave anything on, but seems like you're doing it different than me."

Right. Okay. I left the shoes on and shoved my feet into the suit, which took some doing with the shoes, but I wasn't abandoning my plan. Tyler might prefer to be naked even on a normal, not-going-to-step-on-the-surface-of-a-lava-planet kind of a day. But I wasn't comfortable undressing. Not here. Not now. Not ever. I glanced back at the bots hovering behind us. And not in front of SpaceTech's eyes.

I stepped into the suit and jammed my arms in it to wrench the rest over my shoulders. The suit was much heavier than I realized. I stood there for a minute, trying to do up the front of the suit before giving up. I was going to need Tyler's help. There were three layers of closures—zipper on the bottom layer, and then a series of snaps in the middle, and a seal with a button on the outer-most layer.

Tyler was nice enough to walk me through how to get every-thing secured correctly, which was nearly impossible with the thick gloves. I could barely get my fingers to move, let alone have enough dexterity for the complicated clasps.

By the time it was done, I was exhausted, already sweating, and I didn't even have the helmet on yet. "That was a pain in the ass."

"Why do you think I avoid going out there at all costs?" he asked with a grin.

"The danger?"

"That, too, but the suit is a bitch. Does a good job of protecting you though, and that's all that matters out there."

I really hoped he was right. My stomach was in knots, and I had to get a handle on my nerves. Upchucking that nasty sausage in the suit wasn't going to help anything. I took a step toward him, and it was like my feet were encased in cement, but I took Tyler's word for it. As long as the suit protected me, I wasn't going to complain. Much.

He grabbed something from a hook by the door and turned back to me. "This is what you're spraying out there." It was a belt with a two-liter canister attached and a little handheld nozzle with a trigger. "It's compressed in there, so it's a little heavier than it looks, but should last 'til your break."

Attaching the canister to my waist with the gloves on took me a few tries, but I got it on and gave him a nod. "What's next?" I wanted to get this over with. The longer it took, the sweatier I was getting. Lying to myself that it was just the heat and not nerves wasn't quite cutting it anymore. Soon I'd be out there, risking my life for nothing. Absolutely nothing.

I was trying hard not to let it get to me, but I couldn't stop the anger from rising again and again until I was clenching my teeth hard enough to crack them.

"There are a few buttons on your right wrist. One for AC—on the right. One for the helmet—in the middle. The other button is for your water. Hold it down, and a tube will come out. When you let go, it retracts. But you'll want to use that sparingly. The suit doesn't hold much. They weren't exactly designed to be out there as long as you'll be."

"What?" The scream ripped from me. "What do you mean they're not designed to be out there for long?" My chest constricted and my breath came out in short gasps. I was keeping a handle on the glow even with the anger, but barely. I thought Ahiga approved the suit.

Tyler held up his hands. "Hold on. That didn't come out like I meant. Keep in mind they're made to last longer than their suggested usage. I've just never been out there longer than a few minutes, but you should be fine. They wouldn't assign this job if it wasn't safe."

I wanted to laugh and cry and shout and scream and blow this place up because that was *exactly* why I'd been assigned the stupid job.

I wanted to tell Tyler that but couldn't. I kept my jaw clenched tight, and tried to tell myself that I wasn't walking out there to burn to death but I couldn't do that either.

I'm a di Aetes. I won't quit. Not ever.

That was the mantra that had gotten me through years of running, living on the streets, stealing food, and finally—when we got to Albuquerque—through the stress of years of hiding. It was the same determination and fight that would get me through this stupid job until Declan got here.

I jammed my finger on the middle button, and the helmet came up with a snap. A few displays lit up on the inside of my visor. First was the time, center of the helmet, just above my eye line. The temperature both outside and inside the suit showed on the bottom left, and power and oxygen levels were on the bottom right. Currently, I was at 96 degrees Fahrenheit in my suit and 100 percent for power and O_2.

"You hear me okay?" Tyler's voice came through the helmet.

"Yeah."

"Good. Cams are in the suit, recording everything. SpaceTech likes to keep a record. And when you're out there on your own, I'll be able to check in with you. See your video feed."

In other words, Jason was going to be watching me out there. Perfect. Just perfect.

"Now go ahead and start up the AC. You'll want to give it a head start before we go on out there."

"Sure thing." I hit the one on the right, and freezing air started circulating around my body. It took less than ten seconds for my teeth to start chattering. The temperature readout disappeared for a second and came back as 36 degrees Fahrenheit. "Shit. It's fucking cold." I started shivering and thought about turning the AC off.

"Won't be that way for long. If you're ready, I'm hitting the red button."

I'd never be ready for this, I tried to give him a thumbs-up anyway, but it was a little tricky with the thickness of the gloves and how much I was shaking from the cold.

"Let's get started." He hit the green button, and an alarm blared. The bots came forward, spewing cooling mist around the opening door.

Tyler waved me into the cooling chamber. It was no more than three feet deep. As soon as the door shut behind me, the one in front of me slowly opened. With each inch, it got hotter. Slowly, my teeth stopped chattering. By the time it was open enough for us to walk through, I was already sweating.

A cage elevator hung in front of us, waiting to let us down, but I wasn't too eager to jump in. Tyler gave me a shove, pushing me into it. "Don't want the bay to overheat. Cooling chamber can only do so much for so long." The doors slammed shut behind us, blocking my exit.

"Wow." I couldn't help but be awed by the sight in front of me —so different from anything I'd seen before.

"You'll get used to it. Kinda pretty, right? In a deadly sort of way." Tyler hit the down button, and the metal groaned as it lowered us slowly to the crusted over lava. We were at least fifty meters above the surface.

If I didn't have to go out there, I might've agreed with Tyler about it being pretty. I'd been a little bummed out when I first got here that I didn't get to see the planet, but now I wanted to run back inside. This wasn't a place meant for humans or Aunare or anything alive.

A heavy coating of ash in the air blocked out the light from the two stars in the center of the Abaddon system, which meant the planet was as dark as night, but the lave lit it well enough for me to see off in the distance. I could make out a series of volcanos on the horizon, spewing bright orange, yellow, and red streams into the air and flowing down their sides.

The active lava flow stopped about a quarter of a mile from the base, forming a hard black crust. The base was like an island on a sea of lava. Around the edges, the red-orange ocean pressed against the black, pushing it up from underneath.

I turned back toward the base. Massive round pylons held up the building. I couldn't see what was doing it, but there had to be some serious cooling in the space between the surface and the bottom of the base. Maybe there were cooling mechanisms inside the pylons?

Judging from how far up the base was from the surface—at least a good thirty meters—I figured there was plenty of room underneath in case some of that lava managed to break free of the blackened area, but I wasn't sure how much flow the base could withstand if that happened. And what happened if a volcano formed underneath the base? How far below the surface did they drill the pylons?

I had a lot of questions, but I honestly didn't really care about them. I just wanted to stay alive until I could escape this planet. It wasn't my job to worry about the safety of the whole base. My only job was to survive.

It was silly for me to even worry about the stability of the base for a second. SpaceTech was a lot of things, but they weren't stupid. Not when it came to money and profit margins. I was sure they were confident that the base was going to be fine.

I turned back to see the volcanoes. There were at least twenty small, nine medium, a handful of large, and two massive ones that I could see.

SpaceTech couldn't control this much nature. The fact that SpaceTech thought they could maintain a base here long-term was the height of arrogance. How very like them. I just hoped I was far away when the lava tore this place apart.

I glanced through the grating under my feet. My mouth went

dry as I watched the surface grow closer. My breath sounded harsh and ragged, echoing inside the helmet, as Tyler's words came back to me. About how the suit wasn't built for prolonged exposure.

He was right. There was no way they could be.

This suit wasn't going to be enough. I gripped the railing of the elevator to keep from turning around. From pressing the button to take me back up. Because I didn't have a choice but to keep moving forward.

So I'd keep moving forward. One step at a time.

"You're going to be fine." Tyler's voice sounded inside my helmet.

Maybe. But maybe not.

Six in. Three out. Three in. Six out. Four in.

The cage shook as it jerked to a stop, and with the weight of the suit, I nearly lost my footing, but Tyler held me steady for a second before stepping out onto the surface.

When I didn't move, he yelled back at me, "Come on, girl. No time for dillydallying. Let's get this done and back in the bay quick as we can."

I'd done some stupid things in my life, but this was definitely going to go down as the most iced thing I'd done. It wasn't like it was by choice though. So that was something.

I gave myself one more moment to count my breaths before swallowing down my nerves and stepping into the inferno.

CHAPTER TWENTY

"OVER HERE!" Tyler's voice shouted at me through the helmet's com.

We'd been at it for what felt like ten hours, but I knew from the readout on the inside of my helmet it had only been an excruciating hour, forty-two minutes, and fifty-three seconds. The temp inside my suit had slowly risen to 125 degrees Fahrenheit, and I wouldn't be surprised if my blood were close to boiling at this point.

I was used to heat, but not like this. The helmet made me feel like I was suffocating. It was a miracle of technology that the glass —or whatever it was made out of—hadn't fogged. My breath was hot against my face, and I wanted out of this suit. Off this planet. I wanted to be anywhere but here.

A blast of yellowish-white steam hit my legs, and I looked down. The black crust had started to crack. "Shit!"

"Damn it, girl! You gotta watch where your feet are!"

I stepped slowly back—so as not to crack it more—and aimed my hose where the sulfur plume was shooting from the ground. The foaming chemical concoction was cold enough to turn a human into a Popsicle in five seconds, but it barely made a dent in the heat that was coming up from the ground.

After five minutes, the crust re-formed. The chemicals left a clear film over the patched spot.

I sprayed the surrounding area, and then looked back to the bay. My heart dropped into my toes. We'd only made it about fifty yards from the elevator.

How was that even possible?

The idea that I was supposed to hose down and somehow stabilize the whole area around the base was not only absurd, idiotic, and dangerous, it was hopeless.

Jason Murtagh had given me his version of a Sisyphean task, and the longer I was out here, the more I wondered what his end game was. Why this particular job? What was he trying to accomplish? If he wanted me dead, there were much quicker and easier ways.

But maybe that was the point. A slow, painful, boiling end to my existence.

Suddenly, it wasn't just the suit making me hot. I'd find a way to end Jason Murtagh if it was—

"You gotta keep moving. Remember what I said." Tyler's sharp tone cut through my rising anger. "Walk slow. Spray as you go. This whole area you see has been stabilized by the ice bots, and it needs to stay that way. The pylons cool the area under the base. That area is off limits. Lots of tech doing its thing underneath it, even if it doesn't look too impressive from here, but we have to do it along the perimeter of the base if we want to keep everyone safe. Lava's tricky. It'll find a way to take down the whole area if we give it any room. Your job is not to give it that room. We can't lose the base."

I almost laughed. Unlike SpaceTech's most beloved base, my life was expendable. The ground had opened under my feet six times in less than two hours. "I'll do my best, but bots would be able to cover all the ground in no time. If I was working in twenty-four hour shifts, I might be able to do a full lap around the entire bottom of the base, but that isn't as far out as you said the base needs. And I can't work every day, all day. I won't even make a dent in this."

Tyler's sigh hissed through the tiny speaker in my helmet. "You're right. I don't know why they decommissioned the bots. It's just plain bullshit."

I agreed with him. This was bullshit. "SpaceTech has a long-standing history of doing completely horrible things to all kinds of people and species."

Tyler turned slowly to me, and I wondered if I'd said too much.

"Yes. Yes, they have." Tyler's eyes met mine, and even through the glass of the helmet, I could feel the intensity of his stare, but I didn't know him well enough to know what it meant.

Sweat trickled down my forehead, and I itched to wipe my face but couldn't. Not in the suit. The salty drops stung my eyes, and I tried to blink them away.

"Ten more minutes, and then we get a break."

"Okay." I needed that break. I wasn't even sure I'd last the ten minutes. I had to get out of this suit, even if for only a second. I needed to be able to breathe. And if I wasn't mistaken, it smelled as if my hair was frying in here.

I took a breath, aiming my hose in another direction, counting down the minutes to the break. My breathing technique kept me calm and steady despite my growing anger and unease.

"You want to make sure you keep moving. Maximize the power of the 320zpd."

"Right." The more I moved the liquid around, the less the ground would open up under me. Or that was Tyler's theory. I was doing my best, but it didn't seem to make a difference. Nothing we were doing out here made any difference. Something was off about this whole job.

If the base was really that endangered by this lava, then there would either have to be more than just me out here or I'd have to be scheduled for twenty-four/seven. But neither was happening. There was no way that Jason was going to risk the whole stability of the base just so he could torture me. It didn't make sense.

Which meant that not only was it bullshit that the bots weren't working, it was bullshit that this job was even a thing. I would bet my life that they didn't even need the bots in the first place. That the bots were there to make some risk assessor happy. The base could probably withstand being surrounded by waves of lava.

So I was back to the original question: Why did Jason want me doing this particular job?

I was hot, but on the whole okay out here. Sure, the ground had cracked under my feet, but as long as I stayed aware, I should be okay. It was miserable—I'd give him points for that—but I was mostly safe.

I mimicked Tyler's waving movement with the hose even though the whole process was an exercise in idiocy. I was feeling more bitter by the second, and it didn't help my mood that I was fading in this heat. Fast. Each movement was taking more and more effort.

I tapped a button on my arm, and the water spout came out. The water was warm and tasted like metal, but I didn't care. I was melting in this suit.

By the time the alarm on my suit sounded, signaling our break, I was about ready to drop. We moved carefully back toward the base, icing as we walked. The gray concrete and metal structure reminded me of everything else SpaceTech did—soulless. It towered aboveground, held by countless pylons that disappeared under the black crust of the hardened lava. The base was made up of a central rectangular building with four other rectangular build-ings connected to it by a ring that contained the central corridor. The cargo bay I'd exited was in one rectangle, along with two other bays. The women's quarters and mess were in the central building, along with a whole lot of other things, including the massive hangar.

The base was much bigger than I'd thought, but it didn't make any sense to me. Why waste time and energy to stabilize those corridors? Why not have everything in one building? But then, I wasn't an architect. If I'd built it, I would've put in some windows, but I'd bet money that SpaceTech thought windows were a luxury that could melt in the heat without expensive treatments.

The elevator clanged as we finally reached the cargo bay. We stepped into the cooling chamber, and our suits were coated with cooling mist. The alarm was blaring loud enough to hear even over the hiss of the spray.

When the door finally opened to the cargo bay, the bots were going crazy, spraying their cooling mist into the air around the door. The alarm finally shut off when the doors slammed shut.

Thank God. I pressed the button on my suit to retract my helmet as I collapsed on the ground.

"Shit," Tyler said. "Your face is redder than a tomato, but your suit held or else we would've gotten a warning."

"No warning. All good." I lay back against the lockers. I thought the room was warm before, but now it felt pleasantly cool. My cheek rested against the metal, and I closed my eyes. "This is nice."

There was a bunch of rustling, and I figured Tyler was probably changing out of his suit.

"Here, honey." I opened my eyes to find Tyler squatting in front of me, wearing a looser pair of shorts and nothing else.

I was envious. I wanted out of the suit so badly.

Tyler waved a tube of water in front of my face. "You need to drink all of this before you go back out there."

I tried to sit up to take the water, but the suit made my movements clumsy. It took me a couple tries to grab the tube, but Tyler just stayed there, patiently waiting for me to get the hang of it. The sad smile on his face made me a little uncomfortable. I didn't want anyone's pity.

I broke eye contact and downed half of it in one gulp. "How much longer is my shift?" I asked before taking another gulp.

"You've got two more two-hour sessions out there."

I coughed, choking on the water, and Tyler gave me a couple of hard swats to my back.

"That can't be right, can it?" My voice was raspy. "The heat wiped me out. I won't last that long."

"I hear you. My butt's draggin' already, and I'm damned thankful not to be going out again today."

I didn't have time to respond before he kept on talking.

"And for the record, none of this is right. Regulation says a max of two hours per day on the surface for no more than four days a week."

I wasn't sure whether to laugh or cry. "How many days am I working? Six?"

"Yes. Six. The only reason your shift isn't longer is that it wasn't approved. I saw the order. Higher-ups are working you to death on purpose. I don't know what you did to get sent here, but that ain't right."

"No. It isn't." I tried to be shocked, but I wasn't. Not really.

I drained the tube and then took another from Tyler. I dumped it over my head, and he laughed.

"Now you know why I like to be naked and freshly showered before I put on one of those suits."

"I thought you were just sweaty."

"Maybe now. But before, that was water. Not sweat." Tyler stood up and grabbed something from a locker, tossing it to me. My arms were too tired to catch it, and the packet slammed into my face.

"Oh man. I'm sorry!"

The horrified look on his face made me laugh. "No big. What is it?"

"Concentrated electrolyte packet. You've got as many as you want down here. I made sure of it."

That was nice of him. "Thanks." I ripped open the packet and swallowed down the sickly sweet grape flavored gel. It wasn't as bad as breakfast, but still a little too slimy to be pleasant.

"You do your job, and I'll do my best to keep you alive. Just don't hit a hornet's nest with a short stick while you're out there, okay?"

Hornet's nest? There weren't any hornets out there... Oh, he meant that I shouldn't do anything stupid. It was taking me a second to pick up Tyler's way of speaking, but I was slowly getting it.

I met his bright blue gaze. "I'll do my best."

"Good. I don't love goin' out there. So I'm hopeful the water and electrolytes will keep you going during your shifts." He grinned. "And now that I've seen you, I'm hoping eventually my keeping you alive will lead to me getting laid."

This time I wasn't offended. Tyler had been easygoing out there. His little digs and Southern-sounding sayings kept me moving when all I'd wanted to do was throw down the stupid hose and give up.

"Keep trying," I joked back at him. "Maybe you'll get some-where in the next decade."

"Shit. I knew my luck wasn't that good. I'm out of here in two months." He came back to squat in front of me. He took my wrist in his hand and scanned through my vitals readout on the suit.

I studied his face as he checked on me. The guy was sweet and charming. He seemed too good for this place. "How long have you been here?"

"Couple years. It's not so bad once you get used to it."

"What'd you do?" It was rude to ask, but he was nice. I wasn't getting the murderer-rapist vibe from him at all.

He raised an eyebrow. "Now that's a story that needs a beer to go with it."

"There's beer here?" I didn't drink often, and I'd only been seri-ously drunk once, but I wasn't opposed to it. Especially if it helped get me through my time on Abaddon.

"Nah. On the mining side and for officers, sure. But not for us workers."

"Figures." That would've been too good.

He rechecked my readings, then dropped my wrist. "Vitals are normalizing. Color's getting less tomatoish. How're you feeling?"

I groaned. "Like I don't want to go back out there." I really, seriously wasn't looking forward to it at all.

"It'll get easier I'm sure."

He might be sure, but I wasn't. Not even a little bit.

He patted me on my shoulder. "Ready?"

"Nope." But I took the hand he offered me anyway.

"Tyler!" A man wove through the maze of containers to stand in front of us.

He wore the traditional SpaceTech formal uniform, with the pants and dress shirt despite the heat, but what caught my eye were the gleaming medals—the two silver stars marking him high up in the SpaceTech command—and the way his eyes narrowed with disgust as he stared me down. I had a feeling it had nothing to do with how sweaty I was.

"Yes, sir."

"Status report."

Tyler lumbered over to the comp next to the door controls. "Bays Two, Three, and Seven are at capacity. I just shipped out ten megatons to STB-5612 out this bay, so I've got a bit more room here. Mining has slowed considerably, so we should be good for the next few months unless miners start pouring in again."

"Good. Good." He placed his hands on his hips as he surveyed the room. "I want you to get three tons up to the lab in the next hour. I don't want any delays like last time. Matthew will be here for the transfer, and he doesn't have time to wait around for you."

"Yes, sir," Tyler said. "I'll get it done."

I wanted to hit this SpaceDouche, whoever he was. I hadn't known Tyler for long, but he was a nice guy. He didn't deserve to be condescended to.

"The rest of six will be shipped out in the next two days, so you need to head over there once you get the lucole transfer ready for the labs."

Tyler did a side-glance at me. "Sir? I'm supposed to be supervising—"

"Oh, she's irrelevant. She won't survive the week." He gave me a grin that—even as tired as I was—made me want to step up and smash his face.

He sounded so certain, so confident that I'd be dead soon, that I wanted to beat his cat-ate-the-canary look off of his face.

Punching him would be even stupider than hitting Jason Murtagh, but I really, *really* wanted to.

"You get the lucole ready for the lab. Nothing is more important than that. Especially not her." After a satisfied chuckle as he studied my face, he turned on his heel and marched out of the bay.

My arms shook with the force it took to hold myself back from taking him to the ground. He had to be one of Jason's cronies since he was pleased with how exhausted I was, which gave me the strength to start walking toward the bay doors. "Who was that?"

"General Ystak." He winced. "It'd be best if you forgot everything you heard."

"Sure." I hadn't heard much, except that there was a large amount of lucole headed for a lab.

I wasn't sure why they'd need three tons though. My only thought was for some sort of weapon, but I had war on my brain. Maybe they were testing out a new refinement process to fuel a colony? Or maybe they were using it to test out a new way to travel faster through the galaxy?

But my mind kept going back to war.

Something was going on here. SpaceTech shipped out an entire bay and a half of lucole last week, and now they're shipping out another half of a bay?

Maybe this had nothing to do with the fact that I was here, but what if the two were connected?

I needed to talk to Ahiga, but I couldn't do anything about that right now. The alarm on my suit rang.

"Time for you to get back out there," Tyler said. "I'd go with you, but I got shit to do here." He rubbed a hand down his face.

He'd been all smiles, but the general seemed to have drained all the fun-loving energy out of Tyler with his orders. "You need me, and I'll be out there in a flash. I can get there easy enough from any of the bays, okay? No dying."

Dying wasn't on my to-do list today, no matter what that General SpaceDouche thought. "Okay." I could do this. Really. It wasn't so bad. Just a little hotter than I was used to.

I hit the button on my suit, and the helmet came up. The cold air whirled around my body, and I closed my eyes, relishing the feel of it.

My days would be measured in two-hour chunks. I could do anything for two hours.

I slammed my hand down on the green button. The alarm sounded, and bots buzzed around me, spraying cool mist into the air as I stepped into the cooling chamber.

CHAPTER TWENTY-ONE

HOW I MANAGED to get through my first shift, I wasn't sure. If there hadn't been water and energy bars in my locker on my second break, there would've been no chance of me going back out there for my third and final two-hour block. Tyler had been busy with getting the shipment ready for General SpaceDouche, so I hadn't seen him. But I'd eaten what he'd left out for me, and as soon as the alarm sounded for the end of my break, I'd closed my helmet and gone back out there.

I figured it was mostly pure di Aetes stubbornness that pushed me through the day. Every time I felt like I was going to pass out from the heat, I pictured Jason Murtagh's face. I couldn't—wouldn't—let him get the best of me.

The last alarm sounded, signaling the end of my first day and I almost cried with gratitude. My whole body felt like it was burned. Was it possible to get a sunburn in this thing? I wasn't sure, but my skin felt hot and tender. My internal temp had just started spiking. It was hitting 130, and it felt like the heat was coming from my feet.

Was that sulfur I smelled? No. It couldn't be, because if it was, then that meant my suit had been compromised, and there hadn't been any alarms.

I clenched my jaw as I rushed back to the bay door. I was only a few feet from the elevator, but each step sent a wave of pain up my legs.

I was used to more pain than most Earthers. Nanos were a no-no for Aunare, so growing up I'd had to make do with some archaic medical treatments. Pain had been something that I learned to deal with through breathing and visualization techniques. That was why I picked up so easily on the Aunare breathing technique that Declan had taught me. I usually was able to picture the pain flowing away from any place that felt sore, and with every breath I'd release the pain out of my body. But not today. The pain was stealing my breath, and I couldn't focus enough to visualize on anything but getting out of the heat and finally taking off this suit.

Inside. I needed to be inside. Now.

The blast coolant hit me as I entered the cooldown chamber of the bay doors, and the suit's temperature started dropping instantly, but it was going to take more than that to get my internal temperature down. The small doors opened into the cargo bay, and I hobbled through them as best I could.

"How're you holding up?" Tyler said as soon as the door shut.

I opened my helmet. The cooler air inside the bay felt like a balm against my skin, but it wasn't enough to ease the burning heat on the bottom of my feet. "I—" I fell over with a scream, unable to hold it in anymore.

"Holy hell. What the fuck happened to your suit? I didn't hear any alerts. Did you turn them off? Did you *ignore* them?!"

"No. I didn't get any alerts." A tear rolled down my cheek. I must've looked as bad as I felt. "My feet. When I was maybe thirty seconds from hitting the elevator, something happened. My temp went up and—" My voice cracked. I'd been gritting it out to get inside, but now that I was here, I couldn't hold it together. "Burned. I'm *burning*!"

"Oh shit. Oh *shit*."

He rushed toward me, picking me up, and little starbursts appeared in my vision.

"Don't worry. I'm not gettin' any ideas," Tyler said as he darted around the stacks with me in his arms.

I laughed, but tears were rolling down my face. It felt like blisters were coating the bottoms of my feet, and as much as I wanted the stupid suit off, I was scared to take off the boots, let alone my shoes.

"Where are we going?"

"Med Unit. Faster for me to carry you than wait for an assessment in the bay and have them haul you there. It's close. Hang on."

I wasn't sure I could hang on, but he hustled me through a few hallways and into another room.

He wasn't lying. It was close.

I was trying to keep from crying, but I was hurting and scared and I wasn't sure what I was going to do. I was Aunare. I couldn't do nanos. But I was in so much pain that I knew I needed a miracle.

A desk stood in the center of the room. Waiting chairs pressed against the walls. But it was empty of any people.

"Medic!" Tyler yelled.

A woman hustled out of a back room. "What's going on?" She wore navy scrubs—loose fitting pants and a wrapped top. Her red hair was tied in a tight knot at the base of her neck.

"Thank God, Audrey. Something happened with her suit while she was out there."

"Come on. This way." She spun on her heel, rushing down a short hallway to a door with the large gray number four painted on it. The room had cabinets built into one of the walls. On the opposite wall was an exam table. A third wall was a glass screen.

Audrey took a scan of my tracker and linked it to her computer, giving her a readout of my stats.

"Temperature is dangerously high. Set her down." As soon as

Tyler did, she gasped. "Oh shit." She pointed to my feet. "Ty. Look."

"I know. I saw."

I tried to sit up, but my vision spun. "What? What did you see?" I still had my suit on, so she couldn't see my feet. But something had freaked her out.

"It's worse than I thought," Tyler said as he inspected the soles of my boots. "Why didn't you say anything? Why didn't you just come in?"

"It wouldn't have done any good. I was right there when it happened, and I just had to keep moving or I knew I'd burn alive." I shook my head. "What's wrong with my feet?" The pain was getting worse, and terror made my stomach roll. If I'd had anything in it, I would've already thrown up. It was all I could do to breathe, but I needed answers. I had to know what was wrong.

He pressed his lips together. "The bottom of your boots have melted. Didn't your suit warn you?"

"No." I swallowed. "My suit didn't say anything about it melting."

"Didn't you feel the heat?"

Was he kidding? "It's hot as fuck out there. Of course I felt it." A tear rolled out as I snapped at him.

"Stop it, Ty. She's in pain." Audrey put a hand on my shoulder. "We'll fix this, honey. Hang tight. You just keep on breathing for me. Okay?"

"Okay." My heart was racing so hard, and my ears were ringing, but I was hanging on to consciousness. That was all I could do.

Audrey gave me a nod and hustled off.

"I'm so sorry, Maité." Tyler whispered the words. "The suits... They're only meant for a few hours at most. I didn't even think... We should've traded out suits, but Matt only gave you the one, and with your shoes, you might not have felt the boots being compromised until it was too late, but I don't understand why the suit's internal system didn't warn you long before this happened."

I knew. I *knew* why.

My suit didn't warn me because Jason didn't want it to. He wanted me in pain. He wanted me to suffer. He was punishing me. For hitting him. For being a halfer. For being Amihanna di Aetes. For whatever reason his evil, shitty, microscopic brain could come up with.

I closed my eyes and started my deep breathing. I focused on the pain in my feet and tried to picture it flowing out of me, but it didn't work. Closing my eyes only made the pain worse.

My skin wasn't glowing. I didn't know why, but at least I wasn't totally giving myself away in front of strangers.

Audrey came back. "Okay. Painkillers first."

She was my savior. "Yes. Please." I barely felt the sting of the injection.

"Okay. Those should kick in five seconds."

As soon as she said it, the pain eased a bit. "Thank you. It's already helping."

She patted my arm through the suit. "Of course. This suit is trash, so I'm going to start cutting you out of it." She started with my arm and attached an IV patch as soon as my wrist was free. Cool tendrils ran up my arm as the liquid seeped through the patch and into my body.

"All right. That'll get you hydrated and cooled down. Hang tight, and I'll go grab the nanos. They'll fix you right up."

My heart skipped a beat, and suddenly I was filled with a whole new terror. "I'll be fine. I don't need any nanos."

"The company will pay for them if that's what's concerning you. They consider it part of keeping the workforce going here. It's not in their best interest to have you down, so it's free."

Nothing was free with SpaceTech—even if it got me back to work sooner—there would be a cost involved. "I can't afford for SpaceTech to hold anything else over my head." Plus, I couldn't have nanos. They'd drive me mad before I healed.

"Come on, girl," Tyler said. Concern wrinkled his brow as he squatted down next to me, bringing him down to eye level with me. "You gotta do something about those feet. You're talking about your ability to walk."

My lips tasted bloody as I licked them, trying to find some reason to explain why I didn't want nanos without giving away what I was, but nothing logical or reasonable came to me.

Stall. It's all I could think to do. "We don't even know how bad it is. Maybe they're just a little burned."

"Okay. We'll start with that." Audrey started opening drawers. "I'm sorry I didn't get to say hello this morning. I was out before you were up."

"Oh. Uh." Of course. She must live in the same bunks as I did. "Yeah. No worries. I was wiped after the travel."

"Really?" She looked back at me, and her gaze narrowed as she took a closer look at my face. "Most people have the opposite effect."

Shit. I was going to give myself away. I took a breath and held it for eight. "It'd been a crazy few days before I went into cryo sleep. Maybe it was the stress?"

She tilted her head as she watched me, considering my answer. Her gaze slid all over my face, taking in every feature. She looked down to my feet, taking in my build and height. "Maybe." The way she said it made me think she didn't believe that answer for a second.

My face looked Aunare. My thin frame was typical Aunare, but at five feet, seven inches, I was a little short to be mistaken for full-blood Aunare. That had saved me so many times, but it wasn't enough this time. Not after I'd refused nanos *and* brought up my wonky experience with cryo sleep?

This was amateur hour.

The monitors beeped as my heart rate quickened, and I needed to calm it down.

Four out. Six in. Six out.

Audrey glanced at the screen and then back to me. She held my gaze for a second, trying to tell me something but I didn't know what, and then went back to gathering her tools. "I'm Audrey, as

Tyler said. Been here for six months so far, but it's not so bad. The girls here look out for each other."

I wasn't sure that was accurate. "The woman in the mess hall didn't seem too keen on me."

Audrey snorted. "That's Della. She doesn't like anyone or doesn't seem to, but then she'll horde treats for us, so—"

"What?" Tyler cut in. "Like, what kind of treats?"

"Shut it, Ty. You get plenty."

Tyler grumbled a bit, but quietly.

"Anyway, we'll get you all healed up, and then you'll meet the rest of us tonight."

"Sounds lovely." But even on the chance that I'd be healed by then, I wasn't sure that I'd be fit for company.

Audrey stood up, putting the last of her tools on the countertop. "One sec." She slipped out of the room, coming back with a little metal rolling cart. She rolled it next to me, and I glanced down at it. A few types of laser scalpels, plus some pliers, and a vial of gray liquid.

My breath caught.

Nanos.

Shit. Shit. Just *shit*.

I couldn't let this happen. I wasn't going to let it happen. It wasn't happening. Full stop.

"Okay," she said, finally looking up at me. "So I'm going to try to cut off these boots as best I can without hurting your feet. I'll use a laser cutter, which should cover most of this, but some of the clamps on the suit which would normally release easily look melted. So I brought pliers. I'm worried about your feet. I brought the nanos, but if it's a mild burn, we'll skip. Okay?"

"She's got another pair of shoes under there," Tyler said.

She waved him off. "We'll deal with those when we get to 'em. One step at a time." She grabbed one of the scalpels and flicked it on. The blue laser extended an inch beyond the tip of the metal.

She glanced at me. "Hold still. I don't want to nick you."

"I'll do my best."

It ended up taking her an hour to get my suit off, boots and all. The soles had melted into my shoes, so we ended up cutting around them. I didn't care. I was just glad to be rid of the suit. I wanted to never, ever get into one again, but I knew what I wanted didn't matter. Not here.

I was left lying on the exam table in my tank top, shorts, and what was left of my shoes with their foam and outer soles melted together. I was exhausted, sticky with sweat, stinky, and I just wanted this to be over. To take a shower and go to sleep. To be anywhere but here.

Tyler and Audrey were muttering in the corner about how to get them off, but there was no way around it. They were going to have to come off, and some of my skin might go with it.

"Just pull them off." I was so done. Exhausted and in pain. I wanted this to be over. I wanted everything to be over.

"No," Audrey said, coming to stand beside me. "I refuse to harm a patient when it's not necessary. I'm going to cut around the canvas of the sneakers. I'll leave the soles alone until it's clear what's going on there."

The anxiety of lying there waiting to find out what the hell was wrong with my feet was starting to get to me. I needed something to happen or I was going to go out of my mind. "Honestly, whatever these drugs are, they're good. I can't feel my feet. Just do something."

"The fact that you're awake at all means that you're in a lot of pain. I took an oath, and I intend to stick to it. So—" She wheeled her chair over to my feet and sat. "Here goes."

It took another thirty minutes for her to carefully laser off the top part of one shoe, but it wasn't going to do any good.

"I can see blisters already. We have to get the shoes off, and I'm worried that when we do, your skin will come with it," Audrey said. "I'd like to give you nanos before I do that."

"How in the hell did she not feel that?" Tyler was turning a nice shade of green.

"Heat exhaustion. It can do all kinds of things. She might not have been feeling her surroundings correctly, and with how hot her core temperature was already and how hot the suit was, I'm sure she was miserable. Right?"

"Pretty much. Except on the walk back. I could feel it then, but it was too late, and I was almost inside." I glanced at Tyler, then back to her. "You were a doctor on Earth?"

She nodded. "Because of my arrest, I'm just a medic now, but I still abide by my oath. I won't go against it."

"I don't want any nanos. I don't consent." Any legitimate doctor had to listen to their patient.

"That's not advisable." She put the scalpel down on a tray table next to her. "You might not heal right. You could have a limp forever, be crippled. And for what? You could be healed in a matter of hours."

Yeah. But the nanos would torture me for days. Still, I was probably being stubborn about this. Burns were serious. A broken arm would heal. I'd been lucky with any illnesses, except that one time... But I recovered pretty quickly. Still, I'd never had something like this.

"Tyler?" Audrey said, not taking her gaze from me.

"Yeah?"

I didn't look at him. I kept my gaze on Audrey. She knew. I wasn't sure how she knew, but she knew.

"Can I have a sec with her alone?"

"Uh. Yeah. Sure." He patted my arm. "I'm going to head out. I want to check on the suit and talk to Matthew. It should have warned us there was a problem."

"Okay."

As soon as the door closed, Audrey rolled the chair so she could look me in the eyes.

I swallowed, wanting to avoid the exact conversation that Audrey was going to insist on. "He's nice."

She raised an eyebrow. "Ty?"

I nodded.

"The best." She gave a warm grin.

I wondered what exactly was between the two of them. They seemed like good friends. Their back and forth reminded me of how Roan and I talked to each other.

A tear ran down my cheek, and I slapped my hand over my mouth as a sob slipped free.

Roan. God. I missed him. So much. My chest felt like it was imploding. I needed him here with me. I couldn't do this. I couldn't breathe. I—

Audrey grabbed my arm, hard. "I need you to breathe. I need you to stay with me because I have to ask you a question, and I don't want you to freak."

Six in. Three out. Three in. Six out. I swallowed down the sobs and blinked the tears from my eyes. "Okay."

"Are you—" She mouthed "Aunare." My eyes widened, and she squeezed my hand. "Okay. I can deal with this. I'm going to give you the nanos, but I'm also going to give you a neural inhibitor, okay?"

"That will help?" I hadn't heard of that before.

"Not with everything, but it'll be manageable." She moved her hand to hold mine. "Sort of. With very few side effects."

Very few didn't mean none. "You won't tell—"

"No, and we don't allow monitoring in the rooms. Aside from the bunks and bathrooms, this is the one place you're not watched."

"Why would you help me? Why not turn me in?" She had no reason to help me out like this. If anyone in the company found out that she'd covered up for me, she'd be just as dead as me.

"Because we have to look out for each other." She gave my hand two quick squeezes. "I understand completely what's at stake for you. For both of us."

I took a second to really look at her again. Tall. She was at least a few inches taller than my five feet, seven inches. Slightly pointed chin. Eyes a little too big. The freckles and red hair threw me off. Plus, I'd never met another halfer before. And yet here—of all places—I'd found someone like me.

I wanted to believe that she had a way around the effects nanos had on Aunare, but I wasn't sure. I was in pain, and if there was a choice, I wanted to be able to walk. So I really only had one option.

"Okay." My voice shook. "Let's do it." That came out a little better, but not much.

"Thank you for trusting me." She gave me a sad smile. "You'll be okay. Promise."

I hoped she was right. Otherwise, I was up for a seriously rough night.

CHAPTER TWENTY-TWO

AUDREY LOADED the vial of nanos into the injector. She'd already given me the neural inhibitor and waited thirty minutes for it to take effect, but I didn't feel any different. I wouldn't know if it worked until it was too late.

"Ready?" Audrey held the flat head of the injector against my skin.

I stared at the gray liquid. It held tens of thousands of nanos that would rush through my body, healing me as they worked. But was I ready?

No. I wasn't ready for what I would feel if the inhibitor didn't work. The dread in my stomach felt like a swirling pit of lava.

She said I was going to be okay, but I didn't know that. I'd barely survived the nanos the first time I had them, and now I was tired and hurt, and I wasn't sure how much I had left in me.

"Maité?" Audrey asked again.

Trusting someone—especially a virtual stranger—went against the grain for me, but there was nothing else I could do.

Audrey had used a handheld MRI scope to look through the shoes. I hadn't looked at the screen—I didn't want to know what was under those shoes—but from the way her hand shook as she put down the scope, I knew my feet were basically garbage under those half-melted soles.

I had to have the nanos if I wanted to walk again.

And I wanted to walk. More than that, I wanted to fight. If I couldn't fight, I wouldn't know who I was.

I took one last calming breath and gave her a slow nod. "Do it."

Audrey pushed the button. My arm ached as a pressurized stream of nanos entered my system, and I wanted to throw up.

The problem with nanos was that they worked to repair anything in the body. Not just whatever was recently harmed. They'd keep repairing any damage to the body until they ran out of juice and processed out of the body. Sometimes that took months. I knew that from the one time I'd been injected.

I'd gotten pneumonia when I was eleven, and the antibiotics weren't working. When I started coughing up blood, my mom flipped. Jorge and Roan's mom pitched in for a single dose.

The nanos fixed my pneumonia quickly, but they'd stayed active. I spent six weeks writhing in bed before the damned things ran out of juice. My mom had to strap me down to keep me from trying to claw them out of my veins.

I would've done anything to make the constant crawling and burning under my skin to stop. I couldn't eat. I couldn't hold a glass to drink. I couldn't do anything but scream.

They'd given me an IV to keep me alive. I only slept with the help of sleeping pills, and those only worked for a few hours at a time. By the end of it, I was nearly insane. It'd taken me months to fully recover from the whole ordeal, and sometimes I still had nightmares about it.

After that, we all agreed it was never an option. Unless I was dying or severely injured, I was never using them again.

But I was severely injured now. I needed to be able to walk, and Audrey said these inhibitors would work.

Less than a minute after she injected me, the familiar burn started.

"I thought you said the inhibitor would keep me from feeling the nanos?" It felt like little fire ants were crawling through my veins, biting me as they moved through me. It wasn't unbearable, but they hadn't found my feet yet.

"You can feel them?" The alarm in her voice was almost comical.

The burning buzzing in my veins moved up my arms, down my chest, heading for my feet.

Thirty more seconds. If that. And then…

"Oh God. I can't do this."

I closed my eyes and started focusing on my breaths—not caring about counting. In and out. In and out.

"I can't do this again." My voice was a whisper, a plea, to what I didn't know. But I needed help or… "I'll go crazy."

Audrey's hand gripped mine, and I opened my eyes to see her sitting next to me. "Listen to me. I'm going to get you through it. I didn't give you many. I was *very* conservative. It'll be barely enough to heal your feet. They'll be done by the time the night is over."

"Did you lie? About the inhibitors?"

"No. The inhibitors work fine on me, but…"

"But?" I croaked out the word. They were almost to my feet. The readout on the machine started beeping, warning that my heart rate was kicking up, but there was nothing I could do. Nothing anyone could do.

"I can't do the things that a full Aunare is capable of. Is your other half strong?"

"Yes." The word came out garbled. A wave of pain rose up my legs. I screamed and jerked on the table.

No one would ever dare to call the Aetes line weak.

When I was a year old, my parents took me to Sel'Ani to have my bloodline confirmed. I was much more Aetes than I was human. My mother did her best to tell me what she knew about it, but I knew that my skin could glow, and I was faster and stronger than a human, and tech bothered the hell out of me and—

The burning started, and I gasped. The pain was stealing away my breath, and I bit my lip to stop myself from screaming, tasting the copper of my blood.

"Breathe. You have to breathe."

I sucked in air in fits and starts, but I couldn't get enough. It was like I was walking on the surface again, only this time, my bare feet were on the lava.

"You focus on the feel of my hand squeezing your hand, and you breathe."

A tear rolled down my cheek, and I nodded. I was trying—I really was—but I wasn't sure I could promise anything.

The fire ant bites had turned into blowtorch-level pain. This time I could smell my skin melting, and all I could do was scream and writhe.

Audrey shoved my shoulders into the table when I started to fall off of it.

The door opened and slammed closed, but I didn't care who'd come in. I wanted up. I wanted to be gone. I was going to cut off my own feet. Screw walking.

"What the hell is happening in here?" Tyler yelled, but I could barely hear him over my own screams.

"Help me," Audrey said. "I need to get her strapped down, but I can't hold her still enough."

A heavy weight slammed me back down, and straps shot out from the sides of the medical bed, slid into place, and secured me to the bed.

"No! No! Let me go. Let me *go!*" My skin started glowing.

"Jesus. She's one of them." Tyler started cursing, and Audrey grabbed him, pulling him into a corner.

She shoved him down into a chair. "Sit there and shut up. We'll talk about this later."

I blinked through the tears to see Tyler. He looked from Audrey to me again.

My pain was all-encompassing, but the fear was there, too. Fear of what he would do to me now that he knew what I was.

Another wave of pain hit me, and I screamed. I didn't give a shit about Tyler anymore.

This was so iced. "Make it stop! Audrey! You said this would work! You promised!"

Audrey was suddenly hovering over me, grabbing my chin hard with one hand. "You focus on me. Focus on my words. On my hand in yours." She squeezed it, but I couldn't find the energy to squeeze back. "I got you into this, and I'm not leaving your side until it's done."

I screamed as the fire turned into thousands of pinpricks coming from within my feet. Sweat rolled down my forehead, and Audrey wiped it away with a cloth.

"You focus on my voice. I can't use any drugs to knock you out yet. It'll just make this whole thing take longer. The nanos will split time between healing your feet and processing the drugs out of your body, and it won't help you. Once your feet are mostly healed, I'll put you to sleep. The *second* I can, I promise I will. You hang on until then."

I couldn't help crying. I hated it. I hated feeling weak and right now, I was weaker than I'd been in a long time. But the sob slipped free, and I couldn't help it.

If there were a hell, then I was in it.

The burning faded and then it was like needles sewing my skin. The twitches under my skin made the burning from the implant I'd had seem like child's play.

"I swear, the nanos will burn out with this job in a few hours, tops. Your feet are that bad."

"It-t's o-ok-kay." It came out half-sob.

She patted my shoulder. "Don't worry about talking. Focus on breathing. This first hour will be the worst. Then it'll get better. You ever had them before?"

I nodded, and I'd swore I'd never to have them again.

"If it was because you were sick, then they probably stuck around for a while. But they only last that long with illness, especially common illnesses. With an injury, they burn out much faster.

It's more work for them. I know I told you that you'd be fine and I was wrong, but I'm *not* wrong about this."

The nanos flared, and it felt like a thousand needles ripping into my feet.

I screamed, and she gripped my hand tighter.

"You're feeling your feet and the repair. Humans only feel the injury, and it slowly gets better. But you won't be that lucky. You get injury plus the repair plus the energy imbalance. I'm going to keep on talking. You feel the need to pass out, you go on, but I'm here with you to the end. You listen to my voice." She squeezed my hand. "I was born in New York…"

For the next hour, I heard all about Audrey Faith Paris. How when she was twelve, she and her father managed to hide her mother during Liberation Week but lost her to a common illness a year later. Which prompted Audrey to go into the medical field. With homeschooling and online classes, she moved through high school and was an undergrad in a few years. She knew that there were other halfers out there and she wanted to be there to help them. So she raced her way through medical school.

Wanting to help halfers had gotten her into trouble. It's why she was here, instead of Earth. SpaceTech had found her books and research on Aunare physiology and had thrown her into jail. But she didn't regret what she'd done or what she'd learned because it meant she was here to help me today.

She explained that Aunare bloodlines were complicated. Her bloodline was weak—basically dormant—which allowed her to pass through SpaceTech's scans without being found out. Depending on the bloodline, the effects of the nanos on a halfer could be nothing at all or minor annoyance or extremely excruciating.

She'd had nanos before, and they didn't bother her at all.

Lucky Audrey.

Pain rolled through my body again, and I screamed again and again and again. One scream rolled until the next until my throat was wrecked.

"Okay. You're doing great. You're getting through this."

"Please," I cried. "I can't take it anymore." I was pathetic, but I wasn't beyond begging. Not anymore. I would do anything —*anything*—to make it stop.

"You can do this. I'm right here with you."

Hot tears rolled down my cheeks as I turned my head toward her. "I'm done. I can't do it. End it. Please."

"No!" she yelled. "You're getting through this. Minute by minute. I wish it wasn't like this for you, but a day of pain for a lifetime of walking. It's worth it."

I tried. I really did. But I was so, so tired and I never passed out.

No matter how much I wanted it, begged for it, that sweet darkness never came to rescue me.

AFTER A WHILE, the pain started to ease, but I was still glowing. By the time Audrey asked if I wanted a painkiller, the worst had passed, but I still wanted it. I was tired of hurting.

Audrey left for a minute to grab it, and Tyler came to stand next to me.

"How're you feelin'?" he asked.

The pain wasn't much worse now than getting a tattoo, but the combined hours of suffering plus my shift on the surface of Abaddon had left me feeling jittery and weaker than I'd ever felt before. "Not good." My voice was raspy from all the screaming.

As I looked up at Tyler, I wondered what he made of all of this. Of Audrey's story and what both of us were and my still glowing skin. "Are you going to say anything about me?"

"About you being a halfer?"

I nodded, not trusting my voice.

"You made it this far, that's your business. I don't have any problems with the Aunare."

"Okay." I wanted to know more, but I wasn't going to push.

"I have my issues with SpaceTech." He let out a low huff. "You know, I got hurt a couple of months back, and Audrey fixed me up, but she wouldn't give me the time of day unless I was hurt. Damned near faked an injury to get her to talk to me, but now I guess I know why. You think I have a shot?" He gave me a quick smile and a wink, but then his smile dropped away. "I figure someone already knows what you are. Otherwise, they wouldn't have made up this bullshit job for you. They want you tortured, and they're going to make me feel responsible when you die out there. So I'm not going to let that happen."

I gave myself a second to feel relieved that there wasn't going to be a problem between Tyler and me. I hadn't known him for long, but he seemed like a nice guy. That he cared about me, even though I was a halfer, told me a lot about his character.

Tyler leaned on the table. "Why didn't you say anything while you were out there? Why didn't you tell me you were hurting?"

I licked my lips. The nanos had healed the bite and cracking, but my feet still felt a little dry. "It didn't seem that bad, and I was so close to the elevator, but it got bad fast..." I met his gaze, wanting him to understand that I would never give up. No matter how weak I'd been just now. I was still alive, and that meant I was going to keep going.

"You'll just need to be more careful next time," Tyler said.

The monitor started beeping as my heart rate jumped. I hadn't thought about going back out there. This was only my first day, but I already wanted out of this bullshit duty I'd pulled. I didn't need to go out there again to understand that much.

The general was right. I wouldn't last long out there. Even the suits weren't built for that kind of sustained heat. I had to find a way to talk to Ahiga. Or figure out how to get on the mining runs.

"Don't worry. I have a plan," Tyler said like he'd read my mind. "Matthew and I went down to storage. They have plenty there. Each break, you'll get a new one. We'll inspect the shoes. I won't let you back out there without checking. I'm sorry I wasn't there during your second break. I was—"

There was some yelling from outside the room. Tyler turned toward the door, waiting to hear what was going on, but the voices were either too far away or the walls were too thick. I couldn't make out anything except for the tone of Audrey's voice.

"One second," Tyler said before stepping out into the hallway, closing the door quickly behind him.

If there was someone else out there that wanted to come in, then I was going to have to get my skin to stop glowing.

Six in. Three out. Three in. Six out. Four in. Eight out. Eight in. Four out. Six in. Three out. Three in. Six out. Four in. Eight out. Eight in. Four out.

It wasn't working. Either the pain was setting off the glow, or the nanos' frequencies were, or something else, but Declan's breathing trick wasn't working at all. Not even a little bit.

When the door swung open, both Tyler and Audrey were yelling.

I was still bound to the table. I couldn't get up or run or do anything but wait to see who was on the other side of the door.

I squeezed my eyes shut and hoped this wasn't what Jason wanted. For me to reveal myself to some other SpaceTech goon, who would then execute me. Because that would be a fitting end to my seriously shitty day.

CHAPTER TWENTY-THREE

"WHAT THE FUCK IS GOING ON?" Ahiga's voice was filled with cold fury.

I opened my eyes to see him staring down at me, and his face was turning a lovely shade of purple.

Tyler and Audrey looked ready to shit themselves as they glanced from me to Ahiga and back again.

Ahiga was SpaceTech, and anyone who could see me now, with my glowing skin, knew I was the enemy. Yet Ahiga wasn't doing anything about it.

"It's fine. Close the door," I said to Audrey.

Audrey didn't look convinced, but she'd treated me instead of turning me in. It was her ass on the line, too.

"Trust me." My voice slurred with exhaustion. "This will work out better than the nanos."

He picked up my arm and let go. My arm dropped weightlessly to the table. "You're spent."

"Yeah. I could really use a nap."

Ahiga spun to Audrey. Then looked at me again, before striding to the door. He slammed it shut with such a fury that I was surprised the concrete walls hadn't cracked.

He stepped directly in front of Audrey. "You want to tell me why you gave her nanos, knowing what she is?"

Tyler tried to get between them, but Audrey put a hand on his arm. "I'm confused. You're mad that I treated a patient. Not about *what* she is?"

"You don't know *who* she is, do you? She didn't tell you?"

Audrey's eyes were wide as she looked at me. "She's a halfer."

"She's not just a halfer. Christ. I don't know how I'm going to explain this to him..." Ahiga grabbed the back of his neck. "Someone tell me what happened to her."

Tyler filled in Ahiga quickly on his part of it, and Audrey did the rest. I used the time to relax, letting the chatter lull me into a relaxed state.

And as I was lying there, somewhere between awake and dreaming, I found myself on a beach. Waves lapping at the shore.

"Amihanna!" Lorne's mirth-filled voice was all I could hear. "What's that mess of sand you've got there?"

I couldn't stop the grin. "It's my *beautiful* castle."

"*Beautiful* castle?" Lorne's laughter filled my mind, warming me from the inside. "I think I got here just in time. It looks like a—"

A hand came down on my shoulder, jolting me from my dream with a gasp. I blinked as I tried to figure out where I was.

Med bay. Abaddon. Nanos.

Ahiga gave my shoulder a squeeze, and I met his gaze. "I knew you were going to be a pain in my ass," he said.

"Not funny."

"It's kind of funny." He grabbed the stool that Audrey had been using to sit by me and took her place. "How're you hanging in?"

"Worst is over now, but I can't do this." I was so worn out that I wasn't sure I could sit up on my own. "Please tell me that he's out of cryo." Talking made my throat burn. I'd been screaming way too much, and I was spent. Emotionally. Physically. I wasn't sure how I was going to walk back to my bunk, but I'd figure that out later.

He brushed a hand over my forehead, pushing my hair from my face. "I wish I could."

"What am I going to do?" I couldn't go back out there. The nanos were slowly running out of steam, but the last three hours had been excruciating. I couldn't do this every day.

"I don't know. I—" He stopped himself, and looked back at Tyler and Audrey. "I have files on both of you. I know who and what you are Audrey—"

"How?" She stumbled back a step. "SpaceTech—" Audrey started, but Ahiga silenced her with a look.

"They don't know, but *I* do. I looked into everyone that might come into contact with Maité. The Aunare keep better records of their citizens than SpaceTech. One image dropped into their database and..." Ahiga was quiet as he let that sink in. "Tyler—you now know everything yet stayed quiet today. You shouldn't be here, like many of the workers on Abaddon, but I don't know if I should trust you. And I guess it's a little too late now, but I'll leave it up to Maité to decide how much she wants to tell you or not. But trust *me* when I say we all need her to stay alive."

"You want her alive, you get those bots back out there and her off this job," Tyler said. "You're high up enough. You can get it done."

Ahiga turned back to me. "I'm trying, but her job came from someone much higher up than me."

I nodded my understanding. His talk with the CO hadn't gone well.

"Maité? Who are you?" Audrey stepped around Ahiga to come closer to the bed. "You're a strong bloodline. I know that from your reaction to the nanos and the glow. And someone much higher up wants to torture you? Why would they care? Halfers are executed. Not toyed with. Not tortured. They're *executed*."

"She's not just a halfer." Ahiga's gaze was still on me, as if he were asking me what I wanted to do next.

"It's okay." My voice was more a raspy whisper than anything else. "Tell them." I was too tired to explain it, but I was okay with Ahiga telling them. I didn't have that click. Not with Ahiga. Not with Tyler or Audrey. But that didn't mean they weren't good people. That didn't mean I couldn't trust them.

"She is Amihanna di Aetes." Ahiga's voice was a low, menacing rumble. "Daughter of Rysden di Aetes. The Hand of the Aunare High King. The Leader of the Aunare Military. And Space-Tech knows exactly who they've got here."

"Jesus Christ," Tyler muttered. He reached for Audrey's hand, and she took it.

Audrey's face paled, making her freckles stand out that much more.

"She's a pawn in a game that the Murtaghs are playing with the Aunare. One that will most likely end in war. Especially if she dies. And that's why I'm here. To make sure she doesn't die. And now I'm trusting you to keep her secret and help me keep her alive."

I whimpered as the pain flared again and Ahiga squeezed my arm. "You okay?"

"It's getting better." I stared up at the ceiling, willing the nanos to die.

Ahiga's face came into view above me. He looked ready to kill someone only there was no one he could kill. There was nothing he could do to fix this.

"Right now it probably hurts less than when you got those tattoos all over your face, but let's just say it's been a long few hours and I'm so *tired*." My voice broke on the last word, and my eyes burned with the few tears I had left.

"I bet." He sat back down. "Took me a while to figure out what happened to you when you didn't show in the mess hall. Longer to get away from Jason's men. Otherwise, I would've been here."

"Nothing you could've done." I knew I needed the nanos. Audrey had done the right thing, and if Ahiga had been here he just would've been one more person to watch me at my weakest.

"There's one thing I can do, but I shouldn't do it. Unless you're ready to give up? Unless you're ready for the war to start tomorrow?"

My heart stuttered in my chest. "You'll tell my dad where I am."

"Not him directly. Declan thought it was best I didn't have that information in case I was ever questioned, but there's a chain I can send a message through. It would take a few days, but I think it would reach him. Or someone who could get it to him."

I wanted to beg him to do it. If he had a way to get word to my father, I wanted that to happen now. Today. Immediately.

The nanos flared, and I hissed as a burning heat spread up my legs. I breathed in for six, out for three, in for three, and tried to picture the pain flowing out of me, and it did. The burning and poking and crawling needles were all gone.

I moaned with relief. "Oh thank God." I looked at Audrey, still standing by my feet. "I think that was their last flare. I think they're done."

Audrey went to her computer panel. "Yep. Let's see how your feet are doing."

I held my breath as she pulled off what was left of my shoes. She ran a finger up my foot from heel to toe, and I jerked.

"Hurt?"

"Tickles."

She nodded. "Skin is new, so it'll be a little tender, but you're completely healed."

Audrey was right. A few hours of pain, and I was back to being okay. It was worth it. "I can walk?"

"Jog. Run. Sprint. Kick some ass. You can do whatever you want. The skin is a little thin, like a newborn baby's feet, so be careful with them. The skin would've been thicker if I'd injected more nanos, but I erred on the side of caution with this one."

Nope. I didn't care about that. The fewer nanos used the better. "Thank you. I'll double up on socks."

"I'd tell you it was my pleasure, but it honestly wasn't. I've never felt so helpless as I did today." She sighed. "Let's not do this again, okay?"

"That is something we can both agree on. Can I sit up?"

"Yes. As long as you're not too weak." She pressed a button, and the restraints retracted. "I gave you fluids the entire time, but the nanos depleted you considerably. Take it easy."

Ahiga leaned forward, helping me sit. "You okay?"

The room was spinning, and I felt like death, but I wasn't dead. That was a win. "A little lightheaded and weak, but still breathing." I sighed. "What now?"

"That's up to you. As I said, I can call your dad, but we'll be at war within a week. Are you ready for that?"

"So you call him and a war starts and I put millions of lives at risk?"

"Tens of billions, and that's only counting humans. I don't know exact numbers on the Aunare and their allies."

I swallowed. "That's a lot of lives to put on my shoulders."

"I know."

"But the war is coming anyway?"

"I can't say anything either way because I don't know. I've been friends with Declan for a long time and he's managed to avoid it so far. Every time things get tense, he and Lorne come up with a plan, but that's only going to work for so long. It'll eventually either be war or things will finally fizzle out."

That made this so much worse. How was I supposed to put myself and my survival ahead of so many others?

"You're going to get two days off," Ahiga said after a while. "I'm going to put in for seven—standard for a work-related injury —but they're going to give two."

"That's better than nothing," Audrey said. "If they want her dead, they could refuse it."

"They won't," Ahiga said quickly. "I have a feeling they want her tortured over and over. They're going to want to give her the reprieve so that the torture will be that much more acute. They want her broken. They want her destroyed. The suit is recorded, right?"

Tyler nodded. "From the time the helmet closes until it's opened."

This was so messed up. "SpaceTech will send it to my dad. Make him act out first."

"That's my guess," Ahiga said. "When SpaceTech has all their ducks lined up—whatever they are—they'll release it."

Perfect. "So I need out of here before then, so what—"

"Yes, but we're in a bit of a—"

"Shit," Tyler said.

Ahiga turned to him. "What?"

"The ducks are lining up." His face grew pale as he stared off at nothing for a minute.

I sat taller on the bed. "What do you mean?"

"They've been transferring a lot of lucole to one of the labs for months. Rumor is that they're working on some kind of weapon. Not sure what it does, but something that requires that much lucole isn't good." He crossed his arms. "And the shipments. They've only let minimum rations off the base to supply the colonies and the fleet the three years I've been here. We're talking a few containers here and there leaving the base. They never even made a dent in what's stored. Now you're here, and they've already shipped out an entire bay and a half. In a few days, it'll be two full bays gone. They keep going this way, few weeks and the whole base will be empty and—"

"You can't be serious," Ahiga said.

"Yes. If she's Amihanna, then the Murtaghs are finally going to make their move. It can't be a coincidence."

"No. It can't. Did you know about any of this?" I asked Ahiga.

"No. But..." He looked hard at the ground. "Everyone knows I trained Declan. I was his commanding officer for a while, and that's enough not to trust me fully." He stood up. "Damn it. I need to talk to Matthew."

I wasn't sure what good Matthew was going to do. "Do you think he'll tell you anything?"

"Maybe. He knows everything that's going on here, but I'm not sure which side he's on."

Ice it all to hell. If they were trying to draw my father here... "You can't make that call. If my father comes here with his fleet and they have some sort of new weapon ready for him, then the war could be over before it begins. With SpaceTech *winning*. I can't let that happen."

"I agree. It'd be better if we didn't call him," Ahiga said. "At least not until we know what kind of trap they're setting for your father and what this weapon is, but I'm not sure anyone will tell me anything about it."

This whole situation was the worst. "We should wait for Declan to resurface. It's the only way to avoid a war and not have my father drawn into some sort of trap. I have to hope that Declan will get here before..."

"I agree," Ahiga said. "If Declan's heading here, then depending on when he went into cryo..." He thought for a second. "Worse case—let's say he went into cryo two days ago, right before we woke up. That's the latest it could've been because of the automessage. If he's coming here—and that's what I truly believe because you're his number one priority right now—then it's only twelve more days until he's awake, and he'll be here. Can you—"

"I can last that long." I had to.

"The suit won't fail again," Tyler said. "We'll be careful."

"And if it does, I'll be here," Audrey said. She pressed her right fist to her heart and dipped her head just a tiny bit. An Aunare symbol of respect. "I won't fail you."

"Okay," Ahiga said. "Okay, but the second it becomes too much, I'm sending the message to the Aunare. Their ships are faster. They'd get here in five days—give or take. And it could be that Declan will be here tomorrow. He could've headed here the day after we did. I just don't know—"

"It's okay. I'll be okay." I hoped that was true, but there were no guarantees. The stakes were too damned high for Ahiga to call the Aunare, but I really, seriously, didn't want to die out there. Every scenario I came up with ended in war. It was just a matter of when it happened. But I couldn't let it start with SpaceTech having the upper hand. Not when so many lives were at stake.

I'd clicked with Declan. I trusted him, and I knew he had a plan. I also knew that my slow death on the surface of the lava planet was in *no way* part of his plan, but I'd manage.

Audrey reached below the table into a drawer, pulling out a pair of shorts and a T-shirt. "You'll want these."

I looked down at my sweat-soaked clothes and nodded. "You guys mind?" I waved my pointer finger in a circle, motioning for them to turn around. I might have screamed and cried for the last three hours, but I still had some modesty left.

They did as instructed and I slid off the table. My legs wobbled, and Audrey grabbed my arm to steady me.

"How're the feet?"

"A little weird." They felt tender yet numb.

"That should fade."

"I hope so." I managed to pull off my clothes, replacing them with the looser cut ones Audrey had given me, without falling over. Audrey had helped me keep my balance as I moved, and I was thankful. The last thing I needed was to face-plant on the floor.

She smiled sadly at me. "Not as good as a shower, but better than nothing."

"Okay. I'm decent." I ran my fingers through my hair, and it felt a little crunchy. Damn it. I was right. That smell had been my hair frying. I didn't want to cut it, but I wasn't sure there was enough conditioner in the world to fix it now.

I sat back down on the table before my legs gave out. One thing kept bothering me. "I trust Declan, but what if he wasn't heading here? What if he was taking my mother to Sel'Ani?"

Ahiga's throat bobbed as he swallowed, and I knew that he was afraid of the same thing. It could be weeks or months before

Declan got here. Sel'Ani was a lot farther away than Earth. If he was heading there, then he'd been in cryo for a while.

"You could be right," Ahiga said finally. "So what do you want to do?"

"I don't know, but I need another plan. Something other than putting on a suit. And I'm assuming stealing a ship and running is a bad idea."

Ahiga snorted a laugh. "Epically terrible."

"Would've been too easy and where's the fun in that?" Since transferring my work detail to something else wasn't working, it had to be something that SpaceTech couldn't turn down. Something that would buy Declan enough time to wake up from cryo.

What did SpaceTech want?

Money.

Power.

Lucole.

The miner that was supposed to come on the ship with me and Ahiga chickened out. Which meant they were down one miner on duty right now. Jason Murtagh was messed up enough to find a sick kind of joy in me risking my life to mine lucole—a dangerous job that gave SpaceTech huge profits and could potentially be used in weapons against the Aunare.

I'd already thought of this once before, but my mind kept coming back to it. It seemed crazy, but going back out to the surface of Abaddon in a suit was even crazier.

"What are you planning?" Ahiga stared down at me. "I've trained enough people to know that look. You've thought of something."

"Yeah." But I wasn't even sure if it was possible. "What if I signed up for the mining runs? Do they give the test here?"

"You're nuttier than squirrel shit." Tyler's voice was deep and fierce. "You can't do that. Mining will kill you faster than a faulty suit."

"I don't know about that. Maybe I didn't die today, but I came close." I blew out a breath. "Thoughts?" I asked Ahiga.

Ahiga considered me for a moment. "Can you fly?"

"Yes. Got my Class Y when I was fourteen. Now have an R, T, and L. I was working on my Q. I've spent nearly every dime I've earned on training." I worked hard to be prepared for any eventuality. Any chance I had to get off the third rock from the sun, I wanted to be able to take it. I just never pictured it'd be like this. "I can pass any flight test—practical or simulation or written—but is it an option?"

"Yes. It's an option," Audrey answered me. "They leave it open to workers as this golden carrot to keep us happily working away. Just having the option available boosts morale here, which helps with productivity in the processing plant, which helps their bottom line and costs them nothing." Audrey rolled her eyes, and that told me exactly what she thought of this idea. "Every once in a while some asshat on this side takes the test, but no one has ever passed. I hear they've made it even harder here than it is on Earth or any of the colonies."

"Doesn't matter. I can pass whatever's on that test. I know I can." I've been studying my whole life. I'd done homeschooling for most of it, but my mom and Jorge made sure that my education wasn't lacking anything. If I could take the test, I'd pass it.

Audrey turned to Tyler. "What's her schedule?"

"She's off every Tuesday," he said it with a knowing lilt that made it sound impossible.

"What am I missing?"

"They give the mining qualification test every third Thursday at oh-ten hundred hours," Tyler said. "Smack dab in your first two-hour shift out there."

Son of a space bat. "Right." Because that would be too easy.

"Even if the timing worked out, they made the test impossible to pass." Ahiga looked grim. "I took it the last time I was here, on a lark, and I failed. Miserably. It's got some musical component to it that makes no sense. And if you somehow manage to pass, you have to get the approval of Carl Millander, and there's no chance he'll approve you."

"That old man hates *everyone*," Tyler said. "Spends all his spare time drinking in the bar, gambling away the salary SpaceTech pays him to make sure the miners don't die out there. Losing nearly every pilot that he's trained has hardened him."

"Of course it has. Do you realize how many of those idiots have died mining?" Audrey glared at me. "I didn't put you through the torture of nanos just to watch you commit suicide."

"Is it more suicidal than the job they assigned me?" Because I honestly wasn't sure which was worse.

"A few years ago, I'd have said no," Tyler said. "Mining was much better odds. Used to have about a hundred or two hundred miners here at a time. A good year maybe half would make it through all five runs. A good chunk would drop from the program. The rest… So far this year, only two people have hit the five-runs mark. And there've been how many?" Tyler looked at Audrey and she shrugged. "At least fifty. Maybe even seventy-five. A handful or so dropped out. The rest died."

"But people do still make it?" Because SpaceTech got something right. Like the other workers, I needed a goal—something to work toward that wasn't sweating out my last breath on the surface of Abaddon.

"Yeah. Two. *Two*." Tyler held up two fingers to drive it home. "*Two* out of at least *fifty*."

"Right." There didn't seem to be a good option for me. Maybe today was a fluke, but if my suit had been working properly, then it would've given me some kind of warning that I was in danger. Which meant it failed and I couldn't assume that it was just a broken suit.

Or I could try to get a mining job. Possibly die there. Or possibly make the five runs, and then what? Would Jason let me go home if I completed the job? Maybe not, but it could buy me enough time for Declan to get out of cryo.

Or Ahiga could call my dad. War would start. And billions upon billions of people could die.

There was no answer that I was happy with, so I had to pick

the least-bad option. "I want to say that I can sit around and do my job and wait for Declan to come save me, but that's not my style. I'll go crazy doing that. Even if he shows up tomorrow, I still need to be focusing on saving myself. Especially if I'm stuck with this job. For me, that's mining. I'll work toward that. And if something comes up—if Declan shows or something else happens and we need to get word to my father—then we'll deal with that then."

"I get it," Ahiga said. "I'd be doing the same thing."

"Good." I had a goal. Something that I could actively be working toward. That was a win. "What day is it today?"

"Sunday," Tyler said.

"So when's the next test?" Please God, tell me it's this week.

Tyler winced, and I knew I wasn't going to like his answer. "Next week."

"Damn it." I didn't want to have to deal with this job for another day let alone another week or two.

But it was fine. I'd make it work. An extra week would mean that I had time to plan, which could be better. And maybe the CO would give me the seven days off that Ahiga was going to ask for. "Where do I take the test? And where do I find Carl Millander?"

"The test is given down the hall from the main mess, but there's no way you're getting into the bar to find Carl," Tyler said.

"This is a shit plan," Ahiga said. "But you get to the test and pass, I'll get you in touch with Carl."

Okay. That was something. This was going to work. "If I skip out on work to take the test, it's not like anyone would notice? It's just me out there."

"Shit, girl. I'm your supervisor. You can't ask me about how to skip out on work. If one of the officers finds out, I'll—" Tyler wiped a hand down his face.

Ahiga rose from the stool. "If you won't answer this for her, how am I supposed to believe you'll keep her secret?"

"It's not the same thing." Tyler held his ground as Ahiga stepped toward him.

Oh man. This could get ugly. "You don't want me to die." I slid down off of the bed and stepped gingerly toward Tyler. My feet were still a little numb and tender, but I could walk a couple of steps. So that was something.

I took another step and looked up into his blue eyes. "We both know that my job is a death sentence. I don't want to die, and I know you don't want me to die. Please, just tell me. Once I've checked in, and I'm out there, does anyone look for me? Will you have to monitor me?"

Tyler stared at the ground for a long minute, and I gave him a second to think about what I was asking. If something went wrong and he covered for me, it was his ass on the line, too.

"No one will look for you," he said finally. "But your tracker will give you away."

"I can help with that," Ahiga said.

"But I need to know you won't turn me in or get into trouble if I walk off the job," I said to Tyler.

Tyler stood there, staring me down in silence. I wanted to fidget as I waited for his response, but I forced myself to be patient. I hadn't known him for long, but every time he decided something, he liked to think about it for a second. So I gave him the space he seemed to need.

"Okay," Tyler said, breaking the silence. "I'll help you get to the test, but if you get your five runs, then I'm going to need a favor."

"Tyler, you help me, and I'll make sure it's worth your while. I swear. Even if I don't pass the test." I meant it. I needed his help for this, and if I got away from here alive, I would owe him big.

I could do this. I'd make it happen or die trying. No one was getting the best of me. Not Abaddon. And definitely not Jason Murtagh.

CHAPTER TWENTY-FOUR

I WOKE UP WITH A SCREAM, sweating. Still smelling the scent of sulfur in the air. I gagged and leaned over the bed in case I threw up, but slowly my nausea eased, and I could breathe again.

It was just in my mind. I was safe. In bed. Where I'd been for the last thirty-six hours.

I laid my head back on the pillow and wiped the sweat from my forehead. My body was shaking, but this time it'd been a dream. A nightmare. I wasn't burning on the surface. I didn't even have to put on a suit today.

It took a minute for that to sink in, but once it did, I took one last shuddering breath and felt much better.

Ahiga was right. I didn't get the full seven days he asked for, but I did get two days off. I slept for most of the first day and through the morning of the second. It didn't matter that nanos had healed my feet. The whole experience had left my body so weak, Audrey had to half-carry me to my bunk. It was worse than anything I'd ever experienced before, and I was really hoping this would be the only time I was forced to use nanos here.

With a sigh, I heaved my legs over the edge of my bunk. I'd heard movement and women talking earlier but hadn't found the energy to force open my eyes. My bunkmates were gone now—off to do whatever they did on the base—and I couldn't sit here forever. The couple of times I'd gotten up yesterday, I'd walked very carefully. My feet had been a little tender still. Today, I had to believe that my feet were okay. I held my breath as my feet touched the polished concrete and then took a few steps.

Audrey had been right. They were fine. Tender and sensitive—the cool floor tickled my soles—but my feet were healed. She'd checked on me yesterday, bringing me some food and electrolyte packets. She'd even done my laundry, which was above and beyond, but I couldn't let her keep taking care of me. It was time to face the world again.

I let out the breath I'd been holding and headed for the showers. Tomorrow I was going to have to go back out there. The thought of it made my stomach twist, and my nausea returned worse than before.

I pressed a fist into my stomach and swallowed hard a few times. Starting my day by heaving into a toilet didn't sound awesome. Nervous energy buzzed along my skin—more than any breathing exercises could help—and I knew that if I didn't distract myself, my skin would start to glow.

I quickly dressed in shorts and a tank and braided my now-frizzy hair in two large sections, knotting them up on my head to keep them off my neck. The heat in the women's quarters didn't bother me as much, not after what I'd felt in the suit, but sweat was starting to coat my body. Having my hair up helped cool me down just a little bit.

From what I could tell there was no set weekend. Everyone's schedules overlapped so that there was always someone working, but that meant that it was always someone's day off, too. I wasn't sure what people did on their days off while on Abaddon, but there had to be something to do. With how fit everyone here appeared to be, there had to at least be a gym somewhere.

The map on my wrist unit showed which areas I had access to.

A lot of rooms and areas were off limits, so it was a lot to weed through, but after a few minutes, I found the gym.

The map showed a large room that spanned two levels, plus a few smaller rooms. I wasn't sure what equipment SpaceTech had in their gym or if my body could even take a workout, but I wouldn't know either until I went there. After lying in bed for a day, I had to at least move my body a little bit.

The idea of eating more food from the mess didn't sound appealing, but I was going to have to get over that. I'd been spoiled by my mother's cooking at the diner. A sharp pang hit my chest as I thought of my home that would never be home again. I might never have a meal cooked by her or feel one of her long, tight hugs.

My eyes started to burn, and I ached for my mother and Roan and my warehouse and that stupid shitty apartment in Albuquerque. I even missed the diner. The ache grew into pain, and my heart literally hurt. I stopped walking in the hallway, not caring if someone was watching and closed my eyes. Declan said he'd protect them and I had to believe that he was doing at least that much. I wasn't going to get through this if I let myself get homesick. I was stronger than this.

I shoved all the worry for my mother and Roan way down inside of me until I could breathe again. When this was over, I would see them both again. For now, I needed food.

I went by the mess on my way to the gym. It was technically open all day, but when I got to the food tables, I couldn't help but gag. From the look of things, the food out there was only refreshed during mealtimes. I could barely stomach it when the food was fresh. The old slop that filled the metal pans stank worse than the food I'd pulled from the garbage when we were living on the streets in California.

I snagged a tube of water and a hunk of stale, crumbly bread and avoided the leftover watery eggs that no one in their right mind would ever touch. A few guys were talking at the tables, but no one that I recognized, so I ate as I walked to the gym.

A few wrong turns later, I finally found what I was looking for. The door to the gym was open. I expected it to smell sweaty and rank, especially with how hot it was, and it was a bit rank. But not as bad as some gyms I'd been to.

I spotted Ahiga and Santiago sparring in a ring off to one side. A bunch of guys were leaning on the ropes, yelling. Judging from Ahiga's easy breathing, he had to have been going easy on Santiago. It looked to me like they were working out instead of actually sparring.

Punching bags and speed bags took up the area around the ring. Stairs along the back wall went to a balcony area. Rows of cardio equipment overlooked the ring. A few vidscreens were mounted to the pylons around the room.

A loud slam came from somewhere beyond the cardio equipment, rattling the speed bags hanging from the ceiling. Muffled trash talking filled the gym. I couldn't make out what they were saying, but I knew the tone well enough and figured someone tried to lift a weight that was a little too heavy for them.

A few guys caught me standing at the entrance and puffed up their chests. I almost laughed, but I wasn't sure if they'd take that as encouragement. I was here for a workout, and that was it.

I looked for Audrey's red hair, but she wasn't here. In fact, there were no other women in the gym as far as I could see, but maybe they were upstairs.

I wove through the bags hanging from the ceiling and took the stairs two at a time. The first row of treadmills was occupied, so I went to the second row.

The treadmill was fancier than anything I'd seen before, which didn't seem very SpaceTech-like, but I figured there were enough people here that had a physical requirement to their job for them to spend the money. Healthy employees meant better productivity.

I punched a few buttons—not really sure what any of them did —and hit start.

My muscles protested as I started walking. It'd been forever since I'd worked out, especially counting the time I spent in cryo.

I'd never gone this long without exercise before, but I knew it didn't take long to lose endurance. I knew I should take it easy, but then I hit the button to speed it up to a jog.

And then I hit it again to move into a run.

And then I hit it again.

And again.

I lost track of time. I felt at home pushing myself to move past my limits. The small aches from unused muscles smoothed away. Seeing how far and how fast I could go was a game I'd played all the time. I wished I'd had some music to listen to, but I didn't. So, instead, I listened to the air in my lungs, and let the sounds of the gym fall away. I closed my eyes.

The sound of the air rushing through my lungs started to remind me of the push and pull of the waves on a sandy shore, even though I'd only seen them on vidscreens and recently in my dreams.

I started to picture the ocean. Clear turquoise water. Golden sand. Two suns in the sky, one an orange-pink color, the other a bright white. And I could almost see someone walking toward me.

I breathed out long and slow.

"Amihanna!" Lorne's mirth-filled voice was all I could hear. "What's that mess of sand you've got there?"

I couldn't stop the grin. "It's my *beautiful* castle."

"*Beautiful* castle?" Lorne's laughter filled my mind, warming me from the inside. "I think I got here just in time. It looks like a melted whale."

I picked up a handful of sand and tossed it at him.

He held up a hand. "Hey! Not my fault you're terrible at this."

"I'm a kid. You're supposed to help me."

Lorne bonked my nose with a finger. "I was supposed to come get you for dinner, but I guess I can help you first. Let's see if we can fix this mess."

I wasn't sure if I was dreaming. I could still feel the treadmill under my feet, but ever since cryo, my mind kept coming back to this same dream. Which made me wonder if it was a dream or something else.

I never got to see how it ended. There was always—

The treadmill slowed suddenly, and I opened my eyes, grabbing the rails around me to keep from tripping.

"What the—"

"Hey, girl." Santiago was grinning as he leaned on the rails of my treadmill. "I was wondering—"

"No. You don't want to hurt yourself by having any kind of complicated thoughts."

A snort came from the other side of me, and I turned to find Ahiga two treadmills down, running a fast and steady pace.

"Ignore that giant oaf," Santiago said, drawing my attention back to him. "I thought—since you must be feeling better and all— if you want to head downstairs. Try some moves out on me."

I stood there for a second, trying to figure out what the hell Santiago was doing hitting on me, especially with such a lame pick-up line, before he pointed down. To the sparring square.

Right. That kind of trying some moves. I gave him my best are-you-sure-about-this look. "Seven times not enough?"

He rubbed a hand along his cheek. "It's been a few years. Maybe I've gotten better."

"Maybe have I, too."

He flashed me a bright grin. "Shit. Now I'm rethinking this whole thing."

"Well, you offered." Now that I was warmed up, I knew I'd enjoy kicking his ass again. "You can't back out now."

"Sweet. You done with that?" He motioned to the treadmill.

"I guess I am now."

Ahiga cleared his throat, and I turned to him.

He'd turned off his treadmill and was watching me. "You sure this is a good idea?"

"Probably not, but I'm going out there tomorrow, and the thought of dying without letting myself go for at least a second…"

I couldn't think that way, but martial arts had been my release for so long. It was one of the few things I retained from my early childhood. No matter how bad things got, my mom always found a gym or a secluded section of a park or an abandoned warehouse for me to practice in. And when Jorge had set me up with the warehouse, it was literally the best gift I'd ever been given. For eight years, the only time I'd truly been happy was when I was in that nasty old warehouse. Getting some of that back was just what I needed.

"I have to have something to live for when I'm out there or I won't last."

"And fighting is what you live for?"

"Yes." Moving my body like that, it was as essential as air to me. My mother said my father was the same way.

I wanted to sigh at the confusion that flashed across Ahiga's face, but I knew that look too well. I'd seen the same look from so many people in my life. It should've been my red flag with Haden. He tried to understand why fighting was important to me, but a couple weeks into our relationship, he'd started to resent the fact that I'd choose to spend time at the warehouse rather than hang out with him. Maybe the fact that I was a girl made it hard for him to understand. I should've been playing damsel and waiting for some guy to save me, but that wasn't how my brain worked.

I was a di Aetes. I didn't want or *need* anyone to save me. I would save myself.

The tattoos on Ahiga's face wrinkled as he gave me a grin. "I met someone else like you once before. I think you two were cut from the same cloth." He crossed his arms. "I think I'll enjoy seeing you let loose."

I smiled, but I couldn't feel it. "I can't let loose. Not here." I longed for a time and place when I could have a chance to really learn and push myself. To find a partner that could push me to grow. But that wasn't here. That wasn't today. That wasn't Santiago.

CHAPTER TWENTY-FIVE

I STEPPED down from the treadmill and stretched my arms.

Ahiga walked over and gave my shoulder a squeeze. "Come on. Santiago is already down there warming up."

I walked to the front of the balcony and leaned over the railing to see him below stretching, getting ready for our fight.

"Don't you chicken out on me!" he yelled up.

I shook my head at his taunt. "Wouldn't dream of it." Without overthinking it, I ran toward the stairs. When I hit the edge of the first one, I jumped and tucked my body. I twisted halfway down, spotting my landing. My feet hit the floor, and I breathed a full breath for the first time since Declan had shown up in my apartment.

No. Longer.

I'd been hiding and afraid my whole life, but the worst had already happened. SpaceTech had found me. They had complete control over my life and were using me in their game against the Aunare. So how much hiding did I really have to do?

I wasn't about to go around spilling my guts, but maybe Ahiga was right. Maybe I could let loose just a little bit.

I smiled—a real smile—as I approached the ring. There were

maybe four or five guys who'd been working downstairs that were now quietly watching me approach Santiago. I looked behind me to see Ahiga coming down the stairs. A few guys were leaning over the railing watching.

Ahiga gave me a wide-eyed look that said *what was that*, and I shrugged.

Maybe my acrobatic trick was a little showy—okay, a lot showy —but it'd been fun.

"You're freaking me out with that smile," Santiago said. "And what the hell was that move? You took the entire staircase in one go?"

I kicked off my shoes and shoved my doubled-up socks into them. I hoped my feet would hold up while I sparred. The skin was a little thin, but they'd held up fine while I was running. So I figured this should be okay. "My version of a warm-up." I slid between the ropes. "You ready?"

Santiago was wearing a pair of loose work-out shorts and no shoes or shirt. His matador tattoo made me laugh as he bounced from foot to foot, his hands in fists. "I'm not going to let you push my face into the mat an eighth time."

"I don't think it's a matter of letting me do it." I closed my eyes, letting air fill my lungs. This moment, right before sparring, is when I felt the most whole. To me, sparring was fun. Invigorating. The essence of life.

I opened my eyes. "Okay." I gave him a little bow, and he mimicked the move.

I came up and waited.

Santiago started circling, so I started circling, too.

"Come on. Make a move," someone shouted from outside the ring.

I shook my head. "No. I never make the first move. Not unless I have to."

"Why not?" another voice called out.

"Because it will be the last move, and I don't want it to end that quickly."

That got people laughing and trash talking—asking Santiago if he was going to let a *girl* take him down, telling me I was all talk, booing and hollering for us to start the fight already. It was a huge improvement from the silence.

I could tell the moment Santiago decided to make his move. His arm tensed and he rose up on the ball of his left foot. A look of determination crossed his face. His ever-present smile gone.

Game on.

He punched, and I moved to the left. He moved again, and I moved. Every time he lashed out, I dodged. Until it looked a bit like we were dancing.

I hadn't raised my arms yet. No need to block. Santiago was telegraphing his moves clearly before he made them, so I didn't need to do anything but mirror him to avoid getting hit.

It took a few minutes, but he started laughing. The smile was back, and he paused, putting his fists on his hips. "What the hell is this?"

I shrugged. "You tell me. You're the one giving away all your moves. Whatever you've been doing the last few years, you've gotten worse. It's really pathetic."

"Then you show me how it's done."

Someone whistled, and I glanced around. The crowd had grown. Someone must've gone to find the rest of the workers and miners. I didn't see any other SpaceTech people, aside from Ahiga, but Audrey and Tyler were in a back corner.

"Are you sure?" I asked.

"Hell, yes. That's why I asked you in here."

This time I brought my hands up. "It'll be done in three moves, but you're killing all my fun."

Santiago had time to give me a half-laugh before I kicked his legs out from under him, grabbed his wrist as he fell to the ground like a sack of potatoes, and wrenched it behind his back. When his face hit the ground, I was on him. My knee sunk into the small of his back. My grip on his arm had him at my mercy. "That's eight times I've beat you." I eased up on him. "Want to go for nine?"

"Shit." His voice was muffled by the mat. "I didn't even see you move."

I grinned. "I know." I'd moved fast. Not as fast as I could move, but fast enough to take him down without a real fight.

As soon as I stood up, Santiago flipped onto his back and groaned. "That was embarrassing."

"Don't feel bad." I gave him a little nudge with my foot. "I've been practicing."

"With who? I'm good. I can hold up against Ahiga, and no one else here can."

I shrugged. "Roan."

"Bullshit with Roan." Santiago groaned again as he sat up. "No way Roan is that good."

"He's gotten better." I'd trained him to be my sparring partner. It'd taken me *years* to get Roan to the point where he could keep up with me, but he couldn't push me. He wasn't Aunare. "Fighting with you was more like running drills than pushing myself, but there aren't many people willing to really try sparring with me." I held my hand out and helped him to his feet.

"How'd you do it?" Santiago looked me up and down. "I mean —you didn't even sweat. You didn't even really move much."

He might've thought he'd been practicing, but his teacher had been total crap. "You give away everything you're going to do."

"No." He rubbed the top of his head. "I do?"

I nodded.

"I didn't see him telegraphing shit," someone yelled behind me. "His fighting was legit."

I slipped into teaching mode. I liked it almost as much as I loved sparring. "We're going to try this again."

"We are?" Santiago said, sounding worried.

I raised a brow at him. "Who's chicken now?"

He rubbed the top of his head again. "Okay. Fine. Shit. I guess we're doing this then."

I almost laughed at his nerves. All the cockiness had drained from the man. "This time, watch closely as he tries to hit me," I said to the crowd. "Watch his shoulder. His feet. Where does he put his weight? What muscles are tensing? You have to pay attention to every part of your opponent, even when you're just sparring. Otherwise, when you're in a real fight, you won't be ready. That's what training and practice are all about." I waved Santiago forward. "Try something."

I saw him tense his thigh and I jumped. I was in the air before his foot rose from the ground, easily avoiding the kick. I turned around, not sure who had asked the question. "Did you see his thigh? He tensed it. You have to trust your gut and your eyes. Your focus has to be on the fight and—"

I felt the vibrations in the mat behind me and the shift in the air and sidestepped.

Santiago plowed right by me and into the ropes.

"And you should never turn your back on an opponent." I shook my head at him. "Weak sauce, cheap move, dude."

Santiago let out a surprised laugh. "Unless you have eyes in the back of your head, you couldn't see me coming."

"No. But I felt the mat move with your heavy footfalls. You have to use all of your senses in a fight. Sight. Sound. Feeling—gut and physical. And smells." I sniffed the air. "You need a shower, Santiago."

That one got me a few laughs.

"You've gotten better." Santiago nudged me with his elbow.

I wasn't sure if that was true, but I hadn't gotten any worse since I'd last fought him. "I can train you if you want. Jorge had me teaching classes for the last few years."

"And me?" I heard Audrey's voice yell above the chatter and the room quieted. "Will you train me?"

"And me?" Another woman's voice called out. "I… I've never fought before, but I'd like to feel…"

I found a blonde standing on the other side of Tyler from Audrey. "Safe? You want to feel safe. Because being here with SpaceTech, you don't feel safe?"

She looked around the room, her cheeks turning pink. There

were criminals in here, sure. But most were good people who'd been in the wrong place at the wrong time. People who had been taken advantage of.

"I get it. We're all here for one reason or another. Maybe some of you were convicted of a real crime, or maybe you're like me. Maybe you didn't do anything wrong. Maybe SpaceTech is using you."

There were a lot of nods.

Okay. Okay. This I could work with. "We all know how bad it is on Earth and that the company doesn't really give a shit about us down there. I shouldn't say anything about it since we all know that they're watching us—waiting for the chance to exploit us a little more—but it's not like my job here can get much worse." I shrugged. "On Earth, Santiago and I were part of the ABQ Crew. SpaceTech called us a gang or vigilantes, but really we just looked out for those who needed help in our community. I believe that if we're not happy with how our lives are going, it's up to each and every one of us to change. To make a difference. Our motto was Survivors Together, because only *together* will we overcome the hell that SpaceTech has brought into our lives."

Doing something that had meaning would offset my stupid job. It balanced things out. "I used to teach martial arts on Earth. I'd be happy do the same here for anyone who wants to learn. I don't have much time off, but whenever I do, I'll be in here. Ready to teach whoever wants to learn. Don't worry about experience level. We'll do everything in one big group. All you have to do is show up."

"What about me?" Ahiga's deep rumble made me laugh.

"Seriously. You want me to train you? Aren't you Elite IAF? Don't you know, like, twenty forms of martial arts?"

"Yes, I'm Elite and, yes, I've been trained in many forms and types of fighting. But I want you to spar with me. Now."

I'd never sparred with anyone as well trained as Ahiga. "Why are you even here? I don't see any other officers in the gym."

"Ahiga and me go way back," Santiago said. "Ran into him last time he was here. Not a lot has changed since then."

"Aside from him being a highly decorated officer and you being a criminal working off a sentence?"

"Eh." He grinned. "Technicalities. But he comes to hang with me. I'm way better than the rest of those stuffy officer types."

Ahiga strode up to the ring and shoved his massive body through the ropes. "Come on."

I glanced around the room and spotted Matthew standing in the doorway. I looked back at Ahiga, and he nodded.

"Don't let him stop you."

"You sure?"

Ahiga stepped closer to me. "Yes." His voice was barely more than a whisper. "If he sees a little about what you are, then I think he might be more forthcoming. We need information."

"Okay." I stepped back from Ahiga. He was big. Probably bigger than anyone I'd ever fought. He'd move slower, but he was trained. So that could come out in a wash.

This could be fun, but dangerous. If I lost control, if I pushed myself too hard, if I gave in to my instincts, my Aunare would show.

"We'll stop before it becomes an issue."

My mouth opened to ask him what he meant, but I knew what he meant. He was thinking the same thing I was, but he was going to stop the fight before I showed too much of my hand to the watching crowd. I wasn't sure if I'd be able to stop myself, but maybe hiding didn't matter anymore. "Okay."

Santiago quickly headed out, and Ahiga made the first move before Santiago was clear of the ring.

My body moved as I anticipated Ahiga, but damn it, he was fast. His fist grazed my cheek, and I spun, kicking my leg out, nailing Ahiga in the stomach.

He caught my foot and twisted.

I moved with it and flipped.

I started to move faster and faster. Watching and anticipating.

My body grew warm, and I felt at home. At peace as our fight became a true dance.

I was lost in the moment and started to really let go.

Ahiga held his arms in the air. "Done!" He yelled as he took five quick steps back and bowed.

I froze. What? Why?

The energy from the fight buzzed under my skin.

Shit.

I quickly squeezed my eyes shut.

Six in. Three out. Three in. Six out. Four in. Eight out. Eight in. Four out. Six in. Three out. Three in. Six out. Four in. Eight out. Eight in. Four out.

"That's it?" Santiago said.

I opened my eyes and looked to the doorway. Matthew lifted his chin a little before turning around.

I shrugged and mouthed "Thank you" to Ahiga.

"That's it." Ahiga's gaze stayed locked with mine.

And in that instant—in that one solid look from Ahiga—the click happened. My gut said to trust him, and I did.

It hadn't happened with Tyler or Audrey yet. Maybe it would still. But I trusted Ahiga with my life. I was lost in the dance of it, seconds away from showing my true nature, and when I would've pushed harder—would've shown everyone in the room how Aunare I could be—he stopped the fight.

Even when trying to keep Matthew's attention. Even while locked in a fight with me. Ahiga had kept me safe.

Just like my mom had kept me safe. Just like Jorge and Roan had kept my secret. Just like I knew that Declan came into my life to help me, even if it'd gone sideways. Ahiga was someone I could count on, and in this place, that meant everything.

He gave me a small, almost imperceptible nod.

"Thank you," I said aloud this time.

Another small nod and he turned, ducking between the ropes, and left the room without another word.

CHAPTER TWENTY-SIX

I SPENT the rest of my day off teaching. At dinner, people looked at me differently. Some with respect. Some with fear. A few with disgust. But I didn't care what anyone thought of me. Not anymore. Teaching again felt right. So I was going with that. And if Ahiga ever wanted to spar again, I was more than ready. It'd been fun to see how far I could push myself before my Aunare side kicked in.

That night I woke up three times with nightmares. The first nightmare was bad enough that I'd rushed to the bathroom, puking up what little food I'd eaten at dinner. The scent of sulfur in my dreams had been so real, so strong...

I felt sorry for waking up my bunkmates, but after my second nightmare, Audrey pushed the bunk next to mine close enough so that she could wake me without getting out of her bed.

I woke up in a cold sweat just before the start of my shift, dreading putting on the suit. I threw up again before breakfast. And again after breakfast. But I showed up at Cargo Bay One on time for my shift.

I was a shaking mess as I pulled the damned replacement suit on and stepped out into the elevator. Tyler almost had to come push me out onto the surface, but I managed to save myself that embarrassment, even if it took all my willpower to do it.

The start of my shift was fine. I sprayed the stupid surface. I wasn't going to let SpaceTech know how much this job was already wearing on me, but then the cooling unit in my suit broke.

I was close to the bay elevator, so no harm was done. Barely more than a sunburn. But my second shift scared me. It meant that this wasn't a fluke. It meant that if I'd been farther away…

The nightmares after that were worse.

I wasn't sleeping and keeping food down was next to impossible. I was surviving on a diet of crumbly bread and electrolyte packets.

The day after that, my suit held up, but I didn't. Audrey said the lack of food was a problem, but all the throwing up was worse. An extreme case of dehydration had me spending the night in the med unit getting fluids.

I didn't earn a sick day for that one, but by the next morning, I felt physically okay. Audrey had given me some meds for sleep through the IV. They gave me a wicked headache, but I didn't have any nightmares. Ahiga was on edge, threatening to send word to my father if one more thing went wrong.

By my third day, I knew I had to be prepared for anything. I loaded up on as much disgusting food as I could swallow and drank more water than I thought possible before checking my suit and heading out.

I was only ten minutes away from my second break when my suit got a crack. I'd never been so terrified. Tyler screamed through my com, yelling that he was coming for me, but I was seven hundred meters from the base. I'd thought the pain with my feet was bad on that first day, but I was wrong.

I ended up with second-degree burns that covered most of my body, and my lungs were toast. Which meant nanos again. A heavier dose this time.

Audrey wasn't sure how I'd made it out alive that day, but I was stubborn. The pain kept me moving. If I hurt, then I was still alive, and I couldn't—wouldn't—let Jason Murtagh get the best of me.

I was given a two-day reprieve after that round of nanos.

The nightmares made it impossible to sleep. I was becoming a shell of myself, and only the gym and teaching helped me get through it.

I sometimes wondered why Jason or one of his goons didn't come after me. I honestly didn't see very many SpaceTech officers. Ahiga had been right about that. They were busy doing their own thing. After that, I came to the realization that they didn't *need* to do anything else to me. They were doing exactly what Jason wanted, and that was torture enough.

It was one thing to face an opponent head-on, but this was something entirely different. All I could do was wait for something else to go wrong and hope that whatever it was wouldn't kill me.

Calling my father was looking better and better, but my rescue meant war, and I felt the weight of so many lives on my shoulders. Why should I be responsible for so many? It didn't seem fair or right, but I wasn't sure anything was fair or right anymore. I wasn't sure how much more I could take.

I was living my days in two-hour chunks, concentrating on surviving to the next break or the end of my shift. The sight of the suit made me sick, and I hated—*hated*—everything about this stupid planet.

Today was Tuesday—day eleven on Abaddon—with only two more days until the mining test—and I was back out on the surface.

Sweat trickled down my face. This was my third two-hour window of the day, and it was nearly over. Only eighteen minutes left. I was watching the clock, waiting for it to tell me that I could go back inside.

I hit the button on my arm, releasing the water spout so I could take a drink. I was going to make it without dehydrating this time.

The hiss of the chemicals hitting the hardened crust was mind-numbing. After my second day on the job, I'd started to hear it every time I closed my eyes.

"How's it going out there?" Tyler's voice came over the com. "Suit looks good."

I gritted my teeth. "Don't jinx it." A lot could happen in eighteen minutes.

"Just stay calm. So I was thinking that I need your help."

"Oh yeah?" I asked, thankful for the distraction. "With what?"

"Audrey won't even entertain the thought of a date with me—" I laughed.

"I know. I know. I can't even take Audrey on a real date here, but I thought if Ahiga could hook me up with—"

The alarm went off, and my heart skipped a beat. It wasn't the dinging of the end of my shift. This was the high-pitched squealing alarm that meant something was wrong with my suit.

"Fuck." I dropped the hose, letting it hang at my hip as I started to run.

Tyler had extra coolant in my suit, so it was only 97 degrees inside it, but the alarm wasn't lying.

"I'm grabbing my suit." Tyler's voice came through my helmet. "What's it saying?"

"E94." The code was flashing on the display inside my helmet. "What does that mean?" It was getting hotter. It didn't take a genius to realize I needed to hustle.

I pushed myself—sprinting for the elevator—but I was a good hundred and fifty meters away.

"The suit has a slow leak. Keep running. You'll make it."

Mother icing shit. Not again.

"I am." But I wasn't going to make it.

My lungs were already starting to hurt from the heat—125 degrees.

I wanted to throw up, but that would slow me down. I was already moving slow enough. The suit and the heat made it hard to move, but I pushed myself to run faster.

I punched buttons on the arm of my suit, trying to stop the

alarm, as I moved toward the elevator. I was about to lose this fucked-up game of chicken Jason was playing with me.

"Tyler!"

"I'm already in the elevator, baby girl. I'm on my way down to get you with a truck. You just hang in there for me."

After my first horrific day on the job, Tyler and Ahiga stayed up all night checking the extra suits that Matthew found to replace my melted one. Apparently, my show in the gym had convinced Matthew to be a little more helpful, but he still wasn't spilling about the weapon.

Still, no matter what they did, something always went wrong. Each part of the suit had too much built-in tech. Diagnostics always checked out, but the suits were remotely monitored. It was now clear that someone was watching me during my shifts and causing the malfunctions.

The temperature was at 127. It was rising two degrees every second.

"I'm burning up! Please tell me you're on the surface."

"Almost."

The steam in the suit was thick and hot. The extra coolant was the only thing keeping me alive, but it was also blinding me. And it wouldn't be long before the coolant would run out and the steam started boiling—cooking my skin.

"I don't know where I am anymore. The fog in here is bad." I was moving, but I didn't know if I was even running in the right direction anymore.

"I can see you just fine. You're heading straight for me. Keep moving." His voice was calm and even. I think he thought if he was calm, I would be, too. But I wasn't calm.

I clawed at my helmet as I ran, hoping I was still heading the right way. "Get me the hell out of here. It's too hot! I can't breathe! I can't fucking breathe!" The coolant had run out. I was screwed.

"You wouldn't be talking to me if you couldn't breathe. Hang on for me. I'm there in three. Two." Strong arms caught me as I started to trip.

I let the weight of my body melt into him as he lifted me up. "Tyler. I can't. I can't. I—"

He hopped onto one of the cargo carts with me on his lap and zoomed off. "We're not far. We'll get you out of that suit in a jiff."

"Hurry. Please. I'm frying."

The tears evaporated before they could roll down my cheek, and for some reason that made me even more upset. I leaned against Tyler, counting my breaths. Wishing I could get out of here. Trying to trust that I'd make it to the cargo bay, but the heat was rising with every second. It felt like fire was licking along every inch of my skin.

The only thing I could see was the temperature readout. It rose another ten degrees, and I could hear my skin crackle as the heat rose.

"I can't keep doing this."

"No. I don't reckon you can. We're going to have to do something about it." He drove the cart onto the elevator. It clanged and moaned with the added weight.

"I'm going to let everyone down if I give up." That's what calling my father was—giving up. Like cheating, and gambling the lives of billions on it. And I hated it. But I didn't want to die. And if I died, my father would start the war, and all those billions of lives would be at risk anyway.

I whimpered as my lips cracked and the coppery taste of blood flooded my mouth.

"You're not giving up! You're a goddamned fighter. We can fix all of this." I knew he was looking at the readout of my vitals in his own helmet.

"You're sweet, but you don't need to lie." My voice came out in a rasp. I breathed in shallow breaths, to take in just enough air to keep me alive, but every inhale was like breathing in embers. "I'm not your responsibility. This isn't your fault."

Tyler started cussing up a storm, but I wasn't paying attention. A wave of nausea rippled through me taking all my focus. "Gonna be sick."

"Shit. Don't puke in the suit. I don't want to clean out another one."

I tried to laugh, but it came out more like a croak. I'd vomited the day I'd gotten overheated and dehydrated. Puking purple electrolyte gel had been an experience I hoped I never relived.

"Swallow it down!" Tyler was trying to make me laugh, but the fear in his voice was real and thick.

The cart jolted under us as we entered the cooling chamber. "Five more seconds and that helmet is coming off."

"I don't think I can make it five seconds." The gray dots merged into one growing black dot as my breathing grew shallow. "Passing..." I tried to fight it, but the black dot was getting bigger. "Out..."

"You do what you need to, and Audrey will do what she needs to save you." I heard the words as if they were far away.

I tried to argue, but I couldn't make my mouth move.

I let the darkness take me and hoped that Audrey would hold off on the stupid nanos, whatever was wrong with me this time. I'd already had enough of those little shits to last me the rest of my life.

But when I heard my breath wheezing, I knew that I wasn't going to be that lucky. Not today.

CHAPTER TWENTY-SEVEN

I CAME AWAKE SCREAMING.

"Maité. Please," Audrey's voice pleaded with me. "You have to stop yelling. There are patients down the hall. They're going to hear you."

I couldn't stop, but I was running out of air. My back arched off the table.

"We gotta hold her down or she's going to fall," Tyler said.

"I don't know where to touch her. She's burned everywhere." Ahiga's voice was sharp and fierce.

The air felt cold around my naked body. "Hurts." I sobbed. "Hurts."

Cold hands pressed against my shoulders and the pain tore another scream from me.

"Just hang in there." Audrey was calm, and I had to trust her. "Focus on my words, Maité. Nanos will be done in a few hours. This is bad, but you can do this. You will survive."

I concentrated on breathing, but I wasn't sure she was right. Not this time.

I glanced at Audrey. My breath came in quick gasps, and I could see the tears pooling in her eyes.

If she was crying, then this was bad.

"Need. Pass. Out." My throat ached with the words.

A tear slipped down her cheek. "Don't fight it. Pass out. I got you."

This time, I didn't fight it.

WHEN I WOKE up the second time, the pain was gone. Audrey was curled in a ball, sleeping on a sheet on the floor beside me. I held the thin sheet that covered my naked body to my chest and sat up.

Audrey jumped to her feet.

I held up my hands. "I'm okay."

"Sorry. I just—" She held a hand over her heart. "It's been a long night. Are you in pain?"

I shook my head. "What day is it?" My chest tightened as I waited for her answer. I hoped I hadn't slept too long.

"Wednesday. It's Wednesday night. You've been here for a day and a half."

Tomorrow was the test.

"Nanos must've burnt off." Audrey's face was pale and dark circles hung low under her eyes, and I knew it was because of me.

"Yep." I couldn't feel them at all, which meant they'd spent all their energy fixing me. It wasn't that I hated nanos—I'd been thankful that they existed since I arrived on Abaddon—but they were so painful.

I wiped my face with my hand, and my skin felt rough. I stared down at my hands. "What's up with my hands?"

Audrey stepped toward me, inspecting them. "Some of the blisters formed calluses. They're not very thick—they probably won't impede your movement or hand control—but I could give you another round of na—"

I pulled my hand away from her. "Don't you dare!"

She smiled. "They don't look perfect. There could be more damage underneath, and if you've got them on your hands, you might have them other places."

"So I won't have silky smooth skin in some spots. Who cares?" If anyone was going to judge me by the texture of my skin, then I wanted nothing to do with them. "How late is it?"

"Late. Tyler left already. We should get going, too. I'd love to sleep on something that's not concrete."

"Sorry. You didn't have to stay."

She grabbed my wrist. "I didn't mean it like that. Even if it wasn't my job, I was happy to stay with you, but let's go get some rest. You're going to need it."

There was a knock on the door and a fraction of a second later, Ahiga slipped inside the room. The concern on his face eased as he saw me sitting up. "How are you?"

"I survived." The pain had been excruciating, but the memory of it would fade—eventually. I hoped the nightmares would, too.

"Good." He grabbed one of the rolling stools and sat down in front of me. "I'm making the call. I'm starting the process of getting you out of here, however your people see fit. I just… I can't sit by and watch you die. The more I've thought about it, the more I realized I should've called already. I made a mistake—"

"No." He couldn't think that. I wouldn't let him. "No, you didn't. We didn't know how bad this job was going to go. And for a few days, nothing happened out there."

"But it was bad this time. You…You dying means war. Us calling means war, but you live. It's a no-brainer at this point."

I swallowed down the failure that I felt. Going out there day after day wasn't helping anyone. It wasn't my failure. I wasn't quitting. I was just leaving a losing game.

"Okay."

"I can only send words—no images or video. That would be too easy to intercept. Is there anything you can think of—any saying or something your dad told you or anything that only you would know about your dad—that could help prove that you're really here and that I'm not trying to trick them."

I thought hard but came up with nothing. I couldn't remember my father. "No. There's nothing."

"That's okay. It was a stretch with you being so young when…" His gaze moved over my body as if to check to make sure I was okay.

I was alive. That was as okay I was going to get right then.

"It might take a day for them to get my message through these channels," Ahiga said. "For it to be authenticated, maybe another day. Hopefully, you're out of here in five. Not as fast as Declan would get it done, but it's better than waiting for him to wake up from cryo."

God. I hated that it came to this.

"When will you know?" Audrey asked. "I'd rather not have any more torture sessions."

"I don't know." There was a twinge of helplessness in his voice, and it killed me to see someone so strong feel that way. It reminded me too much of how I felt.

"Have you found out about the weapon?"

Matthew had come around to our side, but he didn't want to compromise his position. He liked being in-the-know on the base and talking to Ahiga was dangerous for him.

Ahiga shook his head. "No. Even Matt doesn't know what it is, but they transferred more lucole to the lab yesterday. He says they've taken something off site a couple of times in the last week, too. We're assuming it's for testing, but all we know is that lucole goes into the labs and doesn't come out. But he did notice something interesting—a few ships that have left here were later tagged as destroyed."

I didn't like the sound of that.

"Whatever it is, they're testing it, and I don't think it's going well."

That was a win. One we needed, badly. "So it's not ready yet?"

"That's my hope." He paused for a second. "Probably good for you to know that Bay Six and Two are now empty, and half of Bay Seven."

That was fast. "Something tells me that I need to be gone before they've emptied all the bays."

"Sounds like it," Audrey said. "This is coming together fast. What are you going to do?"

"I'm going to keep my plan." I had to stay the course. I didn't have a lot of other options. "The test is tomorrow. I only need to be in the suit for an hour." But even thinking about putting it on again and going back out there made my heart race and my breath short and my stomach feel like it was being tossed and turned.

"You can do it." Ahiga leaned forward until all I could see was his face. "You can do this. You hear me?"

I nodded, blinking back the tears before they could fall.

"I already took care of the tracker I implanted in the courtroom."

The tracker. I'd forgotten. "It's still working?" I never felt any updates. At this point, I figured it was more for show than anything else.

He leaned back from me and waggled his hand in the air. "Eh. More or less." He shrugged, and it didn't fill me with confidence. "It's something that Declan and his friend had been working on. More compatible for your kind, but still syncs with our systems."

"I could take out the chip in your finger," Audrey said. "It's just dead tech right now. Why keep something implanted that you don't need?"

It was a pain to get it, and I'd hated the thing with every fiber of my being, but it'd been such a pain to get it put in... What if I needed it again? "It's fine. I think I've got enough to worry about without thinking about the dead chip."

"Let's focus on the test," Ahiga said. "You pass that, you'll get thrown into training. Usually takes a day or two before you have to do your first run. Maybe more. It could buy us some time to get you out of here without another dose of nanos."

"Okay." I had to make this work. I had to pass the test. Ahiga had managed to get me a copy of a practice test, but it wasn't the version that was given here. So the fact that I did fine on the practice test didn't necessarily mean anything.

"I'll be around. Watching, as always." He pulled me against his chest.

I held onto the sheet with one hand and leaned into him. The fact that Ahiga was hugging me told me how bad it'd gotten. I didn't remember the last time I'd been really hugged hard like this.

"You scared me this time."

I patted his back. "I scared me, too." It was something I didn't want to repeat.

He leaned back. "All else fails, I'm not opposed to stealing a SpaceTech ship and trying to make a run for it."

That was an incredibly dumb idea, and we both knew it. "We wouldn't make it far."

"No. But at least we'd go down with a fight. An honorable death, instead of this shit Jason is pulling."

I almost laughed, but the look on his face was too fierce.

He was out of his mind.

Audrey's eyes were wide, and her face was deathly pale as she looked back and forth between us. "It can't come to that. You... That's just..."

"We'll see." Ahiga stood from his stool and gave my leg a barely there pat. "I'll let you know if there's an update."

"Ahiga?" I asked before he could open the door.

"What?"

"Why are you helping me? Why would you give up your life to help me run?" Stealing a ship from SpaceTech? That was massively insane.

His jaw ticced a few times, and then he let out a long, slow breath. "When you're safely away from here, I'll tell you my story."

"I'll hold you to that."

The door closed behind him, and I looked at Audrey. "Holy shit."

She ran a hand down her face. "Holy shit is right. That was intense. The look he just gave you?"

She was right. The look in Ahiga's eyes was equal parts sorrow, hope, and determination. At least that's what it looked like to me. I wasn't sure I knew him well enough to fully understand him or why he was helping me.

"I'm not going to think about that right now. One thing at a time." I hopped off the table, and my head swam a little. Not wanting to give Audrey any reason to stay here longer than we already had, I shook it off.

Audrey handed me some clothes, and I quickly dressed. I didn't like to stay in the med bay for longer than I had to. I didn't exactly have fond feelings for it.

We were both lost in our own thoughts as we wandered through the hallways, heading up the stairs to our quarters.

"So Tyler left?" I asked after a bit. I needed something to talk about that wasn't so life-or-death or intergalactic war. "You two have a fight?"

She laughed. "Stop trying to play matchmaker. Nothing is happening with us while I'm on this base."

"How much more time do you have?" She'd probably already told me while the nanos were at work, but sometimes it was hard to pay attention to her actual words.

"Three years. Been here a year already."

"Yikes." That was longer than my sentence.

She shrugged. "It's not a bad gig. Plus, I'm here to help you."

"Why not give Tyler a break? At least enjoy the time you have together."

"No." The word left no wiggle room, but I couldn't leave it at that. Not after Tyler had been so awesome to me.

"But—"

"No. I can't." The thread of pain in her voice worried me. "He's done here in a couple months. He'll be back on Earth. He might have a girl back there or he might meet someone when he gets home. Two years of waiting with no contact is a lot to ask. And I don't want to be here pining away. Thinking about what he might be doing. Wondering if he's found someone else. It's hard enough on this base without all that."

"He wouldn't cheat on you." If there was anything I'd learned about Tyler these last few days, it was that he was head over heels for her.

"You don't know that for sure. Neither does he. Life… It takes so many twists and turns. Nothing is guaranteed, and I already care too much. When he leaves, it's going to be tough. I really can't make my stay here any harder than it already is."

"I just want you two to be happy."

She gave me a sad smile. "I don't think that's a real option on Abaddon, but I won't always be here. Maybe once I'm done with my time here, he'll still be single, and we'll see. But not before."

I got what she was saying, but I envied the way that Tyler looked at her. I wished someone felt that way about me. Hell, I wished I felt that way about someone. I'd never had that with anyone—not even Haden—and they were here together for a little while. I hated to see them wasting this time.

"How about you?" Audrey's question shook me free from my thoughts.

"Me?" What was she talking about? "And Tyler? Gross. No."

She stopped walking and bent over. Her shaking breaths were the only indication that she was laughing.

"Well, what the hell did you mean? I'm here talking about you and Tyler, and you ask me that?"

She straightened but held her hands to her stomach as she got control of herself. "No. I meant—" She started laughing again.

I crossed my arms. "Come on. It wasn't that funny."

Audrey wiped her eyes. "It was. You and Tyler. No. Just no."

I rolled my eyes at her. "All right. Cut it out. It's seriously not that funny."

She took a shaky breath. "What I meant was, do you have anyone here or somewhere else?"

I snorted. "Please don't tell me you're one of the people that think I'm with Santiago." At home, everyone assumed Roan and I were a thing. On Abaddon, everyone thought I was with John freaking Santiago. Apparently, it didn't matter where you were, any girl-boy relationship was assumed to be romantic, even if it was anything but.

She shook her head. "No. I don't see you and Santiago together."

"Thank God someone here has half a brain. That's so not happening." No matter what the rumors were. "Why?"

"You don't talk about your life on Earth. I've told you *everything*."

I bumped her shoulder with mine. "Only because you've been talking me through the torture sessions."

"I know, but come on. You have someone back at home. Anyone?"

Declan popped into my head, and I must've been tired because Audrey noticed.

"Aha! I *knew* it. There *is* someone!"

I shook my head. "No. There's no one. Honestly. There was a vague possibility that maybe something might eventually grow into something with this guy I'd just met, but I'm here now. Finding a way out of spending another day in that suit on the surface of Abaddon is all I can care about. I don't know how many times I can burn alive before I lose my mind. I can't even get away from it when I sleep. My nightmares are getting worse and—"

She put her arm around my waist. "You're going to pass the test."

My stomach knotted as we started up the stairs to our quarters. "I have to." There wasn't another option.

"You will. You told me yourself, eleven days ago, that you could do it in your sleep. So do it." She placed her hand on the scanner and waited for the beep before swinging open the door.

Inside, the room was quiet and dark. Everyone was already

asleep. I tiptoed in and stood by my bunk. A shower sounded lovely but might wake everyone up.

I collapsed on my thin mattress and closed my eyes. Tomorrow was everything. It could change my life. Or be the end of any hope I had left.

CHAPTER TWENTY-EIGHT

I FINISHED the last bite of my breakfast and nodded to Ahiga and Santiago. "Later."

Ahiga gave me a long look. I wasn't sure what it meant exactly. To be careful? I was going to do my best. I just hoped that whatever message he'd sent to the Aunare made it.

There was nothing either of us could say to each other, not here, so I got up and walked away.

"*Chica!*" Santiago called before I got to the end of the table.

I raised an eyebrow at him. "What?" I yelled back.

"Be careful out there. Pace yourself. Stronger Together." Santiago had become my big brother on Abaddon, yelling to anyone who would hear him that my job was total bullshit, but he didn't realize there was nothing anyone could do about it. He didn't know that I was going to try to fix this whole mess today.

"Stronger Together," I said back to him and started down the aisle.

"Stay safe!" Someone yelled out, and one of the guys from my classes waved at me. I couldn't remember his name, but he was nice.

"Going to do my best."

I'd taught classes five times so far, and that had gained me some friends. Because I was doing such an unusually shitty job that ended with me at the medic after almost every workday, more and more people seemed to be looking out for me. Or maybe they were just wondering how long I'd survive. I was pretty sure someone on the base was taking bets.

Audrey came out from the kitchen, meeting me halfway to the trash. Ready for her shift, she was wearing a pair of navy scrubs with her hair in a tight bun. The rest of the girls from my bunk were in the kitchen, too. They felt like they could relax back there and not worry about who was coming up behind them, which was totally understandable once I heard some of their stories.

I'd gotten to know a few of the girls, especially Tabitha, the blonde from the gym. She was part of the janitorial crew and was way too sweet to be on Abaddon. Audrey said Tabitha had gotten into trouble a couple times during her shift and came back with bruises and a split lip. There wasn't anything the ladies could do about it though. Aside from the kitchen staff, they were out there alone while they worked.

For better or worse, that wasn't something I had to deal with. No one was going to put on a suit and venture onto Abaddon's surface to harass me, and even if they did, I could take care of myself.

I'd eaten with the women in the kitchen a few times, but I preferred to be in the main room. Aside from the gym, it was the only time I got to see Santiago. He was the highlight of my days on Abaddon. Being with him made me feel like home wasn't so far away. Plus, he cracked me up.

"You ready?" Audrey asked as soon as we entered the hallway.

"I have to be." I wasn't sure how I'd survived the last twelve days, but I'd made it. Today was the day I got off this insane work detail. Sure, I was trading it for suicidal mining duty, but there was no way it was worse than the job that ended nearly every day with me in the med bay.

That mining was safer than my current job still blew me away.

It wasn't that long ago that I was trying to convince Roan how stupid signing up for the mining runs would be, and now I was just praying I could pass the test.

That and the whole not-getting-caught thing.

"If you don't feel ready, you could always wait until next month."

The fact that she thought I could last a month was laughable. "And you think this because I've been doing so well during my shifts?"

I was so drained that I wasn't sure how I was putting one foot in front of the next. My bones felt so heavy that I wondered if they'd turned to metal. I wasn't sleeping. Keeping food down was a real problem. I'd lost more weight than I could afford. And it'd only been twelve days.

No. There was no way I could postpone this. "I'm going to make it work."

"What if you don't pass the test?"

I shook my head. "Not happening."

"But what if?"

"Then I guess I'll have to live long enough to give it another try." But with how my shifts were going, that was a bit of a stretch. "But if something happens to me—"

"I'll be waiting to take care of you." She sighed. "I wish I could do something more."

I swallowed down my nerves. "You can't."

"I could—"

"No. Don't get drawn into something that isn't your fight. You're helping me enough already." She was keeping me alive, even when I sometimes begged her to put me out of my misery. She was strong for me when I wanted to give up, and I owed her my life. I wouldn't have survived without her.

We made our way through the hallways to the cargo bay. Tyler was waiting for us at the front.

"Hey, ladies." A big grin spread across his face as he rubbed his hands together. "You ready for the big day?"

I wished I could share his smile, but with everything going on here I could only drum up a wince. "Ready as I'll ever be."

Audrey pulled me into a hug. "Good luck. Gotta run." She let me go and raced out of the room.

I paused, watching her race down the hall.

That wasn't like her. Usually, she stuck around, flirting with Tyler, before heading to her shift in the med unit. "What's that all about?" I asked Tyler.

"She's just worried for you. Come on," Tyler said. "Let's get you suited up."

My locker had expanded into five, one for each suit. Tyler also had stocked them full of electrolyte packets for my breaks, which usually got me through the end of my shift. After that, I'd head to see Audrey and get on IV until we all headed to dinner. Unless it was a day like yesterday.

I still wore clothes under my suit, even if Tyler thought I was nuts. I wasn't getting naked with all those bots watching. But shoes were a different story. Ever since I burned my feet the first day, I wore the suit without shoes and socks. That way I could be more aware of the heat and hopefully avoid a repeat incident. But this time, I had to leave them on. I'd need them later.

I put one foot in my suit and Tyler came over to lean against the locker.

He put one hand over his mouth like he was scratching his cheek before talking. "You know where you're headed?" he whispered the question.

I didn't glance up. Instead, I squatted down, pretending to mess with the boot. "Cargo Bay Four," I whispered back. "I'll call you on my com, tell you that I'm getting dizzy. You'll tell me to go to four. When I get there, I'll tell Javier that I got turned around and need some water."

"Good. Everyone knows about what's been happening to you. Some even have bets on how long you make it each shift."

I snorted a laugh. I *knew* they were going to be betting on it. I wished someone had at least let me in on it, but they didn't have anything other than desserts to trade around and I wanted none of that.

"I warned the other Cargo Bay Heads to keep an ear out for any alarms going off from our bay. I also spread the word to be on alert in case your suit malfunctions and one of them is closer. They're all good guys and watching out for you in case of something like that."

I slowly stood up, pulling the suit up and over my body as I shoved my arms in it. My hands fumbled with the closure, and a bead of sweat rolled down my cheek, and I looked up at Tyler.

"You need the bucket?"

I swallowed hard. "I don't think so." I didn't like throwing up, but I'd been doing a lot of it lately.

"Okay. This is the last time. You can do it." Tyler straightened. "You ready?"

I quickly closed up the suit, powered it up, and hit the button for my helmet. "Ready as I'll ever be." I grabbed the belt and canister hanging beside the elevator and strapped it on.

"I'll be here if you need me."

My heart raced as I stepped up to the bay's door. Each time I stepped into the elevator, it got harder. My whole body shook as I pushed the green button. Steam rose around me as I was briefly sealed in the cooling chamber. Then I stepped into the elevator to head down.

Fear beat against my brain, making it hard to think about anything else but my suit failing like it always did. The idea of stepping onto the surface again went against every instinct I had, and this time I was going to be walking around the perimeter to the other side of the base.

I'd never gone that far on foot. If I got stranded out there, it'd take precious time for someone to get to me.

If I reached Cargo Bay Four today, I could take the mining test. We knew that someone was watching my suit and Bay One. If I went inside too soon or if I left the bay before my shift was over, that would tell whoever was watching that I was up to something.

I couldn't let them find out until the last possible second. I didn't want anyone to stop me from taking the test, so I had to be sneaky.

I hoped that whoever was watching me was far enough away from Bay Four that they wouldn't get to me until I was already done with the test.

As the elevator reached the surface, I wished I could go under the base. Even if it was more dangerous because of all the cooling systems, it would've been shorter. But there were all kinds of alarms under there, and I couldn't alert anyone to what I was about to do.

The black surface crunched under my feet as I stepped out of the elevator, and I said a little prayer.

Please, God. If there is anyone listening, help me do this.

One foot in front of the other. That's how I went. I sprayed the 320zpd before I stepped anywhere. Slowly but surely making my way around the base.

The shift went by painfully slow. I tried to think that every step away from the safety of Bay One meant that I was one closer to Bay Four. To the test. To my freedom. But I hated this.

Terror made it hard to grip the hose as I sprayed down the hardened lava. I watched for any cracks or sulfur plumes, but there wasn't a damned thing that I could do if my suit failed me again. I was too far away from Tyler.

Walk slow, spray as you go. Over and over in my head I chanted Tyler's words to me from my first day out here. Each minute that passed felt like hours.

"How you doin'?" Tyler's voice came through my helmet for one of his routine check-ins.

"Sweating my ass off as usual."

"You watching the time?"

I wanted to roll my eyes, but I knew he was almost as nervous as I was. The test started in fifteen minutes. It was going to be tight.

"I'm working as fast as I can." I picked up my pace, hoping I made it to Bay Four in time.

"Ain't good to hurry out there."

"I have to." I couldn't miss the test.

"Where are you?"

I came around the side of the base and could finally see the bay door. The elevator was down. Ready. "Feels like the middle of nowhere but—"

The alarm went off in my suit. I froze. My gaze went to the temp panel.

101.

Not bad, but that would change.

105.

108.

I tried not to panic, but the temperature was going up faster than it did yesterday.

I dropped the hose, letting it hang from my hip, and started running.

This wasn't part of the plan.

No. No. No.

"Tyler!" I didn't care about the error code in the suit or wasting precious time trying to figure out why my suit was failing. I had to hurry.

"Alerted Javier. He's putting on his suit. How far are you?"

"I don't know. Not far. Thirty meters. Give or take." It didn't seem like that much, but when the suit failed, it went fast.

112.

I ran as fast as I could. I didn't know this Javier dude. He might be as nice as Tyler said, but he didn't know me. He had no reason to hustle. Especially if he was betting on me.

The visor was starting to fog, but if I just kept moving, I'd get there.

"Baby girl?"

"Yeah?"

"Javier's on the line with us now," Tyler said.

"*Hola, chica,*" Javier said.

"*No me manas*. How far am I from the entrance?" I couldn't see shit now, but I wasn't stopping.

"*Cincuenta pies. Mas o menos.*" I stumbled, and Javier hissed. "*No paras, chica.*"

I didn't need Javier to tell me not to stop. There was literally no chance of that. Especially if I was that close.

115.

117.

"I'm watching you on the monitors," Tyler's voice came through. "Two more steps and you're at the cage."

I stumbled and my knees hit the metal, rattling the cage of the elevator. "Bring me up! Bring me up! Bring me—" The elevator jolted up, and I started counting.

The heat built in my suit, causing the fog to thicken. It was like being in a sauna, and I hated every millisecond of it.

I collapsed, closing my eyes as I breathed fire.

Five more seconds until I was to the cooling chamber.

Four.

Three.

Two.

CHAPTER TWENTY-NINE

I CRAWLED inside the cooling chamber. Then a second later strong arms grabbed me, pulling me into the cargo bay. The alarm was blasting as the bots spewed the coolant. I heard some yelling, and then everything started to quiet down.

I hit the button on my arm, and the helmet retracted.

"*Esta bien, chica?*"

I blinked my eyes open. Javier was leaning over me with his suit half-on and his helmet open. His dark-skinned face was pock-marked, but his eyes were kind.

I took a breath. That had been closer than I wanted, but I was okay. My skin felt hot, but I didn't think I had any burns. At least nothing more than a mild sunburn. No need for nanos. If I'd been even ten more meters away, I wouldn't have—

My heart stuttered in my chest, and I swallowed hard.

"*Chica?*"

"Overheated." My voice was raspy again, but I'd been lucky. So freaking lucky. "I need out of this suit and probably an IV. Help me up?"

He nodded, quickly rising to his feet. He reached a hand down, and I took it. "You just made me a bundle. The wager was high today, but I had you clocking out before your first two-hour block was done."

I wasn't sure how I felt about him betting that I'd be toast so quickly, but he'd just helped me. That meant we were even. "Cool."

I looked around as I started undoing the clasps on the suit. This cargo bay was different than the other one. The containers were different colors—red, yellow, black—and much bigger. More like the haunted shipping containers that lined the old train station back home. And the room was even bigger than Tyler's cargo bay.

"What's in here?" I said as I started to shrug out of the top of my suit.

"Ah. All kinds of things. This half over here is food. Weapons. Medical equipment. The base is a bit of a holding station for a lot of SpaceTech's goods."

That made sense. "And the other half?" I sat down to kick off the boots.

He gave me a look like I was crazy for asking, but answered me anyway. "Lucole."

"Right." Because SpaceTech didn't have more than enough in the other bays, but at least that held up with what Tyler had told me. "There's a lot of stuff in here."

"Enough to supply the colonies for a long while."

Jesus. That was even more than I thought. "I never realized that Abaddon held so much of SpaceTech's assets." This guy seemed to want to spill, and I had about a minute to hear him out.

"Oh yeah. It's important. SpaceTech loses this base, the whole thing goes to shit."

I filed that away as I finished slipping off my suit. "Well, it's a good thing no one is coming up against SpaceTech."

"Only a moron would even try. Those Murtaghs know what the hell they're doing."

I shook my head. He bet against me and was a Murtagh fan? Tyler needed some better friends. "I better get going. Thanks again."

"No worries. *Todo está bien.*"

"Right." Maybe for Javier it was all good, but I was running late. "Mind if I leave this here? It's basically trash now."

"*No preocupes.* Matt's coming by anyhow. I'll give it to him for recycling."

I started to leave, but Javier caught my hand. "What?"

"One second. You're going to need this." I was annoyed as I waited for him to come back, but once I saw what was in his hands, I was glad he'd stopped me.

I took the water tube and electrolyte packet from his hand. "Thank you." I ripped the packet open with my teeth, downed it in one gulp, and chased it with some water.

"No problem. Tyler would be pissed if I let you go without it. Guy's bigger than me, so gotta keep him happy."

I gave Javier a nod and exited the cargo bay, checking my wrist unit as I went. I had two minutes before the test started, and it was two floors up. I started sprinting, and my vision blurred for a second. I twisted open the top of the tube and chugged the water down as I ran.

The door was open. Inside was a small, closet-size room with an old man sitting behind a single desk. It had to be a check-in room. The clock above the desk said I had one minute to spare.

I couldn't believe I'd made it. I was out of breath, but I was there on time. "Maité Martinez. I'd like to take the test."

"You're fifteen seconds late." The old man shook his head at me.

That was total bullshit. "The clock says I'm on time." I pointed behind him.

"My lace says you're late." He didn't even look behind him to check.

No. No fucking way. I wasn't having that. "Please let me take the test."

He leaned back in his chair, clasping his hands over his stomach. "You're late. I can't. That's the rule."

"Even if I was late, which I wasn't, by your count it's fifteen seconds." That barely even qualified as late.

"Getting longer now…" He was weaving his hands through the air, like he was reading something on his lace and not paying attention to me at all.

The image of my fingers wrapping around his neck was vivid enough in my mind that I hardly trusted myself. I crunched the empty water tube in my hand to keep from reaching over the table. "Let me take the test. Please."

He stared me down and I really, really wanted to hit him.

"I won't take up more of your time. You have to sit here during the test time anyway, right?"

He tilted his head to the side.

I hoped this guy ended up in a hell worse than Abaddon. "How many people are taking it?"

"None."

Then what was his problem? "So it won't bother anyone that I start late?"

"It'll bother me. That means I leave here late."

He just made this easy. "Okay. That's fine. I'll take time off the end of the test." When he said nothing, I upped the ante. "I'll finish thirty minutes early."

"You say that now, but you're not going to do that. You're going to need that time." He didn't look convinced, but I didn't care about that.

He wanted to make a deal. I could work with that.

I propped my forearms on the table and leaned forward. "What do you want?" I was desperate, and he knew it.

"You're a woman."

As long as it wasn't anything creepy, I could probably make it work. "I am." But if he thought he was getting any kind of *favors* for this, he was dead wrong. He could go ice himself if that's what he wanted.

"You know the woman in the lunchroom."

Maybe I wasn't his type. "Eh. We're not friends, but I bunk with her. You want a hookup?"

He scrunched up his face, making his wrinkles deepen. "Not like you're thinking. I want extra dessert."

Seriously? This was about the disgusting food? "You can have mine."

His mouth popped open. "Why would you do that?"

I didn't think he'd appreciate that I thought all of the food here was foul and barely edible. And the things they called dessert? They were an affront to all things sweet. "I don't care for sweets."

"Ah. Watching your figure." He gave me a long up-and-down look and the urge to wring his neck was back.

I forced myself to take a second before speaking. Otherwise, I might say something snippy. If dessert was what got me the test, yes. *Yes.* I was watching my figure. "I'll give you all of my desserts for my entire one year sentence." I wasn't going to be here that long, but he didn't have to know that.

He slowly stood from his chair, and I was torn between wanting to pat myself on the back and wanting him to hurry up. "No one's ever passed you know."

"I know."

"So what's a little thing like you doing even trying?" I didn't care for the dismissive tone in his voice and the words he chose, but then again, I didn't like the man at all.

"Does it matter?" Just give me the stupid test already.

He didn't say anything.

I gritted my teeth to keep myself from saying anything rude, but my patience had run out a few minutes ago. "May I just take the test?"

"And you'll finish thirty early?"

This time I rolled my eyes. "Yes. I'll finish early, and you'll get your desserts, but only if we get this rolling *now*."

He finally pushed away from the desk, limping over to a door behind him.

Now I felt guilty for wanting him to hurry up. The table had blocked the poorly fitted prosthetic that stuck out from his shorts. I wondered how he'd gotten it, but that was none of my business. As long as I took the test, the man would get his dessert, and we'd both be happy.

The next room wasn't as big as one of the bays, but it was still pretty sizable. Little ten-foot-in-diameter flight simulation pods took up the room. There were twenty in all.

The man lumbered to the closest one. "In you go."

I didn't hesitate to step into the pod.

He swiped a finger over a panel next to the door. "I'm taking the thirty off the test. You finish before, fine. You don't, lights will come on. That means you're done. Got it."

"Got it. Anything else I should know."

"SpaceTech only allows this test once for workers. You fail, there ain't no second chances."

He started to swing the door shut, and I stopped it with my hand. "What?" Ahiga hadn't said anything about that.

"New rule. Made it about a month ago."

"Why?"

The man looked like he sucked on something sour. "SpaceTech makes the rules. Ask them if you want to know so bad. Time's ticking."

I turned to the pilot's seat and quickly sat as he swung the door shut, sealing me into the pitch-black pod.

A second later the screen lit up. Harness straps came down from the tops of the seat, locking me into place. A keyboard and controls came up from the ground.

"Good morning, Maité Martinez," the AI's voice sounded like a perfectly pleasant English woman. "Today's Mining Proficiency Test will take approximately one hour, thirty minutes. The test covers a variety of subjects and ends with simulation. To pass, you will need to achieve eighty-five percent or better."

I took a breath as the first question popped onto the display. A simple physics question. No problem. There were a few more after that along the same line. Then it switched to music. I had to listen to a sample and find patterns in tones. Each question was timed, and I had to give a quick answer. I went with my gut, and with every answer, felt more and more like a failure. I wasn't sure I'd gotten a single one of them correct.

What the hell did tones have to do with flying a ship? This was so iced. Nothing in the practice tests Ahiga had given me said anything about music or tones or pitch, but I remember him mentioning it in the med bay. I should've asked him more about it.

I kept answering the questions as best I could. Some of them were easy. Others took me a while, and even then, I was sure I got them wrong.

The timer counted down in the bottom right-hand corner of the screen. A cold sweat broke out across my skin, and I felt sick as I thought about what would happen if I failed. If I had to put on the suit again…

This was going worse than I'd thought.

By the time I got to the simulation, an hour had sped by, and I wasn't sure that I should've agreed to give up the thirty minutes. If the flight simulation took a while, I was going to be screwed. I had to at least nail that part of it.

The pod fired up, rocking as it simulated flight. It was much nicer than the ones I'd used on Earth, but it freaked me out a little. There were so many more buttons and features.

I tried to feel prepared for what might come, but there was too much riding on this to be anything but nervous. I had to go through an asteroid field, land on some tricky terrain, take off again—calculating for added weight—but that was it. As the light came on in the pod, the timer still showed I had an extra twenty minutes. Adding in the thirty minutes I'd given up, I was finishing way early. It made me wonder if I'd missed something. Or maybe I bombed it so hard that the test ended early?

Roan was right. I could pass the simulation portion no problem, but he hadn't mentioned anything about the first part of the test. There was no chance I'd passed overall.

The door swung open, and the harness unhooked automatically, releasing back into the seat. "How'd I do?" I asked as I stepped out of the pod.

The old man handed me a piece of paper as he stared at me with furrowed eyebrows. "We don't print much out on paper anymore, but I thought you might want to keep this somewhere you could see it. Maybe in your bunk."

I wiped my hands on my shorts before taking it. "Did I pass?" I asked as I fumbled with it. Stupid shaking hands. I needed this. It was my only shot.

There were some lines and question numbers and a bar graph and percentages for each question on the paper, but none of it was making any sense. I flipped it over, but there was nothing on the back. I couldn't find a total score or percentage. I was exhausted physically from my morning on the job and mentally from the test, and clearly my brain was now kaput.

"I don't understand."

"I don't either." He looked confused as he glanced from the paper back to me.

What? "I meant that I can't tell where my score is."

"Judging from your score, I'd think you could figure it out."

Was he being frustrating on purpose or was that his natural state? "Does that mean I passed?"

He took the paper from me. "See these numbers here?"

I nodded.

"Those are the questions. Overall point values you got are to the right. There'd be marks over here if you didn't get something right. This one here?" He tapped a row on the left. "This is your total marks per question."

"But it's empty. Except for these three."

"Yes."

I skimmed down the paper again. "So you're saying I only got three wrong?"

"Yes. Ninety-two percent."

I felt the grin start from inside me, filling me up. It was like I was suddenly weightless, floating through space, on my way to someplace better.

I wasn't sure how this was possible—I'd guessed on so many of the questions—but this was it. I'd saved myself. I'd bought time. This was everything.

"You said no one ever passes, so how did I score so high?"

"I don't know. I've never even seen anyone pass it. Been here for two years. And you did it fast, too. Time to spare, even with the time I took off the top. I don't know where you got your education, but it's a good one."

I closed my eyes. I'd been homeschooled since I got to Albuquerque. It'd been too dangerous to let me go to school. Jorge helped Mom get the books that she requested, and she pushed me to go beyond the minimum. To learn everything I could.

Thank you, Jorge. Thank you, Mom. You guys just saved my ass big time.

I gave the man a hug, nearly toppling him over. "Thank you!"

He laughed awkwardly and patted me on the back. "I didn't do anything, kid."

I stepped back, holding his shoulders as he got his balance. "You let me take the test even though I was late."

"You'll still need approval from Carl Millander before you can officially transfer. He says no, I still get my dessert."

"Mister, you can have all the dessert you want. I'll even put in a good word with Della for more." Right then that frustrating old fart could ask me for anything, and I'd probably give it to him.

"You'd really—"

A throat cleared, and I turned to find a red-haired SpaceTech officer next to a back entrance to the simulation room. His medals glinted in the light, and the way he was pinching his lips together and narrowing his eyes meant that he was pissed. I didn't recognize him, but I knew this had to be one of Jason's guys.

I spun on my heel and started running. Nothing and no one was going to take this away from me. I might be stuck on this godawful planet for now, but I was fixing this completely shitty situation.

My eyes burned and the smile made my cheeks ache. I wanted to cry because I had real hope.

This was it. This was my break. My big win.

For the first time in what felt like eons, I had hope. I had a real, shiny hope burning deep in my soul, and I wasn't about to let anything or anyone mess that up.

CHAPTER THIRTY

I RACED through the hallways to the med unit so fast that it felt like I was floating in Zero-G. My heart pounded, and it wasn't because I was running. It was because I had hope. Shiny, sparkly, golden hope. Almost enough to wash away the horror of that stupid suit.

The door slammed against the wall as I burst into the med unit. I bent over with my hands on my thighs as I tried to catch my breath. "Audrey?" I said when I had enough air.

"I'm in here!" She poked her head out of an exam room, and I hurried down the hall to her.

"You okay? I heard that your suit..." She paused as I entered the room and closed the door behind me, taking in the way I was breathing and the grin across my face. "Your skin is a little red, but you look fine, aside from that crazy grin. It's kind of freaking me out."

"I did it." I wanted to yell the words but held back. Instead, I held out the paper to her. "I took the test."

She snatched the test results from my hand, scanning it from top to bottom. "I can't... From the way you're practically dancing with joy and that grin, I know you passed, but I have no idea what this says. My medical degree isn't helping me at all right now." She leaned back against the exam table and held the paper out. "Explain."

"That makes me feel better. I couldn't figure it out either." I grabbed it back and explained the scoring system.

"Wait. Are you telling me that you only missed three?"

I nodded, still trying to catch my breath. "Yes." I knew that I could pass the test, but I didn't think I could score this well on it, especially once I was taking the test. That part when I had to pick out the right tone was impossible. The tones played so fast with no option to repeat them. And some of the questions didn't even made sense to me.

She huffed. "Now I'm a little disappointed that you got three wrong. I mean, why not the full hundred percent?"

A surprised laugh slipped past my lips. The giddy was fully bubbling over. "I don't care. All I know is that this is a real shot at me not putting on one of those suits again." This was honestly the best thing that had happened to me in a really long time. Years. I couldn't even remember being this excited about something. Even Declan showing up had been a wash of mixed emotions. Hope that maybe we would get away without ever being caught, disappointment that my father wasn't there, and the anxiety of waiting until we left…

Passing this test was something that I'd achieved on my own. I earned this result. The pride grew inside of me, making me feel like I was about to explode.

Being saved by someone was nice, but being able to save myself, that was a rush.

My skin started to glow, and I didn't care. There were no cameras in here. No one else but me and Audrey. I was giving myself this moment to really feel happy for once.

Acing this test was the first step in truly earning my freedom.

"Congratulations." Audrey pulled me in for a hug for a second before letting me go. "Okay. Okay. You said you'd do it and you did." She let out a breath, trying to calm down. "We gotta get you in to see Carl as soon as possible. He's the one to make it happen for real, and we gotta get it done before Jason finds out about any of this. That means tonight."

The giddy feeling started to drain away along with the glow. "There was some SpaceTech guy that showed up wearing a lot of medals after my test, and it freaked me out."

"Shit."

"I know." It wasn't a done deal. Not yet. But I was determined to make this happen. "Can you message Ahiga?"

She went to the control panel in her wall in the main area. "Done." She turned back to me. "Might as well get you an IV. Tyler told me your suit failed again, which I can see from the rose tint on your skin." She pulled a fluid packet from a drawer under the bed and started placing out her supplies.

"Those suits…" God. I really didn't ever want to put one on again. Just the idea of it made me want to crawl under the exam table and hide. "Thankfully, I wasn't far from Bay Four."

Audrey placed the IV patch on my arm, and I got up to pace.

"The happy smile is gone. You okay?" she asked after a minute.

"Yeah. Just anxious. Every time something good has happened to me recently, something bad follows it. I guess I'm realizing that even if I passed this test, it doesn't mean that anything will change. It doesn't mean that mining won't be hard or just as deadly." My mind started thinking through every possibility, but even if mining was terrible, I honestly didn't think it could be worse than icing down the surface.

But what if it was?

"Don't think that way." Sometimes Audrey surprised me by how well she could read me, but the last couple of weeks had been intense, and she'd been by my side for all of it.

"I'm trying. I want to believe that—"

A knock came at the door, and Audrey opened it. "Thanks for coming so quickly," she said.

Ahiga stepped into the room, closing the door behind him.

"How'd it go?" He looked almost as nervous as I'd felt this morning.

I handed him my test results.

"Hmmm…" He said as he read them.

"You don't understand the results either?"

"No, I understand them fine." He gave me a look with a raised eyebrow. "I just didn't think you'd be able to pull this off."

"Ahiga!" Audrey slapped Ahiga's arm, but her outrage wasn't necessary.

"I wasn't sure I was going to pass either, especially while I was taking it."

Audrey laughed. "Well, you did more than pass. I'll let you two talk while I go tell Tyler the news." She pushed the rolling stool to Ahiga on her way out of the room.

He sat down on the stool and waited for me to talk.

I thought about sitting on the bed, but I was too anxious to be still. "My next step is convincing Carl," I said as soon as the door was shut.

He handed the paper to me. "Come to the officers' bar around twenty-two hundred. He's usually had a few by then, but not too many. I'll leave and swing the door wide. All you have to do is walk in."

"Okay. Any tips on how to convince him?"

Ahiga pressed his lips together for a second. "I bought him a beer couple nights ago, trying to see if I could get him to open up, but he never said a word. He was reading on his implant or playing a game or who knows what. He never even spared me a glance."

That didn't give me a lot of hope for what was coming next. "Thanks for trying." I wondered if I was going to have any better luck getting Carl's attention, but all I could do was try.

"There was an officer—one star, tons of medals, SpaceTech-issue short-cut red hair—that came in after I finished. If Jason doesn't know about it already, he'll know soon enough."

Ahiga's face didn't show any surprise. "We knew this would happen."

"I know. I know." I nervously wrung my hands together as I paced. "But now that I actually passed the test, I need to know that Jason isn't going to mess this up for me."

"There are no guarantees. He could absolutely mess this up."

I finally sat down on the bed. The last of the hope drained out of me. "Don't bother pulling your punches."

"My being overly optimistic won't do you any good." Ahiga crossed his arms as he stared at me. "The guy you described isn't that high up. I don't think he could be the one messing with the suit. He doesn't have the clearance or the knowledge to hack in. There has to be someone else on this base who's working for Jason, but it does give me a few ideas."

I snorted. "Everyone on this base is working for Jason."

"You know what I mean."

He was right. I knew what he meant, but Ahiga's dose of reality was feeling a little too harsh right now. I wanted to stay in my blissful, happy, I-passed-the-test mood, but it'd soured too much. All that was left was nervous energy. I hopped down off the bed and paced over to the wall, resting my head back as I leaned against it.

"I think he's going to be as okay with you doing the mining runs as he was with that mindless lava job."

I tilted my head enough to stare at Ahiga sitting on the stool.

"If killing you in some sort of horrific accident is what he wants, then you've just switched the venue to one you can tolerate a little more."

"Fantastic." But that didn't answer my question. "If anyone can put a stop to this, it's Jason. One word and I'm back out there, icing down the stupid lava when it's a job for bots. So what do I do if that happens?"

"Nothing. You can't do anything about Jason."

That wasn't what I wanted to hear.

"I haven't heard word back from any of your father's people, but I don't expect to until tomorrow or the next day. Once I do, everything will happen fast. Not much longer to wait when you think about it. So stay calm. Focus on getting Carl to approve you for mining. He does that, it buys you two days at least. It might time out perfectly so you don't need to ever step foot on Apollyon or mine a single crystal."

There was a knock on the door, and Audrey slipped back in. "That was fast," I said. "What happened?"

"He's fine. Busy, though, getting more lucole ready for the labs."

I shot a look at Ahiga. "Did you know about this?"

"Matthew warned me. They've apparently made a break-through, but I don't know more than that."

"Apparently they're shipping the weapon out in five days," Audrey said.

Ahiga leaned forward. "How do you know that?"

"Matthew came by while I was with Tyler just now. He's taking stuff up to the labs, and then they're doing their thing to it before shipping it out. He was pretty clear what that meant when he told Tyler."

That was too soon. Especially if it was weapons. "We're running out of time..." I let out a stream of curses as I paced. "What do we do?"

Audrey stepped in front of me, stopping my frantic move-ments. "Can I give you some advice?"

"Sure."

She grabbed my shoulders and gave me a little shake. "Don't worry about any of the shit with the lucole exodus or the weapon."

"How can I ignore that when people could die? When—"

"Stop it." Audrey gave me another sharp shake. "You can't do anything about whatever SpaceTech is doing. You're a worker. That's it. And worrying about all this other crap is just going to distract you. The only thing you need to be thinking about is getting officially transferred to mining duty, and then not *dying* while mining."

I pulled away from her to lean against the wall again, banging the back of my head against it a few times. "I don't know if I can ignore it."

"And what can you do about it?"

I closed my eyes. "Nothing." Absolutely nothing. There wasn't a goddamned thing I could do about any of this, but it still felt like it was my responsibility somehow. I was here. There had to be something I could do...

"Listen to her." Ahiga's sharp tone had me opening my eyes. "Whether you know it or not, your spirit—watching what you've been going through the last thirteen days—has affected just about every person on this base. The ripple you're causing is having a bigger impact than you can see. So you keep kicking ass. You keep fighting and surviving, and trust that I'm doing everything I can on my end about the rest of it."

I didn't know what to say to that, so I just watched him.

He got up and cracked open the door. "Twenty-two hundred. I'll get you into the bar. I'm going to send another goddamned message. See if I can hurry things along somehow."

I nodded. "I'll be there."

"Come on," Audrey said. "Let's go get you some food."

I made a face. "It's between mealtimes. It'll be disgusting."

Audrey scrunched up her nose. "Sure, but it'll be calories. Which you need. I bet Della will sneak you some dessert."

I gagged. "That stuff isn't dessert. It's toxic." As was everything on Abaddon.

Audrey pulled me into the hallway with a laugh. "So dramatic. You make it sound like you've almost died a few times."

I elbowed her, and she laughed harder. Audrey's joke might not have been enough to make me laugh, but it was enough that I smiled. If there was one bright spot out of all of this, it was Audrey.

CHAPTER THIRTY-ONE

THAT NIGHT, I waited just down the hall from the bar. I didn't want to be too close, but I didn't want to miss Ahiga either. I leaned against the wall, tapping my fingers on my leg. The cameras were watching me, but no one had come to tell me to move. I wasn't doing anything wrong by being in the hallway. At least not yet.

Audrey thought I should dress sexy for this, but I didn't agree with her, and I definitely didn't want to wear the tiny biker shorts and tank that I used for under my suit. Instead, I'd borrowed a pair of her navy scrubs. They felt like the more professional option, even rolled at the top to keep them from dragging on the floor.

The way Carl had been described to me I didn't think he'd care about what I was wearing or anything I had to say.

Getting him to hear me out was going to be my biggest challenge. I didn't have much of a plan for how to do that, which made me nervous. I liked a good plan, with a handful of backup plans, but Abaddon left me with almost no options.

My wrist unit went off—thirty seconds until twenty-two hundred—and I started down the hallway. The door to the bar opened as soon as I reached it. Ahiga exited without sparing me a glance.

It was a little obvious, but Ahiga knew as well as I did that we weren't lasting much longer here. SpaceTech had to be wondering why he kept going to the med bay whenever I was there.

Inside, the bar was packed. I expected it to smell like cheap beer and sweat, and that's exactly what it smelled like. Nearly everyone in there wore navy and gray SpaceTech uniforms of some sort—camo, athletic wear, and a few more formal guys in gray button-downs and navy slacks.

I kept my head down as I moved through the room. I wasn't sure what this Carl would look like, only that he was old and sat alone. Which actually helped a lot, because most of the guys in here were young and gathered around tables, playing cards or shooting the shit loudly with each other.

I finally spotted Carl off to the side. As expected, he was at a table by himself, flicking his fingers in the air. His solid white hair made him stick out from all the decades-younger officers in the bar. He was hunched over a pint, not paying attention to any of the noise around him. Instead, focusing on whatever his implant was showing him.

I wondered what he was watching. Did a guy like him still care about the news? Or was he playing a game to take his mind off of the job he hated?

I took a second to gather up my courage, and then made my way to his table. I pulled out the chair across from him, and he barely spared me a glance.

This was already going so well. "Hello."

"Go somewhere else." His face was lined with wrinkles, highlighted by the intense scowl he was giving me.

Okay. So he was grumpy. At least that bit of info was accurate. "I came to talk to you. I have something you might find interesting." I pulled out the test score paper, sliding it across the table to him.

"You don't have anything I want to see." He pushed it back to me.

I slid it back at him. "Please. Just give me a chance. I need—"

"You don't *need* anything from me." He leaned forward. "No one with half a brain would even take that damned test. The fact that you did shows me you're stupider than most. Or maybe just gullible as all hell." He crumpled the paper in his fist and threw it at me.

I barely managed to catch the wadded up paper before it smacked me in the face.

"I'm saving your life here. You can thank me or not. I don't really give a shit."

I wanted to be annoyed and frustrated, but I couldn't be. Carl had a good point—I'd said almost the same thing to Roan a million times—but this was my best shot at survival. It was pathetic that this was what my life had come to. I knew that, but I was desperate. I wouldn't take no from him.

I took the crumpled-up paper and smoothed it down on the table, leaving it between Carl and me. "I won't survive the work detail that I'm on. I don't know if you've heard the rumors, but I'm the one on ice-down duty on the planet's surface. I've nearly died every day I've been out there and, trust me, if I stay out there, I *will* die. I've been denied transfers multiple times already. You're my one shot at living."

He finally looked at me.

"I need the mining gig. I need it badly, and quickly. The odds are much better for me doing twenty runs, than lasting another week out there on the surface."

He sat there, quietly considering me. He took a slow breath, which made me think that I was getting through to him, even though the expression on his face hadn't changed. It was something.

"Just look at my scores, please. I know I can do this, and even if I can't, blowing up on the moon is better than slowly boiling to death out there. It would be a mercy."

He pressed his lips together and started shaking his head.

I wasn't sure what else I could say, but I had to say something. I was desperate. I had to make Carl accept me as a miner. "I don't know what you need to hear, but I—"

A large beast of a man sat in the chair next to me and wrapped his arm around my shoulders. "Looky what I found. A girl. In our bar. From the work crew." He squeezed me against his sweaty body. "Whose dick did you suck to get in here?"

Calm. I had to stay calm. Even if I wanted to rip the man's arm from his socket.

My skin buzzed with fury.

Six in. Three out. Three in. Six out. "Please, move your arm."

"Don't be that way." He squeezed me tighter. "Come on. Play nice."

Carl's gaze locked with mine and he leaned back in his chair. He wasn't going to do anything, but he was watching how I would handle this.

I wasn't sure what he was looking for. If I somehow managed to defuse the situation maybe that would make me look like I was good in a crisis, which would help if anything went wrong while I was on a run.

Or maybe he was trying to see how tough I was. He could be wondering to himself if I could take this asshole down.

I could, and I wanted to, but something told me that might not be the best tactic.

"I'm going to ask you one more time. Please, let me go. I don't want any trouble."

The asshole stank of booze as he leaned against me, running his nose up my cheek before licking my face. "Come on, honey. Let's go somewhere quiet."

Okay. I was done with this asshole. He wasn't going to let me go no matter how nicely I asked, which meant I was going to have to use force.

I didn't take my eyes off Carl as I spoke. "I have to take care of this, but please don't hold it against me."

Carl's eyes widened a little bit, and he gave me a small nod.

"Thanks. I appreciate your understanding."

I slammed my elbow into the asshole's stomach. His grip loosened as he tried to get some air in. I stood up, grabbed his head, and slammed it into the table. I gave him a little nudge, and he fell to the floor, unconscious.

I brushed off my hands on my pants and started to sit again. "I really need—"

"What the fuck." Some guy was crouched over Asshole's unconscious body. He stood up, staring at me, and stepped toward me.

I ignored him. "I really need this job. The thing is—"

Asshole's BFF grabbed my arm, pulling me out of my chair and into his body.

I kept my eyes on Carl. "Excuse me. I'll just be one more second."

I darted out of the way just before the BFF punched me in the face. "Are you sure you want to do this?"

He snarled and came at me again.

I punched him in the face, and he dropped to the ground. I stared at him for a second as he held his nose, but he didn't get back up. Pathetic.

I started to turn back to Carl, but silence gripped the room.

Trouble. This was trouble.

Then there was cursing. Some even called me a few inappropriate names. Chairs scraped against the floor as men got up from their tables. They clearly hadn't heard about the lessons I'd been giving everyone or about my sparring with Ahiga.

I rolled my eyes and held out a finger—asking Carl to wait again—before I turned to the room.

Everyone was now on their feet staring at me. "This one decided to lick my face," I said, pointing to Asshole. "This one tried to defend him." I pointed to Asshole's BFF. "I'm not here for trouble, but I don't enjoy being manhandled."

"Fuck that," someone muttered.

I shook out my arms, relaxing my muscles. "If you want to try me, please do. It would be my pleasure." I'd been training people on my day off and after the shifts when I didn't end up needing nanos, but training and sparring were different than an all-out fight. I wouldn't have to go easy on these men. That had me grinning like it was Christmas.

This was going to be fun.

The first guy started at me, and from then on, time was a blur of fists and blocks.

Two came at me at once, but I dropped down, sliding on the floor between them, and grabbed their ankles and twisted. Bones and tendons snapped.

I kipped up and kept going, one after another after another. One move to the next. Like each opponent was a piece in a larger game.

A man came at me with a bottle. I caught his arm as he swung it at me, spinning myself into his body. I elbowed him in the stomach as I wrenched the bottle out of his grasp and kicked him square in the nuts.

Another grabbed at me, and I swung the bottle at his head. The glass broke as he crumpled to the ground.

The sound of glass breaking seemed to mark a pause in the fighting. I was now holding a weapon, and no one seemed confident enough to come at me anymore. They were all looking around at each other, trying to figure out what everyone else was going to do before acting.

That was lame.

I backflipped, putting some extra power into it. I flew high in the air, landing on the top of the table behind me. "This has been fun! Thanks so much for showing me a good time." I gave them a killer smile. "But if we're done, then I'd love to finish my conversation with Carl." I jerked my thumb behind me. I was a little disoriented, but I was pretty sure he was still at his table sitting behind me somewhere.

The door in the back of the room opened, and I saw Ahiga step through.

He took one look around the room and then stared up at me. "What the *everlovingfuck* is going on here!?"

I spun the neck of the bottle in my hand. "These guys wanted to play." I smiled innocently. "I just don't think we were on the same page about what kind of play I was up for."

The men started yelling all at once. Out of the corner of my eye, I saw one about to pounce on me, but Ahiga's whistle cut through the din.

"Leave the lady alone! That's an order! And clean this place up!"

All but one hopped to Ahiga's orders. I turned to look at him square on. He stood there for a good minute—a look of disgust on his face—before spinning on his heel and leaving the bar.

Five feet ten. Two hundred pounds. Muddy brown hair. Weaselly eyes that were placed far too close together. I'd bet good money that guy was friends with the redhead from earlier.

There wasn't anything I could do about that now, but I would ask Ahiga about him later. I had more immediate things to take care of at the moment.

I jumped down from the table and walked to Carl. He was still sitting there, calmly drinking his pint as he watched me, apparently not bothered at all by the brawl.

My chair had been knocked to the floor at some point, so I bent to pick it up, and then sat in it, saying nothing.

I wasn't out of breath or even sweating much, but I'd said enough already. It was Carl's turn to talk. The paper with my test scores was still on the table in front of him, but as far as I knew he hadn't looked at it.

"That was some show," he said after a moment.

I nodded. It wasn't clear from the way he said it if he meant that as a compliment or not, so I kept my mouth shut.

He leaned forward, whispering. "I know."

I swallowed. I didn't dare say anything. Not with so many ears around, and even though I needed Carl's acceptance, I didn't trust him. Not with confirmation of what he believed I was.

He leaned back in his chair again. "I haven't seen fighting like that since… Well, it's been a while. I had a friend once who was good, but he wasn't as good as you."

I hadn't trained with another Aunare since I was six. I wasn't sure how I'd measure up so *that* I took as a compliment. "Thank you."

"Most people look tired after a battle like that, but you took down damned near twenty IAF, and you look like you're ready to take on a hundred more."

He was right. The fight made my blood sing with energy. It made me feel like I could run ten marathons and not feel it. And despite the violence, it made me feel at peace.

Carl nodded and, finally—after all the craziness—took the paper off the table. His low grunt as he looked it over and quietly folded it, handing it back to me, made my heart race.

He stared at me again, and I waited. It felt like we sat there for hours but was probably only a few minutes at most.

"Okay," he said finally. "You chicken out or wash out, that's it. No second chances. You're back to your old duty. But you want to try this stupidity, far be it from me to stop you. Especially with the shit job you've had so far."

A weight lifted off me, and I could finally breathe again.

I wasn't going to chicken out. This was my shot. I wasn't going to mess it up.

"Meet me in 12WA. Oh-six hundred sharp. Don't be late."

"I won't be." I stood and gave him a nod before stepping over a few guys to get to the door.

As soon as I got to the hallway, I took off running back to my bunk.

My plan had come together. Ahiga had been right. Two days. Everything was coming to a head, and I wasn't going to have to go back out on the planet's surface.

With any luck, I'd be off this godforsaken planet before Jason Murtagh knew what happened.

Hope bloomed brighter in my chest, and I planned to hang onto it for as long as I could.

CHAPTER THIRTY-TWO

MY WRIST UNIT helped me find 12WA after my early breakfast. News had traveled fast on the base about my run-in at the officers' bar, thanks to the bartender. Everyone knew that I'd moved to mining duty, and now the betting had taken a new turn. How many runs would I get in before blowing myself up? How much crystal would I haul in on my first run? Would I quit an hour in?

Their bets didn't bother me. I was trading one danger for another, but I wasn't mining on my first day. Ahiga said to expect a couple days of training, and that meant today wasn't going to be dangerous. But I stood outside of room 12WA and wondered what training would mean exactly.

I stared at the keypad next to the door for a while. No one had told me that I could go into the previously restricted areas—there hadn't been any alerts or updates on my wrist unit—but that didn't mean I needed to knock. Not that it necessarily meant anything bad if I couldn't open the door, but it felt like the beginning to my way out if it opened.

I blew out a heavy breath. It was just a freaking door, and I wouldn't know if I could open it unless I tried.

I pressed my hand against the black pad and got a sharp buzz of energy. A second later, there was a beep. I jumped back and dropped my hand before I realized that the beep was the door unlocking. I tried the knob, and it turned.

Here goes everything...

I stepped into the room and was a little confused. There were rows of desks in a semicircle. The front of the room was a blank vidscreen. It was a classroom?

Carl sat in a chair at the front of it, snoring away. Aside from him, the room was empty.

I walked down the stairs, not worrying about being too loud. I made my footfalls a little heavier than usual, hoping that would wake him up for me. But as I made my way to stand in front of his chair, he just kept on snoring.

Oh man. If I woke Carl up, he could get pissed. To do anything to piss off the man who held my fate in his hands was idiotic. He'd accepted my transfer when no one else would. He figured out I was Aunare, yet hadn't turned me in. And if I was going to survive my mining runs, then it'd be because of his knowledge. Pissing him off—

Another loud snore ripped through the room, and I knew I was going to have to do something more to wake him up. I needed whatever training he could give me too badly to waste time.

"Carl?" I whispered.

Nothing.

"Carl?" I said a little louder.

Nothing.

"Carl!" I expected him to jump at my yell, but he just sat there. Another snore ripped through the room.

Clearly, noise wasn't going to wake him up. I reached out and touched his shoulder. As soon as my fingertips made contact, he grabbed my hand and pulled me toward him as he punched.

I ducked, narrowly missing a fist to my face. "Carl! It's Maité Martinez. It's oh-six-hundred," I said as I broke his grip.

He jumped out of his chair, knocking it to the floor with a bang.

He was still coming at me, but his eyes weren't seeing me. They didn't look focused.

"Hey! Wake up!" I yelled as I continued to block his hits. I didn't want to hurt him, but I wasn't about to let him hurt me either.

After a few seconds, his movements slowed, and then stopped altogether. I kept up my guard as I watched him hunch over, catching his breath. It took him a moment, but eventually he stood upright and nodded at me.

"Sorry about that. Didn't mean to fall asleep." He rubbed his fists roughly into his eyes as if he could wipe away whatever he was seeing. "PTSD can be a real bitch."

I'd heard about it but had never seen it in action. I wondered what had happened to make him wake up like that, but it wasn't any of my business. "Not a problem." He rubbed his forehead as he stared at the ground, and I felt like I should change the subject.

I spread my arms wide. "So, what is this?"

He put his hands on his hips and surveyed the room as if reminding himself where he was and what he was supposed to be doing.

"We're in one of the officers' meeting rooms," he said after a minute. "I like to prepare people as much as possible, and the screen helps." He motioned to one of the desks. "Sit. Then we can go over what you need to know to survive mining on Abaddon's moon, Apollyon."

I moved around the desk and sat down, more curious than anything. This was going to be the first time I flew a ship anywhere, and even if it was dangerous, I was excited to learn something new.

"Do you know the history of the lucole mine?"

I shook my head. "No. Not really."

He tapped a few fingers in a sequence in the air, and the vidscreen behind him came to life. "This is the mine." He jerked his thumb toward the giant hole in the surface of the moon.

"Huh." It wasn't at all what I expected.

"What?"

"I pictured a cave." But it wasn't a cave. It looked like terraces cut into the surface of the moon. The hole spiraled, each terrace a little smaller circle than the one above it until it got to some watery looking stuff at the bottom.

"Lotta different types of mining out there. This is open-pit. Each ring that spirals down strips off another layer of lucole. The pit widens until the top ring has no more lucole, then we expand the bottom ones until it's all cleared out. Only a few spots on Apollyon have the crystal, and we've got five fully excavated mines. This is the sixth. We're currently looking to see if there are any more spots ready for mining."

And if there weren't? SpaceTech had a massive stockpile, but if the crystal on the moon was finite, then what were they going to do when it ran out?

No wonder they wanted the Aunare's tech so badly. They needed something more sustainable, especially if they ended up burning through a lot of lucole in war.

Focus. I had to focus. That wasn't my problem. At least not right now. "How wide is the mine?" There wasn't anything I could see from the image to help me understand the scale of the mine. It could be five meters wide or five hundred, and I wouldn't know.

"About three hundred seventy kilometers."

"*Kilometers*." That was massive. "How big are the others?"

"They average nearly seven hundred kilometers and about that deep all told."

"Shit." Mining out seven hundred kilometers of crystals seemed like a lot, maybe even more than what the bays could hold. "I've been working in Bay One, and it's at capacity. When I got here, most of the other bays were at capacity, too. It seems like SpaceTech should have enough lucole by now. Does SpaceTech even really need to be mining anymore?"

"What's enough?" He shrugged. "There's plenty, but Space-Tech plans to mine this moon until they've got every last crumb of lucole. We store most of it here on the base because they can't use up all this. Not in a couple centuries, even accounting for growth." He paused and stared off at nothing. For a second, I thought he was waiting for any questions from me, but he just kept staring.

A second later, he swiped a finger through the air and kept right on going like nothing had happened.

"Twenty years ago, bots did this job, but it was too costly to keep replacing those that got blown up. So SpaceTech found volunteers."

"Wait. I thought that it took something special from me—or any human—to get the lucole."

"Eh. It's all iffy ethics. A bot can do this, but humans are cheaper." He shrugged that off like it was nothing.

"Iffy ethics is right." I couldn't keep the disgust from my voice. "But maybe I'm bitter because I've already been risking my life doing a job a bot could do."

"SpaceTech at its finest." He looked back at the image of the mine behind him. "But mining the lucole correctly is tricky. Humans have a much better success rate, probably because they value their lives more than a bot controlled by SpaceTech's greed does." He swiped his finger, and the image was now a close-up of the mine. Crystal shards stuck out from the rings carved into the ground.

"Bots ensured no loss of human life, but two billion dollars per robot cut heavily into the bottom line. Especially when they started blowing up faster than they could be replaced. SpaceTech figured if they offered up a high salary, enough desperate people would show up. They were right. The trick is not to get blown up."

"So how do I train for that?"

He tapped his finger, and the image of the mine shifted to a video. It was a compilation of people mining. The miner would tap the crystal with a hammer. Sometimes it was once, and sometimes it was three times. Then he'd either move on or flip the hammer around to use the tiny pickaxe on the other end. They'd carefully tap around the base of the crystal with the axe, while holding onto the crystal with their other hand, chipping until the crystal came free.

It seemed pretty straightforward. I didn't get why a bot had so much trouble doing this.

"The first tap will tell you a lot." He paused the video, rewinding for a second before it started again. "See here." The person tapped once with the hammer side of the tool. "Each bit of rock emits a special frequency—a tone. Tapping the crystal—firmly, yet gently—emits it. Only those with the correct frequency will work for SpaceTech's purposes. The rest? They're unstable." He walked to the side of the room and grabbed a box.

Maybe the test wasn't so random after all. "This is why the test had questions about tones?"

He started walking back to me. "Exactly. I added that. Tone-deaf people can't do this job. Too damned dangerous for them to even try." Something rattled inside the box as he set it on the table in front of me.

I wasn't tone deaf, and being Aunare meant that I knew all different kinds of frequencies, so I *should* be okay, but... "How will I know which crystals have the right tone?"

"The crystals have four specific classifications of tones: neutral, first ring, second ring, and explosive. You have two taps to decide if it's harvestable or not. If it's harvestable, a third tap will make it neutral again. If not, the third tap will make it explode."

That was definitely something I wanted to avoid. "Is that why the miner in the video sometimes only hit it once?"

"Yes. Good observation. Harvestable crystals go through three safe stages: the first ring has a loud, medium-toned hum that makes it *active*. The second ring has a softer, medium-toned hum, which makes it *less active*. Then it goes back to neutral with the third tap, which sounds like hitting a normal rock. Nothing special."

That sounded easy enough to get. "What about the unharvestable ones?"

"They go through *two* safe stages, but they're never neutral.

Their pitch can also vary. They either start out a soft, very high-pitched hum, then get louder and higher-pitched with each tap until they explode. Or they start out at a soft, very low-pitched hum, then get louder and lower-pitched until they explode. The important thing to remember is that with an unharvestable crystal, it starts out as neutral before it's ever touched, but one tap activates it. The second tap makes it even more active—which is the opposite of a harvestable crystal. So, if you hit a crystal and it gets *louder* the second time, then the third tap will make it explode."

"How can I be sure if a crystal is harvestable or not?"

He tapped the box. "Going to show you here once you're done with the questions."

I ran my hands down my face as I tried to think. I definitely had more questions. I needed to find out everything I could before mining. "Do you have to make it neutral to harvest it? Can you just hit it the one time and then take it?"

"No. If you don't hit it three times, then it won't come free from the surrounding bedrock."

I suddenly got why he added all those music questions to the test. If a miner wasn't paying close attention to the pitch or tone of the crystal, then they might easily mistake it as harvestable and blow themselves up. Add in a bit of desperation and nerves, and it was easy to see why so many miners didn't make it.

"Anything else?" Carl asked.

I wasn't sure what questions I had. It all seemed confusing to me, but maybe I'd understand once I started doing it. "What should I know that you haven't told me yet?"

"Ah. No one's ever asked me that." He scratched his cheek as he thought. "Okay. Here's something. Be careful how many unharvestable crystals you tap twice."

"Why?"

"You *can* hit a bad crystal two times, but I advise against it. You really need to know with that first hit. But, if you hit it a second time and it gets louder, walk away. That's fine. You made a mistake. But you don't want to do that too many times in the same area."

"Why not?" I wished I had something to take notes on, but instead, I rubbed my temples, hoping that all the information would somehow stick.

"Because if you make a mistake and one crystal blows up, but the surrounding unharvestable crystals have only been hit one time, you might not die. Only that single crystal you hit three times will explode. You might lose a limb or get a few bruises or a concussion, but you'd have a chance at surviving the blast." He pressed his hands down on the table in front of me. "But if one crystal blows up *and* you've left a bunch of them very active—meaning *two taps*—it'll set off a powerful chain reaction. I've seen a guy leave four crystals double-tapped and when he third-tapped one…" Carl shook his head and looked back at the vidscreen. "They didn't bother to dig his body out of the avalanche."

I sucked in a quick breath.

"So, unless you *know* without a doubt that it's harvestable, don't you dare hit any crystal a second time."

"Okay. I won't." I had one hit to know if a crystal was harvestable or not. That was a lot of pressure.

"Once an unharvestable crystal is activated, it'll take about a day for it to go back to normal from *one* tap. It'll stay *very active* for a few days when it's hit *twice*. No one's been out there in weeks. So everything in that mine is—as of this moment—neutral."

"That's good to know." At least I was starting with a clean slate out there.

"Good. A while back I started giving miners special markers to note which crystals are unharvestable crystals. Put the number one on any that you hit once. The number two on any that you hit twice. If you have twos, you keep them well spaced apart. Just in case. And you can use the marks from previous miners as a bit of a guide. Sometimes the crystals become harvestable later, so it's always good to check, but if you think it might be a volatile crystal and it already has a mark on it, don't hit it again."

I nodded. "Okay."

"Any more questions?"

My mind was trying to keep up with all the information that he'd given me. "I'm sure I will later, but I think I'm just trying to process what you're telling me. I really need to grasp this before I go out there."

"Of course." He patted the top of the box. "I have a bunch of harvested neutral crystals here that you can tap all day if you want. Every crystal sounds a little different, but you'll get a feel for them. After that, we'll do some simulations of unharvestable ones. You'll get a feel for those tones, too. Then we'll do simulations with a mix of crystal types so that you get used to making a choice. We won't leave here today until you've got it. Your first run's tomorrow."

All the air whooshed out of me with his last statement. "Tomorrow?" That seemed too soon. "I thought I'd have more training."

"Usually, it's a couple days of training, then a readiness assessment, and then once you pass that, it'd be time for a first run. But the order is for you to get an accelerated version. It's bullshit, but most of SpaceTech is." He gave me a hard look. "Especially when it comes to *you*."

Right. I wasn't their average volunteer. I gave myself a second to come to terms with that and then soldiered on. "Okay. Tell me everything I need to know."

CHAPTER THIRTY-THREE

AFTER A COUPLE HOURS of Carl and his theories on how to stay alive, my brain was filled to the brim and then some. He was starting to give me a theory about how he thought the crystals might actually be living beings—which was making me question his sanity—when someone knocked on the door.

Carl turned toward the sound. "Come in."

Ahiga entered. "I need to speak with Ms. Martinez."

Carl waved him forward. "Go ahead."

"Alone."

Carl swiped a finger through the air, most likely checking the time. "I guess it's time for a break anyhow. I have some other work to prepare for tomorrow. Meet me back here at thirteen hundred."

I nodded. "I'll be here."

As soon as the door closed behind Carl, I turned to Ahiga as he walked down the stairs to the front of the room.

He always looked serious, but right then the stiffness in his shoulders made me think something awful was about to happen. "What's going on? Did you hear something?"

"Not yet, but I have someone that wants to talk to you." He

made a few motions with his finger, and the screen that had been displaying some frequency charts went black.

I had a second to wonder who it could be before Declan appeared on the screen.

"Maité?" Declan asked.

I leaned back in my chair as I blinked, trying to believe that it was him. He was really there on the screen. I—I couldn't believe it.

"Hi." It was lame, but I didn't have any words. Seeing his face meant that maybe I was going to be okay. Like, really okay. "Is this line secure?"

"Yes," Ahiga said as he walked down the row toward me. "This room is for IAF meetings, and therefore not monitored. We've found that people don't speak up when they know everything is being recorded and could be used against them."

Declan leaned closer to the camera, making his face take up the whole screen. "Why in the *hell* are you on mining runs?" He didn't raise his voice, but he might as well have. He was really pissed.

"Declan—" Ahiga started, but I shut him up with a glance.

"You haven't told him?" I asked Ahiga.

"No, and from this reaction, I don't think he's caught up on any of my messages either." Ahiga leaned against the desk behind me. His matter-of-fact tone told me that he was waiting for me to drop the bomb on Declan. "He woke up, called me, and asked for you first thing. Barely even said hello to me."

I closed my eyes, trying to calm down, but no. Declan didn't get to be pissed about me switching to mining runs. Not after everything I'd been through.

I turned back to the vidscreen. "You told me to survive. This is me surviving."

"Mining is dangerous, and—"

"No. It's actually *less* dangerous than what I was doing *before*." I huffed. "At least if I die now, it'll be because of a choice I made." My tone was vicious, but I was past giving a shit.

"Ahiga's right. I just woke up from cryo." His voice was barely a whisper now. "I left Earth two weeks after you did, meaning I went into cryo just as you were waking up. I ensured your job was set. Kitchen duty. I *triple* checked before I went to sleep. But the first alert I saw when I woke up was your transfer to mining this morning."

"I wasn't on kitchen duty." I didn't like sounding bitter, but I couldn't hold it in. "Did you look at what I transferred from?"

"No…" He drew the word out and began swiping his finger in the air.

I relaxed back in my chair, crossing my arms as I waited. Declan was about to flip his lid.

"Your brother decommissioned all the bots that sprayed 320zpd on the surface around the base."

Ahiga pulled out the chair next to me and sat. "She was out there on the surface six hours a day, and her suits kept failing. I don't have to tell you how bad it got. I'm sure the videos are archived on the SpaceTech database."

Declan's face was pale as he swiped a hand across his forehead. "Jesus. I don't think I can watch them. I don't…" He met my gaze. "How are you alive?"

"Nanos." My voice was heavy with every ounce of disgust I had for those parasites.

"You can't have nanos! You're—" He leaned closer, his face turning red. "Why didn't you do anything to help her, Ahiga?"

"Are you fucking kidding me?" Ahiga's voice was filled with freezing calmness as he slowly rose from his char and leaned over the desk. "I asked, bartered, begged, and blackmailed to try and get her switched. Nothing worked. My cover's pretty much blown at this point. I've been sending you messages, but two days ago, I had enough. I sent a message to her family. This is over. She's not suffering anymore."

I patted Ahiga's arm, and he looked down at me, the fire of his anger still burning in his eyes. "Ahiga did everything he could to help me. We even talked about stealing a ship and making a run for it, but—"

"How did this go so fucking wrong?" Declan put his head in

his hands. "You were supposed to be washing dishes in the kitchen." He looked up at me. "In. The. *Motherfucking. Kitchen.*"

"No. Your brother made sure I wasn't washing dishes."

"I…" He stood up so fast his chair crashed to the ground. He leaned over the desk, head hung down. When he looked up at me, his face was filled with pure rage. "I would've been on the same ship as you, except I needed to get your mother, Roan, and a few others who wanted to go with them to safety. If I left your mother where my brother could find her… The two weeks you were in cryo, I was racing to find a good place to stash them, get them there and then cover my tracks. I sent word to your father, and then I left. And it's *still* not going to be good enough?" He stood up and started pacing back and forth.

I felt cold all over. "What do you mean not good enough? You're not close?"

"Not close enough. I'm two days out. I can maybe speed up a little, which will put me there tomorrow in the middle of the night. I wanted to wake up with enough time to set up our exit. I…I needed time to plan so that I could sneak you out of there with no one knowing."

The ship could only go at top speeds when its passengers were in cryo. The human body couldn't take travel like that.

I blinked a few times as I tried to process. "You slowed down and came out of cryo early?"

"Yes."

I swallowed. Declan couldn't go back into cryo now. The drugs that woke him up needed more time to cycle out of his body.

This was so messed up. He was close, but not close enough to do me any good. I shook my head at him. "It doesn't matter. I'm going on my first run in the morning."

Declan moved off camera. I heard something shatter and I hoped it wasn't anything important.

Ahiga looked down at me and raised a brow.

I shrugged. I knew a freak-out from Declan was coming. I

patted the back of his chair, and Ahiga sat beside me to wait for the sounds of Declan smashing his room to settle down.

There were a few more crashes, and I knew I had to say something, but I wasn't sure how to make this better.

"Declan." His being outraged by all of this made it somewhat easier to bear. "I'll be okay. I can do this."

His hair was sticking out in all directions when he came back to stand in front of the screen. "You still don't get it. You don't understand what it means if something happens to you."

"I understand completely. I also understand that SpaceTech is building some sort of weapon here that—"

"What?" Declan's face grew red again, and I hoped he wasn't going to have a heart attack with all of this.

"I was wondering if you knew about it." Ahiga crossed his arms. "Because I can't find dick all about any new weapon, but the experimental lab is cooking overtime."

"Goddamned-fucking-shit-stain-of-a-brother…" Declan was muttering a string of curses as he bent down to pick up the chair he'd thrown. He placed it back in front of his desk and sat down, his fingers swiping through the air again. "I don't… I can't find anything either." He sighed and closed his eyes as devastation wracked his face. "We have to get you away from there before your father steps into SpaceTech territory. He can't make the first move."

"I know. It'll give SpaceTech the justification that they need to do every terrible thing they want." I let out a breath, but my nerves weren't calming. I needed a plan. "What do we do?"

"I don't know. I just…" He leaned back in his chair and closed his eyes for a second. When he opened them, he was staring straight at me. "I don't know why I'm even trying anymore. It's inevitable at this point. The Aunare are going to cream us, but I thought that if I could just convince my father that this was a bad course, that maybe we could make amends and reinstate some sort of peaceful relationship, then we could stop this war before it started."

"It was never in your control," Ahiga said.

"No. I guess it wasn't." Declan looked up and shook his head before meeting my gaze again. "My father has to know what Jason's doing to you. I bet they're getting a goddamned laugh out of it." Now it was Declan's turn to feel bitter, and I felt terrible for him.

I didn't have it easy the last thirteen years, but at least I had my mom—a parent I could love and I knew would protect me. I wasn't sure Declan ever had that.

"You've been naive to think war could be avoided," Ahiga said. "We both knew it was coming."

"I know. I just thought if I found her in time, then I could somehow make this right. But I've made it worse. Your father will never forgive me for not running with you when I had the chance. I played it safe, and this—your suffering—that's on me."

No. He couldn't think that way. "This isn't your fault. It's Jason's."

"It's also mine." He sighed. "Okay. I'm going to come get you, and I had this plan, but now... Fuck it. We're going to make a run for it to Sel'Ani."

"We?" My voice sounded like it was far away and my heart started pounding in my chest. I was such an idiot. It never occurred to me that I'd be fleeing from one of the most heavily fortified SpaceTech bases with the son of its CEO.

This really might be more stupid than anything that had happened so far. This was the most nonplan plan I'd ever considered. "So we just try to outfly SpaceTech's fleet and hope for the best? That's it?"

"Yes." Declan wasn't quite looking at me as his fingers moved through the air. When he finally looked at me, his face had apologies written all over it. "Day and a half is the soonest I can get there. I can't physically be there any faster. Unless..."

"Yes." Ahiga stood up from his chair. "You have to make that call. I already sent a message to him, but I don't know if it made it, and I wasn't able to include very much information. Just the basics."

"What am I missing?" I said.

A pained look crossed Declan's face, and he pinched the bridge of his nose. "He'll never forgive me for keeping this from him."

"We can't change what's already happened," Ahiga said. "You're like brothers. Brothers fight and they make up. You will, too."

There was some drama here that I didn't understand, but maybe there was an alternative. "Can you move me to kitchen duty? And then we'll figure out something else when you get here. Something less dangerous than running from SpaceTech in a stolen ship."

Declan sighed. "Since Jason had you doing such a dangerous job, he's been watching closely. He's probably not on the base himself, but he's aware of your every move. He could be overseeing the weapon, too. Jason is one of the few people in SpaceTech that outranks me."

"He's really watching?" That felt so much worse than having a crony overseeing me.

"Probably. We have to be careful." His jaw ticced as he leaned back in his chair. "I should just take you and run like I should've done on Earth that very first night."

"None of this was your fault. You can't be held responsible for your brother's actions."

"No, but I can be held responsible for my idiotic lack of action."

This was absurd. "Ahiga." I slapped his shoulder. "Tell him it's not his fault."

"I actually agree with Declan." He didn't look sorry at all. "We should've run with her the second you found her."

"I couldn't. Albuquerque was swarming with officials. There were a million checkpoints. No one was getting through."

"Then Lorne should've come."

I gave Ahiga a shove, but it didn't move him much. "Stop it. This is bad enough as it is."

Ahiga shrugged at me. "I'm not the one who has PTSD."

"*I don't have PTSD.*"

"You don't sleep because of the nightmares. You're so stressed and scared that you upchuck the little bit that you eat—"

"The food here is *disgusting*!"

Ahiga gave me a sad look, and I wanted to slap it from his face.

"I don't need your pity!"

Ahiga wrapped an arm around me and pulled me into his chest. "Stop it. You've been through hell, and you're a mess because of it. You need help, and I don't regret calling your family." He pulled away from me and turned to Declan. "Declan needs to get that through his head. He needs to reach out."

"I *will*," Declan said. "Believe me. No one feels worse about this than I do. I will call Lorne as soon as I hang up with you, but he'll take a few days to get here. So…"

"So nothing's changing. You showing up. Calling Lorne. None of that changes what I have to do." I resigned myself to what I had to do tomorrow. "I'm going on the mining run. It's one run. After that, you'll be here, and we'll take off or wait for Lorne or whatever."

Declan shook his head. "I don't like it."

"And you think I do?"

"No. I'm sorry." He blew out a breath. "Ahiga?"

"I'm listening."

"Tomorrow I want to be looped into her coms. If shit is going to go wrong, I want to know about it before it happens. Maybe I can —" Declan was silent for a second before he started typing something fast. "Lorne got your message. I'm relaying about the possible weapon."

"When you said it was all about to come to a head two days ago in the med bay, you really meant it," I said quietly to Ahiga.

"I rarely say things I don't mean. I knew that Declan had to be awake soon and my message to the Aunare was going to get to someone. It was only a matter of time, and the clock had already been ticking. It's been ticking since we landed on Abaddon."

"All right. I have to go," Declan said. "I need to look into this weapon, and I've got some calls to make. I need to see if I can hold off the Aunare army because Lorne isn't listening to me anymore. He… And then I need to make some preparations for running. We'll need this ship quickly refueled if we have any shot of making it to international space before… It'll be tight, but…"

He looked at Ahiga. "If my father is keeping something this big from me, even with all of our spies, then the whole network is useless. We might have to pull all our people out of SpaceTech. I don't know if anyone's compromised and I won't have time to find out today."

Ahiga grunted. "Might be for the best. I'll get started."

"You'll keep an eye on her?"

"Of course." Ahiga stood up from the desk. "But she doesn't need me to watch over her. Check out the videos."

"From her suit?" Declan paled. "I can't watch those."

"You should because she's a survivor. I don't know if I could've lived through what she did. But there's some from the gym, too," Ahiga said. "Those are worth checking out for sure."

I sent a look to Ahiga that I hope conveyed how fucked up I thought that suggestion was, and then turned to Declan. "Don't look at any of it. I'm fine." I spit out the word. It was a lie, but I didn't care. "No one needs to see me almost boiling to death in those stupid suits, especially not you or my father." I rose from my chair and placed my hands on the desk. I gave him a stare that I hope conveyed that he shouldn't fuck with me on this.

"If you find them, delete them before you watch." My tone was cold but didn't care. "I kept my word. I survived. So you do this for me. You delete them."

"You survived. It's more than I can say for myself." The last bit was more of a soft mutter, and I wasn't sure he intended us to hear him. "Okay."

"Declan—"

"Gotta run, but I'll be with you tomorrow in your coms."

The screen went black, and I sighed. "He's not going to forgive himself for this."

"Should he?"

I stared at the blank vidscreen. "Yes." At least I thought so.

Ahiga grunted. "You're too nice."

I turned to stare at Ahiga. "I've been called a lot of things, but nice isn't one of them."

"Doesn't change it from being true." He gave my shoulder a squeeze. "Come on. Let's get you some lunch. Then you need to finish listening to whatever training Carl has going, but I think your best bet is to move as slow as possible. Only take crystals you know are good to go. And if you don't get a full load, who cares. You get through tomorrow, and all this will be over. No unnecessary risks."

I nodded. "Okay. Sounds easy enough." And that was what I was afraid of.

All those miners hadn't died without a very good reason. I might not have to do the job for all five runs, but I had to live through at least one.

I could survive, but I had to be prepared. For everything. Even if that meant I was running through space being chased by Space-Tech's warships. Because when we finally did run, that was very probably happening, too.

CHAPTER THIRTY-FOUR

THE MORNING TOOK FOREVER to come. I was haunted by a whole new type of nightmares—where I was blown up on Apollyon. Nerves had my stomach churning, and when it was finally time for me to get out of bed, breakfast didn't sound the least bit appealing. I'd made peace with the horrible food—I would've starved otherwise—but today that wasn't happening. So I decided to skip it and hoped that wasn't a mistake.

I didn't bother with a shower. There were too many people still in the bunks when I got up, and I just wanted to get the day over with. I dressed in a pair of leggings that Tabitha loaned me—there was no way I was wearing those shorts when I didn't have to, even if Apollyon was hot—and one of my tank tops, and went straight down to the hangar that Carl had shown me yesterday.

It took me about ten minutes to walk there. Mechanics were already yelling at each other as they scurried around, even though it was early. The clang of metal against metal filled the bay and echoed as they went about their jobs to keep ships running. Spare parts and innards of various ships spilled off tables onto the floor.

The hangar wasn't as big as the one that held the supply ships that were coming and going from the base at all hours. The ceiling was much lower, only about 25 meters, and just barely fit the ten tiny mining ships.

I spotted 42XLV, nicknamed Araña because of the spider painted on its side, in the center of the hangar. I liked the personalization. Whoever took care of the ship clearly took pride in their work. It was a bit shinier and cleaner than the rest in the hangar.

As I approached the small vessel, I was surprised to see a familiar face. "Hey, Santiago. What're you doing here?"

He straightened from where he was bent over an open panel in the side of the ship. Bare wires and circuits spilled from it, nearly touching the floor. "*Hola, chica*. Gettin' this ready for ya. Giving her a little extra juice. Just finishing now. I'll close her up in a sec."

"Thanks. I didn't realize you were a mechanic here."

He nodded as he wiped his hands off on a rag sticking out from the pocket of his navy jumpsuit. "Was on Earth, too. That's why I got offered this job. Figured it'd be a good fit and way better than twiddling my time away in a cell. That would crush my soul, you know?" He frowned at me. "You going out there scares the shit out of me, so I wanted to make sure you had the best. Skipped breakfast and everything."

I was touched. For Santiago, that was quite the sacrifice. Skipping wasn't just about the food, but it was about missing time with other people. He wasn't happy unless he was holding court somewhere. Even on Abaddon. "Appreciate having your help. I hope this ship will do better than she looks right now." I motioned to the wires and parts on the deck. "She seemed to turn on fine yesterday during training." And I wasn't sure that was true anymore.

He grinned. "Oh hell yeah. Got a couple other good ships, but this one is the best of the bunch. She'll run, but I was trying to give you a little more power. Maybe if you had some extra *oomph*, it might make a difference if…" He trailed off as his ever-present grin slid from his face. "Look, Maité." His voice had lost all its humor. I'd never seen him so serious. "I'm just hoping you being what you are, you'll be quicker to react to whatever goes wrong up there. And if the ship is quicker, too, maybe that will make the difference you need to stay alive."

Me being what I was? How in the hell did he know? "Excuse me?"

He stepped closer, saying the words just loud enough for me to hear them over the other mechanics working away. "No twelve-year-old can beat a grown man without being something special."

My mouth dropped open, but I wasn't sure what to say. I couldn't believe that he knew about me and never turned me in. I knew that the Crew had my back, but I didn't realize how much they watched out for me. "You really knew? You *all* knew?"

"Nah. Not all of us knew. Some of the people in the Crew are dumbasses. Can't put two and two together, but a good number of us figured it out. Not that Jorge would confirm." He looked away and pulled out the rag from his pocket, busying himself with wiping his hands again. "Don't you think it's kind of messed up that what you're mining will be used against you?"

"They've got more than enough to fuel their war, so a little more isn't going to make that much of a difference. What choice do I have?" Hopefully, I'd only have to do this one time.

He shoved the rag back into his pocket and met my gaze. "It's just messed up. This whole fuckin' place is messed up. I hear things. Made friends with Matthew while working down here. The shit he's found out—it ain't right."

"I know." But there wasn't anything I could do about it. At least not right at this moment.

I stepped inside the ship. It only had one seat—for the pilot. No copilot. Behind the controls was an empty cavern. Big enough for three speeders. Instead, there was a pile of round containers that were all collapsed to look like a pile of plates, but Carl told me that each of those would need to be filled before I came back or else it wouldn't count as a full run. Apparently, only full runs counted toward the five required to get out of here.

That wouldn't apply to me, but he didn't need to know that.

I glanced over the control panel, and then looked back at Santiago. "I went over the ship yesterday, but you're the mechanic and my friend. What do I need to know? Any quirks?"

He gave me a long look—uncharacteristically sober for Santiago—and turned to the ship. My mouth grew dry. I'd known that this was dangerous, but seeing Santiago scared made it so much worse.

Santiago was thorough in what he told me for the next twenty minutes. How one switch was faulty—to make sure that the light above it turned on, otherwise try it again until it lit. He would almost caress the ship as he talked, and I realized that this was the first time I'd seen him in his element. It wasn't while he was joking or talking to people. That was a side of him for sure, but this—the mechanic—that was a big part of him that I'd never known about.

I noticed a tremor in Santiago' voice as he talked and wondered if he was just as nervous as I was, which made my palms start sweating.

He'd been here for longer, knew what I was up against, and most importantly, he knew *me*.

"So here. Usually, you want to hit this." He pointed to a green button. "But don't. Unless you've got this one lit up." He pointed to a square box with a switch under it. "Flip this, box lights up, you're good to go." He gave me a big smile, but it wasn't his real smile. He was faking it, and that sucked a little bit of hope from me.

"Whatever you do, don't hit the green before you do that. That shit is crazy. It'll eat up the fuel too quick and stall out. You'll be floating dead in space." He paused, solemn as he met my gaze. "Don't forget." His words were deadly serious. "Please, don't forget."

"I won't." I'd been listening to everything he'd said. I wasn't going to forget it.

"Good. You'll be fine then." He smiled, but his look had a twinge of sadness that went against his words. The whole conversation, that look had come again and again. Each time, I felt more and more sure that he didn't think I would come back alive.

That scared me more than anyone else's warning.

By the time he was done, I felt like I was going to be sick.

He patted my shoulder. "Survivors Together. I don't want to tell Jorge you died on my watch, in one of my ships."

"Survivors Together." I was hoping for the same thing. "I'll do my best."

He looked like he was about to say something else, but stopped as Ahiga came in. "Hey. I've got this for you." He held out two wrapped packages.

I peeked into the first, but Ahiga glanced at Santiago.

Right. Don't be obvious about it. I looked in the second. "Food? You knew I skipped breakfast?"

"I waited for you," Ahiga said. "When you didn't show, I figured you were here instead."

I stepped farther into the ship, and Ahiga followed me, blocking Santiago's view of me. I quickly opened the smaller package, taking out the small earbud, tapping it on as soon as it was in place.

Ahiga stepped aside, and Santiago looked at the biscuit in my hand. "What? You didn't bring one for me?"

"Knew you probably had food squirreled away here."

"Who wouldn't?"

"Are they on? You hear me okay?" Declan asked in my ear.

"Yes." I ignored the look Santiago sent my way. "Thank you," I said to Ahiga and took a bite of the biscuit.

"Good," Declan said. "I didn't want anyone overhearing us, so I didn't go through the ship coms, but I can see you from their cams."

I hated being watched all the time. I searched around for cameras, but I couldn't see any inside the ship.

"Keep in mind that they'll still hear your end, so be careful what you say."

I started to answer, and turned it into an *"Mmm,* tasty."

"Good. That's probably best. I have a feeling my brother might be listening, too."

I wouldn't doubt it.

Carl stepped through the door. "What is this? A party? Everyone out but Maité."

Ahiga spared Carl a little glance. "Just wishing her luck." He gave me a nod and left.

"I'll have her ready to go in five," Santiago said. "Just got to get that panel closed up."

"Good," Carl said, dismissing Santiago. "You ready, kid?"

"As ready as I can be." I took a breath. "When do I leave?"

"As soon as Santiago gives you the thumbs-up."

Even though I had no food in my stomach except for a single bite of tasteless biscuit, I was pretty sure I was going to barf. "Okay." I wiped the cold sweat from my forehead.

He patted the pilot's chair. "Get comfortable. I'll let you know when you're cleared."

"Thanks."

Carl stepped out of the ship, closing the door behind him, and the sounds of the launch bay cut off. My heart fluttered in my chest as I sat down in the chair. The vinyl was ripped and patched together, but it was comfortable enough. The faint stench of sweat had seeped into the material, but I didn't care. All I wanted was to make it through the day alive.

I closed my eyes. *Please, let me make it through today alive.*

Six in. Three out. Three in. Six out. Four in.

I wasn't sure what was going to happen on the moon, but I was scared—terrified—of making a wrong move, especially when I was so close to getting away from here.

I glanced back at the stack of flattened containers. Ten of them. Each one would hold ten pounds of crystal.

I couldn't just sit there waiting, so I decided to check over all the equipment. I'd already done that with Santiago, but it couldn't hurt to take another look.

"How're you doing?" Declan's voice startled me. "Your vitals are a little off the charts."

I laughed to keep myself from crying. "If only someone could lie to me and tell me I can get through this..." I muttered softly. I bent down and counted the containers. Ten. It didn't seem like a lot, but I knew it was going to be much harder than I thought.

"I don't need to lie. You're going to be fine. Soon you'll be back with your mom, Roan, and Jorge. In a few months, Abaddon and everything that happened there will all feel like ancient history."

My bottom lip trembled, and I pressed them together. I couldn't stop the sniffle though, or the way my eyes burned when I thought of getting to see my mom again. And I really couldn't stop the way my heart ached when I realized how farfetched and stupid it was for me to really believe I'd get to see her again.

There were so many things that could go wrong. I'd already lost count of how many times I'd almost died on Abaddon, and there were so many more deaths I could die between here and there. I couldn't—

"Breathe. Six in. Three out. Come on. I can't hear you. Six in. Three out."

I stood up and leaned against the wall of the ship. My exhale was shaky, but there.

"Good. Come on. Keep breathing. Three in. There you go. Six out. You'll be okay. I promise. This didn't go how I intended. I hate —*hate*—what's happened. And before you ask, yes, I saw the vids from your suit."

I gasped. *No.* I didn't want anyone to see that. I'd been in pain and weak and defeated. Those vids needed to be deleted. It made me sick with anger that they even existed. When I got away from here, I wanted to shove everything that happened on Abaddon into a deep, dark room in my mind, lock the door, and forget about it. I couldn't do that if everyone *knew*. If they *saw*. If they looked at me with pity.

"I sent them to your father. I know that's not what you want to hear, and maybe I shouldn't have looked, but once I saw—"

I dropped my head down. "Privacy," I whispered fiercely.

"What are you talking about kid?" Carl said in my ear.

"Nothing. Ignore me. I'm just muttering to myself."

"All right. Just a few more minutes," Carl said.

I rubbed my shaking hands through my hair. It was still a little crispy, but I wasn't cutting it. I wouldn't let SpaceTech take one more thing from me.

"I have a lot to apologize to you for, but not this," Declan said. "I hear you on the privacy thing, but he deserves the choice to see the vids. If you think that you have something to be embarrassed about, let me tell you that you don't. What I saw... Your strength. Determination."

"Fear," I whispered the word, not wanting Carl to hear it, but I didn't care.

"Yes. You were afraid and vulnerable. I saw that, too. But you never gave up. You kept putting on that suit, facing it over and over. I don't know how you did it."

I didn't want to think about that. Not ever again. I checked the basket of supplies. Three pickaxe-hammer tools. A scale. A purple marker.

"And when you were teaching, you were talking to your students about more than just fighting technique. You gave them life lessons, hope, a way to make things better." The line hissed as he let out a long sigh. "I feel like you did more on that base in twelve days than I've done in my career at SpaceTech. You showed who you are, Amihanna."

I hissed when he said my name.

"I know you don't feel comfortable with your real name, but you will. This is the last day of Maité Martinez. Once this is over, you're Amihanna di Aetes, and I won't let you down again. I swear it on my life. I'm here for you, Ami. We're here for you, but please, stay safe. We need you to be okay."

We? My hands shook as I kept looking at the supplies. I wasn't okay, but hopefully I would be.

Five tubes of water. Three electrolyte packets. Seven energy bars.

"All right, kid," Carl's voice sounded through the ship's com and my wrist unit.

I swallowed.

"Santiago is all done, and the hangar has been cleared. You're good to go for the next ten. Better get a move on."

I blew out a breath as I sat down in the pilot chair, pressing the button for the safety straps. Not that they would do any good if the whole ship blew up, but they made me feel safer.

My hands were shaking and sweating. I wiped them off on my pants and tried my best to push the fear far enough away to give me room to think—to breathe.

"Powering up now." I pushed the sequence of buttons, and the tiny ship started to vibrate as the engine warmed.

"You take it easy out there, kid," Carl said. "I'm here if you have any questions. We'll be monitoring from the base."

I wondered who the "we" meant, but Declan chimed in. "Carl, Ahiga, and a couple others who are working for my brother. There are a few people in the control room, and I hear they're taking bets."

Probably there to watch me blow myself up. Assholes.

"Don't worry about the control room. Yes, they'll be watching, but who the fuck cares what they think. I know that wounds your di Aetes pride, but let it go. Laugh it off. Stay focused, Ami."

I grinned and hoped it looked confident even though it was one hundred percent fake. "Well, hopefully I don't give all of you too much of a show today." If Jason was listening in, I couldn't let him see my fear. I wouldn't give him that satisfaction. No matter how terrified I actually was. "And if there's betting going on, I want in."

Engaging the thrusters, I felt the ship rise, and I started turning it around. For better or worse, in a few minutes, I'd be out there, flying a ship in space for the first time. It wasn't how I ever thought it'd be. I wasn't fleeing Earth. I hadn't bought this vessel. But I was still about to leave a planet flying my own ship. And that was at least one thing I could cross off my bucket list.

"What're you waiting for? Go!" Carl yelled through the com.

I didn't need to be told twice and gunned it out of the bay. As I rose above Abaddon's sulfuric ashes, the ship shuddered. I lifted up out of my chair for a split second before antigrav kicked in, slamming me back down on the cracked vinyl seat.

It wasn't a long ride to the moon. Only about fifteen minutes, but as I flew there, I realized this might be the last thing I'd ever do. Throwing the ship into a series of loops and twists, I couldn't help but laugh.

"What the hell are you doing?" Carl yelled. "Your ship's going to fall apart before you get there!"

"If I die today, at least I had some fun." I tried to play it off as a joke, but my tone was wobbly at best.

"Shit, kid." Carl's sigh came through the tinny-sounding speakers. "Don't let me stop you."

I wasn't in the habit of letting anyone stop me. My mother always said that was the di Aetes side showing through, but maybe that was just all Amihanna. "Almost there." Apollyon was getting bigger by the second, and I was surprised that it looked more like Earth than I'd thought. I could see patches of green and brown surrounded by oceans of blue. "It's pretty."

"Yeah," Carl said. "Reminds me of home."

Declan snorted. "Except it's much smaller. Not enough oxygen for breathing. Has a shit-ton of carnivorous plants. No real animal predators, but a ton of varmints. But the mines have been cleared of any life forms. You'll have nothing to worry about except the crystals themselves."

"Right."

I slowed down as I approached the thin atmosphere, turning my ship slightly to put less strain on it, then flipped on the autopilot for landing. I could do it myself, but I wanted to be sure I ended up in the right spot since there were multiple mines. Going to one that had already been deemed tapped out wasn't going to help me at all, and the ship's nav systems had the exact spot keyed in where the last miner...

I couldn't think about that. Not right then. "Touchdown in ten seconds."

"Copy that."

The ship strained as it hit the ground. I unclipped my safety harness and moved to the back.

I didn't need a suit—the temperature was just over a hundred degrees—but there was too much nitrogen in the air and not enough oxygen. A mask would filter the air so that the mix was just right for my lungs. The transparent polymer dome fit over my whole face like a mask, giving me 180 degrees of viewing. I pressed the button at the top, and it suctioned onto my face almost painfully, but I'd rather have it too tight than too loose.

I closed my eyes and said a prayer. I wasn't sure anyone was listening. After everything that'd happened, I was pretty sure that any gods I prayed to actively hated me, but I wasn't beyond begging. I needed help if I was going to get through this. "Okay. Grabbing my first container and heading out there."

"Godspeed," Carl said.

I picked up one of the plates and shook it out, expanding it, before opening the door.

The ship had parked itself right on the topmost ridge of the surface mine. The grooves of the mine seemed to spiral so deep into the ground that I wasn't quite sure where it ended, but I could see the glittering black ore jutting out from the walls. Drones flew all around the mine, monitoring it—and now me—from a million different angles.

"Don't let the containers get too heavy before you carry them back to the ship."

"Will do." It'd give me time to breathe while playing this epic game of Russian roulette. I clipped the carrying strap around the handles of the container and hooked it around my waist.

My legs felt like gelatin as I stepped onto the surface and I felt like this couldn't be real. But it was. This was my life, and I'd get through this. "Wish me luck."

"Luck," Declan said, echoed by Carl.

I said one more prayer then, with grim determination and a healthy dose of Aunare stubbornness, I headed to the mine.

CHAPTER THIRTY-FIVE

I GRABBED the rock in front of me, holding it with one hand, and tapped it softly with the tiny hammer end of my tool. The tone that came from it was loud and low enough to rattle my teeth.

Volatile. I didn't need to hit it a second time to be sure.

I held my breath and gently let go, not wanting to disturb the crystal a second time. "Marking that one as explosive." I grabbed the marker, writing a '1' on it.

"Done. Good job, kid." Carl's voice came through my wrist unit. He kept a database of all the crystals tested. There hadn't been a miner down here in weeks, so every crystal here was neutral until I hit them, but there were still some he didn't want me testing. He said the crystals sometimes changed, but if it was marked unsafe on three different mining trips, he labeled it as dangerous for good.

"This one?" I asked, just in case I could avoid hitting it. There were no marks on it, but that didn't mean it wasn't going to hurt.

"Hit it."

Not the answer I wanted.

If the past few hours told me anything, it was that I hated mining. Each time I tested a crystal, it felt like messing with a live bomb. The desperation I'd felt while icing down Abaddon's surface made me forget that only someone seriously dumb or desperate would sign up for this job.

My hands were shaking as I held the hammer. I'd tried to control my fear, but I wasn't sure how much longer I could keep going. The next crystal might blow up in my face, and if it did I'd left a trail of active ones ready to go off all over the mine. Luckily, none of the explosive ones were double-tapped, but there had to be a hundred single-tapped and surely that couldn't be safe. I'd essentially rigged Apollyon to blow up at any second. One wrong move and my flesh would be red mist.

I tried to tell myself I didn't need to make a full load today. I just needed to give Declan enough time to get here, but the longer the day wore on, the more I realized mining wasn't any different than icing down the surface of Abaddon. Switching jobs hadn't changed anything, and that left me with a feeling of hopelessness. Enough of it to drown in.

I was exhausted—mentally and physically—and I wanted to give up. I wanted to get back in that ship and say I was done for the day, but I wasn't sure what would happen if I came back before Carl gave me the okay. Only two things kept me going—Declan's voice telling me not to give up, that he was on his way, that every-thing would be okay—and repeating my mantra.

I'm a di Aetes. I don't quit. Not ever.

I reached for the next crystal and gave it a gentle tap. The tone was a soft, medium-pitched hum like small flutters against my mind. None of the neutral ones hurt. I hit it again and heard the same smooth sound, only a little softer.

Harmless.

I quickly gave it one more tap to neutralize it, and I turned the hammer around to the pickaxe side.

A couple of heavy swats to the bedrock around the crystal released it from the wall of the mine. I placed it carefully in the container hanging at my hip.

One more down and I was still alive.

My face stayed dry thanks to the mask, but sweat dripped down behind my ears, falling onto my neck. I wiped it off with my shoulder as I took a few more steps around the edge of the mine.

I'd descended six of the ten mining levels so far. The dirt had been carefully blasted away from the crystals during the excavation process, leaving the shards exposed along the walls. Each level had fewer and fewer viable crystals. Some I tested, but most Carl instructed me to avoid. I'd only filled two of the ten containers, and I was more than halfway through the mine.

I paused at another grouping.

"How are you doing?" Declan's smooth voice was a balm on my frayed nerves.

My tank top was soaked through, and it wasn't just the heat. "I'm hanging in."

"Good work, kid. You're doing great," Carl said.

"He's right, you know." Declan's voice was soft. "You're doing great."

Great. That was such bullshit. I must've been a good actress because on the inside I was slowly losing it.

Carl said something about energy bars on the ship when I first came out here, but I didn't understand why I'd need them. He'd told me that the mask lasted for twelve hours. I was supposed to stay here until either I'd harvested enough crystal or the mask ran out, but I honestly didn't think mining would take longer than a few hours, which meant I'd never need one of those energy bars or the full twelve hours from the mask.

I was so unbelievably wrong.

Mining was more time-consuming than I could've possibly imagined. Since I didn't plan on taking any unnecessary risks, I was stuck out here for nine more hours. Also known as an eternity.

"Your temp's pretty hot," Declan said. "And your blood pressure is through the roof. I need you to remember to breathe."

I grunted, and I hoped he realized how ridiculous his observations were. Was my heightened blood pressure really a surprise?

"Hurry up, Martinez. You're running out of time, and you're

only twenty percent complete." The voice never identified himself, but I knew that it had to be one of Jason's guys. He'd been nagging me to move faster for the last hour, probably hoping that he could goad me into making a mistake.

I ground my teeth to stop myself from saying anything. I couldn't afford any distractions, especially from this guy. Not when a mistake meant blowing myself up.

"Just take a breath. You're doing great." I took a minute to soak in the sound of Declan's voice.

I wasn't sure why it helped so much, but I was thankful that he was helping me through this. He made me feel like I wasn't so alone, even though I was. It was only me and the drones on Apollyon.

"You're alive, and that's all that matters. You don't need a full load. You just have to last long enough. I want you to be very sure before you swing that pickaxe again, okay? Don't let him rush you."

I sighed.

"Okay," Declan said. "Okay. That's better. Sighing counts. Take another breath. Deep inhale."

I did as he asked, but my hand still shook as I grasped another crystal. It had two "1" marks on it. Each a different color. Two different miners had tested it before me and marked it as volatile. I *hated* testing ones that already had marks on them. Those were the most painful.

Ice it all to hell.

I brought the hammer end down on it. The tone must've been out of my hearing range because I didn't hear anything, but it made my ears pop painfully anyway. The tool slipped from my hand, and I lowered my head and tried to breathe through the pain.

"You okay?" I barely heard Declan's voice over the ringing in my head.

I pressed my hands over my ears and yawned, trying to equalize the pressure. "Mark that one as superhot."

"What about the rest in that cluster?" Carl asked.

Who cares about the rest of the fucking cluster? I wanted to shout it at him. But I couldn't. Not if I wanted to keep up the appearance that I was doing this job.

All of the crystals in the cluster had marks on them. It was safe to say that they'd all be volatile, but I knew the control room didn't give a shit about that.

It took me a second to shove my fear far enough inside me to get my hand to work again. I picked up my tool from the ground, reached out to a crystal, and hit it with the hammer end.

I couldn't hear that one either, but my back molars throbbed. "Volatile."

Carl hadn't said anything about pain when testing crystals, but I couldn't bring it up now. I didn't want to look weak in front of Jason and his tribe of jerks. Especially when I wasn't sure if this was an Aunare-only thing.

It took me a good twenty minutes to finish hitting the rest in the bunch, earning myself a hell of a headache. I made sure to mark each one, but by the end of it, my breath was coming out in quick pants.

When I was done, I squatted down, hanging my head between my knees, waiting for the pain to go away, but it didn't.

This whole mining thing was fucked. Almost all of the crystals were volatile. My head was aching. I was exhausted and sweaty. Most of all, I was done. I wanted to quit, but I couldn't. Declan wasn't here yet. So I had to keep going. I had to be strong.

I'm a di Aetes. I don't quit. Not ever.

"You okay, kid?" Carl's voice held more than a bit of concern.

"I just got a migraine. Nothing too bad." It only felt like my head was being cleaved in half.

"Get up. Now. Or this run is over."

Jason's friends were the *worst*. Cowards. Liars. I hated them with everything I was, and I didn't care if the run was null. I was ready to throw down the damned tool and tell them to go ice themselves. I'd sit here and wait out the remaining time. If they had a problem with it, they could come drag me back.

"I'm linked in to the control room." I heard the strain in Declan's voice as he tried to keep his anger leashed, and I knew that whatever he said next, I wasn't going to like it.

"If you stop before you've hit the load minimum, they're going to put you back on the surface for a six-hour shift. Ahiga's arguing against it, but he's outranked."

I whimpered. "What do I do?"

Carl was talking to me through my wrist unit, urging me to keep going, but I wasn't listening to him.

"One just said if you don't get up, he's going to get you himself, rough you up, put you in the suit, and throw you out onto the surface of Abaddon."

"Shit," I muttered to myself. I couldn't put on the suit again. I couldn't go out on the surface. If Audrey had to give me one more round of nanos...

"You can't put on that suit again and survive," Declan said, echoing my thoughts. "You've got a little over eight hours left on your mask. I don't care why they're yelling. Go slow. Finish your day. Once you're back on the base, relax. Eat. Shower. I'll be there tonight, and we'll leave. It'll all be over soon. I promise. Just get through the next eight hours for me."

I focused on Declan's words, but eight hours seemed like forever and going back to icing the surface wasn't a good alternative.

So I would move slowly, deliberately, knowing the time would run out. I would get through this.

Eight hours and then I was done.

"I'm getting up," I said. "Just give me a minute." I reached for the tool that had fallen to the ground beside me. The tiny tool felt heavy in my hand. I closed my eyes and wished there was another way.

"If you don't get your ass up right now, we're coming to haul you back here. Your old job will look like—" I tuned Jason's crony out. He was trying to piss me off, and I wasn't going to let him have that much control over me.

"Your di Aetes steel is showing, you know," Declan said.

"Huh?" I wanted to ask specifics but couldn't.

"When I was growing up, I would've done anything to be part of your family. Your dad is the opposite of my father, but he takes no shit. The look on your face right now while those assholes are yelling at you? The determination? That's all your father. You're Amihanna *di Aetes,* and it shows."

A tear rolled down my cheek. He didn't know about my mantra. That whenever I wanted to give up, I had to remind myself that I was a *di Aetes.* Hearing that right then, when I was so close to giving up, meant I could keep going.

I stayed still for a second, just breathing in and out, letting the pain from my head flow down my body and out of my limbs.

I'm a di Aetes. I never quit. Not ever.

I rose on shaky feet, dusting myself off. "I'm fine." It was a lie, but it sounded truthful when I said it.

The next cluster was much larger than any of the others I'd seen—over twenty crystals, some as thick as my forearm. One wide, arcing crystal linked the others in the cluster together. It was odd that there was no rhyme or reason as to which ones would be mineable. Some tiny ones gave off the worst tones. Some of the biggest ones were the weakest, but there was no guarantee.

I didn't want to hit it even though it didn't have any marks on it, but my life was filled with doing things I didn't want to do. Mining lucole was just one more thing. One more very dangerous thing.

I licked my lips and picked one to test. The fat arcing one. It was the thickest, and hopefully that meant it was the least harmful. I swung the hammer down.

The high-pitched, whining tone crescendoed until it was all I could hear. The pain hit me hard and fast, and I fell, my back slamming into the ground.

The tone quieted, and my vision started to gray until it was black.

And then I was without sight and sound.

As I lay there, I wondered if this was it. If maybe I'd already died, and if the afterlife was just a dark hole where I'd spend eternity.

For a second, I was relieved. No matter how hard I'd tried to do the right thing, it seemed that I always lost. Maybe quitting wasn't so bad. Maybe having this be done and finished meant that I could rest.

No more hiding. No more waitressing. No more wondering whether today was the day I was going to be discovered as a halfer. No more Jason Murtagh or SpaceTech using me to destroy the Aunare. It all sounded so perfectly lovely.

But then I realized if I were dead, my limbs probably wouldn't hurt anymore. And the rock jabbing my back wouldn't exist.

So I wasn't dead. At least not yet.

That realization was a little disappointing. Because if I wasn't dead, then all I had was more suffering ahead of me.

So I lay there and waited for my hearing and vision to come back. Wondering if they would come back. And if not, what was I going to do next?

CHAPTER THIRTY-SIX

I DON'T KNOW how long I was on the ground, but after a while I blinked my eyes, and I could see light and shadows. It took a few more minutes for my sight to fully come back, but everything was still silent. I couldn't even hear myself breathe.

I rolled onto my side, rubbing my spine, trying to ease the ache away. The rock I fell on definitely left a bruise.

I finally decided to say something. Declan was too far away to help, but he was probably worrying. "I think I'm deaf." I couldn't hear my own words. My heart was racing, but I couldn't hear the whooshing it sometimes made in my ears, especially when I was scared. And right now, I should've been hearing the whooshing. Loudly. Which made the silence that much scarier.

I massaged along my jaw, trying to get my ears to pop, but they wouldn't. "Shit." What was I supposed to do now?

And then there was an excruciating pop in my ears, and I screamed. I reached up and felt liquid running down my lobes and onto my neck. I pulled the tiny earbud out, and my fingers came back red.

It was only then that I realized I could hear Carl, Ahiga, and the rest of the control room yelling at me through the wrist unit. I'd bet money if I put in the earbud, Declan would be, too.

I couldn't understand what they were saying. Their voices were too loud and on top of each other.

I put my hands over my ears. "Stop!" That got everyone to shut up. "Let's mark that one as hot, shall we?" My words were sassy, but my voice was so weak and barely there.

I wiped off my bloody fingers and the earbud on my leggings. There were too many drones hovering around me, watching my every move, so I knew they could probably see the earbud. I tried to be covert about it, but at this point I wasn't sure how much I should care. I was bleeding. I didn't know what that meant, but it couldn't be good.

I bent over and lifted my tank top to wipe off the rest of the blood. After a few wipes, the blood stopped, and the fear pounding through my body eased a little. I tried to hide putting the earbud back, but I was over it. Over Jason and his stupid cronies. Declan would be here soon anyway.

There was a long silence, and I assumed that they were all watching me clean up. After years of hiding, having them see me like this made me feel naked. I told myself that it didn't matter. That I was wearing clothes and that they couldn't read my mind and that I shouldn't feel this way, but it didn't help.

"You scared the crap out of me, kid," Carl said finally. "It's almost like these crystals are hurting you."

I didn't want to admit that they were but damn it—they were more than hurting me. I was pretty sure the crystals were killing me.

"Ami?" Declan's voice had a hint of a quiver to it.

He'd never said my name like that, and I knew that meant he was as scared as I was.

I grunted.

"You okay?"

I couldn't answer that.

"Get your ass up and start mining," Jason's jerkwad of a friend said.

"Ignore him," Declan said. "Cough once if you're okay. Twice if you're hurting."

I coughed twice.

Hurting was laughable. Every bone in my body ached, and my head was beyond pounding. I couldn't even think about how bad my ears felt.

I didn't want to test any more crystals. Not even one. I was terrified of what they were doing to my body. I'd never had a headache this bad before.

"You might be reacting to the crystals. I didn't think about what this would be like for an Aunare. I didn't... I didn't know you'd have this kind of a reaction." Worry made his voice waver. "The bleeding is a bad sign, Ami."

I closed my eyes and let that sink in. At this point, the number of things that had gone wrong since Declan came into my life was laughable.

"And I hate to say it, but it's important that SpaceTech doesn't know how badly the lucole is affecting you."

Was he kidding? How was I supposed to act like it wasn't affecting me? I couldn't get my limbs to move any faster even if I wanted to. I wasn't even sure I could stand up yet, much less mine any more lucole. Especially if it was killing me. What was I supposed to do?

"Stall. Tell them it's the stress. That you're scared."

I hissed, telling Declan just what I thought of his idea. I might be terrified of what was happening to me, but letting the control room know that I was scared was *not* something I wanted to do. I didn't like showing weakness.

"I know. You're a di Aetes, but even your father would agree with this plan. It makes sense. Your blood pressure is dangerously high, and they'll believe that you're too scared to continue. That your fear is giving you a headache. Tell them and sit tight. I have to make a call. I'll be here, but I'm muting myself, okay?"

I whimpered. Declan was my lifeline. I didn't want him to be muted.

"I'll be right back. I promise."

The earbud went silent. I missed the sound of his soft breathing. It'd been a comfort. I'd been alone on the moon four hours, but I'd never felt as alone as I did that moment.

And now I had to tell the base that I was too stressed out—too *afraid*—to continue mining. "I think the stress is getting to me." I bit out the words. "I'm not sure I can do anymore today."

I tuned out the fury from the base and waited for Declan to come back. I didn't care how much the jerks back on Abaddon were yelling at me. Declan was right. I had to quit. I was trying —*really trying*—to make this work, but I couldn't do it. And I couldn't go back to the base. I couldn't put on a suit again. Not today. Not ever.

I wasn't sure what was going to happen next, and I was scared. I counted my breaths as I waited for Declan to come back and prayed for a miracle.

"Hey." Declan drew the word out like a soft sigh.

I shoved down the sob that threatened to break free. I was glad Declan was back. So relieved that I wasn't alone, even if he was light-years away.

"I have a new plan." He sounded defeated, and I hated that.

I wanted to tell him how thankful I was for all the risks he was taking for me, but I needed something else to happen. I needed that new plan, whatever it was.

"I talked to your father and Lorne on the other line."

"Thank you." The words flew out before I could stop them.

"Kid?" Carl said. "You okay?"

"I had to tell them what was happening. I watched you unresponsive on my monitor, and I'd never been so scared. I wish…" Declan was quiet for a moment. "Lorne's so unbelievably mad at me." A long sigh hissed across the com. "And if I'm honest, I'm mad at myself, too. Watching you today was impressive. I'm blown away by your strength and determination, but I'm second guessing every single step that led us here. This never should've happened. I've failed you, and that's the last thing I wanted to do."

Failed me? I had a lot to say about that, but it'd have to wait until we didn't have an audience.

"Lorne is coming to pick you up. He'll be there in a few minutes."

"What?" I sat up. "No!"

"Martinez?" Carl asked. "You okay?"

I heard his question, but it felt like it was a million light-years away. My mind was spinning, and answering Carl didn't matter anymore.

None of this mattered. Nothing that I'd suffered through would matter if Lorne picked me up. That would mean war.

It felt like I'd been kicked in the gut. All the air was gone. Declan couldn't do this to me. Avoiding war was why I went to Abaddon in the first place. It was why I endured working the most idiotic job in the entire godforsaken universe. It was why I tried to find my own way out of it and ended up mining. It was why I'd survived for hours today on Apollyon. Giving up now meant that all of that was for nothing. That I'd suffered for no reason. That *I* was the one who failed.

His new plan was iced. I hated it. I was trying to figure out how to tell him that with the control room listening in when the drones around me smashed to the ground, and the yelling from the base abruptly cut off.

"Ahiga just wiped out communication. He made it look like an accident, but they're going crazy, and it might not last long."

"I don't need saving. Find another way. Negotiate with—"

"It's not up to you or me anymore. Lorne started this way as soon as he got Ahiga's message. Apparently, he was almost here when I called him. I was hoping to do this more delicately. I wanted to somehow keep the peace, but the Aunare have decided that war is inevitable. That SpaceTech crossed the final line. Lorne will be there soon. I'm connecting him to you now."

"Amihanna." That one word from Lorne sent shivers down my

spine. My skin flared, and I was glad Ahiga had already shut down the drones. It wasn't just my name that set me off, but the way he said it, laced with so many layers of emotion.

In one word, Lorne told me everything was about to change. Again. And I wasn't sure I could take anymore change. I wasn't sure I had it in me, and once again I didn't have a choice.

"You need to be out of the mine in the next minute. I can't waste time coming down there and carrying you up if you can climb. We need to be gone before anyone from SpaceTech realizes I'm there. Abaddon's base has me outgunned, and my ship won't last in a fight. I'm taking you and running. So, if you can, get up. Now."

"Damn it. No." I slammed my hand on the ground. "I can't be the cause of a war. I can't live with that on my shoulders. Can't you negotiate with SpaceTech to release me?"

"No. I can't risk what they'd do to you in the interim, and I won't let them use you as a bargaining chip. But I also won't sit by and watch you die for Declan's *idiocy*. Start climbing. Forty-five seconds."

"But—"

"Amihanna. War is *inevitable*. The Aunare know it. SpaceTech knows it. Declan is the only one who thinks it can be stopped. No matter what happens next, the war will never be your fault. I don't know why you're on Apollyon or what happened since I talked to you in that warehouse weeks ago, but I know you're hurt, and I won't risk your life. Thirty seconds and I'm there. Get up. *Now*."

"If we could just—" Declan started, but Lorne cut him off.

"No. We cannot *just* anymore." He paused. "Declan lost visual with you when Ahiga blew the coms. So I can't see you and I don't know how hurt you are, but I need you to hear what I say and try. Please." He was much calmer when he spoke to me. "We're not fighting today, but believe me when I say I'm picking you up. Twenty seconds and I'm there. So do me a favor and get up so that we can leave right away. I want to be gone as soon as physically possible."

I wanted to believe what Lorne said—that the war wouldn't be my fault—but it didn't matter anymore. Lorne was here, and I wanted to live. Maybe that was selfish of me, but I ripped off my wrist unit and slammed my hammer down on it. I was done with SpaceTech and pretending to be something that I wasn't.

"Fifteen seconds." He paused. "You won't be able to see my ship, but you'll feel the wind. Are you almost there?"

"Not yet, but I'm getting up." I tucked my tool in the waist of my pants and pushed my body to stand. Even though I was swaying, I started sprinting.

I'd taken stairs down, but there was only a single staircase on each level, and it was directly across the mine from me. A full mile away. Even with my Aunare speed, I couldn't get there as quick as Lorne wanted. It was impossible, unless...

I sprinted toward the wall. I used one foot on the wall to give me a bit more lift as I jumped up, and gripped onto the top edge. Pulling myself up, I started running again at the next wall, except I didn't make it to the top.

"Shit!" I closed my eyes as I slid down until my feet touched the ground. I leaned my head against the dirt wall. My body was too weak to make it. "I can't. I'm so tired. I'm not strong enough."

"Yes, you are. I'm close enough to see you now. I know it feels far, but you can do this." Lorne's voice urged me on. "I can come down once I get there, but that will take longer. When I open my hatch, the cloaking will turn off, and I'm worried that they'll get their coms rebooted. I'd rather not be caught. Not today. Not with this ship. It wouldn't go well."

It was the plea in his voice that got me moving again. I didn't know what they'd do if SpaceTech had the Aunare crown prince in their hands, but I wouldn't let that happen.

I steadied myself as I stepped away from the wall and then ran back, just barely jumping high enough to grab the top of the wall. I groaned as I heaved my body up onto the next level.

I hit the level after that. And the next.

Lorne started talking in Aunare to Declan. I didn't speak a lick of it, so I just ignored their chitchat and kept going. By the time I hit the fifth level, my abs were screaming. If I'd had a relaxing day, then this would've been a cakewalk. But my bones ached, and my muscles were shaking, threatening to give out.

"Tracker?" I gasped the word. The one Declan had given me wasn't the standard human device, but it still had tracking capabilities. I figured a warning would help Lorne.

"I'm going to overload the chip as soon as you're on board. It'll knock you out, but I'll put you in a healing pod when we're safely away from SpaceTech. When you wake, you'll feel better than you have in years. And this is a promise that will actually come true."

It was a stab at Declan and that pissed me off, but as tired as I was I couldn't deny how amazing that sounded. "Good. My. Bones. Hurt." I grunted out the words as I took one last run at the wall in front of me, leaping with every last bit of strength. I screamed with the effort of pulling myself up. As soon as my feet touched the ground, the air shifted around me.

It swirled faster and faster before abruptly stopping. The illusion broke in one small section, revealing a back hatch opening.

I ran to it, knowing that I'd already taken too long, even if he'd given up on the countdown.

A man was waiting just inside. His black hair was pulled back from his face in a low ponytail. He wasn't dressed as most Aunare I saw on the news though. His slacks were a little too loose and his shirt a little too tight. But his jaw had the typical squareness of Aunare males. His skin was glowing, and the darker teal tattoos peeked out from the bottom of his rolled up sleeves.

He stood there, waiting for me, and I stumbled. He was too fierce. Too handsome. He didn't have the thick muscle that Declan did, but he was more muscular than any Aunare I'd ever seen. And he was beautiful. I kept coming back to that. I just never looked at someone before and thought *whoa*. But this man took my breath away. I would give him everything, and that made him more dangerous to me than the mines of Apollyon and the surface of Abaddon combined.

"Hurry!" he yelled, waving me forward.

I jumped into the ship as it hovered two feet above the ground. I started to lose my balance and fall backward, but Lorne leaped forward and grabbed my arm, steadying me.

"Amihanna."

That word again. It was just my name. It shouldn't make me feel anything other than weird—because my name had been Maité for so long—but his voice saying it? It sent shivers through my body. My skin lit from within, and for the first time I didn't try to stop it.

And then I looked into his eyes and froze.

They were my favorite color. A deep, dark aquamarine.

He gently pulled the earbud from my ear, threw it on the floor, then gripped my bicep, right where my tracker was and I could feel something in his hand pressing against my skin. "I'm sorry to do this now, but we need to get out of here."

"Do what you need to do," I said and meant it.

There was a flash of light and searing pain. I started to fall, but Lorne still held my arm.

"Damn it." Lorne's voice was threaded with worry. "Why aren't you passing out?"

"If only it were that easy." The pain had been sharp, but it was fading, leaving me weaker than I was before.

I rested my head against Lorne's chest, unable to keep it up anymore. I'd used the last bit of strength I had to get to him. "My head is pounding."

He grabbed my chin, tilting my head up, but I couldn't open my eyes.

"Amihanna?" He pulled one eyelid open, then the next.

"Hmm." I felt drunk. I'd only been drunk a couple of times, once really wasted, and that was how I felt now. The room was spinning and my head was hurting and I was sure that I would throw up any second, but I was too far gone to care.

He ran a hand over my head. "The blood wasn't from her ears, you idiot." Lorne yelled something in Aunare, and the ship started to move. "It's from her brain. I can't jump through space with her like this. She's not stable." He swung me up into his arms and started running.

"What do you mean it's from her brain?" Declan's voice came from somewhere in the ship.

"Is he here?" I asked.

Lorne shook his head. "No. He's still in his ship."

"Lorne?" My voice sounded so far away.

"I've got you, Ami."

"Okay." I took a breath. "Might pass out now."

"I'm sorry," Declan said. "Take care of her."

"That's what I'm doing."

I could feel the air against my face as Lorne moved, but I barely felt his footfalls. "Are we floating?"

"Stay with me. You have to promise." He sounded so lost and scared that I wanted to ease his worry.

I tried to laugh to show him that I was okay, but it came out more of a croak than anything else. "Lotta promises happening. Just no nanos. No more nanos. Rather die." My words were slurring, and I wasn't even really sure what I was saying, because everything hurt.

"You're safe with me."

He said it and I believed him.

He lowered me into something soft, and I managed to flutter my eyes open. Lorne filled up my sight as he leaned over me, pressing buttons frantically.

I reached up a lazy hand to touch his face. "You're so pretty."

He held my hand to his cheek for a second, before pressing it down onto the bed. "You're going to feel much better in a bit."

Feeling better sounded good.

"Try to sleep. It will help."

My eyelids felt like they weighed ten pounds each. "Not hard. Tired."

His soft lips brushed against my forehead, and I sighed.

Then I remembered. SpaceTech. "Need to run."

"We're fine. We're cloaked again, and they haven't rebooted coms yet. So we're hidden. We have a little time now. It's more important that you heal."

I felt his hand brush against my face, and he started to sing. It was the same song he'd sung to me in the warehouse the night my skin wouldn't stop glowing. This time it sounded sadder. Slower. More aching.

I wished I knew what he was saying.

I tried to stay awake. I wanted to talk to Lorne. To ask him why he was sad. But no matter how hard I tried, I couldn't fight sleep for one second longer.

CHAPTER THIRTY-SEVEN

I WOKE to the distant sound of people arguing. The blue tinted lights were dim but gave a calming cast to the room. I sat up, and the world swam. I was better—I didn't feel drunk anymore—but the room seemed to sway every time I turned my head, which told me I wasn't fully healed. I must not have been asleep for long.

I almost sighed at having to get out from under the softest blanket I'd ever felt, but the voices rose again. Whatever they were arguing about, I hoped it didn't have anything to do with me, but then I heard my name—*both* of my names—and I quickly gave up that hope.

I didn't want to deal with whatever drama was happening now. I was still weak—physically and emotionally—but I couldn't ignore whatever was going on when it was about me.

I slipped out of the small bed and took measure of how I felt. I was exhausted but pain free. That was an improvement. Maybe some food and water would get me back to normal.

Glancing back at the bed, I noticed a readout glowed along the side of it. This had to be the healing pod Lorne promised me. I ran my fingertips across it, and the display changed, but I couldn't read the swirling letters.

The pod itself wasn't made of plastic or metal, but some sort of beige stone that had been polished until it was as smooth and soft as the blanket inside. There weren't any wires or tubes or needles in sight. I wasn't sure how it'd helped me heal, but I couldn't deny that I was feeling better. I did. Still, I'd never seen stone inside a spacecraft before or in anything SpaceTech built. It wasn't just the material that made it odd or the fact that it was comfortable or had readouts that I couldn't read. It was the whole room and the feeling of calm that I felt while in it.

We were on the run from SpaceTech. I should be anything but calm, but for the first time in my life, it was as if I could breathe. But why?

A counter and cabinets made of dark wood took up most of the wall on the opposite side of the room. The sound of trickling water drew me to a miniature waterfall in one corner. Flat, dark gray rocks were stacked in an imperfect circle. Each stone placed specifically so that the water made the prettiest tinkling sound as it traveled down them. Moss stuck out between the rocks, and around the edges was a fine mist. In the center was a little pool. Squatting down I stuck my fingers in the clear water. A cooling sensation spread up my arm, moving through my body.

I drew my hand out of the water, and the sensation slowly receded.

Did the mist have some sort of medicine in it? Was it making me feel calm?

I tested it again, and the feeling came back. The cooling balm ran up my arm and spread out across my chest. The longer I held it in there, the farther it spread.

"Amihanna."

I jerked my hand out of the fountain and fell back on my butt. "Yes?" I winced at my utter lack of grace as I wiped my hand on my tattered leggings. When I first saw him, I thought he was handsome, but I'd been too tired and in too much pain to really notice how attractive he was. My skin started glowing just looking at him and the desire I felt terrified me.

Those eyes. Every time I looked at them, my chest tightened with need. It ached in a totally unfamiliar way, and I didn't trust it. I had to look away, trying to distract myself.

"You like the water?"

"What's not to like?"

"But you seem confused."

I dared to look back at him. "It's beautiful." And so was he.

I looked away again. That sounded painfully familiar. Did I really say that to Lorne when I was out of it?

"And?" He was waiting, patiently watching and observing, but I couldn't get a read from him. I wasn't sure what he thought of me or if he even thought anything. Maybe he was only here to take me home as a favor to my father. It was silly to assume he felt anything for me at all.

This was stupid. I was attracted to the guy, but that didn't have to mean anything. And I didn't have to become a moron because of it. I should be able to have a rational conversation with him. "Isn't a fountain a waste of space?"

"For a human maybe, but we have a different idea on what's wasteful and what's not."

Focusing on his words was helping me get myself together. "So this is a luxury ship, not one for battle or war?"

"It has some weapons, but mostly defensive. The ship is small and was built for speed and stealth, which is why I chose it." He reached a hand to me, and I let him pull me to my feet before quickly stepping away.

"Is that medicated?" I leaned against the wall to keep from falling over as I motioned to the fountain. "Is that why it makes me feel calm?"

"It's not medicated, but it makes you feel calm?" He tilted his head to the side as he stared at me.

I wasn't answering that. No matter how pretty Lorne was, I wasn't about to give him that much insight into myself. Not when I felt laid bare with every look he gave me and every word he spoke.

So I stayed silent, staring into his dark blue-green eyes. The more I stared, the more I realized the depth of the color. They were hypnotizing.

"To say that this particular vessel is the norm for Aunare would be a lie," he continued when I stayed silent. "It's quite nice, but there's not a single Aunare craft that doesn't have natural elements in them. A recovery room without flowing water would be..." He paused. "Healing is two-fold. Body and spirit. We don't like to ignore the spirit, especially when hurt."

"Okay." So it *was* medicated?

"How are you feeling?"

Better than I had been in a while, which wasn't saying much. "Fine." Admitting more than that made me feel exposed. "How long was I out?"

"About four hours."

That was longer than I'd thought. "So where are we?"

"Hiding on the far side of Apollyon."

I wanted to be much farther away than that. I never wanted to be in SpaceTech's grasp ever again. Now that I was away, I didn't think I could survive it. "Are we safe?"

"For now. SpaceTech is, as of yet, unaware that I showed up to take you home. But testing the crystals with their methods caused some bleeds on your brain, and I couldn't risk making a jump through space before healing you at least a little bit."

"Am I okay?" A bleed on my brain sounded really, *really* bad.

"You need more healing, but you're stable for now."

"You're sure?" The woozy feeling hadn't passed like I wanted.

He pressed his lips together as he thought about it, and my throat went dry. There was something wrong with me.

"I can't lie. It was severe, and I think the pod only took the edge off."

I swallowed.

"I'm worried about how you'll do with jumps through space. I'm coordinating to meet your father somewhere in the middle, so hopefully we won't need very many, and once we're on his ship, a few hours in its better healing pod should set you straight, but you'll need to take it easy until we get there. You should sleep some more if you can."

I shook my head. "I don't want to sleep. Not until we're gone."

"You're perfectly safe right now. Are you sure you can't sleep more?"

"I'm sure." I needed to be far away from SpaceTech. Maybe then I wouldn't have any more nightmares.

There was an awkward silence, and I wasn't sure what to say. Lorne's intense stare made me nervous. I looked down at myself. My leggings were torn in a couple places. Every inch of me was covered in dirt and sweat, and more than a few places were bloody. Maybe that was why I was feeling defensive?

"So, what's the plan?"

He sighed as if he were giving up on trying to convince me to go to sleep. "We're staying put for now. I want to run another test on you before we start traveling and send the results to our doctors. It's not the end of the world if we can't jump. SpaceTech doesn't know we're here, so if we can't we'll go the slow route. I'd rather get home quickly though. It gives us less chance of getting into trouble. Before I run tests, do you want to clean up and have some food?"

My stomach tightened at the mention of eating. "I guess I'm hungry, but a shower sounds amazing. Or whatever it is you have here."

He gave me a small nod and motioned me to follow him. "This way."

I moved after him on unsteady legs. The hallways were curved, something that wasn't normal in a SpaceTech ship. Everything the company did was boxy. Square. Cold, hard lines. All function and no form. But this was so different. Everything was so different. I wasn't sure what to think or how to feel, but I was unsettled.

My skin had a faint glow, but Lorne's skin had the same hint to it. I knew I didn't have to worry about that—not anymore—but I still did. I couldn't shut down the worries that had been ingrained in me over years and years.

And as I followed Lorne, I realized that I had a whole new world of worries to think about.

What was I going to do on Sel'Ani? Would the Aunare accept a halfer easier than Earthers? Was I going to be hated there? And what about Ahiga? Santiago? Audrey and Tyler?

What about the weapon SpaceTech was building on Abaddon?

What about the war?

One worry piled onto the next until I was glowing brightly.

Lorne paused in front of a door. "Are you okay?"

I swallowed. "I don't know."

"Whatever you've been through, you'll need time. Give yourself that time."

I wasn't sure I had time, but I hated that I was so easily read. "I guess it's obvious." I motioned to myself.

"It's not about the glow although, yes, I have eyes." He ducked his head to keep my gaze when I tried to look away. "I can see something's upsetting you, but I don't know what it is or what you feel unless you tell me."

He was quiet, and I knew he was leaving it up to me to let him in, but there was no chance of that. Not when I had so many unanswered questions brewing inside me.

"Later then." Lorne pressed his hand to the center of the door, and it slid open soundlessly. "Only one sleeping quarters. The bathroom is through here."

A large, thick mattress was fitted into the floor. Much bigger than my twin back in my apartment and dwarfing the bunk in the women's quarters. White and cream pillows covered one end, and a thick duvet was folded down, almost inviting me in. The sheets were a little wrinkled, and I wondered if Lorne had slept on top of the covers with the blanket on his way here.

Little pops of color filled the room. A few green and brown pillows on the bed and on the chair beside it. A blue-and-green woven blanket was thrown across the foot of the bed. Green ivy crawled up one wall, and I wondered how they managed to keep it alive on a ship.

The bathroom beyond was so lovely, I almost felt bad about taking a shower in it. I was going to get everything dirty.

Lorne fussed inside the bathroom, placing a fluffy towel on the rail beside the shower. "Soaps are in here. The scents are those I favor so they might not be to your liking, but…" He trailed off as if waiting for me to confirm or deny about what scents I liked, but I couldn't see how that would matter. Any soap was fine.

"Clothes are here," he said when I stayed silent. "Some are mine, but some are spares I had here. You're so thin that…" He went to the closet, pulling out a sweater. "Don't want you to get cold. The clothes might not suit your tastes, but once we're on Sel'Ani, we can get that sorted."

I wanted to laugh, but he was serious. This was all nicer than anything I'd ever had before. Judging from the way he was busying himself around the room, I could've sworn he was nervous about it.

"This is amazing. Thank you."

"You don't need to thank me." He frowned and I almost thought he might've been insulted.

I let out a breath. I was messing this up. "I think I do. I'm not sure I'd have made it out of there—"

"Don't. Please." His glow brightened.

I wasn't sure if he was mad at me. "I'm sor—"

He closed his eyes and the glow faded. When he opened his eyes, I was surprised to see the anger still there. "I'm furious, but not with you. Never with you." He motioned to the door. "I'm going to go check on things. I'll be back in a few."

Lorne left so quickly—before I could even say thank you again —that I wondered if he'd been lying. If some part of him was mad at me. And if he was mad, I wasn't sure how to fix it or if he'd even be around long enough that I should try to fix it.

CHAPTER THIRTY-EIGHT

THE SHOWER WAS warm and amazing. The only thing that got me to leave it was knowing that there probably wasn't an unlimited supply of water on a ship. The soap smelled earthy and a little smoky. It wasn't what I would've chosen for myself, but it was nice and left my skin feeling silky, despite the few spots of calluses, and if I wasn't mistaken, my hair felt less crunchy. I wasn't sure if that was the healing pod or Lorne's conditioner, but either way I'd take it. I sighed as I dried off. Even the towel smelled good.

I'd thought the shower at the spaceport had been nice, but this one was amazing.

A knock sounded at the door. "Ami?"

"One second." I quickly pulled on the clothes. The pants were too long, but I rolled the waist to take up the extra room. The sweater was also too big to be anything other than his, but it was so soft I wanted to live in it. I lifted it and took a big breath in.

Lorne. It smelled like his soap, only better.

When I opened the door, Lorne was leaning against the wall. He stood straight and gave me a nod. "Okay. This way. I don't have much on board, but it's better than nothing."

I smiled at him, trying to ease whatever nerves he was feeling.

As we left the room, I thought of the slimy green mystery food on Earth. "It can't be worse than prison food."

He stopped walking. "Prison?"

I swallowed. I'd meant to lighten the mood, but that had been a dumb thing to bring up. "Um. Yeah. I mean, I didn't really do anything to..." I wanted to play up the fact that I was technically a convict as something funny, but from the look of complete horror on Lorne's face, there was no way he'd ever think it was a joke. "Declan didn't tell you?"

His jaw ticced once. Twice. And a third time before he spoke. "No. No, he's been completely evasive when giving information about you. I got the one phone call with you on Earth, and that was it. The next thing I received was Ahiga's message." He pressed his hand against another door, and it slid open. Inside was the kitchen. There were some cabinets and a storage locker that had to hold food. A small round table with four chairs took up the middle of the room.

Lorne pulled out a chair. "Sit." His word was clipped.

I quickly sat before I could upset him any more than I already had. He'd come here—risked everything—for me, and now he was pissed. I knew I'd messed this up, but I couldn't unsay it. I couldn't change the past. No matter how much I wished prison and Abaddon had never happened, it had. That's why we were both here.

Lorne grabbed a glass bottle from one cabinet. "Water."

The glass was cool in my hand. "Thank you." I wanted to say something else, but he spun back and started messing with some of the cabinets.

I wasn't sure how he did it, but a moment later there was a miniature roasted chicken—although it could've been some other Aunare bird—and what looked like roasted potatoes, along with some purple and red leafy vegetable I'd never seen before. He opened another cabinet and twisted off a chunk of bread.

"This okay?" He asked as he looked back at the kitchen as if wondering what else he could fix me. "I didn't ask if you liked meat, and I could—"

"Please. This is perfect." Roasted chicken was my favorite, and this looked close enough. I stared down at it for a second, twisting the plate while I stalled. "Perfect, but..." I met his anger-filled gaze. "I did something wrong, didn't I?"

"No." He closed his eyes for a second, taking a breath. When he opened his eyes again, his perfectly cool, calm mask was in place. "No. You've done nothing wrong."

I couldn't look at him anymore. He was lying. He said he wasn't mad, but when I looked at him, all I saw was anger still burning in his eyes. I stared at the food in front of me, and suddenly I wasn't sure if I could eat it.

"I'm not mad at you, but I *am* mad. I'm trying to deal with it, horribly if you think this is your fault." He sat across from me and pushed a napkin wrapped around a fork and knife to me. "Please eat. I know you're hungry."

I took the fork in my hand. "Okay, but if I'm eating, you need to tell me why you're mad. It's making me uncomfortable. I can't eat when I'm nervous."

He smiled at me, but it wasn't a real smile. It didn't light up his face because the anger was still there, but he was trying to put me at ease. He waited as I picked up the fork, nodding when I hesitated. "Please."

"You first."

His smile slowly faded, and I wanted it back. Even if it had been tinged with anger, it was still lovely.

"After our call on Earth, Declan left a message saying again that you were fine and he was leaving for Sel'Ani with you the next day. I could get there fast, but not the next day. I was on the other side of the galaxy. So it was silly for me to go to Earth, no matter how hard it was to stay away. To not be doing something to get you home." He paused and leaned back in his chair.

I tried to think of it from his point of view. I hated when I couldn't fix something. It seemed like he and I had some things in common.

"Please eat."

"I will. Keep going."

"Another message came the next day saying that there were some delays, a couple weeks at most. He had to take a roundabout way to get you back. Jason was causing trouble, but everything was fine. Not to worry. So I waited, but more than a couple weeks passed, and I was getting nervous, but then we got word that your mom and some friends were nearby, in the Naustlic System. I hadn't heard back from Declan, so instead of trying to track you down on Earth when there was no guarantee you were still there, I went with Rysden to get them. I thought you were okay with Declan and that your mother would know where you were. I didn't understand why he'd split you up, but I trusted him to make the right call."

My mom. I had to know. "Did you—"

"Your mom and friends are safe with your father."

I hunched over with relief. My mother was okay. Safe. That was huge.

"I was with your father in the Naustlic System, about to pick them up, when I got another message. One from Ahiga. It didn't give much away, except your location. There was no good reason for you to be on Abaddon." His glow started again, and he gave a long sigh. "I got in my ship—it's faster than your father's fleet—with your father following shortly after. I planned to get as close as I could to Abaddon, contact Ahiga, and assess how much force to use when taking you back home. But when I was making my last jump, Declan *finally* called me. Only it was to tell me that you were there mining on Apollyon and very, very sick. I don't understand at all what happened, and he won't tell me." He leaned forward. "Why were you mining?"

I didn't want to break Declan's trust or cause any more problems, but I also didn't understand the secrecy. I wasn't sure how to answer Lorne without getting into the whole nasty story. "None of that matters anymore." It wasn't a lie. I was alive and safe. Hopefully, soon I'd be far away from SpaceTech.

His lips pressed tightly together as he watched me. After a long moment, he shook his head. "You're wrong. It matters very much to me." He tapped the fork. "Will you eat now?"

"Okay." I took it and stabbed a bite of meat. I still wasn't sure if it was chicken, but it tasted like it. I moaned at the perfectly spiced, tender bite, and Lorne grinned. This time it was a real one. It transformed his face from handsome to devastating.

"Good?" Lorne asked.

He had to be joking. "This might be the best thing I've had in a long time. Like since—"

"Prison?"

I took another bite before speaking. "Thankfully, I wasn't in prison for long, but the food on Abaddon wasn't much better." I wanted to leave it at that, but something about the look in his eyes told me that he wasn't going to let this go.

I took a few more bites to see if he'd say something else, but he didn't. Distraction was my only option. "There are a few things you should know before we decide to do anything else."

"I'm listening."

I let out a long breath. "There are seven storage bays on Abaddon. They were filled to the brim with lucole up until the week before I got there, and ever since I've been on base SpaceTech has been emptying them as quickly as they could. There's been an endless stream of ships showing up, only to turn right back around again. The shipments go to different colony planets for storage. And I'm not talking a container or two. It's been hundreds of thousands of *tons* of unprocessed lucole. They used to do all the processing there, but they stopped a few months ago. Carl—the guy who trained me to mine—said there was enough lucole to last SpaceTech for a couple centuries, even factoring in rapid expansion."

Lorne leaned back in his chair as my words sank in. "What are they doing with all of that lucole?"

"You mean beyond powering their cities, fueling their ships, and using it for weapons? I don't know. But I think they were planning to have the base emptied by the time any Aunare showed up to take me." I took another bite. "They're building some sort of new top secret weapon with it, too. Most of the lucole left on the base right now is earmarked for the lab. Matt—the guy in charge of inventory—wouldn't tell Ahiga much, but he did say that whatever the weapon was, it would be enough to take down the Aunare."

He muttered something.

I didn't know what he'd said, but I understood cursing when I heard it. "Not only that, but most of the crystals I found on the moon were unharvestable. They were planning to mine that moon until it was all gone, and I think it's safe to say that's already happened. There are more places they could possibly start new mines, but for whatever reason nearly all of the crystals are volatile. Something on that moon has changed, maybe all of the mining changed the makeup of the crystals themselves?"

Lorne was still, and so quiet.

I played with my food while I talked. "I think I was there to draw you in, except only *after* the base was emptied of supplies. Then you show up, take me—or probably take my body because the way my job was going there, I wasn't going to last much longer. I'd have killed myself before I put on that stupid suit again and—"

Lorne sucked in a big breath as his skin brightened. His tattoos lit along his skin, and he squeezed his eyes shut.

"Are you okay?"

"No, but finish. Please."

"Umm…" I wasn't even sure what I'd been saying.

He opened his eyes, and the glow dulled a little. "I'm just having a little trouble controlling my emotions. When you say that you would've killed yourself, it's hard not to get upset."

I opened and closed my mouth a couple of times before I found the words. "I don't know why you'd care." His glow brightened again with my words, and I knew I was messing this up. I just wasn't understanding why.

He smiled at me, but it was filled with pain and heartache. "Please finish. I show up to find you dead and…"

I swallowed. "And you blow up the base. Which, as far as anyone in the universe would know, was SpaceTech's only source of supplies. No one would know it was decommissioned and that anything of value had already been moved to the colonies. The Aunare would look bad when you blew it up because no one would know that the base would actually be empty."

Lorne let out a breath. "It would be the rallying cry for all of our enemies to join forces to act against us, and then they could use whatever weapon they've built with full support of every known civilization."

"Exactly, except you showed up early. The bays aren't totally empty yet."

"I'm not sure how that changes things. All of this tells me that I should take you and run before anyone sees us."

I was pretty sure he was going to hate this, but I couldn't stop myself. "I don't want to leave the people who helped me, but going back is dangerous. I'd feel better if Declan could check in with Ahiga and make sure everyone is okay before we leave."

"And if they're not?"

I shrugged. "I don't know that I can leave my friends behind if they're in trouble. And if we're sticking around, we should also try to get information about the new weapon they've been developing. And you might consider blowing up the base."

"Even if I could do that—which I can't—why would I do that?"

"Because I have a feeling that when I'm gone, SpaceTech will quickly empty all the remaining storage bays, blow it up, and blame you. Why not beat them to it? Why not make a dent in their resources?"

"Gods above." He leaned back in his chair. "I can't believe I'm actually considering any of this."

Lorne stared off at nothing, but that gave me time to study his face. The way his long dark hair tucked behind his slightly pointed ears. The strong jaw line and full lips. His bright blue-green eyes.

I was staring at the poor guy. Mooning over him. It was so dumb.

And then he turned his eyes on me. The color... Why did they have to be that color? The one that made me feel so calm and at peace that I'd painted my room the same shade.

He raised a brow at me and my cheeks heated. He couldn't know what I was thinking, but it felt like he might.

"I really need to know how you ended up here," he said finally. "I can't seem to focus on anything else. It's driving me mad, and Declan wouldn't tell me anything other than that I had to get here fast or you'd die."

I didn't know why Declan wasn't telling Lorne, but maybe I could tell him a little bit without getting into the details. "It was my fault. We were going to come as planned, but I... I smashed his brother's face in and popped his arm out of its socket."

The grin on Lorne's face made me feel hot all over. "You did, did you?"

"He deserved it, but I did it at work and then was arrested. It caused some complications. I—" I thought back on that morning at the diner. The feel of Jason's hand... "He deserved it." All humor in my voice was gone.

"What did he do to you?" He leaned across the table.

I shook my head slowly. There was zero chance of me telling Lorne about that. I didn't even like thinking about it—how I was manhandled and manipulated—but talking about it? Not happening.

His hair fell a little in front of his face as he reached for my hand. "If Jason attacked you, I should've picked you up immediately. I could've gotten there just as easily as I got here. Even if you were in jail. I would've torn it apart to get you out."

I slid my hand away from his. In that moment, I knew exactly why Declan hadn't called him. "You can't tear apart a jail just because I was arrested. The war—"

"Gods damn this bloody war!" He slammed his hand down on the table, rattling my plate. "How could you possibly believe that you could prevent a war that SpaceTech has wanted for the last twenty-five years? Nothing you could've ever done would've changed that. They were looking for a reason, and this time it was you. But it's been other things before. And if this ploy didn't work, another would have. It wasn't worth your life. *You were almost dead!*"

My skin grew bright. "*Almost doesn't count!*" I yelled it so loudly that my throat burned, but even as my words hung in the silence, I knew it was dumb. It sounded so incredibly dumb, even to me.

I couldn't sit still anymore. I got up from my chair and paced to the wall. I needed to think. I just needed a second. I leaned against the cold stone wall, hoping to find the right words to have it all make sense to Lorne, but I wasn't sure it would ever make sense to him. Maybe none of what I went through mattered, and that was a truly depressing thought. If it all could've been avoided so easily like he said, then I had nothing left to say.

When I turned around, I was a little calmer and a lot more resigned to the situation. "We made the best choices that we could make at the time. If anyone died because I wouldn't take the risk? Because I was too scared to go to Abaddon and wait until Declan got here to quietly take me away?" I shook my head. "I couldn't do that. I'm not worth that."

"Yes, you are." His chair scratched against the floor as he got up. "You're worth everything."

"No. I'm not better than anyone else."

He came toward me, backing me into the wall. I didn't consider myself a short person, but as he approached, I felt small. He was easily pushing seven feet tall, and that lean muscle held power under it.

I swallowed as I tried to push down the attraction and need I felt for him. It was too much—enough to consume me—and I wouldn't be consumed. Not by anything.

He cupped the side of my neck, running his thumb across my racing pulse point. "You are everything to me."

My mouth grew dry, and my heart was pounding. "Why?" I couldn't assume anything about what I thought he meant. I had to know for sure.

There was a bell sound, and Lorne frowned as he stepped back from me. "That's Declan."

The distraction couldn't have been better timed. It gave me a chance to get myself together. "Good. Let's find out what to do now. Getting upset over the past won't help us right now."

"This is far from over." He gave me a nod. "You stay and *eat*. I'll talk to Declan."

I didn't breathe until he was gone. I slid down the wall to sit on the ground as soon as the door closed.

This wasn't going to be easy. None of it was going to be easy. I felt lost and unsure of myself. I'd never felt that way, even when I was using fake names and hiding from SpaceTech. I wasn't sure if my short time on Abaddon had broken me or if I would've always felt so turned around when I found my way back to the Aunare.

And yet, standing in front of Lorne, having him touch me like that, all I could think was that this was too much and that there was something I was forgetting. Something I wasn't understanding. And if I could just remember it, then maybe I wouldn't feel so lost anymore.

But I couldn't deny that Lorne felt familiar. I trusted him. It was different—more than the usual click I got—and I didn't think that was all because of the added attraction I felt for him. I wanted him like I'd wanted nothing else in the world. The kind of desire that made me feel like I was spinning out of control in zero gravity.

I leaned my head back against the wall and realized that there were giant pieces in my mind that were missing because of what my mother did. She'd never lied to me. I knew what was done—I'd agreed to it—but until that moment, having my mind wiped never bothered me.

It more than bothered me now.

From the way Lorne was reacting to me and the things he was saying and from the color of his eyes...

That color. I'd never seen the exact shade in someone's eyes before. It couldn't be a coincidence. Not when I'd also seen his face when I was in cryo and running on the treadmill and—if I was honest with myself—I was pretty sure I'd been dreaming of him off and on for years.

They were the kind of dreams that left me wishing I could fall back asleep, but I never could, and I never remembered what they were about. No matter how long I lay in my bed with my eyes closed, they would slip through my fingers, like trying to grasp fog. I'd spend the rest of the day homesick for the ghosts of my dreams.

As I sat there, trying to figure out what to do next, all I could feel was lost. Because they hadn't been dreams. They were memories.

"Damn it, Mom. What did you do?"

CHAPTER THIRTY-NINE

AFTER MY SMALL FREAK-OUT, I went back to the table and shoveled food into my mouth as fast as I could. I was still feeling weak and a little woozy, but I figured eating had to help. A nap would be better, but I didn't have time for that. Not yet. We were still way too close to SpaceTech. I wasn't going to be able to relax enough to sleep until we were far, far away from here.

Once I was done, it didn't take me long to find Lorne. All I had to do was follow the yelling to its source.

I wasn't sure if the doors were locked, but I pressed my hand to the center like Lorne had at all the other doors, and it slid open.

The room was small, only slightly bigger than my barely-there living room in Albuquerque. Declan's face took up the upper portion of the far wall. His head was hanging down as he spoke rapidly in a language I wished I could understand.

None of this was Declan's fault, but guilt was written across his face. He was taking it all on himself.

Lorne prowled in front of the vidscreen. His movements were so fluid. I could nearly feel the power rippling inside of him, begging to break free. His skin was flickering, and I wondered what that meant. I was so frustratingly clueless of everything

Aunare. My skin would grow bright when I was scared or stressed or emotional, but I didn't know if that served some sort of purpose —other than being a full-body mood ring.

There was a long, narrow desk built into the floor in the middle of the room, nearly cutting the room in half. A captain's chair was pushed about a meter back from the desk. The walls were all the same smooth beige stone-like material. Aside from the desk and chair, the room was empty. This had to be the bridge of the ship, but there were no buttons or switches or blinking lights. Where were the ship's controls?

Something Declan said must've pissed off Lorne because he spun—facing Declan—his voice fierce as he spoke the lilting and sibilant Aunare words. A harsh fricative cut in, and I wondered if he was cursing.

I wasn't sure what they were arguing about, but there was a very good possibility that it had to do with me.

Lorne said my name, and I corrected my thoughts. This was absolutely to do with me.

"Hey," I said, trying to get their attention, but when they kept going, I said it louder.

Nothing.

I stuck two fingers into my mouth and whistled. *That* shut them up. "What's going on?"

"Your color is better, but how're you feeling?" Declan asked. His gaze kept traveling over me like he couldn't believe I was standing there.

"Better." I let out a breath. "Not a hundred percent, but I don't feel like I'm going to fall over anymore. The food helped."

His smile was sad and aching. "That's good," he said.

Lorne looked between Declan and me, and then he shoved his hands into his pockets. His shoulders hunched for a second and I couldn't tell if he was tired or disappointed, but I didn't like either if I was the cause of it.

"What's the plan? We're so close to SpaceTech, and I'm worried about Ahiga and the others. I know Lorne wanted to run a test on me, but…but if we're going to do anything, then I want to do that now and get the hell out of here before anything else can go wrong."

"That's what we're arguing about," Declan said. His gaze darted to Lorne for a second, but then came back to me.

Why was he staring at me like that?

"Well then maybe I can be a tiebreaker." I stepped in front of the desk to stand beside Lorne. If there was a choice to be made, I wanted to be part of the decision process. "Who wants what?"

"Lorne doesn't want you to go back to the planet, but I'm still far away. Ahiga's worried about what Jason might do once he realizes that Lorne has you, and he can't find Audrey or Tyler."

"That's not good."

"I know. I have a really bad feeling about it. Ystak said something while you were mining that set me off, too. I'm pretty sure he knew I was listening. I…"

He was quiet, and I knew I wasn't going to like whatever he said next. The look on his face as he scrunched his eyebrows together said he felt pity for me and guilt and I hated both of those things.

"What? Just say it."

He gave me one small, slow nod before speaking. "While you were in the healing pod, I searched through the records again for recordings and found more. A lot more. They were in the classified folders, and the ones with you and Audrey in the med—"

"No! No. There were no cameras in—"

"They were there. Hidden. So small I'm sure you'd never find them unless you knew where to look."

Revulsion made me stumble to the side, away from Lorne, until I hit the wall. It felt like a real, physical kick in the stomach, and I was so angry that I was finding it nearly impossible to breathe.

Lorne took a step toward me, but I held out a hand to stop him. I didn't want comforting. I didn't want someone to tell me it was okay. Because it wasn't okay.

"Please, he didn't—please tell me he wasn't watching me." I

hated the hint of whine in my voice, but I couldn't stop it. It was bad enough knowing that he'd been watching while I was in the suits, but the stuff in the med bay was private. It was *private*. I'd been weak and vulnerable and in pain and sometimes mostly naked.

"I think he's played us, and—"

I gasped in air. "Me. He played *me*. If he was watching the whole time, then he knew about everything. About the test. About my plan to switch to mining. He knew it all." I never even considered that he could've been watching me when I'd been told those areas were off limits, but I should've realized.

With a couple exceptions, I never ran into any officers on the base. Aside from someone messing with my suits, I wasn't aware of Jason or any of his accomplices actively coming after me. No one got in my face. No one bothered me. No one physically attacked me. It'd been so unbelievably easy to focus on surviving my stupid job instead of thinking one step ahead of Jason's plans. I'd completely ignored the bigger picture.

I covered my face with my hands.

"How could you let this happen?" Lorne's words were pure ice, but for the first time, I agreed with him. This had all been one terrible mistake after another.

"I don't think I'll ever get the sound of you screaming out of my head." Declan ignored Lorne entirely.

I dropped my hands from my face. Declan's face was pale and his eyes were wide. That was why his gaze kept darting to me. "You didn't." If he watched those videos, I didn't know what I was going to do.

"I had to." Pity. It was pity on his face now.

I didn't want his pity. I didn't need that.

"You screamed for hours and hours in that room. And the burns. The first vid file I found from the med bay—the day your shoes melted to your feet—that had been horrible, but it got so much worse. Your skin. The way your lungs rattled the third time you were in there. I had to watch it on fast forward. I couldn't stand it. You were dead for a minute and thirty-seven seconds and—"

There was a flash of brightness in the room and I glanced at Lorne.

His eyes were closed as he leaned back against the desk. His hands gripped the edge so tightly his knuckles turned white.

I stepped toward him, but he shook his head without looking up.

"I just need a second." Lorne's voice was strained. "Please. Just a second."

Declan said something softly, but Lorne cut him off with a single, sharp word.

The sleeves of Lorne's shirt were pushed up above his elbows. His muscles were corded as he held onto the table and I wanted to touch his bright skin. The tattoos ran up his arms, and I knew they probably covered most of his upper body, but I couldn't see them all.

I took a small step toward him. "What do they mean?" I asked, hoping to distract him.

Lorne turned to me slowly. "What does what mean?" he asked a little too softly.

"The glow? The tattoos? What do they mean? Why do you glow?"

He squeezed his eyes shut and hung his head low. "My heart breaks that you have to ask."

It was humiliating, but it was more important that I knew. "I know I'm ignorant, and I can't stay that way, so I have to ask. If my mom knew anything about it, she didn't tell me, and I couldn't trust any information that I found."

"Of course you have to know, and when we have a moment it would be my honor to explain what it means, how it's used, and why. Right now, I seem to be having a hard time controlling myself when I should be old enough to…"

"I'm sor—"

His eyes opened, and he gave me a sharp look that had me

backing away. "Don't you dare apologize for something that was not your doing. You are a *di Aetes*. Don't apologize. Ever."

Declan cleared his throat. "As much as I hate to interrupt, we need to make a decision," he said. "I know that you're mad at me, Lorne, but we'll deal with that later. Right now, we're running out of time."

He was probably right, and I wanted to get the hell away from Jason, but I couldn't leave. Not yet. "Audrey. She's a halfer. She helped me through all the nanos sessions. If Jason watched me while I was with her, then he knows about her. And if Ahiga can't find her, then she's in trouble. I can't leave her to die."

Lorne's glow dimmed just a little bit, and he let go of the desk to cross his arms. They started talking in English, but I wasn't listening. Everything went quiet in my head.

I had an idea. A stupid, crazy idea.

It would take SpaceTech down a notch and get Audrey, Tyler, and Ahiga back.

I was vaguely aware that the guys had stopped talking and were watching me, but I was working through the details quickly in my head. It was going to be a massive risk. For me. For Declan and Lorne. For the Aunare. But if I could at least do this...

"Did you mean what you said?" I asked, still staring off at nothing.

"Who are you asking?" Declan asked.

I blinked to free myself from my thoughts and turned to Lorne. "Did you mean it? What you said?"

A small crease formed between his eyes, but he nodded anyway. "I would never lie to you, but I don't know what you mean."

"About the war. About it being inevitable." I had to know before we did anything that could make the situation between Aunare and SpaceTech worse than it already was.

Lorne straightened from the desk. His skin dulled a little more. "Yes. I wanted to go find you on Earth myself. I thought waiting to find you was stupid. The day they slaughtered tens of thousands of Aunare, all diplomatic relations should've ended. The war is coming and—"

My hands shook, and I clasped them together to hide my fear, but Lorne glanced down at them.

Damn it. Lorne knew. How could he read me like that?

It didn't matter. I realized what I needed to do. "I have a plan, but it means that the war isn't just starting soon. If this goes badly, I might start it right now."

There was a bell. Two sharp tolls. Lorne pressed his hand on the desk behind him, and the screen split. Another man appeared. One I recognized.

I didn't know what to do or say, so I stood there, rigidly holding my breath as I tried to figure out what to say to him.

Every thought I had slipped through my fingers as I stared at my father. A man I was supposed to know but didn't. He was looking at me with all of his expectations racing across his face, and I was left with nothing but empty space in my mind for a moment. I hadn't expected this to be the first time I'd talk to him, and I was pretty sure that he wasn't going to like my plan.

CHAPTER FORTY

"RYSDEN," Lorne said, but my father didn't acknowledge him. Lorne said something else in Aunare, but my father shook his head.

"Amihanna." My father stood tall, but his eyes glittered with the shine of unshed tears. "It is so..." His throat bobbed as he swallowed. "It is so good to finally see you."

I'd seen clips of him on the news before, talking to different leaders in the galaxy and meeting with SpaceTech officials. But seeing him in front of me...

I wasn't sure what to feel. I was supposed to call him Dad or Father, but those names didn't feel right. He was a stranger, and seeing him only made me miss my mother that much more. She'd know what to do. What I should say. She would help me through this.

My mother was supposed to be here when I met my father. I never thought I'd be doing this alone.

After a moment, "Hi," was all I managed to say.

Lorne cleared his throat. "I'm sorry for leaving so quickly, but—"

"Declan sent me the videos." My father's eyes were on me. "I don't know—"

I let out a hiss and turned to Declan. "I told you to delete the ones you'd already found when we talked in the IAF meeting room, and instead you go looking for *more*, and then *shared* them with *more people!*"

"Yes. I ignored what you wanted and sent them to your father. You don't have anything to be ashamed about. We might need to use them to—"

"Like hell we'll need them. *No one* needs them. No one needs to see me like that. Delete them." I hated the burning in my eyes. I wouldn't cry. Not here. Not now.

And then a new horror cooled my heated skin. "You didn't show him the footage from the diner, did you?"

Declan's silence said everything.

I couldn't look at him. At any of them. I turned away. My skin was glowing out of control—brighter than Lorne's—and I wanted to hide. I wanted to be alone. I wanted none of this to ever have happened.

"Amihanna, please. I had to know. I'm your father. I..." He sighed, and I was tempted to turn around, but I couldn't. "I'm on my way with Teams Four and Seven, plus my own personal fleet. We're about three hours out. Less if you're ready to start jumping back this way."

What? I spun to face the screen. "You can't come here. You can't —" I started to say, but his gaze turned to fire.

"Yes, I can. I've dealt with SpaceTech for years after they brutally slaughtered so many Aunare. There were many reasons we didn't immediately crush them, but one reason—a very personal reason—was you and your mother. Your mother and some friends of yours are here with me now, but you are not. I've watched you tortured because you're my daughter and I will *not* stop until I have you safely at home."

My mother. He had Mom. The relief I felt was thick and heavy. "She's okay?"

He gave me a small smile. "She's worried about you, but fine."

I wanted to see her so badly. I closed my eyes, letting it sink in that she was really okay. Safe. With my father like she always wanted.

And still, I had a question. "She didn't—"

"No," he said quickly, cutting off my question before I could even ask it. "Declan advised me not to watch them, that no one should see them—as you requested—but I had to know the full story." He held his closed fist over his heart. "You were only a child when I left, and I wanted to see you." His voice broke, and he took a breath. "I wanted to know you, even if it was only the horrible parts. And watching the recordings—watching you in pain and tortured—only to pick yourself up, head held high, and do it all again—"

I gave a bitter laugh and looked away. He was making me sound admirable. I was anything but that. "I don't think my head was very high. Especially today." On that moon, I'd been so done. I wasn't sure I could've kept going if it weren't for Declan's calm, soothing voice in my ear.

"I don't know everything that you've gone through, but—" He paused for a moment. "One friend is quite vocal about getting you back. He's sent yet another message to me about how he needs an ETA."

"Roan." Only Roan would make demands from someone like my father without fear.

I missed him. The ache was real and physical. I tried not to think about Roan while I was on Abaddon, but now as my father spoke about him, I needed my best friend. He'd know how to handle this better than I did, and I could tell him more than I could my mother. He wouldn't judge or worry about what had already happened. He'd help me focus on what's next. That's what I needed right now.

"He's okay?"

"I should say so." My father grinned for the first time, and it was nice to see it. "Interesting character, that one."

I grinned back. It was the first real smile I'd had in a while. "He's the best."

My father gave me a small, slow nod. "I wouldn't expect otherwise from a friend of my daughter, but Lorne just messaged about an argument he and Declan were having."

I really, really didn't want to start out getting to know my father with a fight, but if that's what had to happen then that's what I'd do. "I survived the last couple weeks thanks to some friends. Declan found out they might be in trouble, and I won't leave them behind." I didn't leave any room for negotiation in my tone.

He let out a long sigh. "Ah. I see. I saw them in the videos, but *you* going back now is idiocy." He frowned and I knew I wasn't going to like what he said next. "Not everyone can be saved in war."

"Maybe not, but I have to try. And I wasn't planning on stepping foot on Abaddon again."

Lorne and Declan looked at me.

"You weren't?" Lorne asked.

"No. I have another plan." I huffed a soft laugh. "Might be a crazy one, but I think it's pretty solid considering…"

"Go on," Rysden said.

"How far from Abaddon are you, Declan?"

"Six hours and change."

That wasn't what I wanted to hear. "You're too far away for what I need. I want to do this quickly. Can you get to his ship?" I asked Lorne. "Can you tow it to Abaddon while cloaked?"

His eyebrows went up. "I can tow him and get it very close undetected, yes."

I knew he was okay with seeing where I was going with this, but I wondered if he'd back me up on my insane plan. I couldn't do it without him. My father was too far away to stop us, but Lorne could.

"Good." I focused back on Declan. He leaned back in his chair and crossed his arms as he waited, looking ready to take whatever punch I was going to throw his way.

I was going to manipulate him, and maybe I'd feel bad about that later, but if it meant Audrey had a chance to live, especially after everything she'd done for me, then I'd worry about that later. "I did everything you asked of me in that courtroom. I survived, but it was hard. I know that when all of this is done, I will forever have nightmares about my time on Abaddon. I hear my skin sizzling as I fall asleep every night. I smell sulfur as I wake. It was hard, but I did it. And now I need you to do something for *me*."

He dropped his arms to his sides. "What do you want me to do?"

"Your ship is still SpaceTech, and you haven't technically defected yet, right?"

"Yes."

"Good. Lorne is going to drop me off on the surface of the moon, I'll make a very big distraction, and in the chaos, *you* need to land on Abaddon and get my friends."

Declan shook his head slowly. "This is a bad—"

"You don't get to say no." I was pissed at him, and I was going to use that to fuel what I had to do next. "You grab Ahiga, Audrey, Tyler, Santiago, and anyone else who Ahiga thinks should come. No one stays behind who could be killed because of me. You get them out of there, then sound the evacuation alarm."

"What kind of distraction are you going to make?" Lorne asked.

This was the part that was bad. I'd barely survived the moon the first time around, and I was about to tell them I wanted to go back for more. What they couldn't know was how dangerous this could be for me. Otherwise, they'd never let me go.

I took a moment and tried to muster up all the confidence I had left. "I know where all the volatile crystals are. The ones I hit are still active. They'll be active for hours yet. All I need to do is hit them one more time, and then find a crystal big enough to set off all the others, and I think I know the one. I'm going to blow up the moon from the inside, and if we're lucky it'll smash into Abaddon and take the base with it."

My father shook his head. "I don't know Amihanna. This sounds—"

"We'll stay cloaked, but it won't take a genius for SpaceTech to figure out what happened. And if anything goes wrong—"

Lorne laughed in shock. "Gods above. You're mad."

Maybe I was crazy. I was asking Lorne and Declan to risk their lives for me. My only plan was to blow up a moon. I should be worried that hitting those crystals had nearly killed me the first time, and I was about to go back for round two when I still wasn't fully healed, but I wasn't. If I didn't come back from this, I was okay with that.

I should also be worried about starting a war, but I wasn't anymore. What Lorne had said about the war being inevitable had set in. He'd made sense. SpaceTech was evil. It had to be stopped.

Above and beyond everything else, I couldn't carelessly leave good people to die.

Ahiga. Audrey. Tyler. Santiago. They'd be traitors for helping me. For hiding me. I couldn't run when I could save them. No matter what happened to me, I was going to save them.

"Lorne and Rysden both said the war is coming. We might as well start things off with a bang." I shrugged, trying to play off the enormity of what I was saying, but I couldn't really. I'd never blown up anything, and I'd definitely never started a war.

"And blowing up the moon qualifies?" my father asked.

"I'd say so. Should be a pretty loud bang when it's all done, which should give Declan more than enough time to get away from the base with my friends. There should also be enough time for SpaceTech to evacuate the rest of the base if the moon crashes into the planet, but it's a gamble."

"Doesn't hurt that it might be fun to beat Jason at his own game, too." Lorne grinned. "I'm in."

"Declan?" I asked.

He gave me a grave nod. "Anything you need. I'm there. I owe you. I'll never stop owing you. But this? This is easy. We can make this work. I don't want to leave Ahiga there any more than you do."

"It means leaving SpaceTech." And his family. He'd once said that he didn't feel any allegiance to them, and I wondered if that was true.

"It was only a matter of time, really. I wish I'd been able to change things, but I can help more with the Aunare now. But I do have one problem with your plan." He leaned toward the camera, his gaze staring into me. "Are you well enough to do this?"

I opened my mouth to tell him that I was fine, but Declan held up his hand.

"No. No. Don't you dare lie to me. I watched you on that moon. I was with you the whole time." His voice was cold and furious. "I *know* what it did to you."

I straightened up, ready to defend myself. "I don't lie."

"And how many times did you say you were okay in the suit when you weren't? How many times did you say this was going to be *a piece of cake* to Tyler before you closed the helmet—only it was hell out there? Do *not* lie to me right now."

I stepped toward the screen. My skin was still glowing, and I didn't care that it was giving away how mad I was. "Don't you dare use that against me. *Ever*. I'm fine. I'll keep being *fine* until my friends are here and we're safe. Until that base and all the lucole and everything it stood for is gone. I'm *fine*!"

Lorne said something, and Declan leaned away from the camera, surrendering the argument. "Okay, Ami. If you say you're fine, then you're fine. You know your limits."

I let out a long breath. I felt a little bad about fooling them, but I was determined enough. I'd make this work. "Is this okay with you, Rysden?" His name came stumbling out, and I wasn't the only one wincing at the sound of it.

"Dad or Father, please. Not Rysden. I'm your *father*." There was heartbreak on his face, but I couldn't say the word no matter how much he wanted me to. I could think it in my head, but I didn't feel it in my heart.

"I know… I…" I didn't know how to explain it to him without feeling like a total jerk.

"It's okay. I understand. But you need my approval for this?" my father asked.

I didn't. My father was too far away to really stop me, but I didn't want to start off our relationship badly if I didn't have to. I gave him a small shake of my head. "But it'd be nice to have."

"All right then, I'll keep my mouth shut, but you're going to have to run fast. From my limited knowledge about the base, it's extremely protected. I'm speeding up. We'll meet in the middle somewhere. Hopefully sooner than later, but Lorne—you'll keep me apprised."

"You know I will." Lorne stood tall, held his hand over his heart, gave my father a small nod. "You've got my word on it."

"Then let's get this done and get back to Sel'Ani. I want to have a long talk with my daughter."

I swallowed. "About?"

"Everything." He tilted his head to the side as he studied me. "I missed it all. But also, about not calling me Father. We're going to have to work on that."

Man. I should've just made myself say the word, even if it felt wrong. "Okay." It came out as a squeak.

He gave a nod, and the screen blinked back to just Declan.

I blew out a long breath. Lorne watched me as I realized what was going to happen, and he gave me a small smile. My skin went from a dull glow to painfully bright.

I swallowed, not wanting to think too hard about why a simple smile from Lorne was making my skin glow so intensely. Or how when he said my name it made me feel like I was falling. Or how basically anything he did set me off in a way that I could only call uncomfortable. I didn't have the capacity to handle someone like him. Not right now. Maybe not ever.

I glanced at Declan. He didn't make my skin glow, and it didn't give me a rush when he said my name, but he made me feel safe. He was what I needed.

This was so iced. Roan was going to make so much fun of me when I told him about how I was freaking out over some guy when I was about to risk my life. Again. "I guess it's time to start a war."

"I guess so." Lorne's words hummed through me, setting my glowing skin on fire.

No. This was so not fair. He didn't glow when I talked.

Lorne's grin widened, and my glow brightened even more, making it so much worse.

I closed my eyes.

He was doing it on purpose. *Damn him.*

CHAPTER FORTY-ONE

IT TOOK ALMOST no time for us to get to Declan's ship. Instead of moving from point A to point B as quickly as possible, the Aunare ships did a series of jumps through space. That's how Lorne had moved through the galaxy in a few days, while it'd taken us weeks to go from Earth to Abaddon on a SpaceTech ship.

One jump and we were to Declan's ship. Easy-peasy.

Lorne was running his hands along the desk in front of him as he set up his ship to tow Declan's. He was standing, eyes darting from the screen to the desk and back again. I couldn't quite figure out what he was doing exactly. I couldn't even see what was on the desk. No specific buttons. No keyboard. I had to be missing something, but he was busy. I filed my questions away to ask later.

"Coupled," Lorne said. "We'll be there in ten minutes or so. Jumping while towing is a little more complicated. Takes a bit for the ship to enter in all the variables. I set it to drop us just a little outside of SpaceTech's detection. We'll swing around to the moon while you land and wait for your signal."

"Sounds good," Declan said. His image only took up a small corner of the vidscreen now. He was busy getting stuff ready in his ship.

There wasn't much for me to do, so I started pacing. Staying still wasn't something that I did very well, especially when I was nervous. I wasn't sure about this plan, but I wasn't turning back. My friends were worth the risk. And beating Jason at his own game? I *needed* that.

I ran my hands along one of the stone walls as I paced, and a light caught my eye. I stepped back, touching it again. When I turned my head, the light was gone. Only when I stood right in front of it could I see the lights and commands. They were bright blue-white against the dark sand-colored stone. The lights rippled and swirled. I wondered what would happen if I touched one of them, but I didn't dare try. The Aunare's swirling script was indecipherable to me. It was beautiful and lovely but completely foreign.

I looked over my shoulder to find Lorne watching me. I couldn't read anything on his face. That made me want to shake him. I wanted to know what he was thinking, but I was too chicken to ask.

Lorne stayed that way—watching. Observing. Waiting. For what I didn't know, but his gaze made me feel exposed. I'd been hiding most of my life, and now that was suddenly over.

I turned away, not able to look at him anymore. I seemed to do that a lot with him, and it was starting to get on my nerves. I didn't back down. I wasn't a chicken. But with him, I was.

Maybe that's where the exposed feeling was from. Maybe it wasn't even him making me feel this way. He wasn't looking at me and seeing Maité. He looked at me, and he saw Amihanna di Aetes. Daughter of Rysden di Aetes. The lost di Aetes heir.

I wasn't sure who I was anymore, let alone how to be Amihanna. I'd lost her so long ago.

I glanced back, but he was still watching me. This was getting awkward. Him just watching me in silence, so I turned to him and asked a question that had nothing to do with my feelings or the Aunare or being Amihanna or anything emotionally intense at all.

I motioned to the wall. "I can only see it when I stand directly in front of it. Is that how the control panel is with you? No buttons or switches?" My voice cracked, and I cleared my throat, but he didn't seem to notice or care.

He nodded. "Yes, but it's also keyed to certain people. Only me and a few trusted others can fly this ship."

"Is that why I can't see anything on that desk?"

"Yes." He leaned back into the desk, still patiently studying me.

I didn't want to think too hard about what he was seeing when he looked at me. "But I can see this?" I pointed to the wall. I didn't understand the difference.

"It's not ship operations. Or not critical operations. I assume you can't read it?"

I didn't want to piss him off again. He'd been so upset by how little I knew about the Aunare, but I wasn't going to lie. I shook my head. "Is it your fingerprint that unlocks it?" I motioned to the desk.

"No." He gave me a small smile. "Everyone has a unique signature—frequency might be a better description, but there's no human word for it. The ship's keyed to detect who's in it at all times and adjust accordingly."

A soft beeping started, and Lorne turned back to his desk, silencing the sound. "You ready?" he asked Declan.

"Yes. Go ahead. Turning off the video. I'll have audio on mute."

"Disengaging now," Lorne said.

The ship shuddered, and I glanced at the screen.

Abaddon was straight ahead. From up here, the planet looked like a swirling ball of gray and black and red. It was beautiful. If I didn't know better, I would've thought it might be fun to visit, but that planet would haunt me. Looking back at it, I knew with every part of my being that I would rather die than walk the surface of Abaddon one more time.

I was glad I wasn't the one to be going back there. "Be careful, Declan."

After a second, his audio came back on. "Don't worry about me. I'll be in and out."

He could say that, but I was still going to worry. "Just don't forget to tell us if you need anything," I said.

"Will do. Muting again."

"I'm muting as well, but we'll leave the line on if you need us." Lorne pressed his hand against the control panel. "We'll give him a few minutes, and then head to the moon."

I nodded. "Do you have some shoes for me? And maybe something better for being on the surface of the moon?" Although I didn't want to give up the sweater. The scent of his soap was comforting, and the woven material was softer than anything I'd ever felt before. I wondered if he'd notice if I kept it.

"This way." Lorne motioned for me to follow him.

He led me back through the hallway to the bedroom. The door slid open, and he grabbed a jumpsuit for me. It was a deep forest green, with some Aunare writing sewn over a pocket on the left chest of it and...

A bright red firedrake spewing golden fire from its mouth.

My breath caught and I rubbed my thumb over the ridges of the embroidered dragon. I pressed my free hand to the inside of my left hip.

It was the exact same one I'd drawn for the tattoo artist. The *exact* same one. It'd faded with all the burns and nanos, but it was still there. When I noticed it'd faded, I made a plan to get it fixed as soon as I was off Abaddon, but why was it here? On his clothes?

I tried to tell myself that dragons were popular. That so many different people and cultures used them as logos and icons and legends. Maybe this was just something my subconscious pulled up. A general Aunare thing. It didn't mean that it was specific to Lorne.

"What does it mean?"

He glanced at the embroidery. "House of Taure. Each member of the Taure bloodline is given a special symbol. This particular firedrake is mine."

Lorne bent down and picked up a pair of slip-ons, and I was glad that he wasn't looking at my face right then. I wasn't sure what it meant or why out of all the things in the world, I'd picked Lorne's personal symbol to tattoo on my hip.

He stood up and I tried my best to wipe all the emotions from my face. He never had to know about my tattoo.

"This is my personal ship, although I keep some clothes and shoes in various sizes in case of emergencies."

"Emergencies?" I asked, trying to focus on what he was saying. "You pick up half-dead girls from moons a lot?"

He laughed, and from the look on his face, I wasn't sure who was more surprised by it—him or me. "I shouldn't have laughed. That wasn't funny."

"Too soon?"

He shook his head. "No. I don't pick up half-dead girls a lot. This is a first for me." His grin. God. That smile. It stole my breath.

I cleared my throat, not wanting to seem as affected as I was by him or the firedrake or the sound of his laugh. "Right. So other, more normal types of emergencies."

But I wondered why he needed the clothes. He'd asked a lot about my past back in the warehouse. Roan had practically spilled my whole dating history, the jerk. It should've been fair play to ask about his, but I wasn't sure I wanted to hear his answer.

I looked into his eyes, and that aquamarine gaze saw right through me. I didn't know how, but he did. "You can ask."

My cheeks heated. Would I feel jealous if I knew the answer? I didn't want to find out. "It's none of my business."

He raised a brow but offered nothing, so I took the jumpsuit and shoes from him and went back into the bathroom to change.

I threw the clothes by the sink, leaned against the wall, and closed my eyes. I needed a second. The man threw me off balance. My glow had dimmed, but it was still there. I couldn't get control of myself around him at all.

I hoped all the Aunare weren't like this. I wasn't sure I could live on Sel'Ani if this wasn't just a Lorne side effect.

Get it together, Mai— I didn't even know what to call myself in my head. I slammed my hand down on the counter. I had to get it together before I made a complete fool of myself or worse—got us killed.

I snatched up the clothes and quickly changed. This plan was going to be hard enough to pull off. I had to force all my worries and lingering questions out of my mind. I couldn't be distracted. Not when I was about to do something so incredibly insane.

CHAPTER FORTY-TWO

I FOUND Lorne a few minutes later on the bridge. The panel in front of him still looked blank to me, but I knew he could see something on it. He slid his fingers over it as if there were buttons and keys he was touching.

I went to stand behind him, trying to watch whatever he was doing by leaning to the side, but I couldn't see anything on the desk.

"I've entered in the coordinates," Lorne said. "Declan?"

"Pulling in now. I have Ahiga on a coded line. He's trying to round up everyone."

"Good."

The moon came into view, and I let out a loud sigh. Lorne turned to look at me. I kept staring at the little piece of rock that powered all of SpaceTech. It seemed so tiny and harmless, but the moon had the ability to destroy everything.

It would've been better if SpaceTech had never found it. The moon gave them too much power too quickly, and they'd done evil things with that power.

"You okay?" Lorne stepped closer me.

"Sure."

Even if bitterness was brewing inside me. I had a hatred for SpaceTech—well earned—but hating something this much wasn't healthy. I knew it, but I couldn't help myself from hating it either.

I could see him putting in a few more commands out of the corner of my eye before he turned me to look at him.

He muttered something in Aunare as he stepped closer to me. "You're not going down there alone."

I wanted to roll my eyes at him and step back, but I held my ground. "No. I'm not afraid of going down there. I'm just angry."

"Why?" He thankfully stepped back to lean against the desk and crossed his arms. I think he knew I didn't want him to come closer. He was intimidating enough a few feet away.

"So many reasons. I can't even…" I wasn't even sure why I was mad anymore. "It doesn't matter." The words were barely more than a whisper.

"What?" He stood up from the desk. "Why would you being mad not matter? You matter."

I couldn't look at him. He was wrong. Sure. I was Amihanna di Aetes, and that was supposed to be a big deal, but I didn't feel like her. Maybe everything that'd happened the last couple of weeks weighed on me more than I thought, but—

He turned to press a few more buttons and then gave it a nod as if to say he was done. "Come here," he said as he stepped toward me.

"No."

I was feeling too many things, and being around him made it so much worse. I couldn't put a finger on why, but I didn't need him poking at my emotions. Not when they were so raw, and we were about to do something insane and dangerous.

"Come here, *please*."

When I started to back away, he grabbed my arm and half-lifted me into the captain's chair.

He'd moved so fast. My chest moved up and down as I tried to breathe, but he caged me in with his arms, leaning down into the chair. "Why are you mad? Why do you think you don't matter?

Please. Before you go out there and risk your life, I need to understand that much."

"No." I wasn't telling him anything. I knew I had to calm down before I hyperventilated, but I didn't want to tell him anything.

"Please." His nose nearly brushed mine as he begged me to open up, but I couldn't. If I started talking, he might realize that I wasn't so sure I'd be okay on the moon again. I'd be an idiot not to be scared. Not when I'd barely survived it the first time.

"Stop treating me like a child."

"Stop acting like one and talk to me." He rose up, crossing his arms. "Why are you mad?"

"Why do you care?"

"Gods above." He stared up at the ceiling for a second.

Then his gaze was on mine. I'd never felt so bare before someone, and I hated it. I was feeling too much, and that was dangerous. I had to keep it in. All of it. That's how I'd stayed alive all these years. I hid *everything*.

Lorne leaned forward until his forehead rested against mine and I couldn't hide when he did that. "I care for a lot of reasons, but mostly because you're Amihanna di Aetes and I've waited for you all my life."

I leaned back into the chair as far as I could. "What do you mean you've waited for me all your life?" He couldn't be serious with that.

He grinned, and it wasn't a happy one. "Oh no. I'm not going to spill any of my secrets until I know one of yours. Why are you mad? Tell me. Make your skin glow with it. Show me."

"I don't want to glow." I spat out the words at him, not caring if it hurt his feelings. For so long, glowing meant death. It was something I'd avoided at all costs, and I couldn't be okay with glowing. I wanted it to stop. I wanted to go back to hiding.

Except I couldn't.

Not anymore.

But letting go of the habits I'd developed to survive years in hiding wasn't going to happen overnight. I had to take baby steps. He'd said that I should take time, but he was so pushy.

Lorne knelt in front of me. Seeing him, a powerful man, on his knees in front of me, did something to me. It made me want to give in to him.

"I'm Aunare," he said. "I love seeing your skin glow. I want to see the patterns on your skin. I want to read your glyphs."

He closed his eyes, and a second later I was blinking. The light was so bright, I could even see the outlines of the tattoos on his chest through his shirt.

"I want to know why you're mad."

I gritted my teeth. "I don't know."

"Please." The word hummed and rolled through me.

I closed my eyes, but I could still see the glow. It felt safe and warm and like home, and that made me weak. So I gave him what he wanted.

"I'm mad for a lot of reasons." I kept my eyes tightly shut. "I hate SpaceTech. Everything they've done makes me burn with anger. I hate how they've made me live. Scared. Hiding. Alone. We barely survived, and there were so many close calls. So many times when…"

I opened my eyes, and Lorne was still there. Glowing brightly as he listened to me. "*That* makes me angry. We did our best to make a life on Earth, but it was hard. Every second was tainted with fear that SpaceTech was seconds away from finding me. And then Jason did." I needed to get up. I pushed Lorne away from me, and he moved so that I could get by.

I walked to the vidscreen and then spun back to him. He'd stood slowly, watching me from behind the desk.

"I thought it couldn't get worse than that night in the diner— the assault and humiliation and being covered in his blood—but it got worse. So much worse. The last few weeks have been hell, and I just want to get through this." I took a long, shaky breath. "And then I want to rest. Because I'm tired of hiding and running and fighting. I can't do it anymore. I can't pretend and…"

His face was so carefully blank. Not an ounce of pity on his face.

Good. I didn't want that. Not at all.

"I hate that Jason's fucked with me so badly and that everything I did was exactly what he wanted. It makes me burn with so much anger that I feel sick." I strode to him. "I hate that now I'm here ranting at you when all I want is to get this over with. So that maybe I can just be me for one second. But I don't even get that much because I don't know who I am anymore. You say I'm Amihanna, but that feels like someone else. Maité feels like a lie, too. And the other twenty names I had? So, yes, I'm angry, but I'm going to go out there and do this *one more thing*. Because maybe— just maybe—if I save my friends, if I take down this base, then maybe all of my life filled with terror and pain will be worth it. Because if I don't have a reason for why all of this happened—if I can't find that—then I'm scared that I'll always feel lost. That I'll never know who I am. That all I'll ever have is pretending that I'm fine, and I'm not sure I can live like that anymore. I'm not sure I can do it anymore. I don't know what to do and—"

My breath was coming too fast again, and the pressure was building in my eyes, but I didn't have any tears. Not right now.

"Is that enough? Is that enough for you?" I gasped. "Please. Let it be enough. Let me go out there and do this one more thing. Help me make this work. Please—"

He pulled me into him, wrapping his arms around me, stopping me from speaking before I embarrassed myself any more.

"Yes. Yes, it's enough." He rested his cheek on the top of my head. "Amihanna."

His voice. My name. It was too much, and yet the glow settled down. For the first time since he'd picked me up, it was almost gone.

How did he do that? What did it mean?

I tried to pull back to ask him, but he held on tight.

"This will get easier. I swear. I'll do whatever I can to help you. I promise. You're not lost. Not anymore. You're home." His glow was still there. Not as bright as it had been, but it was just enough to show the faint outline of his tattoos.

"I'm not your responsibility." I touched one symbol on his arm that looked like a bird flying, and he tightened his grip on me.

"Yes. You are."

I pulled back, and this time he let me go. Once I was free of his arms, I regretted it, but I was too stubborn to go back to him, so I hugged my arms around myself. "I don't understand. Why would I be your responsibility?"

"You and I are—"

The ship started making a soft dinging sound, and I stared at the vidscreen. We were closing in on the surface of the moon, but there were a bunch of red dots on it. "What are those?"

"Those are people on the surface of the moon. No doubt they're investigating what happened to you."

"I thought that they'd left?"

"They did, but while we left to get Declan they must've come back."

My mouth went dry, and I realized that I couldn't blow up the moon while there were people on it. "What now?"

"I don't know." He slid his fingertips across the desk. "Declan?"

"I'm having some issues." There were sounds of fighting. "Audrey's in bad shape. Got info on the weapon. Bad news all around. Need that distraction or we're not getting out of here alive."

I met Lorne's gaze and swallowed. This was tricky. So very tricky. "Your ship is fast, right?"

"Very."

"And weapons."

He shook his head. "Just some light defensive ones. The ship was built for speed. Weapons add weight."

Okay. The speed would have to be enough. "Uncloak the ship. That will draw their attention while I get down there to set off the crystals."

Lorne placed his hands on the desk and closed his eyes. "If I do, you won't have much time before SpaceTech will rally their squadrons. We'll be floating dead if—"

"I'll be fast. I know what crystals to hit. We have to help Declan—"

"I'm not saying we're leaving him." He turned his head to give me a slashing look. "I just want to give you a clear picture of what you're asking. I sped here from the Naustlic System. I made it in *three* days."

I gasped. I knew the Aunare ships were fast, but I never imagined they were *that* fast.

"Exactly. You can imagine how much fuel I burned doing that. I exhausted what I could spare healing you, and *then* I towed Declan's ship. And it's not small."

Fear gripped my heart and twisted. I hadn't known we'd be so close. I wasn't sure if it would change my plan if he'd told me, but I...

"If we uncloak, I'm not sure we can make it across the galaxy without getting caught before your dad meets us. They'll anticipate our jumps. They know we have to go through some heavily populated systems and they'll have ships waiting. I'm not sure..." He stood up and ran his hands through his dark hair. "Gods above. I can't believe I'm actually thinking about doing this. I honestly can't think of an alternative."

We were getting closer to the moon. I could see Spider and the SpaceTech IAF officers inspecting it.

I stepped toward him. I was scared and angry and worried that this was more dangerous than I'd thought, but we couldn't stop now. Not with Declan fighting for his life on Abaddon. And he was forgetting something big.

I was going down there to activate crystals. If Lorne could barely jump with how I was now, how were we going to get away *after* I hit the crystals?

"If you're going to do something, do it now! I—I need help.

Now! Shit!" Declan's voice came through the com before it cut off abruptly.

I couldn't think about anything but helping him. I didn't care if I was hurt by the end of it. "Do it. We'll make it." We didn't have another choice.

"My father will have my head for this."

My mouth dropped open for a second. Lorne's father was the King. "You mean literally?"

Lorne gave me a wicked grin that sent shivers down my spine. "No. Not literally. But he'll be mad."

I let out a breath and laughed. "Blame me. That's fine." I'd survive. Somehow. But I wasn't sure how much of me would be left after this.

"Never." His grin faded and he was all business. "If I uncloak it, then you *are* going down there alone. It seems like Ahiga managed to wipe out the cameras for good, but the rest of the weapons on Apollyon are active. I need to be here." He closed the distance between us. "I know you don't remember me, but I also know you don't feel nothing." He caressed my neck, and my skin burned bright.

He stepped back from me. "I need you to give us a chance. And to do that, I need you *alive*. So be careful."

I nodded, not really agreeing to the rest of it, but I really hoped the alive part was happening. "I will be." I hoped he didn't hear the uncertainty in my voice.

"Take these." He pulled an earbud out of his pocket and held it out for me. "I don't care if you blow up the moon or not. Do what you can and straight back here. No unnecessary risks."

This was all one massive risk—one I was willingly taking—but he didn't have to know that.

I grabbed the earbud from him and took off running.

The ship wasn't big enough that I'd get lost. I pushed the earbud in place, followed the hallway to the hatch, and waited. My mask and tool were still on the floor. I picked up the mask and flipped it on. The suction was slightly less painful this time since I knew what to expect. It had hours left on it, but if I needed more than ten minutes, we were going to be dead.

Lorne was right about one thing: no unnecessary risks.

"I'm opening the hatch now," Lorne said through the earbud. "They'll know we're here when I do it."

"I'm ready." I felt the ship lower and bent down to pick up the tool. A soft plink sounded behind me.

"What the hell?" Another came right after it from outside the hatch.

An officer stood twenty feet in front of me, weapon out, and fired again. I dropped to the ground.

Some guy was actually firing at me?

I looked back up. Just like I'd seen on the vidscreen, the ship that Santiago had prepared for me—Spider—was still where I'd left it. Three SpaceTech officers were near it, watching me with their weapons out, and more officers were inspecting where I'd fallen. One had my broken wrist unit in his hand.

My heart sped up and I was instantly flooded with the need to move.

"Hurry, Amihanna! Now!" Lorne's voice kicked me into motion.

Running toward gunfire was a special kind of idiocy, but I did it anyway.

Because, after all the times I'd nearly died, risking my life to save my friends and take down SpaceTech? That was an easy choice to make. If I lived, then good. And if I died? What an honorable way to go.

CHAPTER FORTY-THREE

I RAN AS FAST as I could out of Lorne's uncloaked ship and landed ten meters away from the edge of the mine. I couldn't believe I was back on Apollyon, but it was better than being on Abaddon. My short time in the pod had definitely helped. I had a lot more energy than I did before, but this was still pretty damned stupid.

I ran toward the SpaceTech officers firing at me, heading for the edge of the mine, and yelled, "Get to your ships. If you don't want to die, leave. Now!"

One of the officers shot at me again, but I kept moving.

"I'll take care of them," Lorne said through the earbud. "You take care of the crystals."

The officers all stopped shooting to find cover as Lorne started firing at them from the ship.

I jumped down two levels into the mine and then got to work.

I pulled out the tool and hit crystals that I knew were bad—the ones I'd only hit once. The ones with my purple marks.

I moved down the mine, running along the edges. As I activated more and more crystals, my head started to throb. I stumbled and nearly fell, but I gripped the crystals on the wall to stay upright. I took only enough time for my vision to clear a bit and then kept going.

Each crystal I activated was more excruciating than the one before it.

My vision started to double and dim, but I kept moving. The memory of Declan's cry for help kept me rushing along as fast as I could. I didn't give myself time to deal with the pain. And as I moved, I wondered if a part of Carl knew what I was going to do.

He'd given me the key to destroying this whole moon. If anyone hated this moon more than me, it had to be the guy who'd trained all the volunteers only to watch them die.

Two hits to make them volatile. Set one crystal off and the whole place would be blown. Add in his method of marking them up, and I had a recipe for how to destroy Apollyon.

Still, it'd be hard to time the explosion right. Carl's endless afternoon training had drilled into me how unstable lucole were and also unpredictable—they didn't necessarily always blow up right away. Sometimes the vibrations would crescendo, which could take from thirty seconds to ten minutes.

There was a cluster in particular that I was looking for. It was the one that had nearly killed me. It was highly volatile and bigger than any other cluster in the mine. If I could get that one to blow, it should produce an explosion big enough to tear the moon apart. Add in the rest of the activated crystals, and I'd have one hell of a distraction. I wasn't sure if the timing and orbit would work out for the debris to land on the base itself, but even if it landed on the other side of the planet, that should be enough to cause the whole lava surface to destabilize. No matter what technology was built into the base's pylons, it couldn't combat that.

I hit more. And more. And more crystals as I searched for the one I was looking for. Ignoring the shaking of my legs. Ignoring the blood dripping from my nose. Ignoring the sounds of gunfire around me. I kept going, trusting Lorne to have my back.

The more crystals I hit, the worse the pain got, and I knew I should stop, but I couldn't make myself stop. I couldn't get this far only to fail. So I kept hitting crystal after crystal. The *thwump-thwump* in my head grew and grew. Just like when I'd been here earlier. Even if I felt better after the pod, I knew what Lorne had said. I needed another healing session, which meant I was going to be in bad shape before this was done, and I couldn't even begin to worry about the fuel we needed to get away.

I jumped down another level and slipped. My back hit the ground, and I wanted to stop, but I thought of Audrey. Of how she saved my life. Of how she held my hand in the med bay, telling me her life story. I had to help her.

I'm a di Aetes. Di Aetes never quit. Not ever.

I got moving again, slower this time. The one I needed had a unique formation. One of the crystals in the group had arced instead of spiking out of the bedrock. The ones around it grew out of the arc. It looked like a spiky, black-and-white rainbow. The fat arc crystal. It nearly killed me the first time I hit it.

Two more taps and Apollyon would be dust.

Shots rang out around me, but I trusted Lorne to do what he said. To protect me. And I knew that he was going to keep me safe. So I kept running, hoping that my vision wasn't too messed up to actually find the right one.

There.

I blinked a few times, making sure I actually saw it.

Yes. There.

Right freaking there.

I spotted the one I wanted, but I was on the wrong level. Not surprising since the mining had been hard and every level looked the same, but I found it.

I jumped down to the sixth level, and my knees ached with the impact.

"Stop! Don't! You'll blow the whole moon!" A SpaceTech officer held a gun, pointed straight at me. He was one level above me.

That was exactly the point.

"I've got him." Lorne fired from the ship, and the man fell to the ground. "Do what you need to do."

I didn't look back to check on the officer who would've killed me. I did what I had to do. I brought the hammer end down on the crystal with a loud *thwack*.

The high-pitched tone felt like a spike being dug into my head. I moaned as hot blood ran down my cheeks, and it felt as if one of my molars had cracked in two.

"Are you okay?" Lorne said. "We're about to have more company."

I had blood running out my ears and nose, my muscles would barely hold me, and my vision was cutting in and out. "I'm fine." Liar. I was such a liar.

"There's blood running out of your ears." I didn't have to know him very well to hear the cold fury in his voice.

I wiped it away. "I'm fine," I gritted out the words, knowing I was anything but. "Be ready to pick me up. I might pass out again."

"You better not pass out on this godforsaken moon! Get your ass back to this ship."

"Sorry. I might've lied to you and Declan about how I was feeling." My words were slurring. "And I'm way worse now than I was the last time you picked me up."

Lorne let out a stream of curses in two languages, but I didn't regret it. No matter what anyone said, I would never regret going back to help the people that kept me alive on Abaddon.

"Wait," Lorne said. And then started yelling in Aunare.

"What?" I blinked, trying to clear my vision, but it was like I was drunk. I gripped the crystals as the moon spun.

"Declan doesn't have a ship. He says that it was already loaded up and SpaceTech took off with it."

I knew there was going to be something that messed this up, but I didn't think of that. It was too fast. How did SpaceTech get his ship refueled already? It hadn't been that long.

I needed to think of something. There had to be a way. There had to— "Santiago's ships. There were two other fast ones he was working on. Use one. It won't get them far, but it's better than nothing. Then we'll pick them up. Either tow the ship or transfer them to ours."

"Towing is out. My ship can't tow while running from Space-Tech's fleet *and* not being able to jump because your *brain is bleeding, again.*"

"I'm *not* arguing with you. Tell Declan what I said! And then tell Rysden to pick up the pace. I'm hitting this crystal the third time. Be ready!"

I took a steadying breath and slammed the hammer down for the last time.

I was blind again. My ears were ringing. I wasn't sure what had happened, but I was pretty sure that was the ground digging into my back. I'd fallen. I wasn't sure how long I'd been lying there, and I was pretty sure I wasn't going to be able to get back up.

"Move! Now! Now!" I could hear Lorne faintly yelling through my battered ears, but I couldn't move.

Everything was black.

I couldn't see.

I couldn't move.

We were so fucked.

"Get up or I'm coming down! Right now!"

I blinked my eyes open, surprised that I could see again, even if things were still blurry and spinning, but I wasn't sure I could move. "Just leave me here."

"Like hell. I'm dropping a line. You have to grab it. And we have to go."

A second later something shiny appeared in front of my face.

"Grab it."

My arms felt like they were filled with impossibly heavy lucole, but I managed to hold onto it. Something warm wrapped around my body and then I was flying fast toward the ship above me, making me so dizzy I started gagging. Before I could take another breath, Lorne was picking me up off the line.

"You hang in there." He ripped off my mask and ran with me in his arms.

Lorne yelled something in Aunare, and I felt the ship jolt under him, but he didn't pause or falter. Not even for a second. Not even while carrying my limp body.

He gently placed me on the floor against the side wall in the bridge. He took a second to press two fingers to my pulse point while he stared into my eyes. "Stay here, okay?"

"I can't move. I think I'll just watch the show from here."

"Good." He stood up and went to his desk. "We're to you in five. You run!"

I wasn't sure who he was talking to, but I assumed it wasn't me because I wasn't in shape to run anywhere. Not for a while.

I slid my gaze up to see the vidscreen. One screen showed us moving fast toward Abaddon, entering its atmosphere. A second screen was zoomed in on seven figures running across the crusty lava. Cracks opened up as they ran.

They were on foot? "Where's Santiago's ship?"

"Blocked," he said. "You've got five more seconds, and then I'm leaving without you."

He couldn't. He had to pick them up. My heart pounded.

The ship rocked as something hit it. My head slammed back into the wall, and I winced. "What was that?" I tried to sit up, but the pounding in my head grew worse, so I gave that up.

"Your plan worked. The moon's gone. Good job." His tone was so sharp, I wondered if he was joking.

I closed my eyes. "Really?"

"Yes. You did what you set out to do." He shook his head at me. "I'm not sure I'm happy with the cost though."

A tear rolled out of my eye, and I didn't care enough about wiping it away. "Will it hit the base?"

"No. It should mostly land on the other side of planet, but that will destabilize it. And Declan set up his own bombs down there just to make doubly sure."

My lungs grew tight, and I wasn't sure what I was feeling—if it was relief or exhaustion or just overloaded emotions—but I opened my eyes to watch the screen. I'd worry later about how I was supposed to feel about destroying a moon and a base. I'd wait until I heard if everyone made it out okay.

The ship rocked again.

"What was *that*? Another moon exploded?"

Lorne gave me a small laugh. "I wish. Base's security drones are firing at us. We have to go. Support ships are heading our way now."

Declan was so close. My friends. So close.

Lorne lowered the ship in front of them. "Hatch is open, Dec. Move your ass!"

One of the figures stumbled, and I gasped. No. I couldn't tell who was who in the suits, but I didn't want anyone left behind.

One of the others grabbed the stumbler, half dragging them toward the ship, and I breathed easier.

The screen shifted in front of Lorne, showing the drones firing at us. "We need to get out of here. Oh gods. Hurry, Dec! We need to go!"

I'd been focused on the bottom square—the seven figures in suits running into the hatch—but now I looked at the bigger picture.

I propped myself up on my elbow and my vision blurred for a second before I saw what Lorne saw.

He was right. More ships were coming from patrols. At least fifty.

An alarm started ringing, and I knew we were screwed.

Footsteps ran down the hall, and I grunted as I heaved myself off the ground, leaning against the wall to keep me upright. I needed to see my friends. I needed to know that they were okay.

Declan was the first to appear, and I closed my eyes. *Thank God.*

"What the hell, Lorne?" Declan asked. "Why aren't we jumping?"

I swallowed down the guilt. It was going to be my fault if we didn't get away now.

"We can't," Lorne said. The ship swayed before speeding up, maneuvering between SpaceTech's fleet.

"What? That one hit was too much—"

"Look at her." Lorne's voice was full of anger, and I knew he meant me.

I wanted to apologize, but I didn't dare. That would only piss off Lorne more.

Audrey dropped down beside me, still in her suit. Her face was pale, and her left eye was swollen. "You can't leave her like this. She needs nanos!" Audrey yelled.

"No!" Lorne and I said at the same time.

"I can't do that. Not again," I said. The idea of it made me want to give up and die right then and there.

"Even if they wouldn't torture her, they'd take too long to repair her brain. We have a perfectly good healing bed on her father's ship. I can't use mine. Not if we want a shot at staying alive. I need everything this ship has left focused on speed. Just hang on."

He flew and flew fast. The ship rocked as it was hit. Over and over. But the damage wasn't enough to slow it down. Not yet.

I held on to Audrey, trying to keep myself stable, and looked around the room. My vision was still a little blurry, but I could make out the forms well enough. Tyler was standing next to Audrey, pulling off his suit. Ahiga, Santiago, and Matthew were still in their suits with their face shields open. They stood against the wall by the door. Tabitha and some guy I didn't know—also in their suits—were sitting on the floor against the back wall, watching the vidscreen with wide eyes. I wasn't sure what to make of Matt and the other guy, but I had to trust that Declan and Ahiga wouldn't bring any Aunare enemies with them.

I twisted to look back at Declan, and the room swam. Audrey caught me when I started to fall, and I mouthed *thank you* at her.

Declan had shed his suit and was standing at the desk next to Lorne, doing something else. Firing weapons? I wasn't sure. But I had to assume that Lorne's ship was keyed to Declan. I knew they were close, but hearing how they talked to each other and worked as one—I hoped that Lorne could get over his anger.

Audrey grabbed my head and looked into my eyes. "She's got brain trauma. Her pupils are a mess. She needs help."

"She'll be okay," Declan said.

"She might not be," Audrey said. She stood up enough to wiggle out of her suit, and I noticed a rash along her skin.

"You okay?" I knew she'd been missing for a while. The color of her skin and the swelling eye and now a rash? Something was wrong.

"Don't worry. Right now I'm better off than you." Audrey kicked her suit to the side and sat beside me.

I grabbed her hand. "I'll be fine. I survived this long."

"I don't know how, but you're stubborn." She coughed a few times, then shook her head. "Find me a bucket and water and some washcloths."

I heard someone get up, but I couldn't look away from the vidscreen.

More SpaceTech ships appeared.

We were iced. It was done. If we didn't get away now, we weren't getting away. That couldn't happen. I'd rather die than be under Jason Murtagh's thumb again. I wouldn't live through it a second time. The base was going to be gone soon, but there were so many other ways Jason could torture me. I didn't want to see what he'd dream up next.

Another hit rocked us, and I slid down to the ground. It was too hard for me to stay upright, even with Audrey's help.

"How far out are we?" Declan asked.

"We'd need three jumps." Lorne's gaze slid to me. "I can't risk it."

"If we don't try it..."

"What's the dilemma?" I asked. "If I'm the problem, I should get to help decide what we do."

Declan came to kneel in front of me. "We need three jumps to get to your father. We can't outrun them. Not without jumping. We get to your father, and we're free. Right now we're one small ship. SpaceTech's happily engaging with us. But your father's ship plus two other squads? That's big time. They can't engage without officially committing to war. My brother needs my father and the *entire* board to agree before he can do that. And our allies might not look kindly on that, especially now."

We had to jump. We had to get to my father, but the last thing Declan said took a second to process. I didn't understand. "What do you mean especially now?" I swatted away a drop of blood dripping from my nose.

"Your father released a statement and small news reel just in case something went wrong. The clip from the diner and a few select clips from Abaddon."

My skin felt cold. *No. No.* Bright dots sparked in my vision as I tried to understand why my father would do that to me. He heard me yelling at Declan about showing him. How could he do that to me? "Who saw it?"

"Everyone."

All the air whooshed out of my lungs, and I didn't think I'd ever be okay again. I never wanted anyone to see any of that. I'd sacrificed everything I ever was to stay safe. To remain hidden. To prevent this stupid war. And my father had just released some of my most humiliating and private moments for everyone in the universe to see.

I looked at Audrey, and she squeezed my hand.

"It was for our allies. So that they'd know why we were running from SpaceTech. And to warn anyone allied with Space-Tech to stay out of our way. I know you're going to be upset about it, but you have nothing to be ashamed of. I hope one day you'll understand that. But right now, we're too close to the Hestalon and Zktra systems, otherwise..."

Another blast hit the ship, and an Aunare voice started speaking.

My eyes grew wide as I saw the fear on Declan's face. "What's it saying?"

"Our shields are almost done," Lorne said. "I'm diverting power, but..."

No. I wasn't getting captured by SpaceTech. Neither was Declan. Neither was the *crown prince* of the Aunare.

I licked my lips. "How long does a jump take?"

"Seconds."

I took a breath. "I can hold on." I really hoped I wasn't lying, but even if I was, I didn't care.

"It'll be excruciating!" Lorne yelled.

"I can do anything for a few seconds. I know that much by now." That wasn't a lie.

"She can take it," Declan said as he stood up.

Lorne stormed over to us, shoving Declan. "You miserable piece of—"

"She can take it." Audrey gripped my hand in hers.

We'd been through this before. We could do it again.

"She can take it." Ahiga stepped forward.

I took a breath.

Lorne had to jump. He had to believe them.

"I wouldn't say it if it wasn't true," Tyler said, and I could've kissed him for it. "Girl has been through a hell of a lot. I can't pretend to know what you're talking about, but if it's pain, she can take it."

Lorne looked at me. "I can't risk it. I *can't*."

I was scared. There was no doubt about that. I didn't want to die, but more than that, I couldn't take any more of what Space-Tech was going to give me. I was too tired. Too weak. There wasn't another choice. It was run or die.

"I can't be taken by them again. Please, get us away from here and know that I will hang for as long as I can. I know I'm not looking fantastic right now, but I'm strong, and I'm stubborn. Jumping will save all of us. Please, *please* do this. Don't let me down. Don't break your promise."

He closed his eyes, and I saw him taking the breath—the count of six, out for three. He strode back to the desk. His fingers moved fast along the surface. "Ready in three. Two. One."

He hit the button, and it felt like my brain was exploding. The pain ran through my whole body, and for a second I thought I was dying. I screamed and clutched my head.

And then it was over. The ringing was worse though. At least I thought it was worse. All I knew was I didn't think I'd ever felt this bad.

I panted a few breaths, letting the pain flow out of my body. Hot tears rolled down my cheeks, dripping onto the floor.

Lorne looked at me, and I could feel his pain as if it were mine. I knew I was forcing his hand, and I hoped that eventually, he'd forgive me. Especially for the lying, because I had a feeling that this was about to go terribly wrong for me.

But we had to keep going. Nothing had changed. We couldn't be captured. Not now. Not ever. I would sacrifice everything to make sure at least that much happened.

I nodded at Lorne and then winced from the pain of moving my head. "Do it." My voice was shaky, but I was okay.

"Ready in three. Two. One." He hit the button.

I thrashed on the ground, rolling into a ball as I clutched my head. My throat burned as the scream ripped from my throat.

It took me a second to catch my breath. The stone floor was cold against my face, and I needed a second as the sobs wracked through me.

Just one more second.

One more.

"They're coming. We're too close to Zktra's base." Declan said. "Hit it again."

"No." Lorne's voice was cold and vicious.

"Do it!"

"No," he said quietly. I couldn't see him, but I knew that he was giving up. I could hear it in his voice. "It's over. She's in too much pain. I can't... And the ship... It's barely holding together. The healing chamber won't work. There's not enough power left even if I... I...I won't be able to save her."

Audrey was murmuring to me, wiping my face with a cool,

damp washcloth. I felt Lorne come over. I knew I had to be the one to tell him, but I wasn't sure I could find the words.

He ran his hand down my back. I was still in a ball on the floor. My forehead resting against the ground. I could hear the plop-plop-plop of my blood as it dripped out of my ears.

I'm a di Aetes. Di Aetes never quit. Not ever.

I closed my eyes and thought of Jason in that diner. Of the feel of his fat fingers digging into my arm. Of his hand weaseling its way into my underwear. And I turned my head just enough to catch Lorne's gaze.

I could handle it. I knew I could. Jason wasn't winning. "Do it."

His jaw ticced. "No."

He had to do it. I would do anything—say anything—to convince him. "Please. I don't want to go back there."

"No." He shook his head slowly. "I can't watch you die."

"Declan?"

There was pain in Lorne's eyes as I asked for Declan. He must've thought I was picking Declan over him, but I wasn't. I just wanted to get away from SpaceTech.

"Can you do it?"

Lorne gave me a sad smile as he brushed my hair from my face. "No. He can't. I changed the jump controls before I left the desk. I won't risk you, and I don't trust Declan with your safety. Not anymore."

Okay. That was out. I had one last thing I could do, but I didn't want to do it. I really, seriously didn't want to. But I didn't want to find out what SpaceTech would do to us if they caught us. I couldn't take that. Anything but that.

I looked at Audrey and her swollen eye.

It wasn't just my life on the line here. If they caught us, we were all dead. I couldn't let Lorne sacrifice everyone because one last jump *might* kill me. I wasn't afraid to die.

"Declan?" My voice shook.

Lorne's eyes widened.

"Yes, Ami?" Declan's voice was wary, and I got it. But he was going to do whatever I asked.

"Play him whatever my father showed everyone." My voice was raspy but sounded clear and confident.

"No," Lorne said. "You didn't want me—"

I laughed. "Apparently everyone's seen them. You're just one more person."

"You sure?" Declan asked. "You got pretty mad about that earlier…"

I rolled onto my back and met Declan's gaze. "Yeah." A tear roll down my cheek, and Lorne caught it with his thumb.

I heard it start and I squeezed my eyes shut. I didn't need to see it. I'd lived it.

Jason's pervy voice filled the bridge. I heard my voice asking him to stop. I could feel his hands on me again, and then I heard the sick crunch his face made as I smashed my fist into it.

Then I heard myself yelling, begging for it to stop. Begging for Audrey to sedate me. I heard Audrey and Tyler's fight. That had to be the first nanos session.

"Christ. Stop. Declan, stop." Lorne's forehead rested against mine. "You're breaking my heart, Amihanna."

"Please. I can't go back there. I can't live through all of that again." My chin shook, and tears streamed from my eyes, but I wasn't above begging. "I know I'm in terrible shape. I can feel it. But don't make all of what I went through up to this point mean nothing. You can help me. Get us to my father. Please."

His tears dripped onto my cheek, mixing with mine, and he pulled back. "Okay, but you hang in for me. I can't lose you again."

"I haven't come this far to die now." The truth was that I wasn't sure I could keep that promise. I'd try, but I was in so much pain. All I could think about was getting away from SpaceTech and the pain finally being over. One way or another.

Lorne closed his eyes. A burst hit the ship again, and the walls glowed with a red light.

He stood up and went back to the desk. "In three." His voice cracked. "Two." I could barely stand to hear it. "One." The word whispered so softly in the quiet.

I knew I was screaming—the air was ripped from my lungs—but I couldn't hear it. I couldn't feel anything, except for pain. It was like a meat grinder in my head, and all I could think was that I'd lied. I couldn't survive this.

And when the ship stopped, I couldn't stop screaming.

I don't know how long I was like that before I could hear something. My own screams. It was faint, but I heard them and tried to stop.

Then my father's voice yelling.

Someone picked me up and ran.

I felt the air shift. Just like I had in the mine when I'd been sucked into the ship.

And then I heard my mother screaming.

My mother?

Was I dying?

"I'm sorry, Mom." My voice was little more than a croak, and I heard her answering sob, but I couldn't make my eyes open. I couldn't stand the pain. So I did the only thing left that I could do.

I let go.

CHAPTER FORTY-FOUR

I was warm...
Safe...
Loved...

The light was so bright, so white that it should've hurt to look at it, but it didn't.

Being here was like being wrapped in a warm blanket made of love. Cozy and perfect.

I let out a slow breath and felt the weight of over a decade of fear and pain and sorrow disappear as if it were a trillion light-years away. Finally, I was free. Truly free.

Maybe I should've been scared or upset that I was gone—that my life had ended so painfully short—but I wasn't. Death was true peace, and I wanted to stay here forever.

A low hum rumbled through my soul, and I felt myself being called back, except I didn't want to go back.

I didn't want to go…

I didn't want to—

CHAPTER FORTY-FIVE

I WASN'T DEAD. I didn't hurt. And I was disappointed that I was alive.

Those were the first three things that came into my mind.

I didn't want to wake up. I'd really, truly thought I was going to die on Lorne's ship, and I'd made peace with it. When I begged Lorne to make that last jump to my father's ship, the eternal beyond hadn't scared me. Not after everything I'd been through. I might have begged for death a few times when Audrey was giving me nanos, but each time I'd woken okay with having made it through, and I'd been glad.

This time was different.

If I was alive, then that meant I had light-years to go. Light-years upon light-years to go before I could ever be free again, and I wanted to be back in that bright, warm, safe place. I wanted it like nothing I'd wanted before.

And as I lay there silently listening to my mother murmur to my father in hushed conversations, I knew I should be thankful to be alive, but I wasn't. I wasn't sure I had the strength left to survive much more.

Living on Earth had been a daily struggle. Sometimes the fear threatened to swallow me whole. Eventually, I'd gotten used to it. Dealing with fear was essential to surviving. But Jason's assault and Abaddon and Apollyon changed things. It changed me. Even as I was going through it, I didn't realize how much worse it'd been than the years and years of terror I'd already lived through.

The pain of slowly dying over and over had whittled away the little bit of myself I had left.

I didn't think I'd ever not smell sulfur on me or feel the heat of the boots burning into my feet or hear the crackle of my skin burning.

I was empty. Done.

That made me a coward—and I hated it—but I was so *tired*, so incredibly exhausted and bone weary, that I wasn't sure I cared about being brave anymore. I just wanted to fade away, back into that calm, warm place filled with peace.

I squeezed my eyes shut, hoping that no one would notice that I was awake.

Dying on the ship had felt like a nice end to all the fear and pain and millions and millions of lies I'd told everyone. Giving my life so that my friends could make it to safety? That felt like a good, decent way to end my short, miserable life.

I held my breath until I couldn't hold it anymore. I was so scared that if I breathed, that I'd cry. I didn't want to cry. I didn't want to give into the sob crawling its way up my throat, but I wasn't sure I could stop it.

I held the air inside me until my lungs burned. Until my body fought for life. And then the sob slipped free.

All the little whispered conversations stopped.

I kept my eyes tightly shut and rolled over in the bed, hiding my face. I felt my mother's hand on my back as she told me it was okay. But it *wasn't*. It *wasn't okay*.

Being awake meant that I was going to have to figure out how to be Aunare enough for them to accept me.

Being awake meant that I was going to have to face war and bloodshed and all the horrors that came with it.

Being awake meant that I was going to have to fight for my freedom again in an entirely new way, and I wasn't sure I had it in me to figure out a new way to be me.

"Are you in pain?" my mother asked. Her worry was thick in her voice.

"No." Not the kind she meant.

"What's the matter then?"

"I..." I couldn't say it. I opened my eyes and saw Lorne sitting in a chair beside my bed. He was wearing a pair of dark gray pants and a shirt that had three buttons at the top. The long sleeves were rolled up to his elbows, revealing the tattoos around his forearms. His skin was glowing with a golden aura, bright enough to light the whole room.

His face was so carefully blank as he watched me. No judgment there. No pressures to be something that I wasn't. He just watched in that quiet way he had. So different from the man who had caged me in his captain's chair. Different from the one that pressed his forehead against mine, knowing what I was asking of him, but willing to do it anyway.

Him, I could tell. Not anyone else.

He didn't move as I cried. He never tried to comfort me. He just watched me, waiting. For what, I didn't know. But he sat in the chair beside my bed.

I wasn't sure where we were or what was going on. All I knew was that I was alive. When... "I was ready to die."

Lorne moved then. Not much. Just closed his eyes. My mother blocked him from view as she quickly moved around the bed and lay down beside me, wiping tears from my face.

"No, *mija*. You're fine. You didn't die."

She didn't understand.

I sat up, needing to see Lorne. To know if he knew what I meant. When I met his gaze again, his eyes were open, dark blue-green calling to me.

He let out a long, slow breath, and I knew. He knew exactly what I meant.

He got up and walked away.

The *swoosh* of the door sliding open made my heart ache. Stupid. I was so stupid to think Lorne would get it. That he'd understand. He didn't know me. My own mother didn't get it. Maybe Roan… Maybe Roan would understand.

The bed I was in was big, but not big enough to scoot away from my mother without upsetting her. There were chairs on either side, but I wasn't sure if someone had brought those from another place in the room or from somewhere else. I looked back at the one Lorne had been sitting in, a red blanket was thrown over the back, and a pillow was crunched against the side, and I wondered if he'd been sleeping in it. But he was gone.

He was gone now.

I pulled my knees into my chest and rested my head on them to hide my seemingly endless stream of tears. I wondered how I could ask for Roan without pissing off my mother. She'd be hurt that I wasn't confiding in her, but her constant stream of questions was making this so much worse.

"Everyone leave." Lorne's voice cut through the whispers and my mom's pleading tone as she stroked my hair, and the thick, swirling emotions threatening to drown me. "Give us a moment. Please." The please felt tacked on at the end like he'd only just remembered to be polite.

I lifted my head, and he was there. At the foot of the bed. Watching me. And just like that, the tears stopped.

Declan started to object, but Lorne's glow flashed painfully bright and the look he gave Declan—like he would slit Declan's throat if he could and be happy doing it—I never wanted to be on the receiving end of a look like that. Not from anyone.

"You don't want me to go, do you?" Mom's face was full of concern and worry, which was nice, but I did want her to go. There was just no way I'd ever be able to tell her that though. So I took the coward's way out. I looked at Lorne.

"Please, Liz. I need a moment alone with her." His gaze stayed glued to mine as he spoke to my mom.

"*Now?*" Declan spat the word. "She just woke up from a coma, and you're picking *now* to talk to her. Can't you just give her—?"

"No. I can't *just*. Leave now," Lorne said, without even looking at Declan.

Declan looked like he wanted to punch Lorne, but my father pulled him away.

My father. This was a hell of a first impression, but I couldn't help myself. He was watching Lorne and me very carefully, and then he said something in Aunare. Lorne whispered something back.

Ha shalshasa ni meha.

The words felt important. They echoed in my mind.

Ha shalshasa ni meha.

Ha shalshasa ni meha.

I didn't know what that meant, but it seemed to simultaneously piss off Declan while my father nodded slowly and stepped back.

"Come, Elizabeth. She'll be okay. Lorne will come get us in a moment."

I wanted to laugh as my mother nodded. She was giving up that easily?

What the hell did *ha shalshasa ni meha* mean? Because if that's all I needed to say to get everyone to back off, it was now my new favorite phrase.

Everyone left without another word, leaving me alone with Lorne.

It was quiet with them gone. Too quiet. I'd wanted them to leave, but now I felt more empty and alone, and I wasn't sure what to say to Lorne. The silent space between us felt like a chasm, one I had no idea how to cross. So instead I finally looked at where I was.

The room was pretty large. It could've fit our old Albuquerque apartment in here. There was a sitting area next to some windows, and it looked like there were spots where two armchairs would fit nicely. Thick curtains covered the windows, blocking out whatever was beyond them.

The only light in the room was coming from the lamps on either side of the bed, the massive chandelier hanging from the ceiling, and Lorne. His glow was still so bright, I wasn't sure I needed any other lights in the room.

I dried my face. It felt like I could breathe again. "Thanks." It wasn't much, but that was all I could manage.

"Hmm," Lorne said as he sat on the foot of my bed, keeping his gaze glued to mine. "I don't think you're going to be thanking me at the end of this."

I wiped my hands on the sheets, suddenly ashamed of everything I was feeling. "I bet you're pretty mad at me." He'd said he would never lie to me, but that's exactly what I'd done to him. I'd lied. And with what I'd said after waking up, he knew it.

"Mad doesn't even begin to describe what I'm feeling right now." His voice was filled with heat, and I knew I had to fix this somehow. "You knew you were going to die?"

"I didn't know for sure, but..." I nodded. Lorne cleared the room—saved me from all the questions and fretting from my mother—which meant I owed him the truth. "I hadn't felt pain like that before, and after the last few weeks, I pretty much knew what it was like to come close to death. But I..."

I didn't know how to make him understand, but I couldn't take the emotionless look on his face as he waited for me to finish. I wanted to tell him to scream at me. To show me what he was feeling. But he was back to the quiet Lorne.

I hoped that being honest with him might help him understand. "I just didn't want to be caught. They were so close, and if SpaceTech had me, they would've given me nanos only to torture me again. I'd had enough of that. And maybe I could've held on until my father bargained for me, but maybe not. In the meantime, you would've been caught, along with Declan and Audrey and everyone else. That couldn't happen. So I chose the lesser evil. I wasn't sure I would die, but I wasn't really sure I'd live either."

"Okay," he said the word, and I knew that he didn't mean it.

His voice was too cold and flat and his face... I wasn't sure how he could keep it so blank.

The hope that he would understand and forgive me died. "What happened?"

I wouldn't have known that whatever he was going to say was upsetting to him if I hadn't noticed the short breath he took and the swallow, as if he was pushing down his emotions to keep his calm mask over his face.

"You stopped breathing in my arms as I was running with you to your father's ship. The doctor was there at the door waiting for us. He kept you from dying until we got you into their healing chamber. You've been out for a week. At first, they thought you might be a vegetable, but—"

"But I'm okay." I was speaking clearly, and even if I hadn't stood up yet, I could wiggle my toes. I knew all I had to do was try to stand and I would.

"Yes. Physically, you're fine. You'll be a little weak at first, but you'll get that back with a little work. Exercise should help everything get a little clearer for you."

He barely knew me, but he could see through me. When I woke up, I'd needed that. I'd needed his help. But now, I wasn't sure I liked being transparent at all. "How did you know?"

He raised an eyebrow. "How did I know what?"

"What I meant when I woke up? To send everyone away? How did you know? You were going to leave, but you stopped..." I should've been embarrassed asking him that, but I didn't care. I wanted to know.

"I wasn't leaving." He was quiet for a long minute. We just sat there staring at each other as I waited for him to answer. Finally, he shook his head. "Ask me again when you're not feeling so raw. Until then, let's just say I have excellent gut instincts, especially when it comes to you."

"Is that an Aunare thing?" Because the click I felt with some people could be called a gut instinct.

"Yes, and before you ask me anything else, I have to tell you that there are a number of things you should be worrying about. Like where you are? What's been happening while you were asleep? And the war?"

I almost laughed at his words. I'd said nearly the same kind of thing to him in the kitchen of his little ship when I wanted to distract him from asking more personal questions. "Okay. I'll play. Where am I? What happened? What's the deal with the war?"

He got up and moved to the chair beside my bed, scooting it closer to me. He leaned forward, his elbows on his thighs as he spoke. "You are on Sel'Ani. Specifically, in your father's house. I've also lived here with him for the last seven years, so it's become my home, too."

Interesting. I didn't know what to think about that, so I put it away. I slid out from under the covers to face him fully.

"While you were out of it, I spent a little time with the people we picked up from Abaddon and from the Naustlic System. Your father was right. Roan is interesting, and I was surprised how much I like him."

I laughed. "He's my speedy teddy bear. Whenever I was really scared or afraid or life was really shitty, he was always there to make it easier. He has this amazing ability to make anything fun."

He leaned back in the chair and gave me a sad smile. "Then I guess I owe him a great deal." He paused. "I quite like Ahiga, too. I've met him briefly a few times before, but I seem to see eye to eye with him on most things. He feels truly terrible that he wasn't able to do more for you."

I shook my head. "It wasn't his fault."

"No. No, it wasn't."

I didn't like the way he said that, with a hint of threat. "It wasn't Declan's either."

He raised a brow. "I'll agree to disagree on that one."

I wasn't sure there was anything I could say to change his mind. "Okay." I sighed. "How's Audrey?"

He nodded, as if glad to be done with the topic of Declan. "She was given some poison, but she's okay. Thankfully, SpaceTech is still in the testing phase for their newest weapon. A few modifications to the formula and Audrey might not have been so lucky." He said the last quickly before I could worry.

"The weapon? You found out more about it?"

"Yes. It's bio in nature. They've turned their lucole into a powder, and it won't be good for anyone with Aunare blood if it's released." He took a long, steadying breath. "We've been busy with our allies. The next few weeks will be interesting, but war is imminent. We finally all agree on that count. The videos of you on Abaddon—"

"No." I wasn't talking about those videos. I hated—*hated*—that parts had been released when we were racing from SpaceTech, but I understood. "Please tell me you didn't release more of them."

"We did." This time he couldn't keep the emotion from his face.

He was guilty, but not sorry. The way he never looked away from my gaze told me that. "Our allies asked to see more before deciding to go to war. So I went through all the recordings, showed them enough, and Declan, Ahiga, and I spoke on your behalf. We also exposed our side of what was dubbed Liberation Week on Earth. Your mother spoke of the suffering of the Aunare and halfers across the colonies."

"You went through all of them?" My voice cracked at the end, but I couldn't help it. I already felt stripped bare with him. If he'd seen those videos, I wasn't sure I could ever feel anything but exposed around him. I stared at the sheets, unable to look at him.

"Declan said you have nothing to be ashamed of, and in this, I agree. You don't look weak. I wish you could see them like I—"

I glanced back at him. "No. I'm never watching them. I lived through it." That alone was enough to give me nightmares forever.

I hated that everyone knew what Jason had done to me in that diner. Everyone in the known universe got to hear me begging to die as the nanos worked their way through my system. They'd seen me afraid and alone and at my most vulnerable.

It'd been bad enough that I'd shown him any of it while on his ship, but now he'd seen *everything*.

"Stop." Lorne's sharp tone cut through my thoughts like he could read my mind plain as day. "Your suffering rallied our allies. If that upsets you, try to remember that having our allies back us in this war will only strengthen us when we take down SpaceTech."

I swallowed down my embarrassment. "You watched them. That's why you understood what I meant?"

"No. That's not how I knew." I wanted to ask more questions, but he kept talking. "All of your friends from Abaddon have been what I believe you call under house arrest, but they should be cleared soon."

He didn't want to talk about it—maybe he was still mad about my lie—so I let it go. "Can I see them?"

"You may, yes, but you'll face media as soon as you leave here. Are you ready for that?"

The idea of facing cameras or talking to anyone about what happened was so far beyond anything that I could even begin to think about.

"I thought as much." He crossed his arms. "Your friends are anxious to hear from you, but they can wait until you're ready or they're cleared to come here."

I wanted to ask how long that would be, but it didn't really matter. I wasn't leaving here. Not for a while. I glanced at the door.

"I know it seemed like your father left this room easily, but he's barely left your side."

I wasn't sure what to think about my father. I figured that Lorne must be close with him if he'd lived under my father's roof for the last seven years, but I wasn't even sure what to say to him or where to start. So I pushed that subject away, too.

Even if talking to Lorne had helped, there was someone else I needed. "Where's Roan?" He'd better not be under house arrest, too. For him, I might brave the media.

"Training on the grounds here, but on his way. I sent someone to fetch him when you woke up crying."

"That's why you got up?"

Lorne nodded.

"How did you know?" Lorne saw too much, and I didn't understand how.

"Roan said you told him almost immediately who and what you were."

"I… Yeah. I did." I wasn't sure how that related to my question.

"You're Aunare. That *click* as you call it, that's an Aunare thing. I told you before that each person has a frequency at which they resonate, although frequency isn't a good translation and really doesn't do it justice. It's too simplified, but we'll call it that for now. You and Roan resonate on what I'll call harmonizing frequencies. He balances you."

I nodded. That tracked. "Yes. He does."

"I want to be jealous, but then we have a different kind of connection, and you already told me you don't have feelings for him, and he's told me the same is true for him."

It never failed. Everyone always questioned it, but Roan and I were on the same page. "No. That's not something either of us has ever wanted. He's like a best friend and brother in one. He's more than family."

"I know. It's like Declan and me. We were eight when we met and were instantly family. I trusted him implicitly, even though I had no reason to befriend a Murtagh." He frowned for a second. "Or I guess that's how we were."

"Please, don't stay mad at him for—"

"Don't worry. We'll work it out or we won't." He shrugged. "Friends sometimes come and go."

It didn't have to be that way.

"Roan's going to be mad he missed you waking up," Lorne said, changing the subject. "He and Ahiga have been working with some of my guards. Apparently, he thinks our *faksano* is totally frosty."

A surprised laugh slipped free. I wasn't sure what a *faksano* was, but him using our slang was awkward. "Don't. That sounds so wrong coming from you."

Lorne grinned, and I was shocked by how it transformed his face. The calm, serious mask melted away and what was left was the most beautiful man I'd ever seen. His blue-green eyes glittered, and I knew I could sit there forever and stare into them.

"Frosty sounds wrong?"

I nodded my head. The grin on my face felt foreign but good. "It just does."

Lorne started to say something, but the door swooshed open, and Roan raced through, tackling me to the bed.

"You had me so fucking scared." He pulled away for a second. His hair was extra poofy, and he was sweaty, but I didn't care. Not even a little bit. My best friend was here. The one who knew me better than anyone. I didn't think I'd ever see him again, and here he was.

I squeezed him tighter as my eyes burned.

"You're okay?" Roan asked quietly in my ear.

"No. I'm not." My voice broke as I stifled a sob.

"You will be," he said softly. "You've got me here, and one hell of a frosty house. Did you know that you're freakin' loaded?"

I rested my head against Roan's shoulder and laughed. I couldn't help myself. "No, but I can't wait for you to tell me about it."

"Dude. This house is so beyond frosty that we need a new word for it." He pulled back to sit next to me. "You gotta check it out. And I can't wait for you to see…"

I tilted my head in time to see Lorne slipping out of the room. He glanced over his shoulder at me.

"Thank you," I mouthed to him.

He shoved his hands in his pockets and gave me a small nod. "My pleasure." The words were little more than a whisper. I shouldn't have been able to hear them over Roan's chattering, but I did.

As the door closed behind Lorne, I wondered how that man could understand me so well, yet I felt so lost around him.

CHAPTER FORTY-SIX

A LITTLE WHILE LATER, Roan left me to shower. He stank, and I wanted a shower, too. I'd been in new clothes when I'd woken up, but according to Lorne, it'd taken days in the healing beds for me to fully recover. I wasn't sure who had changed me and put me in these clothes, but it didn't really matter. Not anymore.

I was going to have to find a way to keep going. Lorne said I'd been asleep for a week, but I felt like I could sleep for another month straight. I knew that not all of my exhaustion could be blamed on my physical state, although I realized as I showered that I was thinner than I'd ever been before and that was saying something. There were a few times when we'd been on the run that food had been pretty scarce. I could easily count my ribs and when I spotted my back in the mirror while undressing, I could see the little knobs on my spine.

I knew I hadn't been eating great while on Abaddon, especially since I'd been burning through so many calories on the surface and during my nano treatments, but I didn't realize it'd gotten this bad.

Lorne was right. I was going to need to work to get my body back to speed. The exercise would help me get my mood balanced, too, but as I rinsed the soap from my body, I realized that I needed something to fight for. Something to do. Because the lost feeling that was threatening to drown me wasn't going to go away easily.

After a while, I stopped hoping that the shower would somehow fix everything and shut off the stream of hot water. I wrapped myself in a soft, green towel and went in search of clothes.

I couldn't find any closet or dresser in the bedroom, so I walked back to the bathroom. I'd assumed the door in it was a linen closet, but when I opened it, I found a walk-in closet filled to the brim with clothes.

I almost stepped out, not wanting to use clothes that weren't mine, but I had to wear something. I couldn't hide in my room wrapped in a towel forever, no matter how appealing that was. I had to start living again. I just didn't know what that meant, but I'd figure it out somehow.

I stepped deeper into the closet and noticed they were all women's clothes. All my size. All in the Aunare style of long flowing dresses or loose pants and endless styles of sleeveless or tank tops. After a bit of searching, I found a pair of fitted pants that had more give than I'd expected and a black top. I didn't realize that there was a large cut-out in the back before I put it on. It was more revealing than I'd like, but the cut felt elegant and the material had to be something like silk. It was so soft against my skin.

I was pulling my hair into a ponytail when there was a beep from my door. "Hello?" I yelled as I stepped out of the bathroom.

The door swished open, and Rysden di Aetes entered.

My father.

My skin started giving off a low glow. My nerves were literally showing on the outside, and I hated that. I did the breaths that Declan had taught me, and the glow went down a bit, but I couldn't fully quench it.

Rysden came to stand in front of me with a smile on his face. It was a nice, warm smile on the surface, but it set me on edge. He wanted something. I knew it. Otherwise, my mother would've been here.

Rysden's blond hair hung to his shoulders. His eyes were blue, like a bright summer day. He was taller than I imagined—and bigger—but I should've known that the head of the Aunare military and chief advisor to the king would be intimidating.

"It's nice to see you awake," he said after a moment.

I nodded, unable to find any words for him. I stepped deeper into the bedroom and sat on the bed.

"I don't want to push you, but that's—unfortunately—the road ahead for us." He sighed.

My heart ached at the sound of it. I'd given up hope that I'd ever be reunited with my father so long ago, but when I was a girl, I used to dream about this. Of him coming to save my mom and me. And yet, now that I was here with him on Sel'Ani, I wasn't sure what to say or how to feel about him. All I knew was that I didn't know this man in front of me. He hadn't gone through what mom and I had, and it felt too late for us to try to have a relationship. I was past the point of needing him.

But maybe that wasn't fair. It wasn't my father's fault. He didn't want to leave us. So I kept quiet before I could say anything that couldn't be unsaid.

"A lot of Aunare are asking questions, not all of them nice ones. I want you to be prepared. Who and what you are put you at risk, and before you set foot out of this house—out of this room—I need you to understand what you're up against. If we could make a statement together today, that would be best. The longer we wait, the more distrust will brew."

I swallowed down my nerves. At least my father was being honest with me, but making a statement? No. That wasn't who I was. I hid. I lied. I fought. That was it. I didn't want to be in the spotlight. I wasn't up for that.

If my mom were here, she'd be so pissed off. That's why he was here alone. And this—*this*—was exactly why I'd been upset when I woke up. In that moment, I craved the peace that I'd felt so briefly in that safe, warm place before I woke up.

I didn't know what to say to him, but this time I couldn't lie. Not anymore. "I need time. *Please*."

His brows creased, and I knew I was disappointing him, but that didn't change anything.

He blew out a breath. "Your mother said the same, and we can wait a day. Two at most."

Was he insane? Time didn't mean a day. I'd just woken up. I jumped up off the bed to tell him as much, but he held up a hand to stop me.

"The statement can be short. I have an advisor for you. He will help you through this."

"I don't want his help." I backed away from him. "I want to be left alone."

He sat down on the edge of the bed—where I'd just been sitting —and looked up at me. In that one look, I realized my father might be as lost in this conversation as I was, but he was doing the practical thing—preparing me for life—when I wanted something else. Anything else.

"We need to bring your memories back or you will need to quickly learn what it is to be Aunare."

I backed up another step, hitting the wall, and he stood from the bed.

"I have tutors ready, but... You don't remember me at all do you?"

"No." I wished I had another answer for him, but I didn't.

His face crumpled and he ran a hand down it. "I knew it was too much to hope when your mother said, but... This is bad timing. All of this. It's gone so much worse than I'd ever dreamed, and we're at war now, and I don't have time to ease you into this."

He shook his head and stood up like he was shoving all his emotions back down inside of himself. I'd seen Lorne do the same thing, and I wondered if my father had taught him that or if it was an Aunare thing.

Either way, the devastation was gone, and in front of me stood a leader.

"You have a place to take. I know what I'm asking of you, and I'm not expecting this to be easy between you and me because of it, but—"

"No." If there were a door that I could slam in his face, I would've. "No. I'm not taking any place. I'm—"

"Please, Amihanna. I—"

The anger was back, and my skin started to glow. "No. You don't get it. I don't even know who Amihanna is. Whoever you think I am or whatever place you think I'm going to take, I'm not. I just clawed my way out of that hellhole, and you're coming at me *now* to tell me that I'm in danger and hated here and—" I cut myself off before I could say anything else. I didn't know him, and clearly, my father didn't know me. At all.

"I understand." He held out his hands to me, pleading with me to listen to him, but I wasn't sure I could. Not now. "I do. I really, truly do understand. And if we weren't going to war or if you were anyone else, I would give you more time, but *you* have to understand that you are the long-lost heir to the di Aetes line, and the betrothed of—"

"No." I felt like I was falling. He couldn't have just said what I thought he said. "*Betrothed*? I can't. No." My words were fierce whispers as the horror of what he said hit me. I couldn't marry some random person.

My father gave me a sad smile. "Don't you even want to know who you're betrothed to?"

I moved to the chair beside the bed before my legs could give out. "No. I don't know. It doesn't matter who—" Oh shit. The look on my father's face. The smile. It was someone I knew already. Someone…

My heart raced, and I knew. I knew who it was. I knew deep inside of me who I was tied to. "Lorne," I whispered.

"You remember?" My father sounded hopeful.

"No." But Lorne said he'd been waiting for me. He couldn't mean… "No. I didn't remember anything. When did this happen and why wasn't I told?"

This was a nightmare. I couldn't be forced into marriage with anyone, even if it was Lorne. He was…beautiful and strong and he made me feel too much and he was the *crown prince.*

Someone like him could swallow me whole, and I couldn't be with him when I was still so lost. I didn't know what it was to be Amihanna anymore, and to have all that added pressure of being…

Horror crashed over me.

I couldn't be the crown princess. The Aunare would never accept a halfer as a ruler. I'd be hunted for the rest of my life. I'd never be safe again, and I'd already done all the pretending I could handle. I didn't have anything left to give.

"It happened a long time ago, when—"

"A long time ago?" Was he insane? I pressed my fist into my stomach to quiet the fluttering inside. "I was *six* when I saw you the last time. How could you tie me to someone at that age? How could you ask—?"

"I'm doing this poorly." He took a breath. "This is *not* my first choice of a conversation with my daughter. I want to hold you, but I sense you don't want that. Not from me. I want to tell you about how I've missed you. How I've worried and prayed for you. That the Lady would hold you in her light. That the di Aetes line would be strong."

His eyes shimmered with unshed tears. "And the Gods take it all, you are everything I dreamed and imagined. And so beautiful. You've got your mother's eyes and her kindness. Teaching those kids on Earth. That's her I see in you." He let out a breath. "But I have to warn you of the weight that's coming. You're not some everyday waitress here, and outside of this door, people are waiting and pushing and crowding to see who you really are. To test what mettle you're made of. I won't see you fail. I won't see you harmed again. So I have to prepare you. That is my job as your father, even if you hate me for it."

"I… I don't know how to be the Amihanna di Aetes that you want me to be, and I don't know if I want to be her. The only thing

I ever wanted was to live my own life. To be free. And now I've woken up to a whole new nightmare."

His face paled. "You are free."

"Not if I'm betrothed to a *stranger*!" I tried to calm down, I really did. I stood up and paced around the room. "Not if I'm supposed to be someone I'm not. I can't be his wife. I can't be a princess."

"The future queen."

I hissed as I spun to face him. "That's even worse! I can't pretend anymore. I don't have any pretending left in me. The last of it burned away on Abaddon."

He held his fist to his heart and stepped toward me again. "I know you. You are my daughter in every way. You might not realize it right now, but you are Amihanna di Aetes. You were born to rule. The Aunare will burn bright in you, but you're going to need to learn—"

No. He wasn't listening. He wasn't—

I tried to breathe through the panic, but it was building in me. Too strong. Too swiftly. The walls were caving in, and I couldn't dig myself out fast enough. So I ran.

I ran out the door. I didn't know where I was heading and I didn't care. All I knew was that I couldn't be there. I couldn't talk to my father for one second longer.

CHAPTER FORTY-SEVEN

MY FATHER HADN'T BEEN LYING. There were people literally waiting outside my bedroom door. Not a lot, but a few men that had to be soldiers. A woman in a beautiful flowing dress, looking down her nose at me.

They were quiet for a second and then they all started talking at once. In Aunare.

My father came from my room and stood behind me.

I spotted an opening down the hallway, and I started running. My muscles screamed at being pushed, and I wobbled a little, but I forced myself to keep going. I had to get out of here. Faster and faster. One foot in front of the other, with a hand to the wall occasionally to keep me from falling over. I was getting away from here.

I wouldn't be trapped in another life I didn't want.

I didn't really see my surroundings. I wasn't looking at my father's house. I was looking for a door. A way out.

And then I saw it. Windows. A door with windows. I ran outside and stumbled to a stop. I pressed my hands into my thighs as I hunched over, gasping for enough air to fill my lungs. I'd never been this out of shape, but I'd get my body back. Some food and exercise. I could fix it. I had to fix it.

I placed my hands on top of my head as I straightened, finally taking in my surroundings.

The grounds were amazing. Flowers bloomed. The scents blended together to create the most delicate perfume. The sky held two suns and planets that were so large, triple the size of a harvest moon on Earth.

I turned, staring at the building behind me. The stone melded perfectly with the surroundings. Sounds of animals—birds, something that sounded like monkeys maybe, I wasn't sure—but it was all so much. So rich. So lush. So different than anything that I'd ever seen before.

No cement. No smog in the air. No crush of people and speeders and pods. Just a house and nature.

There was a stone path in front of the doorway, so I took that as quickly as my aching muscles would move. I wasn't sure if Rysden or anyone else was following me, so I had to keep moving. I didn't want to finish that conversation. Not right now.

When I stepped on the path, I realized I wasn't wearing shoes.

Too late to turn back now.

Plus, I couldn't find my way back to that room even if I wanted to, but I didn't want to go back.

I followed the path, not really caring where it led. I just wanted to get away. To have a moment by myself. The stones zigzagged through the gardens to a fountain surrounded by benches.

I wished the sound of water drew me toward the fountain, not the man sitting in front of it.

Lorne.

I almost laughed. Almost.

I'd run away from my father's house—away from a conversation about Lorne—only to run right into him.

If I believed in signs, then maybe I'd read too much into this. But it was a coincidence. Only a coincidence. It didn't mean anything.

The house stood on a hill overlooking the fountain. The farther away I got, the bigger it seemed. Weird.

The gardens surrounding the fountain were massive. The floral scents of the bright blooms filled the air.

Lorne watched me as I strode toward him. He was still glowing, but not as bright as he was in my room.

"I hear we're betrothed," I said when I got close enough to talk to him.

He relaxed back against the bench, resting his arms wide against the back. "Indeed we are. And that has you in a mad panic, running through your father's grounds like the hounds of hell are at your feet—and no shoes?" He gave me a wicked grin, and I knew he was teasing me.

I didn't like to show any weakness, but after everything we'd been through, he didn't count. He'd already seen me at my worst. "It does. I don't like to be forced to do anything."

"I would imagine not. You're very di Aetes."

"I don't know if that's a compliment or not." He'd said it blandly, but I wasn't sure.

"You think I'd insult you?" His eyes were wide as he waited for me to answer.

Those eyes. My favorite color. I wondered if part of me had remembered them—remembered *Lorne*—if that was why I'd painted my room that color. But that was a silly thought. "No. I don't think you'd insult me."

I wanted to sit down, but the way he was stretched out, I'd have to sit next to him. It felt childish not to take the seat just because I was betrothed to him, so I sat next to him, and as he tucked me to his side, I instantly regretted it. I wondered if he'd been planning that move.

"Am I that awful?"

He might have intended for the question to come off as teasing, but his glow brightened a bit, giving him away. I knew with one answer I could break this man, but would it be the truth or was I saying it just to fight something I didn't understand?

I closed my eyes. I wouldn't lie to Lorne again. "No, but I'm... I don't know who I am." I opened my eyes and hoped he'd understand. "I can't give away my freedom. Not after I've fought so hard for it. I've lived in fear for so long, hiding and hoping that no one would ever find me. And then Declan did. It was exciting and frustrating and scary on another level as I waited to leave, but then Jason... And Abaddon and..." The panic was rising up in me, and he gave my hand a squeeze. "My father came to talk to me."

"He did?" He didn't sound surprised at all. Instead, he started weaving his fingers through mine.

My heart fluttered and my breath stuttered and it was hard to focus on anything other than the touch of his fingers. This—this was one big reason why I had to stay away. Lorne holds my hand, and I lose it?

Next thing I knew, I was going to turn into my ex, Haden. All needy and calling and making a nuisance of myself.

Embarrassing.

I tried to pull my hand away, but he held on tighter.

I opened my eyes to see Lorne staring at me, a small smile on his face. He knew what he was doing. He always did.

"Your father came to talk to you?"

I almost groaned as he brought me back to the topic at hand.

My father. We'd been talking about my father. "Yes. He did." It had gone worse than I'd imagined.

"What did he say?" I figured that knowing my father better than I did, he'd know what my father came to talk to me about, but he sounded genuinely curious.

I didn't really feel like rehashing it, but I summed it up as best as I could. "That I need to take up my place and that it's going to be hard because people don't like me and—"

The smile was instantly gone, and I missed it. "Don't listen to him," Lorne said.

"What? I thought you'd—"

"Your father means well, but let's take this one day at a time.

No more panicking. And, at the very least, you need to build up your strength before you try to run away again. Also, shoes."

I laughed. "Is running away a possibility?" Because that seemed doable and appealing.

"It is. Where are we running to?"

Oh man. I hung my head. "What do you want from me?" I'd learned the hard way that nothing came without a cost.

Lorne squeezed my hand again and I looked up at him, nearly getting lost in his gaze. "Everything."

I hissed out a breath and tried to pull away. Lorne wanted my freedom just as much as my father did.

"I'll back off—for now—because you need a friend more. I've been waiting this long. I think I can manage a little while longer. Especially now that I know you're safe."

"Thanks so much," I said, my tone dripping in sarcasm.

Declan came down the path and stopped walking as he saw us sitting together. He didn't have the calm mask that Lorne did. We were easily thirty meters away and I could still clearly see the hurt on his face.

Declan had to know I was betrothed, yet...

Maybe I'd misread things. For a second on Earth, I'd thought that there was something between Declan and me. Even with Declan's evil family, being with him would be easier than being with Lorne.

Lorne squeezed my hand one last time before letting go, and I turned back to him.

"If you change your mind about running away with me, let me know. The Rayshani beaches were always your favorite." He started to stand, but I stopped him, grabbing his wrist.

"What's the matter?" he asked as he sat down again.

He sounded worried, but I just needed a second. Something he said...

Beaches?

Something about that was familiar.

I tilted my head as I remembered something. I'd dreamt of him. I'd dreamt of the beach and of him and a sandcastle.

"I...I..." I looked away from him as I tried to remember. "I had a dream about the beach. I think you were there. And I think I made a sandcastle, but it didn't look much like a castle..."

And I'd seen him—a foggy, blurry version of him—while I was running on the treadmill on Abaddon, too. It was a fragment at best. More like an impression. I couldn't describe anything about it, only the feeling of being happy.

I looked back at him. "What does it mean?"

He grinned, and his eyes grew glassy. "It wasn't a dream."

He was wrong. "No. I swear I had this dream and—"

"It was a *memory*, Amihanna. We used to go there every Earth winter." He leaned down and pressed a kiss to my forehead. "This is a very good sign. It gives me hope that your memory will come back."

"But I don't remember anything important. Just one day on the beach. What good does that do?"

"It's one piece."

"And if I don't remember anything else? If that's all I ever get?" I couldn't take disappointing him, and I wasn't going to think too hard about that.

He tucked a piece of hair behind my ear and gave me a small smile. "Then we'll make more memories and the tutors will teach you Aunare and everything will be okay. Don't push yourself. Just relax. Enjoy the fountain. Every gods' damned ridiculous thing your father was going on about can wait." He got up again, and I dropped his wrist. "If you need me or want to talk, I'll be here."

I nodded quietly, staring at the fountain again.

When I'd found him sitting here, I was annoyed. I wanted to be alone. But now, I was sad that he was leaving. My head was officially a mess.

Lorne's footsteps sounded heavy on the stone as he walked away, and I had to stop myself from asking him to come back. I'd already leaned on him once today when I woke up. I couldn't keep doing that.

Lorne stopped in front of Declan. They had been as close as brothers once. That's what Declan said back on Earth and what Lorne had told me, but I couldn't see that now. Lorne's hands were tight fists at his side. I couldn't make out the words exchanged— the water crashing around the fountain drowned out the words— but the tone—the tone Lorne used was vicious.

Declan took Lorne's abuse with his chin held high, then Declan said something equally harsh.

One second Lorne was standing there, hands in his pockets. The next, he was glowing bright and slamming his fist into Declan's face.

I jumped up from the bench, wondering if I should step in, but I didn't know who to defend.

Declan held his jaw with his hand, and I could see that he was holding on by a thread.

Lorne looked back at me, and he looked tired and pained.

"What?" I mouthed to him. "Is it my fault?"

Lorne shook his head, then said to Declan loud enough so I could hear, *"Ha shalshasa ni meha."*

Declan jerked back, as if absorbing a second hit. "I know. Believe me, I *know*."

Lorne started down the path, and I wasn't sure if I should go after him. I wasn't sure if I should check on Declan. So I stood there frozen with my mouth open.

Declan gave me a half-hearted smile. It was fake and pained and tried to shove aside whatever had happened between him and Lorne.

I turned away. That fight had been about me, and I didn't like it. Not even a little bit. I wasn't something to be fought over.

I stared at the fountain for the first time.

There was an ornate statue in the center. A woman stood tall. Her hands held two short batons. The water seemed to move and swirl as it flowed around her. Almost like the water was forming people. Like there was a fight going on in the fountain with water-formed men.

When I got to her face, it felt as if the ground disappeared beneath my bare feet.

It was me.

What the hell was a statue of me doing in the gardens?

I looked back toward the house. Lorne was almost to the turn in the path, but he seemed to sense my gaze and glanced back at me. "She's your destiny," he yelled. "As am I."

I spun back to the fountain and watched the water crashing around her.

I had a destiny?

I stumbled back until the bench pressed against me and sat before my legs gave out.

"You okay?" Declan asked.

He settled down beside me, and I felt the stirrings of panic.

I needed my memory back. I needed to figure out what being Aunare was. And I needed to figure out how I fit into this world. Because, like it or not, I was here. "What am I going to do?"

"Don't worry too much. You'll figure it out." Declan nudged my shoulder with his. "You're going to be fine."

For a second, I believed him. I took a deep breath and let it out slowly.

"There you go. See? It'll be okay."

But as I sat there, staring at that stupid fountain, I stopped believing it.

It was so easy for Declan to say everything will be fine. That I'd be okay. That I'd figure it out. But he wasn't the one who had to do the work.

How? How was I supposed to be okay? *That's* what I *needed* to know.

But all I knew was how to be Maité Martinez—a waitress, ABQ Crew member, and martial arts instructor.

I'd been on the run for most of my life, forced to make choices based on survival. That was over. I was supposed to be able to live my life how I chose now, but I was slowly realizing that my life might never be that easy. Especially when I was supposed to become the Aunare Queen.

How was I supposed to figure *that* out?

And then there was Lorne. Handsome. Funny. Kind. He pushed-pulled me with his quiet yet bossy nature. He probably was a good match, but I didn't ask for it. And I definitely couldn't marry someone I didn't love. And I couldn't be a queen.

All I wanted to do was fade into the background and have a normal life, but I'd never get to do that beside him.

"You okay?" Declan asked again.

I leaned back against the bench. "Shouldn't I be asking you that question?" His face had a big red mark that I was sure would be a nasty bruise by morning.

"I'll be fine."

He would, but that didn't mean it didn't hurt. "What was that about?"

"You really need to ask?"

I shook my head. "No. I guess I don't." It'd been about me. I wished I could convince them that I wasn't worth fighting over, but I didn't think either of them would listen.

"You don't have to, you know?"

I looked at him. "Don't have to what?"

"Marry him. If you don't want to."

I blew out a long, slow breath. Declan was worrying about the wrong thing.

"Do you want to?"

It was so iced that he was even asking. "Marry Lorne? How the hell am I supposed to know? I thought I was going to die, and now suddenly I'm not. My head is spinning from all the change, and you're asking me if I want to wear a white dress and put on a crown and rule people that are honor-bound to hate me?" I laughed and went back to watching the fountain. "No. Maybe. Kind of in theory, but also I have *no fucking idea*."

Declan's laugh was rich and deep. "Well, when you put it that way, it sounds like you've got it clear in your mind."

I huffed a soft laugh.

Declan got quiet, and I was thankful for it. I wanted a second to catch my breath. That's why I'd come out here. I wasn't sure I'd even really begun to process everything that'd happen. Lorne was right, it was going to take time.

Damn it. Was Lorne always right? That was going to piss me off.

My skin started glowing, and I got up. I might've been weak, but I wouldn't get stronger by sitting there.

"Can I ask you a question?" Declan asked before I could walk away.

I wanted to say no. I'd already had multiple emotional conversations, but what was one more? "Sure."

"Where are your shoes?"

The last month had been an unmitigated disaster, but as the laugh slipped free, I was thankful for Declan. He was easy to talk to, and I knew he'd be a good sounding board when things got crazy. And if I was right, things were going to get crazy.

I wasn't mad at Declan for what had happened. It wasn't his fault or mine. We both did our best and, yes, things had gone horribly wrong, but I'd ended up here. Safe. With my family. With Roan and a few new friends. And, as Roan pointed out, I was apparently loaded now. So maybe things were looking up?

I laughed quietly to myself at that thought.

I wasn't sure what was going to happen with the Aunare or the war or my apparent betrothal, but I was alive. Someday I hoped to find the peace I was looking for. But for now, I was still breathing, and that meant I'd keep fighting.

I'm a di Aetes. I don't quit. Not ever.

The story continues with *Off Balance*, book two in the Aunare Chronicles series coming early 2020!

For updates on the series and everything Aileen, check her out on Instagram (@aileenerin) or Facebook (@aelatcham)!

And join her Ink Monster Superfans group on Facebook. (www.facebook.com/groups/InkMonsterFans)

TO MY READERS

Thank you so much for reading *Off Planet*! This book was a long time coming. I've been working on it off and on since 2012. I'm so excited to have it finally out in the world!

And don't worry! I'm already well into writing *Off Balance*, the second book in the Aunare Chronicles. There's more to come for Amihanna, Lorne, Declan, and Roan. You're not going to want to miss it!

I'll be posting updates on my books on Instagram (@aileenerin), Facebook (@aelatcham), as well as my blog!

There's also an Ink Monster Superfans group on Facebook! (www.facebook.com/groups/InkMonsterFans) I post on there the most, so come and join in on the fun!

I absolutely love hearing from you. So, please reach out on social media or email me: aerin@inkmonster.net

xoxo
    Aileen

ACKNOWLEDGMENTS

I was living in Albuquerque during the production of Marvel's *The Avengers* (which my husband, Jeremy, produced) when I first learned of Spaceport America, Richard Branson's cutting-edge commercial space endeavor.

The notion of the glitz and wealth of the burgeoning space-exploration industry contrasted with the staggering poverty of present-day New Mexico led me to imagine a world where private concerns end up replacing the governments of the world. A world where commerce replaced democracy.

Off Planet is what came from all of that inspiration. I was writing in our little rented house off of Central Ave, and I could hear the jets landing at the Air Force base. I needed 10K words for my fifth writing residency for my MFA at Seton Hill University, and what came out was a version of the diner scene.

I took it to that June 2011 residency and got critiqued by an AMAZING group of people, including Dr. Nicole Peeler. I got such good feedback, and everyone encouraged me to keep working on it. One other classmate (David W.) pulled me aside afterward and asked me to send him anything else that I wrote for this story. I was so excited, so when I met with my new mentor, Maria V.

Snyder, I decided expand the diner scene into a whole book. I'd already finished *Becoming Alpha* with Dr. Lee McClain, and was so excited to build a whole new world for Maité.

For that whole semester with Maria, I think I learned more than I did in all the other semesters combined about how to world build. She kicked my ass BIGTIME, and I'm so incredibly grateful that she accepted me as a mentee.

This book has gone through so many versions—one where she became IAF, ones where Lorne came instead of Declan, ones where she didn't know she was a halfer... But I finally found the right version and cut 50K words last year. Somehow, I still ended up over 140K, nearly double the average length of one of my Alpha Girls books. Whoa, mama! And I couldn't have done it without a TON—I mean a TON—of help. So here's the list of everyone that helped! Be prepared. It's a long one!

Thank you to Lola Dodge, Maria V. Snyder, Margie Lawson, Mary Karlik, Cheri Patton, John McDevitt, and everyone else who has given me feedback on this book through its many versions.

Thank you to Kime Heller-Neal. Your feedback was so thorough and organized. Your editing made this book shine, and I'm so thankful that you were able to fit this book into your schedule!

Thank you to Sharon Garner, my copyeditor. I'm so thankful that someone can catch all my typos, and so stoked that you enjoyed the read, too. :)

Thank you to my amazing mother-in-law, who came to watch Isabella while I hosted Margie Lawson's Immersion Master Class. My writing improved so much from that, and I'm so thankful to have such a supportive mother-in-law! I appreciate it so much.

To Kelly, Ana, Katie, Allison, and all the rest at INscribe, thank you for all your hard work! Your support of Ink Monster and our books is invaluable. You're AMAZING!

To my family, for being so supportive of all of my books! Thank you for the cheers and encouragement. I love you all.

To our nanny, Nicky G. Without you taking such good care of

our Isabella, I wouldn't be able to work. Thank you for that daily gift.

Jeremy. You're the best partner. Thank you for reading every single draft and always telling me to keep going. I'm so thankful for you. For taking Isabella on weekends when I'm on deadline to staying up late reading revisions to making me dinner and shooing me off to finalize the final-final files. I love you the most.

Isabella doesn't understand what I do yet (she's only 2.5!), but I hope she reads this one day and enjoys it. If today is that day, know that I love you so much and I hope you enjoyed it. Taking time away from you isn't easy, but you're always in my heart and on my mind. Maité's strength comes from you.

ABOUT THE AUTHOR

Aileen Erin is half-Irish, half-Mexican, and 100% nerd—from Star Wars (prequels don't count) to Star Trek (TNG FTW), she reads Quenya and some Sindarin, and has a severe fascination with the supernatural. Aileen has a BS in Radio-TV-Film from the University of Texas at Austin, and an MFA in Writing Popular Fiction from Seton Hill University. She lives with her husband and daughter in Los Angeles, and spends her days doing her favorite things: reading books, creating worlds, and kicking ass.

f facebook.com/aelatcham

🐦 twitter.com/aileen_erin

📷 instagram.com/aileenerin

Made in the USA
Las Vegas, NV
13 June 2023